ARNOLD B1

GU00363943

The Lion's Share

Elibron Classics
www.elibron.com

THE LION'S SHARE

The Lion's Share

BY

ARNOLD BENNETT

CASSELL AND COMPANY, LTD
London, New York, Toronto and Melbourne

First Published 1916.

CONTENTS

CONTENTS

THE LION'S SHARE

CHAPTER I

AUDREY had just closed the safe in her father's study when she was startled by a slight noise. She turned like a defensive animal to face danger. It had indeed occurred to her that she was rather like an animal in captivity, and she found a bitter pleasure in the idea, though it was not at all original.

"And Flank Hall is my Zoo!" she had said. (Not that she had ever seen the Zoological Gardens or visited London.)

She was lithe; she moved with charm. Her short, plain blue serge walking-frock disclosed the form of her limbs and left them free, and it made her look younger even than she was. Its simplicity suited her gestures and took grace from them. But she wore the old thing without the least interest in it—almost unconsciously. She had none of she preoccupations caused by the paraphernalia of existence. She scarcely knew what it was to own. She was aware only of her body and her soul. Beyond these her possessions were so few, so mean, so unimportant, that she might have carried them to the grave and into heaven without protest from the authorities earthly or celestial.

The slight noise was due to the door of the study, which great age had distorted and bereft of sense, and, in fact, almost unhinged. It unlatched itself, paused, and then calmly but firmly swung wide open. When it could swing no farther it shook, vibrating into repose.

Audrey condemned the door for a senile lunatic, and herself for a poltroon. She became defiant of peril, until the sound of a step on the stair beyond the door threw her back into alarm. But when the figure of Miss Ingate appeared in the doorway she was definitely reassured, to the point of disdain. All her facial expression said: "It's only Miss Ingate."

And yet Miss Ingate was not a negligible woman. Her untidy hair was greying; she was stout, she was fifty, she was plain, she had not elegance; her accent and turns of speech were noticeably those of Essex. But she had a magnificent pale forehead; the eyes beneath it sparkled with energy, inquisitiveness, and sagacity; and the mouth beneath the eyes showed by its sardonic dropping corners that she had come to a settled, cheerful conclusion about human nature, and that the conclusion was not flattering. Miss Ingate was a Guardian of the Poor, and the Local Representative of the Soldiers' and Sailors' Families Association. She had studied intimately the needy and the rich and the middling. She was charitable without illusions; and, while adhering to every social convention, she did so with a toleration pleasantly contemptuous; in her heart she had no mercy for snobs of any kind, though, unfortunately, she was at times absurdly intimidated by them—at other times she was not.

To the west, within a radius of twelve miles, she knew everybody and everybody knew her; to the east her fame was bounded only by the regardless sea. She and her ancestors had lived in the village of Moze as long as even Mr. Mathew Moze and his ancestors. In the village, and to the village, she was Miss Ingate, a natural phenomenon, like the lie of the land and the river Moze. Her opinions offended nobody, not Mr. Moze himself—she was Miss Ingate. She was laughed at, beloved and respected. Her sagacity had one flaw, and the flaw sprang from her sincere conviction that human nature in that corner of Essex, which she understood so profoundly, and where she was so perfectly at home, was different from, and more fondly foolish than, human nature in any other part of the world. She could not believe that distant populations could be at once so pathetically and so naughtily human as the population in and around Moze.

If Audrey disdained Miss Ingate, it was only because Miss Ingate was neither young nor fair nor the proprietress of some man, and because people made out that she was peculiar. In some respects Audrey looked upon Miss Ingate as a life-belt, as the speck of light at the end of a tunnel, as the enigmatic smile which glimmers always in the frown of destiny.

"Well?" cried Miss Ingate in her rather shrill voice, grinning sardonically, with the corners of her lips still lower than usual in anticipatory sarcasm. It was as if she had said: "You cannot surprise me by any narrative of imbecility or turpitude or bathos. All the same, I am dying to hear the latest eccentricity of this village."

"Well?" parried Audrey, holding one hand behind her.

They did not shake hands. People who call at ten o'clock in the morning cannot expect to have their hands shaken. Miss Ingate certainly expected nothing of the sort. She had the freedom of Flank Hall, as of scores of other houses, at all times of day. Servants opened front doors for her with a careless smile, and having shut front doors they left her loose, like a familiar cat, to find what she wanted. They seldom "showed" her into any room, nor did they dream of acting before her the unconvincing comedy of going to "see" whether masters or mistresses were out or in.

"Where's your mother?" asked Miss Ingate idly, quite sure that interesting divulgations would come, and quite content to wait for them. She had been out of the village for over a week.

"Mother's taking her acetyl salicylic," Audrey answered, coming to the door of the study.

This meant merely that Mrs. Moze had a customary attack of the neuralgia for which the district is justly renowned among strangers.

"Oh!" murmured Miss Ingate callously. Mrs. Moze, though she had lived in the district for twenty-five years, did not belong to it. If she chose to keep on having neuralgia, that was her affair, but in justice to natives and to the district she ought not to make too much of it, and she ought to admit that it might well be due to her weakness after her operation. Miss Ingate considered the climate to be the finest in England; which it was, on the condition that you were proof against neuralgia.

"Father's gone to Colchester in the car to see the Bishop," Audrey coldly added.

"If I'd known he was going to Colchester I should have asked him for a lift," said Miss Ingate, with determination.

"Oh, yes! He'd have taken *you!*" said Audrey, reserved. "I suppose you had fine times in London!"

"Oh! It was vehy exciting! It was vehy exciting!" Miss Ingate agreed loudly.

"Father wouldn't let me read about it in the paper," said Audrey, still reserved. "He never will, you know. But I did!"

"Oh! But you didn't read about me playing the barrel organ all the way down Regent Street, because that wasn't in any of the papers."

"You *didn't!*" Audrey protested, with a sudden dark smile.

"Yes, I did. Yes, I did. Yes, I did. And vehy tiring it was. Vehy tiring indeed. It's quite an art to turn a barrel organ. If you don't keep going perfectly even it makes the tune jerky. Oh! I know a bit about barrel organs now. They smashed it all to pieces. Oh yes! All to pieces. I spoke to the police. I said, ' Aren't you going to protect these ladies' property?' But they didn't lift a finger."

"And weren't you arrested?"

"Me!" shrieked Miss Ingate. "Me arrested!" Then more quietly, in an assured tone, "Oh no! I wasn't arrested. You see, as soon as the row began I just walked away from the organ and became one of the crowd. I'm all *for* them, but I wasn't going to be arrested."

Miss Ingate's sparkling eyes seemed to say: "Sylvia Pankhurst can be arrested if she likes, and so can Mrs. Despard and Annie Kenney and Jane Foley, or any of them. But the policeman that is clever enough to catch Miss Ingate of Moze does not exist. And the gumption of Miss Ingate of Moze surpasses the united gumption of all the other feminists in England."

"Oh no! Oh no! Oh no!" repeated Miss Ingate with mingled complacency, glee, passion, and sardonic tolerance of the whole panorama of worldly existence. "The police were awful, shocking. But I was not arrested."

"Well, *I* was—this morning," said Audrey in a low and poignant voice.

Miss Ingate was startled out of her mood of the detached ironic spectator.

"What?" she frowned.

They heard a servant moving about at the foot of the stairs, and a capped head could be seen through the interstices of the white Chinese balustrade. The study was the only immediate refuge; Miss Ingate advanced right into it, and Audrey pushed the door to.

"Father's given me a month's C.B."

Miss Ingate, gazing at the girl's face, saw in its quiet and yet savage desperation the possibility that after all she might indeed be surprised by the vagaries of human nature in the village. And her glance became sympathetic, even tender, as well as apprehensive.

"'C.B.'? What do you mean—'C.B.'?"

"Don't you know what C.B. means?" exclaimed Audrey

with scornful superiority over the old spinster. "Confined to barracks. Father says I'm not to go beyond the grounds for a month. And to-day's the second of April!"

"No!"

"Yes, he does. He's given me a week, you know, before. Now it's a month."

Silence fell.

Miss Ingate looked round at the shabby study, with its guns, cigar-boxes, prints, books neither old nor new, japanned boxes of documents, and general litter scattered over the voluted walnut furniture. Her own house was old-fashioned, and she realised it was old-fashioned; but when she came into Flank Hall, and particularly into Mr. Moze's study, she felt as if she was stepping backwards into history—and this in spite of the fact that nothing in the place was really ancient, save the ceilings and the woodwork round the windows. It was Mr. Moze's habit of mind that dominated and transmogrified the whole interior, giving it the quality of a mausoleum. The suffragette procession in which Miss Ingate had musically and discreetly taken part seemed to her as she stood in Mr. Moze's changeless lair to be a phantasm. Then she looked at the young captive animal and perceived that two centuries may coincide on the same carpet and that time is merely a convention.

"What you been doing?" she questioned, with delicacy.

"I took a strange man by the hand," said Audrey, choosing her words queerly, as she sometimes did, to produce a dramatic effect.

"This morning?"

"Yes. Eight o'clock."

"What? Is there a strange man in the village?"

"You don't mean to say you haven't seen the yacht!"

"Yacht?" Miss Ingate showed some excitement.

"Come and look, Winnie," said Audrey, who occasionally thought fit to address Miss Ingate in the manner of the elder generation. She drew Miss Ingate to the window.

Between the brown curtains Mozewater, the broad,

shallow estuary of the Moze, was spread out glittering in the sunshine which could not get into the chilly room. The tide was nearly at full, and the estuary looked like a mighty harbour for great ships; but in six hours it would be reduced to a narrow stream winding through mud flats of marvellous ochres, greens, and pinks. In the hazy distance a fitful white flash showed where ocean waves were breaking on a sand-bank. And in the foreground, against a disused Hard that was a couple of hundred yards lower down than the village Hard, a large white yacht was moored, probably the largest yacht that had ever threaded that ticklish navigation. She was a shallow-draft barge-yacht, rigged like a Thames barge, and her whiteness and the glint of her brass, and the flicker of her ensign at the stern were dazzling. Blue figures ran busily about on her, and a white-and-blue person in a peaked cap stood importantly at the wheel.

"She was on the mud last night," said Audrey eagerly, "opposite the Flank buoy, and she came up this morning at half-flood. I think they made fast at Lousey Hard, because they couldn't get any farther without waiting. They have a motor, and it must be their first trip this season. I was on the dyke. I wasn't even looking at them, but they called me, so I had to go. They only wanted to know if Lousey Hard was private. Of course I told them it wasn't. It was a very middle-aged man spoke to me. He must be the owner. As soon as they were tied up he wanted to jump ashore. It was rather awkward, and I just held out my hand to help him. Father saw me from here. I might have known he would."

"Why! It's going off!" exclaimed Miss Ingate.

The yacht swung slowly round, held by her stern to the Hard. Then the last hawser was cast off, and she floated away on the first of the ebb; and as she moved, her mainsail, unbrailed, spread itself out and became a vast pinion. Like a dream of happiness she lessened and faded, and Lousey Hard was as lonely and forlorn as ever.

"But didn't you explain to your father?" Miss Ingate demanded of Audrey.

"Of course I did. But he wouldn't listen. He never does. I might just as well have explained to the hall-clock. He raged. I think he enjoys losing his temper. He said I oughtn't to have been there at all, and it was just like me, and he couldn't understand it in a daughter of his, and it would be a great shock to my poor mother, and he'd talked enough—he should now proceed to action. All the usual things. He actually asked me who ' the man ' was."

"And who was it?"

"How can I tell? For goodness' sake don't go imitating father, Winnie! . . . Rather a dull man, I should say. Rather like father, only not so old. He had a beautiful necktie; I think it must have been made out of a strip of Joseph's coat."

Miss Ingate giggled at a high pitch, and Audrey responsively smiled.

"Oh dear! Oh dear!" murmured Miss Ingate when her giggling was exhausted. "How queer it is that a girl like you can't keep your father in a good temper!"

"Father hates me to say funny things. If I say anything funny he turns as black as ink—and he takes care to keep gloomy all the rest of the day, too. He never laughs. Mother laughs now and then, but I never heard father laugh. Oh yes, I did. He laughed when the cat fell out of the bathroom window on to the lawn-roller. He went quite red in the face with laughing . . . . I say, Miss Ingate, do you think father's mad?"

"I shouldn't think he's what you call mad," replied Miss Ingate judicially, with admirable sang-froid. "I've known so many peculiar people in my time. And you must remember, Audrey, this is a peculiar part of the world."

"Well, I believe he's mad, anyway. I believe he's got men on the brain, especially young men. He's growing worse. Yesterday he told me I musn't have the punt out on Mozewater this season unless he's with me. Fancy skiffing

about with father ! He says I'm too old for that now. So
there you are. The older I get the less I'm allowed to do.
I can't go a walk, unless it's an errand. The pedal is off
my bike, and father is much too cunning to have it repaired.
I can't boat. I'm never given any money. He grumbles
frightfully if I want any clothes, so I never want any.
That's my latest dodge. I've read every book in the house
except the silly liturgical and legal things he's always
having from the London Library—and I've read even some
of those. He won't buy any new music. Golf! Ye gods,
Winnie, you should hear him talk about ladies and golf ! "

"I have," said Miss Ingate. "But it doesn't ruffle me,
because I don't play."

"But he plays with girls, and young girls, too, all the
same. He's been caught in the act. Ethel told me. He
little thinks I know. He'd let me play if he could be
the only man on the course. He's mad about me and
men. He never looks at me without thinking of all the
boys in the district."

"But he's really very fond of you, Audrey."

"Yes, I know," said Audrey. "He ought to keep me in
the china cupboard."

"Well, it's a great problem."

"He's invented a beautiful new trick for keeping me in
when he's out. I have to copy his beastly Society letters for
him."

"I see he's got a new box," observed Miss Ingate,
glancing into the open cupboard in which stood the safe.
On the top of the safe were two japanned boxes, each
lettered in white : "The National Reformation Society."
The uppermost box was freshly unpacked and shone with all
the intact pride of virginity.

"You should read some of the letters. You really
should, Winnie," said Audrey. "All the bigwigs of the
Society love writing to each other. I bet you father will
get a typewriting machine this year, and make me learn it.
The chairman has a typewriter, and father means to be the

B

next chairman. You'll see. . . . Oh! What's that? Listen!"

"What's what?"

A faint distant throbbing could be heard.

"It's the motor! He's coming back for something. Fly out of here, Winnie, fly!"

Audrey felt sick at the thought that if her father had returned only a few minutes earlier he might have trapped her at the safe itself. She still kept one hand behind her.

Miss Ingate, who with all her qualities was rather easily flustered, ran out of the dangerous room in Audrey's wake. They met Mr. Mathew Moze at the half-landing of the stairs.

He was a man of average size, somewhat past sixty years. He had plump cheeks, tinged with red; his hair, moustache and short, full beard, were quite grey. He wore a thick wide-spreading ulster, and between his coat and waistcoat a leather vest, and on his head a grey cap. Put him in the Strand in town clothes, and he might have been taken for a clerk, a civil servant, a club secretary, a retired military officer, a poet, an undertaker—for anything except the last of a long line of immovable squires who could not possibly conceive what it was not to be the owner of land. His face was preoccupied and overcast, but as soon as he realised that Miss Ingate was on the stairs it instantly brightened into a warm and rather wistful smile.

"Good morning, Miss Ingate," he greeted her with deferential cordiality. "I'm so glad to see you back."

"Good morning, good morning, Mr. Moze," responded Miss Ingate. "Vehy nice of you. Vehy nice of you."

Nobody would have guessed from their demeanour that they differed on every subject except their loyalty to that particular corner of Essex, that he regarded her and her political associates as deadly microbes in the national organism, and that she regarded him as a nincompoop crossed with a tyrant. Each of them had a magic glass to see in the other nothing but a local Effendi and familiar guardian angel of Moze. Moreover, Mr. Moze's public smile and public manner were irresistible—until he lost his temper. He might have had friends by the score, had it not been for his deep constitutional reserve—due partly to diffidence and partly to an immense hidden conceit. Mr. Moze's existence was actuated, though he knew it not, by the conviction that the historic traditions of England were committed to his keeping. Hence the conceit, which was that of a soul secretly self-dedicated.

Audrey, outraged by the hateful hypocrisy of persons over fifty, and terribly constrained and alarmed, turned vaguely back up the stairs. Miss Ingate, not quite knowing what she did, with an equal vagueness followed her.

"Come in. Do come in," urged Mr. Moze at the door of the study.

Audrey, who remained on the landing, heard her elders talk smoothly of grave Mozian things, while Mr. Moze unlocked the new tin box above the safe.

"I'd forgotten a most important paper," said he, as he relocked the box. "I have an appointment with the Bishop of Colchester at ten-forty-five, and I fear I may be late. Will you excuse me, Miss Ingate?"

She excused him.

Departing, he put the paper into his pocket with a careful and loving gesture that well symbolised his passionate affection for the Society of which he was already the vice-chairman. He had been a member of the National Reformation Society for eleven years. Despite the promise of its name, this wealthy association of idealists had no care for reforms in a sadly imperfect England. Its aim was anti-Romanist. The Reformation which it had in mind was Luther's, and it wished, by fighting an alleged insidious revival of Roman Catholicism, to make sure that so far as England was concerned Luther had not preached in vain.

Mr. Moze's connection with the Society had originated in a quarrel between himself and a Catholic priest from Ipswich who had instituted a boys' summer camp on the banks of Mozewater near the village of Moze. Until that quarrel, the exceeding noxiousness of the Papal doctrine had not clearly presented itself to Mr. Moze. In such strange ways may an ideal come to birth. As Mr. Moze, preoccupied and gloomy once more, steered himself rapidly out of Moze towards the episcopal presence, the image of the imperturbable and Jesuitical priest took shape in his mind, refreshing his determination to be even with Rome at any cost.

CHAPTER II

THE THIEF'S PLAN WRECKED

"THE fact is," said Audrey, "father has another woman in the house now."

Mr. Moze had left Miss Ingate in the study and Audrey had cautiously rejoined her there.

"Another woman in the house!" repeated Miss Ingate, sitting down in happy expectation. "What on earth do you mean? Who on earth do you mean?"

"I mean me."

"You aren't a woman, Audrey."

"I'm just as much of a woman as you are. All father's behaviour proves it."

"But your father treats you as a child."

"No, he doesn't. He treats me as a woman. If he thought I was a child he wouldn't have anything to worry about. I'm over nineteen."

"You don't look it."

"Of course I don't. But I could if I liked. I simply won't look it because I don't care to be made ridiculous. I should start to look my age at once if father stopped treating me like a child."

"But you've just said he treats you as a woman!"

"You don't understand, Winnie," said the girl sharply. "Unless you're pretending. Now you've never told me anything about yourself, and I've always told you lots about myself. You belong to an old-fashioned family. How were you treated when you were my age?"

"In what way?"

"You know what way," said Audrey, gazing at her.

13

"Well, my dear. Things seemed to come very naturally, somehow."

"Were you ever engaged?"

"Me? Oh, no!" answered Miss Ingate with tranquillity. "I'm vehy interested in them. Oh, vehy! Oh, vehy! And I like talking to them. But anything more than that gets on my nerves. My eldest sister was the one. Oh! She was the one. She refused eleven men, and when she was going to be married she made me embroider the monograms of all of them on the skirt of her wedding-dress. She made me, and I had to do it. I sat up all night the night before the wedding to finish them."

"And what did the bridegroom say about it?"

"The bridegroom didn't say anything about it because he didn't know. Nobody knew except Arabella and me. She just wanted to feel that the monograms were on her dress, that was all."

"How strange!"

"Yes, it was. But this is a vehy strange part of the world."

"And what happened afterwards?"

"Bella died when she had her first baby, and the baby died as well. And the father's dead now, too."

"What a horrid story, Winnie!" Audrey murmured. And after a pause: "I like your sister."

"She was vehy uncommon. But I liked her too. I don't know why, but I did. She could make the best marmalade I ever tasted in my born days."

"I could make the best marmalade you ever tasted in your born days," said Audrey, sinking neatly to the floor and crossing her legs, "but they won't let me."

"Won't let you! But I thought you did all sorts of things in the house."

"No, Winnie. I only do one thing. I do as I'm told—and not always even that. Now, if I wanted to make the best marmalade you ever tasted in your born days, first of all there would be a fearful row about the oranges. Secondly, father would tell mother she must tell me exactly what I was to do. He would also tell cook. Thirdly and lastly, dear friends, he would come into the kitchen himself. It wouldn't be my marmalade at all. I should only be a marmalade-making machine. They never let me have any responsibility—no, not even when mother's operation was on—and I'm never officially free. The kitchen-maid has far more responsibility than I have. And she has an evening off and an afternoon off. She can write a letter without everybody asking her who she's writing to. She's only se enteen. She has the morning postman for a young man now, and probably one or two others that I don't know of. And she has money and she buys her own clothes. She's a very naughty, wicked girl, and I wish I was in her place. She scorns me, naturally. Who wouldn't?"

Miss Ingate said not a word. She merely sat with her hands in the lap of her spotted pale-blue dress, faintly and sadly smiling.

Audrey burst out:

"Miss Ingate, what can I do? I must do something. What can I do?"

Miss Ingate shook her head, and put her lips tightly together, while mechanically smoothing the sides of her grey coat.

"I don't know," she said. "It beats me."

"Then *I'll* tell you what I can do!" answered Audrey firmly, wriggling somewhat nearer to her along the floor. "And what I shall do."

"What?"

"Will you promise to keep it a secret?"

Miss Ingate nodded, smiling and showing her teeth. Her broad polished forehead positively shone with kindly eagerness.

"Will you swear?"

Miss Ingate hesitated, and then nodded again.

"Then put your hand on my head and say, 'I swear.'"

Miss Ingate obeyed.

"I shall leave this house," said Audrey in a low voice.

"You won't, Audrey!"

"I'll eat my hand off if I've not left this house by to-morrow, anyway."

"To-morrow!" Miss Ingate nearly screamed. "Now, Audrey, do reflect. Think what you are!"

Audrey bounded to her feet.

"That's what father's always saying," she exploded angrily. "He's always telling me to examine myself. The fact is, I know too much about myself. I know exactly the kind of girl it is who's going to leave this house. Exactly!"

"Audrey, you frighten me. Where are you going to?"

"London."

"Oh! That's all right then. I am relieved. I thought perhaps you wanted to come to *my* house. You won't get to London, because you haven't any money."

"Oh, yes, I have. I've got a hundred pounds."

"Where?"

"Remember, you've sworn. . . . Here!" she cried suddenly, and drawing her hand from behind her back she most sensationally displayed a crushed roll of bank-notes.

"And who did you get those from?"

"I didn't get them from anybody. I got them out of father's safe. They're his reserve. He keeps them right at the back of the left-hand drawer, and he's so sure they're there that he never looks for them. He thinks he's a perfect model, but really he's careless. There's a duplicate key to the safe, you know, and he leaves it with a lot of other keys loose in his desk. I expect he thought nobody would ever dream of guessing it was a key of the safe. I know he never looked at this roll, because I've been opening the safe every day for weeks past, and the roll was always the same. In fact, it was dusty. Then to-day I decided to take it, and here you are! He finished himself off yesterday, so far as I'm concerned, with the business about the punt."

"But do you know you're a thief, Audrey?" breathed Miss Ingate, extremely embarrassed, and for once somewhat staggered by the vagaries of human nature.

"You seem to forget, Miss Ingate," said Audrey solemnly, "that Cousin Caroline left me a legacy of two hundred pounds last year, and that I've never seen a penny of it. Father absolutely declined to let me have the tiniest bit of it. Well, I've taken half. He can keep the other half for his trouble."

Miss Ingate's mouth stood open, and her eyes seemed startled.

"But you can't go to London alone. You wouldn't know what to do."

"Yes, I should. I've arranged everything. I shall wear my best clothes. When I arrive at Liverpool Street I shall take a taxi. I've got three addresses of boarding-houses out of the *Daily Telegraph,* and they're all in Bloomsbury, W.C. I shall have lessons in shorthand and typewriting at Pitman's School, and then I shall get a situation. My name will be Vavasour."

"But you'll be caught."

"I shan't. I shall book to Ipswich first and begin again from there. Girls like me aren't so easy to catch as all that."

"You're vehy cunning."

"I get that from mother. She's most frightfully cunning with father."

"Audrey," said Miss Ingate with a strange grin, "I don't know how I can sit here and listen to you. You'll ruin me with your father, because if you go I'm sure I shall never be able to keep from him that I knew all about it."

"Then you shouldn't have sworn," retorted Audrey. "But I'm glad you did swear, because I had to tell somebody, and there was nobody but you."

Miss Ingate might possibly have contrived to employ

some of that sagacity in which she took a secret pride
upon a very critical and urgent situation, had not Mrs.
Moze, with a white handkerchief wrapped round her forehead, at that moment come into the room. Immediately
the study was full of neuralgia and eau-de-Cologne.

When Mrs. Moze and Miss Ingate at length recovered
from the tenderness of meeting each other after a separation
of ten days or more, Audrey had vanished like an illusion.
She was not afraid of her mother; and she could trust
Miss Ingate, though Miss Ingate and Mrs. Moze were
dangerously intimate; but she was too self-conscious to
remain in the presence of her fellow-creatures; and in spite
of her faith in Miss Ingate she thought of the spinster
as of a vase filled now with a fatal liquor which by any
accident might spill and spread ruin—so that she could
scarcely bear to look upon Miss Ingate.

At the back of the house a young Pomeranian dog,
which had recently solaced Miss Ingate in the loss of a
Pekingese done to death by a spinster's too-nourishing
love, was prancing on his four springs round the chained
yard-dog, his friend and patron. In a series of marvellous
short bounds, he followed Audrey with yapping eagerness
down the slope of the garden; and the yard-dog, aware
that none but the omnipotent deity, Mr. Moze, sole source
of good and evil, had the right to loose him, turned
round once and laid himself flat and long on the ground,
sighing.

The garden, after developing into an orchard and
deteriorating into a scraggy plantation, ended in a low
wall that was at about the level of the sea-wall and
separated from it by a water-course and a strip of very
green meadow. Audrey glanced instinctively back at the
house to see if anybody was watching her.

Flank Hall, which for a hundred years had been called
"the new hall," was a seemly Georgian residence, warm
in colour, with some quaint woodwork; and like most such
buildings in Essex, it made a very happy marriage with

the landscape. Its dormers and fine chimneys glowed amid
the dark bare trees, and they alone would have captivated
a Londoner possessing those precious attributes, fortunately
ever spreading among the enlightened middle-classes, a
motor-car, a cultured taste in architecture, and a desire
to enter the squirearchy. Audrey loathed the house. For
her it was the last depth of sordidness and the common-
place. She could imagine positively nothing less romantic.
She thought of the ground floor on chill March mornings
with no fires anywhere save a red gleam in the dining-
room, and herself wandering about in it idle, at a loss
for a diversion, an ambition, an effort, a real task; and
she thought of the upper floor, a mainly unoccupied wilderness of iron bedsteads and yellow chests of drawers and
chipped earthenware and islands of carpets, and her mother
plaintively and weariedly arguing with some servant over
a slop-pail in a corner. The images of the interior, indelibly
printed in her soul, desolated her.

Mozewater she loved, and every souvenir of it was exquisite—red barges beating miraculously up the shallow
puddles to Moze Quay, equinoctial spring-tides when the
estuary was a tremendous ocean covered with foam and the
sea-wall felt the light lash of spray, thunderstorms in
autumn gathering over the yellow melancholy of deathlike
sunsets, wild birds crying across miles of uncovered mud at
early morning and duck-hunters crouching in punts behind
a waving screen of delicate grasses to wing them, and the
mysterious shapes of steamers and warships in the offing
beyond the Sand. . . . The sail of the receding yacht
gleamed now against the Sand, and its flashing broke her
heart; for it was the flashing of freedom. She thought of
the yachtsman; he was very courteous and deferential; a
mild creature; he had behaved to her as to a woman. . . .
Oh ! To be the petted and capricious wife of such a man,
to nod commands, to enslave with a smile, to want a thing
and instantly to have it, to be consulted and to decide, to
spend with large gestures, to be charitable, to be adored by

those whom you had saved from disaster, to increase happiness wherever you went . . . and to be free ! . . . .

The little dog jumped up at her because he was tired of being ignored, and she caught him and kissed him again and again passionately, and he wriggled with ecstasy and licked her ears with all the love in him. And in kissing him she kissed grave and affectionate husbands, she kissed the lovely scenery of the Sound, and she kissed the magnificent ideal of emancipation. But the dog had soon had enough of her arms ; he broke free, sprang, alighted, and rolled over, and arose sniffing, with earth on his black muzzle. . . .

He looked up at her inquiringly. . . . Strange, short-frocked blue figure looking down at him ! She had a bulging forehead ; her brown eyes were tunnelled underneath it. But what living eyes, what ardent eyes, that blazed up and sank like a fire ! What delicate and exact mirrors of the secret traffic between her soul and the soul of the world ! She had full cheeks, and a large mouth ripe red, inviting and provocative. In the midst, an absurd small unprominent nose that meant nothing ! Her complexion was divine, surpassing all similes. To caress that smooth downy cheek (if you looked close you could see the infinitesimal down against the light like an aura on the edge of the silhouette), even to let the gaze dwell on it, what an enchantment ! . . . She considered herself piquant and comely, and she was not deceived. She had long hands.

The wind from afar on her cheek reminded her poignantly that she was a prisoner. She could not go to the clustered village on the left, nor into the saltings on the right, nor even on to the sea-wall where the new rushes and grasses were showing. All the estuary was barred, and the winding road that mounted the slope towards Colchester. Her revolt against injustice was savage. Hatred of her father surged up in her like glittering lava. She had long since ceased to try to comprehend him. She despised herself because she was unreasonably afraid of him, ridiculously mute before him. She could not understand how anybody

could be friendly with him—for was he not notorious? Yet
everywhere he was greeted with respect and smiles, and he
would chat at length with all manner of people on a note of
mild and smooth cordiality. He and Miss Ingate would
enjoy together the most enormous talks. She was, however,
aware that Miss Ingate's opinion of him was not very
different from her own. Each time she saw her father and
Miss Ingate in communion she would say in her heart to
Miss Ingate: "You are disloyal to me." . . .

Was it possible that she had confided to Miss Ingate her
fearful secret? The conversation appeared to her unreal
now. She went over her plan. In the afternoon her father
was always out, and to-morrow afternoon her mother would
be out too. She would have a few things in a light bag that
she could carry—her mother's bag! She would put on her
best clothes and a veil from her mother's wardrobe. She
would take the 4.5 p.m. train. The stationmaster would be
at his tea then. Only the booking-clerk and the porter
would see her, and neither would dare to make an observa-
tion. She would ask for a return ticket to Ipswich; that
would allay suspicion, and at Ipswich she would book again.
She had cut out the addresses of the boarding-houses. She
would have to buy things in London. She knew of two
shops—Harrod's and Shoolbred's; she had seen their
catalogues. And the very next morning after arrival she
would go to Pitman's School. She would change the first
of the £5 notes at the station and ask for plenty of silver.
She glanced at the unlimited wealth still crushed in her
hand, and then she carefully dropped the fortune down the
neck of her frock. . . . Stealing? She repulsed the idea
with violent disdain. What she had accomplished against
her father was not a crime, but a vengeance. . . . She
would never be found in London. It was impossible. Her
plan seemed to her to be perfect in each detail, except one.
She was not the right sort of girl to execute it. She was
very shy. She suspected that no other girl could really be
as shy as she was. She recalled dreadful rare moments with

her mother in strange drawing-rooms. Still, she would execute the plan even if she died of fright. A force within her would compel her to execute it. This force did not make for happiness; on the contrary, it uncomfortably scared her; but it was irresistible.

Something on the brow of the road from Colchester attracted her attention. It was a handcart, pushed by a labourer and by Police Inspector Keeble, whom she liked. Following the handcart over the brow came a loose procession of villagers, which included no children, because the children were in school. Except on a Sunday Audrey had never before seen a procession of villagers, and these villagers must have been collected out of the fields, for the procession was going in the direction of, and not away from, the village. The handcart was covered with a tarpaulin. . . . She knew what had happened; she knew infallibly. Skirting the boundary of the grounds, she reached the main entrance to Flank Hall thirty seconds before the handcart. The little dog, delighted in a new adventure, yapped ecstatically at her heels, and then bounded onwards to meet the Inspector and the handcart.

"Run and tell yer mother, Miss Moze," Inspector Keeble called out in a carrying whisper. "There's been an accident. He ditched the car near Ardleigh cross-roads, trying to avoid some fowls."

Mr. Moze, hurrying too fast to meet the Bishop of Colchester, had met a greater than the Bishop.

Audrey glanced an instant with a sick qualm at the outlines of the shape beneath the tarpaulin, and ran.

In the dining-room, over the speck of fire, Mrs. Moze and Miss Ingate were locked in a deep intimate gossip.

"Mother!" cried Audrey, and then sank like a sack.

"Why! The little thing's fainted!" Miss Ingate exclaimed in a voice suddenly hoarse.

CHAPTER III

AUDREY and Miss Ingate were in the late Mathew Moze's study, fascinated—as much unconsciously as consciously—by the thing which since its owner's death had grown every hour more mysterious and more formidable—the safe. It was a fine afternoon. The secondary but still grandiose enigma of the affair, Mr. Cowl, could be heard walking methodically on the gravel in the garden. Mr. Cowl was the secretary of the National Reformation Society.

Suddenly the irregular sound of crunching receded.

"He's gone somewhere else," said Audrey.

"I'm so relieved," said Miss Ingate. "I hope he's gone a long way off."

"Are you?" murmured Audrey, with an air of surprised superiority.

But in secret Audrey felt just as relieved as Miss Ingate, despite the fact that, her mother being prostrate, she was the mistress of the situation, and could have ordered Mr. Cowl to leave, with the certainty of being obeyed. She was astonished at her illogical sensations, and she had been frequently so astonished in the previous four days.

For example, she was free; she knew that she could impose herself on her mother; never again would she be the slave of an unreasoning tyrant; yet she was gloomy and without hope. She had hated the unreasoning tyrant; yet she felt very sorry for him because he was dead. And though she felt very sorry for him, she detested hearing the panegyrics upon him of the village, and particularly of those persons with whom he had quarrelled; she actually stopped

23

Miss Ingate in the midst of an enumeration of his good qualities—his charm, his smile, his courtesy, his integrity, et cetera; she could not bear it. She thought that no child had ever had such a strange attitude to a deceased parent as hers to Mr. Moze. She had anticipated the inquest with an awful dread; it proved to be a trifle, and a ridiculous trifle. In the long weekly letter which she wrote to her adored school-friend Ethel at Manningtree she had actually likened the coroner to a pecking fowl! Was it possible that a daughter could write in such a strain about the inquest on her father's body?

The funeral had seemed a function by itself, with some guidance from the undertaker and still more from Mr. Cowl. Villagers and district acquaintances had been many at the ceremony, but relatives rare. Mr. Moze's four younger brothers were all in the Colonies; Mrs. Moze had apparently no connections. Madame Piriac, daughter of Mr. Moze's first wife by that lady's first husband, had telegraphed sympathies from Paris. A cousin or so had come in person from Woodbridge for the day.

It was from the demeanour of these cousins, grave men twice her age or more, that Audrey had first divined her new importance in the world. Their deference indicated that in their opinion the future mistress of Flank Hall was not Mrs. Moze, but Audrey. Audrey admitted that they were right. Yet she took no pleasure in issuing commands. She spoke firmly, but she said to herself: "There is no backbone to this firmness, and I am a fraud." She had always yearned for responsibility, yet now that it was in her hand she trembled, and she would have dropped it and run away from it as from a bomb, had she not been too cowardly to show her cowardice.

The instance of Aguilar, the head-gardener and mechanic, well illustrated her pusillanimity. She loathed Aguilar; her mother loathed him; the servants loathed him. He had said at the inquest that the car was in perfect order, but that Mr. Moze was too excitable to be a good driver. His evidence was true, but the jury did not care for his manner. Nor did the village. He had only two good qualities—honesty and efficiency; and these by their rarity excited jealousy rather than admiration. Audrey strongly desired to throw the gardener-mechanic upon the world; it nauseated her to see his disobliging face about the garden. But he remained scathless, to refuse demanded vegetables, to annoy the kitchen, to pronounce the motor-car utterly valueless, and to complain of his own liver. Audrey had legs; she had a tongue; she could articulate. Neither wish nor power was lacking in her to give Aguilar the supreme experience of his career. And yet she did not walk up to him and say: "Aguilar, please take a week's notice." Why? The question puzzled her and lowered her opinion of herself.

She was similarly absurd in the paramount matter of the safe. The safe could not be opened. The village, having been thrilled by four stirring days of the most precious and rare fever, had suffered much after the funeral from a severe reaction of dullness. It would have suffered much more had the fact not escaped that the safe could not be opened. In the deep depression of the day following the funeral the village could still say to itself: "Romance and excitement are not yet over, for the key of the Moze safe is lost, and the will is in the safe!"

The village did not know that there were two keys to the safe and that they were both lost. Nobody knew that except Audrey and Miss Ingate and Mr. Cowl. The official key was lost because Mr. Moze's key-ring was lost. The theory was that it had been jerked out of his pocket in the accident. Persistent search for it had been unsuccessful. As for the unofficial or duplicate key, Audrey could not remember where she had put it after her burglary, the conclusion of which had been disturbed by Miss Ingate. At one moment she was quite sure that she had left the key in the safe, but at another moment she was equally sure that she was holding the key in her right hand (the bank-notes being in her left) when Miss Ingate entered the room; at still another

C

moment she was almost convinced that before Miss Ingate's arrival she had run to the desk and slipped the key back into its drawer. In any case the second key was irretrievable. She discussed the dilemma very fully with Miss Ingate, who had obligingly come to stay in the house. They examined every aspect of the affair, except Audrey's guiltiness of theft, which both of them tacitly ignored. In the end they decided· that it might be wiser not to conceal Audrey's knowledge of the existence of a second key; and they told Mr. Cowl, because he happened to be at hand. In so doing they were ill-advised, because Mr. Cowl at once acted in a characteristic and inconvenient fashion which they ought to have foreseen.

On the day before the funeral Mr. Cowl had telegraphed from some place in Devonshire that he should represent the National Reformation Society at the funeral, and asked for a bed, on the pretext that he could not get from Devonshire to Moze in time for the funeral if he postponed his departure until the next morning. The telegram was quite costly. He arrived for dinner, a fat man about thirty-eight, with chestnut hair, a low, alluring voice, and a small handbag for luggage. Miss Ingate thought him very interesting, and he was. He said little about the National Reformation Society, but a great deal about the late Mr. Moze, of whom he appeared to be an intimate friend; presumably the friendship had developed at meetings of the Society. After dinner he strolled nonchalantly to the sideboard and opened a box of the deceased's cigars, and suggested that, as he was well acquainted with the brand, having often enjoyed the hospitality of Mr. Moze's cigar-case, he should smoke a cigar now to the memory of the departed. Miss Ingate then began to feel alarmed. He smoked four cigars to the memory of the departed, and on retiring ventured to take four more for consumption during the night, as he seldom slept.

In the morning he went into the bathroom at eight o'clock and remained there till noon, reading and smoking in continually renewed hot water. He descended blandly, begged Miss Moze not to trouble about his breakfast, and gently assumed a certain control of the funeral. After the funeral he announced that he should leave on the morrow; but the mystery of the safe held him to the house. When he heard of the existence of the second key he organised and took command of a complete search of the study, and in the course of the search he inspected every document in the study. He said he knew that the deceased had left a legacy to the Society, and he should not feel justified in quitting Moze until the will was found.

Now in these circumstances Audrey ought certainly to have telegraphed to her father's solicitor at Chelmsford at once. In the alternative she ought to have hired a safe-opening expert or a burglar from Colchester. She had accomplished neither of these downright things. With absolute power, she had done nothing but postpone. She wondered at herself, for up to her father's death she had been a great critic of absolute power.

The heavy policemanish step of Mr. Cowl was heard on the landing.

"He's coming down on us!" exclaimed Miss Ingate, partly afraid, and partly ironic at her own fear. "I'm sure he's coming down on us. Audrey, I liked that man at first, but now I tremble before him. And I'm sure his moustache is dyed. Can't you ask him to leave?"

"Is his moustache dyed, Winnie? Oh, what fun!"

Miss Ingate's apprehension was justified. There was a knock at the study door, discreet, insistent, menacing, and it was Mr. Cowl's knock. He entered, smiling gravely and yet, as it were, teasingly. His easy bigness, florid and sinister, made a disturbing contrast with the artless and pure simplicity of Audrey in her new black robe, and even with Miss Ingate's pallid maturity, which, after all, was passably innocent and ingenuous. Mr. Cowl resembled a great beast good-humouredly lolloping into the cage in which two rabbits had been placed for his diversion and hunger.

Pulling a key from the pocket of his vast waistcoat, he said in his quiet voice, so seductive and ominous :

"Is this the key of the safe?"

He offered it delicately to Audrey.

It was the key of the safe.

"Did they find it in the ditch?" Audrey demanded, blushing, for she knew that the key had not been found in the ditch; she knew by a certain indentation on it that it was the duplicate key which she herself had mislaid.

"No," said Mr. Cowl. "I found it myself, and not in the ditch. I remembered you had said that you had changed at the dressmaker's in the village and had left there an old frock."

"Did I?" murmured Audrey, with a deeper blush.

Mr. Cowl nodded.

"I had the happy idea that you might have had the key and left it in the pocket of the frock. So I trotted down to the dressmaker's and asked for the frock, in your name, and lo! the result!"

He pointed to the key lying in Audrey's long hand.

"But how should I have had the key, Mr. Cowl? Why should I have had the key?" Audrey burst out like a simpleton.

"That, Miss Moze," said he, with a peculiar grin and in an equally peculiar tone, "is a matter about which obviously you are better informed than I am. Shall we try the key?"

With a smooth undeniable gesture he took the key again from Audrey, and bent his huge form to open the safe. As he did so Miss Ingate made a sarcastic and yet affrighted face at Audrey, and Audrey tried to send a signal in reply, but failed, owing to imperfect self-control. However, she managed to say to Mr. Cowl's curved back:

"You couldn't have found the key in the pocket of my old frock, Mr. Cowl."

"And why?" he inquired benevolently, raising and turning his chestnut head. Even in that exciting instant Audrey could debate within herself whether or not his superb moustache was dyed.

"Because it has no pocket."

"So I discovered," said Mr. Cowl, after a little pause. "I merely stated that I had the happy idea—for it proved to be a happy idea—that you might have left the key in the pocket. I discovered it, as a fact, in a slit of the lining of the belt. . . . Conceivably you had slipped it in there—in a hurry." He put strange implications into the last three words. "Yes, it is the authentic key," he concluded, as the door of the safe swung heavily and silently open.

Audrey, for the first time, felt rather like a thief as she beheld the familiar interior of the safe which a few days earlier she had so successfully rifled. "Is it possible," she thought, "that I really took bank-notes out of that safe, and that they are at this very moment in my bedroom between the leaves of 'Pictures of Palestine'?"

Mr. Cowl was cautiously fumbling among the serried row of documents which, their edges towards the front, filled the steel shelf above the drawers. Audrey had never experienced any curiosity concerning the documents. Lucre alone had interested the base creature. No documents would have helped her to freedom. But now she thought apprehensively: "My fate may be among those documents." She was quite prepared to learn that her father had done something silly in his will.

"This resembles a testament," said Mr. Cowl, smiling to himself, and pulling out a foolscap scrip, folded and endorsed. "Yes. Dated last year."

He unfolded the document; a letter slipped from the interior of it; he placed the letter on the small occasional table next to the desk, and offered the will to Audrey with precisely the same gesture as he had offered the key.

Audrey tried to decipher the will, and completely failed.

"Will you read it, Miss Ingate?" she muttered.

"I can't! I can't!" answered Miss Ingate in excitement. "I'm sure I can't. I never could read wills. They're so funny, somehow. And I haven't got my spectacles." She flushed slightly.

"May *I* venture to tell you what it contains?" Mr. Cowl suggested. "There can be no indiscretion on my part, as all wills after probate are public property and can be inspected by any Tom, Dick or Harry for a fee of one shilling."

He took the document and gazed at it intently, turning over a page and turning back, for an extraordinarily long time.

Audrey said to herself again and again, with exasperated impatience: "He knows now, and I don't know. He knows now, and I don't know. He knows now, and I don't know."

At length Mr. Cowl spoke:

"It is a perfectly simple will. The testator leaves the whole of his property to Mrs. Moze for life, and afterwards to you, Miss Moze. There are only two legacies. Ten pounds to James Aguilar, gardener. And the testator's shares in the Zacatecas Oil Development Corporation to the National Reformation Society. I may say that the testator had expressed to me his intention of leaving these shares to the Society. We should have preferred money, free of legacy duty, but the late Mr. Moze had a reason for everything he did. I must now bid you good-bye, ladies," he went on strangely, with no pause. "Miss Moze, will you convey my sympathetic respects to your mother and my thanks for her most kind hospitality? My grateful sympathies to yourself. Good-bye, Miss Ingate. . . . Er, Miss Ingate, why do you look at me in that peculiar way?"

"Well, Mr. Cowl, you're a very peculiar man. May I ask whether you were born in this part of the country?"

"At Clacton, Miss Ingate," answered Mr. Cowl imperturbably.

"I knew it," said Miss Ingate, and the corners of her lips went sardonically down.

"Please don't trouble to come downstairs," said Mr. Cowl. "My bag is packed. I have tipped the parlourmaid, and there is just time to catch the train."

He departed, leaving the two women speechless.

After a moment, Miss Ingate said dryly:

"He was so very peculiar I knew he must belong to these parts."

"How did he know I left my blue frock at Miss Pannell's?" cried Audrey. "I never told him."

"He must have been eavesdropping!" cried Miss Ingate. "He never found the key in your frock. He must have found it here somewhere; I feel sure it must have dropped by the safe, and I lay anything he had opened the safe before and read the will before. I could tell from the way he looked."

"And why should he suppose that I'd the key?" Audrey put in.

"Eavesdropping! I'm convinced that man knows too much." Audrey reddened once more. "I believe he thought you'd be capable of burning the will. That's why he made you handle it in his presence and mine."

"Well, Winnie," said Audrey, "I think you might have told him all that while he was here, instead of letting him go off so triumphant."

"I did begin to," said Miss Ingate with a snigger. "But you wouldn't back me up, you little coward."

"I shall never be a coward again!" Audrey said violently.

They read the will together. They had no difficulty at all in comprehending it now that they were alone.

"I do think it's a horrid shame Aguilar should have that ten pounds," said Audrey. "But otherwise I don't care. You can't guess how relieved I am, Winnie. I imagined the most dreadful things. I don't know what I imagined. But now we shall have all the property and everything, just as much as ever there was, and only me and mother to spend it." Audrey danced an embryonic jig. "Won't I keep mother in order! Winnie, I shall make her go with me to Paris. I've always wanted to know that Madame Piriac—she does write such funny English in her letters."

"What's that you're saying?" murmured Miss Ingate, who had picked up the letter which Mr. Cowl had laid on the small table.

"I say I shall make mother go to Paris with me."

"You won't," said Miss Ingate. "Because she won't go. I know your mother better than you do. . . . Oh! Audrey!"

Audrey saw Miss Ingate's face turn scarlet from the roots of her hair to her chin.

Miss Ingate had dropped the letter. Audrey snatched it.

"My dear Moze," the letter ran. "I send you herewith a report of the meeting of the Great Mexican Oil Company at New York. You will see that they duly authorised the contract by which the Zacatecas Oil Corporation transfers our property to them in exchange for shares at the rate of four Great Mexican shares for one Zacatecas share. As each of the Development Syndicate shares represents ten of the Corporation shares, and as on my recommendation you put £4,500 into the Syndicate, you will therefore own 180,000 Great Mexican shares. They are at present above par. Mark my words, they will be worth from seven to ten dollars apiece in a year's time. I think you now owe me a good turn, eh?"

The letter was signed with a name unknown to either of them, and it was dated from Coleman Street, E.C.

CHAPTER IV

MR. FOULGER

HALF an hour later the woman and the girl, still in the study and severely damaged by the culminating events of Mr. Cowl's visit, were almost prostrated by the entirely un-expected announcement of the arrival of Mr. Foulger. Mr. Foulger was the late Mr. Moze's solicitor from Chelmsford. Audrey's first thought was: "Has heaven telegraphed to him on my behalf?" But her next was that all the solicitors in the world would now be useless in the horrible calamity that had befallen.

It is to be noted that Audrey was no worse off than before the discovery of the astounding value of the Zacatecas shares. The Moze property, inherited through generations and consisting mainly in farms and tithe-rents, was not in the slightest degree impaired. On the contrary, the steady progress of agriculture in Essex indicated that its yield must improve with years. Nevertheless Audrey felt as though she and her mother were ruined, and as though the National Reformation Society had been guilty of a fearful crime against a widow and an orphan. The lovely vision of immeasurable wealth had flashed and scintillated for a month in front of her dazzled eyes—and then blackness, nothing-ness, the dark void! She knew that she would never be happy again.

And she thought, scornfully, "How could father have been so preoccupied and so gloomy, with all those riches?" She could not conceive anybody as rich as her father secretly was not being day and night in a con-dition of pure delight at the whole spectacle of existence.

Her opinion of Mathew Moze fell lower than ever, and fell finally.

The parlourmaid, in a negligence of attire indicating that no man was left alive in the house, waited at the door of the study to learn whether or not Miss Moze was in.

"You'll *have* to see him," said Miss Ingate firmly. "It'll be all right. I've known him all my life. He's a very nice man."

After the parlourmaid had gone, and while Audrey was upbraiding her for not confessing earlier her acquaintance with Mr. Foulger, Miss Ingate added :

"Only his wife has a wooden leg."

Then Mr. Foulger entered. He was a shortish man of about fifty, with a paunch, but not otherwise fat; dressed like a sportsman. He trod very lightly. The expression on his ruddy face was amiable but extremely alert, hardening at intervals into decision or caution. He saw before him a nervous, frowning girl in inelegant black, and Miss Ingate with a curious look in her eyes and a sardonic and timid twitching of her lips. For an instant he was discountenanced; but he at once recovered, accomplishing a bright salute.

"Here you are at last, Mr. Foulger!" Miss Ingate responded. "But you're too late."

These mysterious words, and the speechlessness of Audrey, upset him again.

"I was away in Somersetshire for a little fishing," he said, after he had deplored the death of Mr. Moze, the illness of Mrs. Moze, and the bereavement of Miss Moze, and had congratulated Miss Moze on the protective friendship of his old friend, Miss Ingate. "I was away for a little fishing, and I only heard the sad news when I got back home at noon to-day. I came over at once." He cleared his throat and looked first at Audrey and then at Miss Ingate. He felt that he ought to be addressing Audrey, but somehow he could not help addressing Miss Ingate instead. His grey legs were spread abroad as he sat very erect on a chair, and between them his dependent paunch found a comfortable space for itself.

"You must have been getting anxious about the will. I have brought it with me," he said. He drew a white document from the breast-pocket of his cutaway coat, and he perched a pair of eyeglasses carelessly on his nose. "It was executed before your birth, Miss Moze. But a will keeps like wine. The whole of the property of every description is left to Mrs. Moze, and she is sole executrix. If she should predecease the testator, then everything is left to his child or children. Not perhaps a very businesslike will—a will likely to lead to unforeseen complications, but the sort of will that a man in the first flush of marriage often does make, and there is no stopping him. Your father had almost every quality, but he was not businesslike—if I may say so with respect. However, I confess that for the present I see no difficulties. Of course the death duties will have to be paid, but your father always kept a considerable amount of money at call. When I say 'considerable,' I mean several thousands. That was a point on which he and I had many discussions."

Mr. Foulger glanced around with satisfaction. Already the prospect of legal business and costs had brought about a change in his official demeanour of an adviser truly bereaved by the death of a client. He saw the young girl, gazing fiercely at the carpet, suddenly begin to weep. This phenomenon, to which he was not unaccustomed, did not by itself disturb him; but the face of Miss Ingate gave him strange apprehensions, which reached a climax when Miss Ingate, obviously not at all at ease, muttered:

"There is a later will, Mr. Foulger. It was made last year."

"I see," he breathed, scarcely above a whisper.

He thought he did see. He thought he understood why he had been kept waiting, why Mrs. Moze pretended to be ill, why the girl had frowned, why the naively calm Miss Ingate was in such a state of nerves. The explanation was that he was not wanted. The explanation was that Mr. Moze had changed his solicitor. His face hardened, for he and his uncle between them had "acted" for the Moze family for over seventy years.

He rose from the chair.

"Then I need not trouble you any longer," he said in a firm tone, and turned with real dignity to leave.

He was exceedingly astonished when with one swift movement Audrey rose, and flashed like a missile to the door, and stood with her back to it. The fact was that Audrey had just remembered her vow never again to be afraid of anybody. When Miss Ingate with extraordinary agility also jumped up and approached him, he apprehended, recalling rumours of Miss Ingate's advanced feminism, that the fate of an anti-suffragette Cabinet Minister might be awaiting him, and he prepared his defence.

"You mustn't go," said Miss Ingate.

"You are my solicitor, whatever mother may say, and you mustn't go," added Audrey in a soft voice.

The man was entranced. It occurred to him that he would have a tale to tell and to re-tell at his club for years, about "a certain fair client who shall be nameless."

The next minute he had heard a somewhat romantic, if not hysterical, version of the facts of the case, and he was perusing the original documents. By chance he read first the letter about the Zacatecas shares. That Mathew Moze had made a will without his aid was a shock; that Mathew Moze had invested money without his advice was another shock quite as severe. But he knew the status of the Great Mexican Oil Company, and his countenance lighted as he realised the rich immensity of the business of proving the will and devolving the estate; his costs would run to the most agreeable figures. As soon as he glanced at the testament which Mr. Cowl had found, he muttered, with satisfaction and disdain :

"H'm ! He made this himself."

And he gazed at it compassionately, as a cabinetmaker might gaze at a piece of amateur fretwork.

Standing, he read it slowly and with extreme care. And when he had finished he casually remarked, in the classic legal phrase:

"It isn't worth the paper it's written on."

Then he sat down again, and his neat paunch resumed its niche between his legs. He knew that he had made a tremendous effect.

"But—but——" Miss Ingate began.

"Not worth the paper it's written on," he repeated. "There is only one witness, and there ought to be two, and even the one witness is a bad one—Aguilar, because he profits under the will. He would have to give up his legacy before his attestation could count, and even then it would be no good alone. Mr. Moze has not even expressly revoked the old will. If there hadn't been a previous will, and if Aguilar was a thoroughly reliable man, and if the family had wished to uphold the new will, I dare say the Court *might* have pronounced for it. But under the circumstances it hasn't the ghost of a chance."

"But won't the National Reformation Society make trouble?" demanded Miss Ingate faintly.

"Let 'em try!" said Mr. Foulger, who wished that the National Reformation Society would indeed try.

Even as he articulated the words, he was aware of Audrey coming towards him from the direction of the door; he was aware of her black frock and of her white face, with its bulging forehead and its deliciously insignificant nose. She held out her hand.

"You are a dear!" she whispered.

Her lips seemed to aim uncertainly for his face. Did they just touch, with exquisite contact, his bristly chin, or was it a divine illusion? . . . She blushed in a very marked manner. He blinked, and his happy blinking seemed to say: "Only wills drawn by me are genuine. . . . Didn't I tell you Mr. Moze was not a man of business?"

Audrey ran to Miss Ingate.

Mr. Foulger, suddenly ashamed, and determined to be a lawyer, said sharply :

"Has Mrs. Moze made a will?."

"Mother made a will? Oh no!"

"Then she should make one at once, in your favour, of course. No time should be lost."

"But Mrs. Moze is ill in bed," protested Miss Ingate.

"All the more reason why she should make a will. It may save endless trouble. And it is her duty. I shall suggest that I be the executor and trustee, of course with the usual power to charge costs." His face was hard again. "You will thank me later on, Miss Moze," he added.

"Do you mean *now*?" shrilled Miss Ingate.

"I do," said he. "If you will give me some paper, we might go to her at once. You can be one of the witnesses. I could be a witness, but as I am to act under the will for a consideration somebody else would be preferable."

"I should suggest Aguilar," answered Miss Ingate, the corners of her lips dropping.

Miss Ingate went first, to prepare Mrs. Moze.

When Audrey was alone in the study—she had not even offered to accompany her elders to the bedroom—she made a long sound : "Ooo!" Then she gave a leap and stood still, staring out of the window at the estuary. She tried to force her mood to the colour of her dress, but the sense of propriety was insufficient for the task. The magnificence of all the world was unfolding itself to her soul. Events had hitherto so dizzyingly beaten down upon her head that she had scarcely been conscious of feeling. Now she luxuriously felt. "I am at last born," she thought. "Miracles have happened. . . . It's incredible. . . . I can do what I like with mother. . . . But if I don't take care I shall die of relief this very moment!"

CHAPTER V

THE DEAD HAND

AUDREY was wakened up that night, just after she had gone to sleep, by a touch on the cheek. Her mother, palely indistinct in the darkness, was standing by the bed-side. She wore a white wrap over her night attire, and the customary white bandage from which emanated a faint odour of eau-de-Cologne, was around her forehead.

"Audrey, darling, I must speak to you."

Instantly Audrey became the wise directress of her poor foolish mother's existence.

"Mother," she said, with firm kindness, "please do go back to bed at once. This sort of thing is simply frightful for your neuralgia. I'll come to you in one moment."

And Mrs. Moze meekly obeyed; she had gone even before Audrey had had time to light her candle. Audrey was very content in thus being able to control her mother and order everything for the best. She guessed that the old lady had got some idea into her head about the property, or about her own will, or about the solicitor, or about a tombstone, and that it was worrying her. She and Miss Ingate (who had now returned home) had had a very extensive palaver, in low voices that never ceased, after the triumphant departure of Mr. Foulger. Audrey had cautiously protested; she was afraid her mother would be fatigued, and she saw no reason why her mother should be acquainted with all the details of a complex matter; but the gossiping habit of a quarter of a century was too powerful for Audrey.

In the large parental bedroom the only light was Audrey's

candle. Mrs. Moze was lying on the right half of the great bed, where she had always lain. She might have lain luxuriously in the middle, with vast spaces at either hand, but again habit was too powerful.

The girl, all in white, held the candle higher, and the shadows everywhere shrunk in unison. Mrs. Moze blinked.

"Put the candle on the night-table," said Mrs. Moze curtly.

Audrey did so. The bedroom, for her, was full of the souvenirs of parental authority. Her first recollections were those of awe in regard to the bedroom. And when she thought that on that bed she had been born, she had a very queer sensation.

"I've decided," said Mrs. Moze, lying on her back, and looking up at the ceiling, "I've decided that your father's wishes must be obeyed."

"What about, mother?"

"About those shares going to the National Reformation Society. He meant them to go, and they must go to the Society. I've thought it well over and I've quite decided. I didn't tell Miss Ingate, as it doesn't concern her. But I felt I must tell you at once."

"Mother!" cried Audrey. "Have you taken leave of your senses?" She shivered; the room was very cold, and as she shivered her image in the mirror of the wardrobe shivered, and also her shadow that climbed up the wall and bent at right-angles at the cornice till it reached the middle of the ceiling.

Mrs. Moze replied obstinately:

"I've not taken leave of my senses, and I'll thank you to remember that I'm your mother. I have always carried out your father's wishes, and at my time of life I can't alter. Your father was a very wise man. We shall be as well off as we always were. Better, because I can save, and I shall save. We have no complaint to make; I should have no excuse for disobeying your father. Everything is mine to do as I wish with it, and I shall give the shares to the Society. What the shares are worth can't affect my duty. Besides, perhaps they aren't worth anything. I always understood that things like that were always jumping up and down, and generally worthless in the end. . . . That's all I wanted to tell you."

Why did Audrey seize the candle and walk straight out of the bedroom, leaving darkness behind her? Was it because the acuteness of her feelings drove her out, or was it because she knew instinctively that her mother's decision would prove to be immovable? Perhaps both.

She dropped back into her own bed with a soundless sigh of exhaustion. She did not blow out the candle, but lay staring at it. Her dream was annihilated. She foresaw an interminable, weary and futile future in and about Moze, and her mother always indisposed, always fretful, and curiously obstinate in weakness. But Audrey, despite her tragic disillusion, was less desolated than made solemn. In the most disturbing way she knew herself to be the daughter of her father and her mother; and she comprehended that her destiny could not be broken off suddenly from theirs. She was touched because her mother deemed her father a very wise man, whereas she, Audrey, knew that he was nothing of the sort. She felt sorry for both of them. She pitied her father, and she was a mother to her mother. Their relations together, and the mystic posthumous spell of her father over her mother, impressed her profoundly. . . . And she was proud of herself for having demonstrated her courage by preventing the solicitor from running away, and extraordinarily ashamed of her sentimental and brazen behaviour to the solicitor afterwards. These various thoughts mitigated her despair as she gazed at the sinking candle. Nevertheless her dream was annihilated.

D

CHAPTER VI

THE YOUNG WIDOW

It was early October. Audrey stood at the garden door of Flank Hall.

The estuary, in all the colours of unsettled, mild, bright weather, lay at her feet beneath a high arch of changing blue and white. The capricious wind moved in her hair, moved in the rich grasses of the sea-wall, bent at a curtseying angle the red-sailed barges, put caps on the waves in the middle distance, and drew out into long horizontal scarves the smoke of faint steamers in the offing.

Audrey was dressed in black, but her raiment had obviously not been fashioned in the village, nor even at Colchester, nor yet at Ipswich, that great and stylish city. She looked older; she certainly had acquired something of an air of knowledge, assurance, domination, sauciness and challenge, which qualities were all partly illustrated in her large, audacious hat. The spirit which the late Mr. Moze had so successfully suppressed was at length coming to the surface for all beholders to see, and the process of evolution begun at the moment when Audrey had bounced up and prevented an authoritative solicitor from leaving the study was already advanced. Nevertheless, at frequent intervals Audrey's eyes changed, and she seemed for an instant to be a very naive, very ingenuous and wistful little thing—and this though she had reached the age of twenty. Perhaps she was feeling sorry for the girl she used to be.

And no doubt she was also thinking of her mother,

who had died within eight hours of their nocturnal interview. The death of Mrs. Moze surprised everyone, except possibly Mrs. Moze. As an unsuspected result of the operation upon her, an embolism had been wandering in her veins; it reached the brain, and she expired, to the great loss of the National Reformation Society. Such was the brief and simple history. When Audrey stood by the body, she had felt that if it could have saved her mother she would have enriched the National Reformation Society with all she possessed.

Gradually the sense of freedom had grown paramount in her, and she had undertaken the enterprise of completely subduing Mr. Foulger to her own ends.

The back hall was carpetless and pictureless, and the furniture in it was draped in grey-white. Every room in the abode was in the same state, and, since all the windows were shuttered, every room lay moribund in a ghostly twilight. Only the clocks remained alive, probably thinking themselves immortal. The breakfast things were washed up and stored away. The last two servants had already gone. Behind Audrey, forming a hilly background, were trunks and boxes, a large bunch of flowers encased in paper, and a case of umbrellas and parasols; the whole strikingly new, and every single item except the flowers labelled "Paris via Charing Cross and Calais."

Audrey opened her black Russian satchel, and the purse within it. Therein were a little compartment full of English gold, another full of French gold, another full of multicoloured French bank-notes; and loose in the satchel was a blue book of credit-notes, each for five hundred francs, or twenty pounds—a thick book! And she would not have minded much if she had lost the whole satchel —it would be so easy to replace the satchel with all its contents.

Then a small brougham came very deliberately up the drive. It was the vehicle in which Miss Ingate went her ways; in accordance with Miss Ingate's immemorial command, it travelled at a walking pace up all the hills to save the horse, and at a walking pace down all hills lest the horse should stumble and Miss Ingate be destroyed. It was now followed by a luggage-cart on which was a large trunk.

At the same moment Aguilar, the gardener, appeared from somewhere—he who had been robbed of a legacy of ten pounds, but who by his ruthless and incontestable integrity had secured the job of caretaker of Flank Hall.

The drivers touched their hats to Audrey and jumped down, and Miss Ingate, with a blue veil tied like a handkerchief round her bonnet and chin—sign that she was a traveller—emerged from the brougham, sardonically smiling at her own and everybody's expense, and too excited to be able to give greetings. The three men started to move the trunks, and the two women whispered together in the back-hall.

"Audrey," demanded Miss Ingate, with a start, "what are those rings on your finger?"

Audrey replied:

"One's a wedding ring and the other's a mourning ring. I bought them yesterday at Colchester. . . . Hsh!" She stilled further exclamations from Miss Ingate until the men were out of the hall.

"Look here! Quick!" she whispered, hastily unlocking a large hat-case that was left. And Miss Ingate looked and saw a block toque, entirely unsuitable for a young girl, and a widow's veil.

"I look bewitching in them," said Audrey, relocking the case.

"But, my child, what does it mean?"

"It means that I'm not silly enough to go to Paris as a girl. I've had more than enough of being a girl. I'm determined to arrive in Paris as a young widow. It will be much better in every way, and far easier for you. In fact, you'll have no chaperoning to do at all. I shall be the chaperon. Now don't say you won't go, because you will."

"You ought to have told me before."

"No, I oughtn't. Nothing could have been more foolish."

"But who are you the widow of?"

"Hurrah!" cried Audrey. "You are a sport, Winnie! I'll tell you all the interesting details in the train."

In another minute Aguilar, gloomy and unbending, had received the keys of Flank Hall, and the procession crunched down the drive on its way to the station.

CHAPTER VII

THE CIGARETTE GIRL

AUDREY did not deem that she had begun truly to live until the next morning, when they left London, after having passed a night in the Charing Cross Hotel. During several visits to London in the course of the summer Audrey had learnt something about the valuelessness of money in a metropolis chiefly inhabited by people who were positively embarrassed by their riches. She knew, for example, that money being very plentiful and stylish hats very rare, large quantities of money had to be given for infinitesimal quantities of hats. The big and glittering shops were full of people whose pockets bulged with money which they were obviously anxious to part with in order to obtain goods, while the proud shop-assistants, secure in the knowledge that money was naught and goods were everything, did their utmost, by hauteur and steely negatives, to render any transaction possible. It was the result of a mysterious "Law of Exchange." She was aware of this. She had lost her childhood's naive illusions about the sovereignty of money.

Nevertheless she received one or two shocks on the journey, which was planned upon the most luxurious scale that the imagination of Messrs. Thomas Cook & Son could conceive. There was four pounds and ninepence to pay for excess luggage at Charing Cross. Half a year earlier four pounds would have bought all the luggage she could have got together. She very nearly said to the clerk at the window : "Don't you mean shillings?" But in spite of nervousness, blushings, and all manner of sensitive reactions to new experiences, her natural sang-froid and instinctive knowledge of the world saved her from such a terrible lapse, and she put down a bank-note without the slightest hint that she was wondering whether it would not be more advantageous to throw the luggage away.

The boat was crowded, and the sea and wind full of menace. Fighting their way along the deck after laden porters, Audrey and Miss Ingate simultaneously espied the private cabin list hung in a conspicuous spot. They perused it as eagerly as if it had been the account of a *cause célèbre*. Among the list were two English lords, an Honourable Mrs., a baroness with a Hungarian name, several Teutonic names, and Mrs. Moncreiff.

Audrey blushed deeply at the sign of Mrs. Moncreiff, for she was Mrs. Moncreiff. Behind the veil, and with the touch of white in her toque, she might have been any age up to twenty-eight or so. It would have been impossible to say that she was a young girl, that she was not versed in the world, that she had not the whole catechism of men at her finger-ends. All who glanced at her glanced again—with sympathy and curiosity; and the second glance pricked Audrey's conscience, making her feel like a thief. But her moods were capricious. At one moment she was a thief, a clumsy fraud, an ignorant ninny, and a suitable prey for the secret police; and at the next she was very clever, self-confident, equal to the situation, and enjoying the situation more than she had ever enjoyed anything, and determined to prolong the situation indefinitely.

The cabin was very spacious, yet not more so than was proper, considering that the rent of it came to about six-pence a minute. There was room, even after all the packages were stowed, for both of them to lie down. But instead of lying down they eagerly inspected the little abode. They found a lavatory basin with hot and cold water taps, but no hot water and no cold water, no soap and no towels. And they found a crystal water-bottle, but it was empty. Then a steward came and asked them if they wanted anything, and because they were miserable poltroons they smiled and said "No." They were secretly convinced that all the other private cabins, inhabited by titled persons and by financiers, were superior to their cabin, and that the captain of the steamer had fobbed them off with an imitation of a real cabin.

Then it was that Miss Ingate, who since Charing Cross had been a little excited by a glimpsed newspaper contents-bill indicating suffragette riots that morning, perceived, through the open door of the cabin, a most beautiful and most elegant girl, attired impeccably in that ritualistic garb of travel which the truly cosmopolitan wear on combined rail-and-ocean journeys and on no other occasions. It was at once apparent that the celestial creature had put on that special hat, that special veil, that special cloak, and those special gloves because she was deeply aware of what was correct, and that she would not put them on again until destiny took her again across the sea, and that if destiny never did take her again across the sea never again would she show herself in the vestments, whose correctness was only equalled by their expensiveness.

The young woman, however, took no thought of her impressive clothes. She was existing upon quite another plane. Miss Ingate, preoccupied by the wrongs and perils of her sex, and momentarily softened out of her sardonic irony, suspected that they might be in the presence of a victim of oppression or neglect. The victim lay half-prone upon the hard wooden seat against the ship's rail. Her dark eyes opened piteously at times, and her exquisite profile, surmounted by the priceless hat all askew, made a silhouette now against the sea and now against the distant white cliffs of Albion, according to the fearful heaving of the ship. Spray occasionally dashed over her. She heeded it not. A few feet farther off she would have been sheltered by a weather-awning, but, clinging fiercely to the rail, she would not move.

Then a sharp squall of rain broke, but she entirely ignored the rain.

The next moment Miss Ingate and Audrey, rushing forth, had gently seized her and drawn her into their cabin. They might have succoured other martyrs to the modern passion for moving about, for there were many; but they chose this particular martyr because she was so wondrously dressed, and also perhaps a little because she was so young. As she lay on the cabin sofa she looked still younger; she looked a child. Yet when Miss Ingate removed her gloves in order to rub those chill, fragile, and miraculously manicured hands, a wedding ring was revealed. The wedding ring rendered her intensely romantic in the eyes of Audrey and Miss Ingate, who both thought, in private :

"She must be the wife of one of those lords ! "

Every detail of her raiment, as she was put at her ease, showed her to be clothed in precisely the manner which Audrey and Miss Ingate thought peeresses always were clothed. Hence, being English, they mingled respect with their solacing pity. Nevertheless, their respect was tempered by a peculiar pride, for both of them, in taking lemonade on the Pullman, had taken therewith a certain preventive or remedy which made them loftily indifferent to the heaving of ships and the eccentricities of the sea. The specific had done all that was claimed for it—which was a great deal—so much so that they felt themselves superwomen among a cargo of flaccid and feeble sub-females. And they grew charmingly conceited.

"Am I in my cabin? " murmured the martyr, about a quarter of an hour after Miss Ingate, having obtained soda water, had administered to her a dose of the miraculous specific.

Her delicious cheeks were now a delicate crimson. But they had been of a delicate crimson throughout.

"No," said Audrey. "You're in ours. Which is yours? "

"It's on the other side of the ship, then. I came out for a little air. But I couldn't get back. I'd just as lief have died as shift from that seat out there by the railings."

Something in the accent, something in those fine English words "lief" and "shift," destroyed in the minds of Audrey and Miss Ingate the agreeable notion that they had a peeress on their hands.

"Is your husband on board?" asked Audrey.

"He just is," was the answer. "He's in our cabin."

"Shall I fetch him?" Miss Ingate suggested. The corners of her lips had begun to fall once more.

"Will you?" said the young woman. "It's Lord South-minster. I'm Lady Southminster."

The two saviours were thrilled. Each felt that she had misinterpreted the accent, and that probably peeresses did habitually use such words as "lief" and "shift." The corners of Miss Ingate's lips rose to their proper position.

"I'll look for the number on the cabin list," said she hastily, and went forth with trembling to summon the peer.

As Audrey, alone in the cabin with Lady Southminster, bent curiously over the prostrate form, Lady Southminster exclaimed with an air of childlike admiration :

"You're real ladies, you are !"

And Audrey felt old and experienced. She decided that Lady Southminster could not be more than seventeen, and it seemed to be about half a century since Audrey was seventeen.

"He can't come," announced Miss Ingate breathlessly, returning to the cabin, and supporting herself against the door as the solid teak sank under her feet. "Oh yes ! He's there all right. It was Number 12. I've seen him. I told him, but I don't think he heard me—to understand, that is. If you ask me, he couldn't come if forty wives sent for him."

"Oh, couldn't he !" observed Lady Southminster, sitting up. "Couldn't he !"

When the boat was within ten minutes of France, the remedy had had such an effect upon her that she could walk about. Accompanied by Audrey she managed to work her way round the cabin-deck to No. 12. It was empty, save for hand-luggage ! The two girls searched, as well as they could, the whole crowded ship for Lord Southminster, and found him not. Lady Southminster neither fainted nor wept. She merely said :

"Oh ! All right ! If that's it. . . . ! "

Hand-luggage was being collected. But Lady Southminster would not collect hers, nor allow it to be collected. She agreed with Miss Ingate and Audrey that her husband must ultimately reappear either on the quay or in the train. While they were all standing huddled together in the throng waiting for the gangway to put ashore, she said in a low casual tone, à propos of nothing :

"I only married him the day before yesterday. I don't know whether you know, but I used to make cigarettes in Constantinopoulos's window in Piccadilly. I don't see why I should be ashamed of it, d'you? "

"Certainly not," said Miss Ingate. "But it *is* rather romantic, isn't it, Audrey? "

Despite the terrific interest of the adventure of the cigarette girl, disappointment began immediately after landing. This France, of which Audrey had heard so much and dreamed so much, was a very ramshackle and untidy and one-horse affair. The custom-house was rather like a battle-field without any rules of warfare ; the scene in the refresh-ment-room was rather like a sack after a battle ; the station was a desert with odd files of people here and there ; the platforms were ridiculous, and you wanted a pair of steps to get up into the train. Whatever romance there might be in France had been brought by Audrey in her secret heart and by Lady Southminster.

Audrey had come to France, and she was going to Paris, solely because of a vision which had been created in her by the letters and by the photographs of Madame Piriac. Although Madame Piriac and she had absolutely no tie of blood, Madame Piriac being the daughter by a first husband of the French widow who became the first Mrs. Moze—and speedily died, Audrey persisted privately in regarding Madame Piriac as a kind of elder sister. She felt a very

considerable esteem for Madame Piriac, upon whom she had
never set eyes, and Madame Piriac had certainly given her
the impression that France was to England what paradise is
to purgatory. Further, Audrey had fallen in love with
Madame Piriac's portraits, whose elegance was superb. And
yet, too, Audrey was jealous of Madame Piriac, and
especially so since the attainment of freedom and wealth.
Madame Piriac had most warmly invited her, after the death
of Mrs. Moze, to pay a long visit to Paris as a guest in her
home. Audrey had declined—from jealousy. She would not
go to Madame Piriac's as a raw girl, overdone with money,
who could only speak one langauge and who knew nothing
at all of this our planet. She would go, if she went, as a
young woman of the world who could hold her own in any
drawing-room, be it Madame Piriac's or another. Hence
Miss Ingate had obtained the address of a Paris boarding-
house, and one or two preliminary introductions from political
friends in London.

Well, France was not equal to its reputation; and Miss
Ingate's sardonic smile seemed to be saying : "So this is
your France ! "

However, the excitement of escorting the youngest
English peeress to Paris sufficed for Audrey, even if it did
not suffice for Miss Ingate with her middle-aged apprehensions. They knew that Lady Southminster was the
youngest English peeress because she had told them so. At
the very moment when they were dispatching a telegram for
her to an address in London, she had popped out the
remark : "Do you know I'm the youngest peeress in England? " And truth shone in her candid and simple smile.
They had not found the peer, neither on the ship, nor on the
quay, nor in the station. And the peeress would not wait.
She was indeed obviously frightened at the idea of remaining
in Calais alone, even till the next express. She said that her
husband's "man" would meet the train in Paris. She ate
plenteously with Audrey and Miss Ingate in the refreshment-
room, and she would not leave them nor allow them to leave

her. The easiest course was to let her have her way, and she had it.

By dint of Miss Ingate's unscrupulous tricks with small baggage they contrived to keep a whole compartment to themselves. As soon as the train started the peeress began to cry. Then, wiping her heavenly silly eyes, and upbraiding herself, she related to her protectresses the glory of a new manicure set. Unfortunately she could not show them the set, as it had been left in the cabin. She was actually in possession of nothing portable except her clothes, some English magazines bought at Calais, and a handbag which contained much money and many bonbons.

"He's done it on purpose," she said to Audrey as soon as Miss Ingate went off to take tea in the tea-car. "I'm sure he's done it on purpose. He's hidden himself, and he'll turn up when he thinks he's beaten me. D'you know why I wouldn't bring that luggage away out of the cabin? Because we had a quarrel about it, at the station, and he said things to me. In fact we weren't speaking. And we weren't speaking last night either. The radiator of his— our—car leaked, and we had to come home from the Coliseum in a motor-bus. He couldn't get a taxi. It wasn't his fault, but a friend of mine told me the day before I was married that a lady always ought to be angry when her husband can't get a taxi after the theatre—she says it does 'em good. So first I told him he mustn't leave me to look for one. Then I said I'd wait where I was, and then I said we'd walk on, and then I said we must take a motor-bus. It was that that finished him. He said : ' Did I expect him to invent a taxi when there wasn't one? ' And he swore. So of course I sulked. You must, you know. And my shoes were too thin and I felt chilly. But only a fortnight before I was making cigarettes in the window of Constantinopoulos's. Funny, isn't it? Otherwise he's behaved splendid. Still, what I do say is a man's no right to be ill when he's taking you to Paris on your honeymoon. I knew he was going to be ill when I left him in the cabin, but he stuck me out he wasn't. A man that's so bad he can't come to his wife when *she's* bad isn't a man—that's what I say. Don't you think so? You know all about that sort of thing, I lay."

Audrey said briefly that she did think so, glad that the peeress's intense and excusable interest in herself kept her from being curious about others.

"Marriage ain't all chocolate-creams," said the peeress after a pause. "Have one?" And she opened her bag very hospitably.

Then she turned to her magazines. And no sooner had she glanced at the cover of the second one than she gave a squeal, and, fetching deep breaths, passed the periodical to Audrey. At the top of the cover was printed in large letters the title of a story by a famous author of short tales. It ran :

"MAN OVERBOARD."

Henceforward a suspicion that had lain concealed in the undergrowth of the hearts of the two girls stalked boldly about in full daylight.

"He's done it, and he's done it to spite me !" murmured Lady Southminster tearfully.

"Oh no ! " Audrey protested. "Even if he had fallen overboard he'd have been seen and the captain would have stopped the boat."

"Where do you come from?" Lady Southminster retorted with disdain. "That's an *omen*, that is "— pointing to the words on the cover of the magazine. "What else could it be? I ask you."

When Miss Ingate returned the child was fast asleep. Miss Ingate was paler than usual. Having convinced herself that the sleeper did genuinely sleep, she breathed to Audrey :

"He's in the next compartment ! . . . He must have hidden himself till nearly the last minute on the boat and then got into the train while we were sending off that telegram."

Audrey blenched.

"Shall you wake her? "

"Wake her, and have a scene—with us here? No, I shan't. He's a fool."

"How d'you know?" asked Audrey.

"Well, he must have been a fool to marry her."

"Well," whispered Audrey. "If I'd been a man I'd have married that face like a shot."

"It might be all right if he'd only married the face. But he's married what she calls her mind."

"Is he young?"

"Yes. And as good-looking in his own way as she is."

"Well——"

But the Countess of Southminster stirred, and the slight movement stopped conversation.

The journey was endless, but it was no longer than the sleep of the Countess. At length dusk and mist began to gather in the hollows of the land; stations succeeded one another more frequently. The reflections of the electric lights in the compartment could be seen beyond the glass of the windows. The train still ruthlessly clattered and shook and swayed and thundered; and weary lords, ladies and financiers had read all the illustrated magazines and six-penny novels in existence, and they lolled exhausted and bored amid the debris of literature and light refreshments. Then the speed of the convoy slackened, and Audrey, looking forth, saw a pale cathedral dome resting aloft amid dark clouds. It was a magical glimpse, and it was the first glimpse of Paris. "Oh!" cried Audrey, far more like a girl than a widow. The train rattled through defiles of high twinkling houses, roared under bridges, screeched, threaded forests of cold blue lamps, and at last came to rest under a black echoing vault.

Paris!

And, mysteriously, all Audrey's illusions concerning France had been born again. She was convinced that Paris could not fail to be paradisiacal.

Lady Southminster awoke.

Almost simultaneously a young man very well dressed

passed along the corridor. Lady Southminster, with an awful start, seized her bag and sprang after him, but was impeded by other passengers. She caught him only after he had descended to the platform, which was at the bottom of a precipice below the windows. He had just been saluted by, and given orders to, a waiting valet. She caught him sharply by the arm. He shook free and walked quickly away up the platform, guided by a wise instinct for avoiding a scene in front of fellow-travellers. She followed close after him, talking with rapidity. They receded. Audrey and Miss Ingate leaned out of the windows to watch, and still farther and farther out. Just as the honeymooning pair disappeared altogether their two forms came into contact, and Audrey's eyes could see the arm of Lord Southminster take the arm of Lady Southminster. They vanished from view like one flesh. And Audrey and Miss Ingate, deserted, forgotten utterly, unthanked, buffeted by passengers and by the valet who had climbed up into the carriage to take away the impedimenta of his master, gazed at each other and then burst out laughing.

"So that's marriage!" said Audrey.

"No," said Miss Ingate. "That's love. I've seen a deal of love in my time, ever since my sister Arabella's first engagement, but I never saw any that wasn't vehy, vehy queer."

"I do hope they'll be happy," said Audrey.

"Do you?" said Miss Ingate.

CHAPTER VIII

EXPLOITATION OF WIDOWHOOD

THE carriage had emptied, and the two adventurers stood alone among empty compartments. The platform was also empty. Not a porter in sight. One after the other, the young widow and the elderly spinster, their purses bulging with money, got their packages by great efforts down on to the platform.

An employee strolled past.

"*Porteur?*" murmured Audrey timidly.

The man sniggered, shrugged his shoulders, and vanished.

Audrey felt that she had gone back to her school days. She was helpless, and Miss Ingate was the same. She wished ardently that she was in Moze again. She could not imagine how she had been such a fool as to undertake this absurd expedition which could only end in ridicule and disaster. She was ready to cry. Then another employee appeared, hesitated, and picked up a bag, scowling and inimical. Gradually the man, very tousled and dirty, clustered all the bags and parcels around his person, and walked off. Audrey and Miss Ingate meekly following. The great roof of the station resounded to whistles and the escape of steam and the clashing of wagons.

Beyond the platforms there were droves of people, of whom nearly every individual was preoccupied and hurried. And what people! Audrey had in her heart expected a sort of glittering white terminus full of dandiacal men and elegant Parisiennes who had stepped straight out of fashion-plates, and who had no cares—for was not this

E   57

Paris? Whereas, in fact, the multitude was the dingiest she had ever seen. Not a gleam of elegance! No hint of dazzling colour! No smiling and satiric beauty! They were just persons.

At last, after formalities, Audrey and Miss Ingate reached the foul and chilly custom-house appointed for the examination of luggage. Unrecognisable peers and other highnesses stood waiting at long counters, forming bays, on which was nothing at all. Then, far behind, a truck hugely piled with trunks rolled in through a back door and men pitched the trunks like toys here and there on the counters, and officials came into view, and knots of travellers gathered round trunks, and locks were turned and lids were lifted, and the flash of linen showed in spots on the drabness of the scene. Miss Ingate observed with horror the complete undoing of a lady's large trunk, and the exposure to the world's harsh gaze of the most intimate possessions of that lady. Soon the counters were like a fair. But no trunk belonging to Audrey or to Miss Ingate was visible. They knew then, what they had both privately suspected ever since Charing Cross, that their trunks would be lost on the journey.

"Oh! My trunk!" cried Miss Ingate.

Beneath a pile of other trunks on an incoming truck she had espied her property. Audrey saw it, too. The vision was magical. The trunk seemed like a piece of home, a bit of Moze and of England. It drew affection from them as though it had been an animal. They sped towards it, forgetting their small baggage. Their *porteur* leaped over the counter from behind and made signs for a key. All Audrey's trunks in turn joined Miss Ingate's; none was missing. And finally an official, small and fierce, responded to the invocations of the *porteur* and established himself at the counter in front of them. He put his hand on Miss Ingate's trunk.

"Op-en," he said in English.

Miss Ingate opened her purse, and indicated to the

official by signs that she had no key for the trunk,
and she also cried loudly, so that he should comprehend:

"No key! . . . Lost!"

Then she looked awkwardly at Audrey.

"I've been told they only want to open one trunk
when there's a lot. Let him choose another one," she
murmured archly.

But the official merely walked away, to deal with the
trunks of somebody else close by.

Audrey was cross.

"Miss Ingate," she said formally, "you had the key
when we started, because you showed it to me. You can't
possibly have lost it."

"No," answered Winnie calmly and knowingly. "I
haven't lost it. But I'm not going to have the things in
my trunk thrown about for all these foreigners to see. It's
simply disgraceful. They ought to have women officials
and private rooms at these places. And they would have,
if women had the vote. Let him open one of your trunks.
All your things are new."

The *porteur* had meanwhile been discharging French
into Audrey's other ear.

"Of course you must open it, Winnie," said she.
"Don't be so absurd!" There was a persuasive lightness
in her voice, but there was also command. For a moment
she was the perfect widow.

"I'd rather not."

"The *porteur* says we shall be here all night," Audrey
persisted.

"Do you know French?"

"I learnt French at school, Winnie," said the perfect
widow. "I can't understand every word, but I can make
out the drift." And Audrey went on translating the porter
according to her own wisdom. "He says there have been
dreadful scenes here before, when people have refused to
open their trunks, and the police have had to be called

in. He says the man won't upset the things in your trunk at all."

Miss Ingate gazed into the distance, and privately smiled. Audrey had never guessed that in Miss Ingate were such depths of obstinate stupidity. She felt quite distinctly that her understanding of human nature was increasing.

"Oh! Look!" said Miss Ingate casually. "I'm sure those must be real Parisians!" Her offhandedness, her inability to realise the situation, were exasperating to the young widow. Audrey glanced where Miss Ingate had pointed, and saw in the doorway of the custom-house two women and a lad, all cloaked but all obviously in radiant fancy dress, laughing together.

"Don't they look French!" said Miss Ingate.

Audrey tapped her foot on the asphalt floor, while people whose luggage had been examined bumped strenuously against her in the effort to depart. She was extremely pessimistic; she knew she could do nothing with Miss Ingate; and the thought of the vast, flaring, rumbling city beyond the station intimidated her. The *porteur,* who had gone away to collect their neglected small baggage, now returned, and nudged her, pointing to the official who had resumed his place behind the trunks. He was certainly a fierce man, but he was a little man, and there was an agreeable peculiarity in his eye.

Audrey, suddenly inspired and emboldened, faced him; she shrugged her shoulders Gallically at Miss Ingate's trunk, and gave a sad, sweet, wistful smile, and then put her hand with an exquisite inviting gesture on the smallest of her own trunks. The act was a deliberate exploitation of widowhood. The official fiercely shrugged his shoulders and threw up his arms, and told the *porteur* to open the small trunk.

"I told you they would," said Miss Ingate negligently.

Audrey would have turned upon her and slain her had she not been busy with the tremendous realisation of the fact that by a glance and a gesture she had conquered the customs official—a foreigner and a stranger. She wanted to be alone and to think.

Just as the trunk was being relocked, Audrey heard an American girlish voice behind her:

"Now, you must be Miss Ingate!"

"I am," Miss Ingate almost ecstatically admitted.

The trio in cloaked fancy dress were surrounding Miss Ingate like a bodyguard.

CHAPTER IX

MISS THOMPKINS and Miss Nickall were a charm to dissipate all the affrighting menace of the city beyond the station. Miss Thompkins had fluffy red hair, with the freckles which too often accompany red hair, and was addressed as Tommy. Miss Nickall had fluffy grey hair, with warm, loving eyes, and was addressed as Nick. The age of either might have been anything from twenty-four to forty. The one came from Wyoming, the other from Arizona; and it was instantly clear that they were close friends. They had driven up to the terminus before going to a fancy-dress ball to be given that night in the studio of Monsieur Dauphin, a famous French painter and a delightful man. They had met Monsieur Dauphin on the previous evening on the terrace of the Café de Versailles, and Monsieur had said, in response to their suggestion, that he would be enchanted and too much honoured if they would bring their English friends to his little "leaping"— that was, hop.

Also they had thought that it would be nice for the travellers to be met at the terminus, especially as Miss Ingate had been very particularly recommended to Miss Thompkins by a whole group of people in London. It was Miss Thompkins who had supplied the address of reliable furnished rooms, and she and Nick would personally introduce the ladies to their landlady, who was a sweet creature.

Tommy and Nick and Miss Ingate were at once on terms of cordial informality; but the Americans seemed to be a little diffident before the companion. Their voices, at the introduction, had reinforced the surprise of their first glances. "Oh! *Mrs.* Moncreiff!" The slightest insistence, no more, on the "Mrs."! Nothing said, but evidently they had expected somebody else!

Then there was the boy, whom they called Musa. He was dark, slim, with timorous great eyes, and attired in red as a devil beneath his student's cloak. He apologised slowly in English for not being able to speak English. He said he was very French, and Tommy and Nick smiled, and he smiled back at them rather wistfully. When Tommy and Nick had spoken with the chauffeurs in French he interpreted their remarks. There were two motor-taxis, one for the luggage.

Miss Thompkins accompanied the luggage; she insisted on doing so. She could tell sinister tales of Paris cabmen, and she even delayed the departure in order to explain that once in the suburbs and in the pre-taxi days a cabman had threatened to drive her and himself into the Seine unless she would be his bride, and she saved herself by promising to be his bride and telling him that she lived in the Avenue de l'Opéra; as soon as the cab reached a populous thoroughfare she opened the cab door and squealed and was rescued; she had let the driver go free because of his good taste.

As the procession whizzed through nocturnal streets, some thunderous with traffic, others very quiet, but all lined with lofty regular buildings, Audrey was penetrated by the romance of this city where cabmen passionately and to the point of suicide and murder adored their fares. And she thought that perhaps, after all, Madame Piriac's impression of Paris might not be entirely misleading. Miss Ingate and Nick talked easily, very charmed with one another, both excited. Audrey said little, and the dark youth said nothing. But once the dark youth murmured shyly to Audrey in English:

"Do you play at ten-nis, Madame?"

They crossed a thoroughfare that twinkled and glittered from end to end with moving sky-signs. Serpents pursued burning serpents on the heights of that thoroughfare, invisible hands wrote mystic words of warning and invitation, and blazing kittens played with balls of incandescent wool. Throngs of promenaders moved under theatrical trees that waved their pale emerald against the velvet sky, and the ground floor of every edifice was a glowing café, whose tables, full of idle sippers and loungers, bulged out on to the broad pavements. . . . The momentary vision was shut off instantly as the taxis shot down the mouth of a dark narrow street; but it had been long enough to make Audrey's heart throb.

"What is that?" she asked.

"That?" exclaimed Nick kindly. "Oh! That's only the *grand boulevard*."

Then they crossed the sombre, lamp-reflecting Seine, and soon afterwards the two taxis stopped at a vast black door in a very wide street of serried palatial façades that were continually shaken by the rushing tumult of electric cars. Tommy jumped out and pushed a button, and the door automatically split in two, disclosing a vast and dim tunnel. Tommy ran within, and came out again with a coatless man in a black-and-yellow striped waistcoat and a short white apron. This man, Musa, and the two chauffeurs entered swiftly into a complex altercation, which endured until Audrey had paid the chauffeurs and all the trunks had been transported behind the immense door and the door bangingly shut.

"Vehy amusing, isn't it?" whispered Miss Ingate caustically to Audrey. "Aren't they dears?"

"Madame Dubois's establishment is on the third and fourth floors," said Nick.

They climbed a broad, curving, carpeted staircase.

"We're here," said Audrey to Miss Ingate after scores of stairs.

Miss Ingate, breathless, could only smile.

And Audrey profoundly felt that she was in Paris. The mere shape of the doorknob by the side of a brass plate lettered "Madame Dubois" told her that she was in an exotic land.

And in the interior of Madame Dubois's establishment Tommy and Nick together drew apart the curtains, opened the windows, and opened the shutters of a pleasantly stuffy sitting-room. Everybody leaned out, and they saw the superb thoroughfare, straight and interminable, and the moving roofs of the tram-cars, and dwarfs on the pavements. The night was mild and languorous.

"You see that!" Nick pointed to a blaze of electricity to the left on the opposite side of the road. "That's where we shall take you to dine, after you've spruced yourselves up. You needn't bother about fancy dress. Monsieur Dauphin always has stacks of kimonos—for his models, you know."

While the travellers spruced themselves up in different bedrooms, Tommy chattered through one pair of double doors ajar, and Nick through the other, and Musa strummed with many mistakes on an antique Pleyel piano. And as Audrey listened to the talk of these acquaintances, Tommy and Nick, who in half an hour had put on the hue of her lifelong friends, and as she heard the piano, and felt the vibration of cars far beneath, she decided that she was still growing happier and happier, and that life and the world were marvellous.

A little later they passed into the café-restaurant through a throng of seated sippers who were spread around its portals like a defence. The interior, low, and stretching backwards, apparently endless, into the bowels of the building, was swimming in the brightest light. At a raised semi-circular counter in the centre two women were enthroned, plump, sedate, darkly dressed, and of middle age. To these priestesses came a constant succession of waiters, in the classic garb of waiters, bearing trays which they offered to the gaze of the women, and afterwards throwing down coins that rang on the marble of the counter. One of the women wrote swiftly in a great tome. Both of them, while performing their duties, glanced continually into every part of the establishment, watching especially each departure and each arrival.

At scores of tables were the most heterogeneous collection of people that Audrey had ever seen; men and women, girls and old men, even a few children with their mothers. Liquids were of every colour, ices chromatic, and the scarlet of lobster made a luscious contrast with the shaded tints of salads. In the extreme background men were playing billiards at three tables. Though nearly everybody was talking, no one talked loudly, so that the resulting monotone of conversation was a gentle drone, out of which shot up at intervals the crash of crockery or a hoarse command. And this drone combined itself with the glittering light, and with the mild warmth that floated in waves through the open windows, and with the red plush of the seats, and with the rosiness of painted nymphs on the blue walls, and with the complexions of women's faces, and their hats and frocks, and with the hues of the liquids—to produce a totality of impression that made Audrey dizzy with ecstasy. This was not the Paris set forth by Madame Piriac, but it was a wondrous Paris, and in Audrey's esteem not far removed from heaven.

Miss Ingate, magnificently pale, followed Tommy and Nick with ironic delight up the long passage between the tables. Her eyes seemed to be saying: "I am overpowered, and yet there is something in me that is not overpowered, and by virtue of my kind-hearted derision I, from Essex, am superior to you all!" Audrey, with glance downcast, followed Miss Ingate, and Musa came last, sinuously. Nobody looked up at them more than casually, but at intervals during the passage Tommy and Nick nodded and smiled: "How d'ye do? How d'ye do?" "*Bon soir,*" and answers were given in American or French voices.

They came to rest near the billiard tables, and near an aperture with a shelf where all the waiters congregated to shout their orders. A grey-haired waiter, with the rapidity and dexterity of a conjurer, laid a cloth over the marble round which they sat, Audrey and Miss Ingate on the plush bench, and Tommy and Nick, with Musa between them, on chairs opposite. The waiter then discussed with them for five minutes what they should eat, and he argued the problem seriously, wisely, helpfully, as befitted. It was Audrey, in full view of a buffet laden with shell-fish and fruit, who first suggested lobster, and lobster was chosen, nothing but lobster. Miss Ingate said that she was not a bit tired, and that lobster was her dream. The sentiment was universal at the table. When asked what she would drink, Audrey was on the point of answering "lemonade." But a doubt about the propriety of everlasting lemonade for a widow with much knowledge of the world, stopped her.

"I vote we all have grenadines," said Nick.

Grenadine was agreeable to Audrey's ear, and everyone concurred.

The ordering was always summarised and explained by Musa in a few phrases which, to Audrey, sounded very different from the French of Tommy and Nick. And she took oath that she would instantly begin to learn to speak French, not like Tommy and Nick, whose accent she cruelly despised, but like Musa.

Then Tommy and Nick removed their cloaks, and sat displayed as a geisha and a contadina, respectively. Musa had already unmasked his devilry. The café was not in the least disturbed by these gorgeous and strange apparitions. An orchestra began to play. Lobster arrived, and high glasses full of glinting green. Audrey ate and drank with gusto, with innocence, with the intensest love of life. And she was the most beautiful and touching sight in the café-restaurant. Miss Ingate, grinning, caught her eye with joyous mockery. "We are going it, aren't we, Audrey?" shrieked Miss Ingate.

Miss Thompkins and Miss Nickall began slowly to differentiate themselves in Audrey's mind. At first they were merely two American girls—the first Audrey had met. They were of about the same age—whatever that age might be—

and if they were not exactly of the same age, then Tommy
with red hair was older than Nick with grey hair. Indeed,
Nick took the earliest opportunity to remark that her hair
had turned grey at nineteen. They both had dreamy eyes
that looked through instead of looking at; they were both
hazy concerning matters of fact; they were both attached
like a couple of aunts to Musa, who nestled between them
like a cat between two cushions; they were both extraordinarily friendly and hospitable; they both painted and both
had studios—in the same house; they both showed quite
a remarkable admiration and esteem for all their acquaintances; and they both lacked interest in their complexions
and their hair.

The resemblance did not go very much farther. Tommy,
for all her praising of friends, was of a critical, curious, and
analytical disposition, and her greenish eyes were always at
work qualifying in a very subtle manner what her tongue
said, when her tongue was benevolent, as it often was.
Feminism and suffragism being the tie between the new
acquaintances, these subjects were the first material of conversation, and an empress of militancy known to the world
as "Rosamund" having been mentioned, Miss Ingate said
with enthusiasm :

"She lives only for one thing."

"Yes," replied Tommy. "And if she got it, I guess no
one would be more disgusted than she herself."

There was an instant's silence.

"Oh, Tommy ! " Nick lovingly protested.

Said Miss Ingate with a comprehending satiric grin :

"I see what you mean. I quite see. I quite see. You're
right, Miss Thompkins. I'm sure you're right."

Audrey decided she would have to be very clever in
order to be equal to Tommy's subtlety. Nick, on the other
hand, was not a bit subtle, except when she tried to imitate
Tommy. Nick was kindness, and sympathy, and vagueness.
You could see these admirable qualities in every curve of her
face and gleam of her eyes. She was very sympathetic, but

somewhat shocked when Audrey blurted out that she had not come to Paris in order to paint.

"There are at least fifty painters in this café this very minute," said Tommy. And somehow it was just as if she had said: "If you haven't come to Paris to paint, what have you come for?"

"Does Mr. Musa paint, too?" asked Audrey.

"Oh *no!*" Both his protectresses answered together, pained. Tommy added: "Musa plays the violin—of course."

And Musa blushed. Later, he murmured to Audrey across the table, while Tommy was ordering a salad, that there were tennis courts in the Luxembourg gardens.

"I used to paint," Miss Ingate broke out. "And I'm beginning to think I should like to paint again."

Said Nick, enraptured:

"I'll let you use my studio, if you will. I'd just love you to, now! Where did you study?"

"Well, it was like this," said Miss Ingate with satisfaction. "It was a long time ago. I finished painting a dog-kennel because the house-painter's wife died and he had to go to her funeral, and the dog didn't like being kept waiting. That gave me the idea. I went into water-colours, but afterwards I went back to oils. Oils seemed more real. Then I started on portraits, and I did a portrait of my Aunt Sarah from memory. After she saw it she tore up her will, and before I could get her into a good temper again she married her third husband and she had to make a new will in favour of him. So I found painting very expensive. Not that it would have made any difference, I suppose, would it? After that I went into miniatures. The same dog that I painted the kennel for ate up the best miniature I ever did. It killed him. I put a cross over his grave in the garden. All that made me see what a fool I'd been, and I exchanged my painting things for a lawn-mower, but it never turned out to be any good."

"You dear! You precious! You priceless!" cooed Nick. "I shall fix up my second best easel for you to-morrow."

"Isn't she just too lovely!" Tommy murmured aside to Audrey.

"I not much understand," said Musa.

Tommy translated to him, haltingly, and Audrey was moved to say, with energy:

"What I want most is to learn French, and I'm going to begin to-morrow morning."

Nick was kindly confusing and shaming Miss Ingate with a short history and catechism of modern art, including such names as Vuillard, Bonnard, Picasso, Signac, and Matisse—all very eagerly poured out and all very unnerving for Miss Ingate, whose directory of painting was practically limited to the names of Raphael, Sir Joshua, Rembrandt, Rubens, Gainsborough, Turner, Leighton, Millais, Gustave Doré and Frank Dicksee. When, however, Nick referred to Monsieur Dauphin, Miss Ingate was as it were washed safely ashore and said with assurance: "Oh yes! Oh yes! Oh yes!"

Tommy listened for a few moments, and then, leaning across the table and lighting a cigarette, she said in an intimate undertone to Audrey: "I hope you don't *mind* coming to the ball to-night. We really didn't know——" She stopped. Her eyes, ferreting in Audrey's black, completed the communication.

Unnerved for the tenth of a second, Audrey recovered and answered:

"Oh, no! I shall like it very much."

"You've been up against life!" murmured Tommy in a melting voice, gazing at her. "But how wonderful all experience is, isn't it. I once had a husband. We separated—at least, he separated. But I know the feel of being a wife."

Audrey blushed deeply. She wanted to push away all that sympathy, and she was exceedingly alarmed by the revelation that Tommy was an initiate. The widow was the merest schoolgirl once more. But her blush had saved her from a chat in which she could not conceivably have held her own.

"Excuse me being so clumsy," said Tommy contritely. "Another time." And she waved her cigarette to the waiter in demand for the bill.

It was after the orchestra had finished a tango, and while Tommy was examining the bill, that the first violin and leader, in a magenta coat, approached the table, and with a bow offered his violin deferentially to Musa. Many heads turned to watch what would happen. But Musa only shrugged his shoulders and with an exquisite gesture of refusal signified that he had to leave. Whereupon the magenta coat gracefully retired, starting a Hungarian dance as he went.

"Musa is supposed to be the greatest violinist in Paris —perhaps in the world," Tommy whispered casually to Audrey. "He used to play here, till Dauphin discovered him."

Audrey, overcome by this prodigious blow, trembled at the contemplation of her blind stupidity.

Beyond question, Musa now looked extremely important, vivid, masterful. She had been mistaking him for a nice, ornamental, useless boy.

CHAPTER X

FANCY DRESS

JUST as the café-restaurant had been an intensification of ordinary life, so was the ball in Dauphin's studio an intensification of the café-restaurant. It had more colour, more noise, more music, more heat, more varied kinds of people, and, of course, far more riotous movement than the café-restaurant. The only quality in which the café-restaurant stood first was that of sustenance. Monsieur Dauphin had not attempted to rival the café-restaurant in the matter of food and drink. And that there was no general hope of his doing so could be deduced from the fact that many of the more experienced guests arrived with bottles, fruit, sausages, and sandwiches of their own.

When Audrey and her friends entered the precincts of the vast new white building in the Boulevard Raspail, upon whose topmost floor Monsieur Dauphin painted the portraits of the women of the French, British, and American plutocracies and aristocracies, a lift full of gay-coloured figures was just shooting upwards past the wrought-iron balustrades of the gigantic staircase. Tommy and Nick stopped to speak to a columbine who hovered between the pavement and the threshold of the house.

"I don't know whether it's the grenadine or the lobster, or whether it's Paris," said Miss Ingate confidentially in the interval; "but I can scarcely tell whether I'm standing on my head or my heels."

Before the Americans rejoined them, the lift had returned and ascended with another covey of fancy costumes, including a man with a nose a foot long and a girl with bright green hair, dressed as an acrobat. On its next journey the lift held Tommy and Nick's party, and it held no more.

When the party emerged from it, they were greeted with a cheer, hoarse and half human, by a band of light amateur mountebanks of both sexes who were huddled in a doorway. Within a quarter of an hour Audrey and Miss Ingate, after astounding struggles in a dressing-room in which Nick alone saved their lives and reputations, appeared in Japanese disguise according to promise, and nobody could tell whether Audrey was maid, wife, or widow. She might have been a creature created on the spot, for the celestial purpose of a fancy-dress ball in Monsieur Dauphin's studio.

The studio was very large and rather lofty. Its walls had been painted by gifted pupils of Monsieur Dauphin and by fellow-artists, with scenes of life according to Catullus, Theocritus, Propertius, Martial, Petronius, and other classical writers. It is not too much to say that the walls of the studio constituted a complete novelty for Audrey and Miss Ingate. Miss Ingate opened her mouth to say something, but, saying nothing, forgot for a long time to shut it again.

Chinese lanterns, electrically illuminated, were strung across the studio at a convenient height so that athletic dancers could prodigiously leap up and make them swing. Beneath this incoherent but exciting radiance the guests swayed and glided, in a joyous din, under the influence of an orchestra of men snouted like pigs and raised on a dais. In a corner was a spiral staircase leading to the flat roof of the studio and a view of all Paris. Up and down this corkscrew contending parties fought amiably for the right of way.

Tommy and Nick began instantly to perform introductions between Audrey and Miss Ingate and the other guests. In a few moments Audrey had failed to catch the names of a score and a half of people—many Americans, some French, some Argentine, one or two English. They were all very talented people, and, according to Miss Ingate, the most

F

characteristically French were invariably either Americans or Argentines.

A telephone bell rang in the distance, and presently a toreador stood on a chair and pierced the music with a message of yells in French, and the room hugely guffawed and cheered.

"Where is the host?" Audrey asked.

"That's what the telephoning was about," said Tommy, speaking loudly against the hubbub. "He hasn't come yet. He had to rush off this afternoon to do pastel portraits of two Russian princesses at St. Germain, and he hasn't got back yet. The telephone was to say that he's started."

Then one of the introduced—it was a girl wearing a mask—took Audrey by the waist and whirled her strongly away and she was lost in the maze. Audrey's first impulse was to protest, but she said to herself: "Why protest? This is what we're here for." And she gave herself up to the dance. Her partner held her very firmly, somewhat bending over her. Neither spoke. Gyrating in long curves, with the other dancers swishing mysteriously about them like the dancers of a dream, and the music as far off as another world, they clung together in the rhythm and in the enchantment, until the music ceased. . . . The strong girl threw Audrey carelessly off, and walked away, breathing hard. And there was something in the strong girl's nonchalant and curt departure which woke a chord in Audrey's soul that had never been wakened before. Audrey could scarcely credit that she was on the same planet as Essex. She had many dances with men whom she hoped and believed she had been introduced to by Tommy, and no less than seventeen persons of either sex told her in unusual English that they had heard she wanted to learn French and that they would like to teach her; and then she met Musa, the devil.

Musa, with an indolent and wistful smile, suggested the roof. Audrey was now just one of the throng, and quite unconscious of herself; she fought archly and gaily on the spiral staircase exactly as she had seen others do, and at last they were on the roof, and the silhouettes of other fantastic figures and of cowled chimney pots stood out dark against the vague yellow glow of the city beneath. While Musa was pointing out the historic landmarks to her, she was thinking how she could never again be the girl who had left Moze on the previous morning. And yet Musa was so natural and so direct that it was impossible to take him for anything but a boy, and hence Audrey sank back into early girlhood, talking spasmodically to Musa as she used in school days to talk to the brother of her school friend.

"I will teach you French," said Musa, unaware that he had numerous predecessors in the offer. "But will you play tennis with me in the gardens of the Luxembourg?"

Audrey said she would, and that she would buy a racket.

"Tell me about all those artists Miss Nickall spoke of," she said. "I must know about all the artists, and all the musicians, and all the authors. I must know all about them at once. I shan't sleep until I know all their names and I can talk French. I shan't *sleep*."

Musa began the catalogue. When a girl came and chucked him under the chin, he angrily slapped her face. Then, to avoid complications, they descended.

In the middle of the studio, wearing a silk hat, a morning coat, striped trousers, yellow gloves, and boots with spats, stood a smiling figure.

"*Voilà* Dauphin!" said Musa.

"Musa!" called Monsieur Dauphin, espying the youth on the staircase. Then he made a gesture to the orchestra: "Give him a violin!"

Audrey stood by Musa while he played a dance that no-body danced to, and when he had finished she was rather ashamed, under the curtain of wild cheering, because with her Essex incredulity she had not sufficiently believed in Musa's greatness.

"Permit your host to introduce himself," said a voice behind her, not in the correct English of a linguistic Frenchman, but in utterly English English. She had now descended to the floor of the studio.

Emile Dauphin raised his glossy hat, and then asked to be allowed to put it on again, as the company had decided that it was part of his costume. He had a delicious smile, at once respectful and intimate. Audrey had read somewhere that really great men were always simple and unaffected—indeed that it was often impossible to guess from their demeanour that, etc., etc.—and this experience of the first celebrity with whom she had ever spoken (except Musa, who was somehow only Musa) confirmed the statement, and confirmed also her young instinctive belief that what is printed must be true. She was beginning to feel the stealthy oncomings of fatigue, and certainly she was very nervous, but Monsieur Dauphin's quite particularly sympathetic manner, and her own sudden determination not to be a little blushing fool gave her new power.

"I can't express to you," he said, moving towards the dais and mesmerising her to keep by his side. "I can't express to you how sorry I was to be so late." He made the apology with lightness, but with sincerity. Audrey knew how polite the French were. "But truly circumstances were too much for me. Those two Russian princesses—they came to me through a mutual friend, a dear old friend of mine, very closely attached also to them. They leave to-morrow morning by the St. Petersburg express, on which they have engaged a special coach. What was I to do? I tried to tear myself away earlier, but of course there were the portrait sketches to finish, and no doubt you know the usage of the best society in Russia."

"Yes," murmured Audrey.

"Come up on the dais, will you?" he suggested. "And let us survey the scene together."

They surveyed the scene together. The snouted band was having supper on the floor in a corner, and many of the guests also were seated on the floor. Miss Ingate, intoxicated by the rapture of existence, and Miss

Thompkins were carefully examining the frescoes on
the walls. A young woman covered from head to foot with
gold tinsel was throwing chocolates into Musa's mouth, or
as near to it as she could.

"What a splendid player Mr. Musa is!" Audrey in-
augurated her career as a woman of the world. "I doubt
if I have ever heard such violin playing."

"I'm so glad you think so," replied Monsieur Dauphin.
"Of course you know I'm very conceited about my
painting. Anybody will tell you so. But beneath all that
I'm not so sure. I often have the gravest doubts about
my work. But I never had any doubt that when I took
Musa out of the orchestra in the Café de Versailles I was
giving a genius to the world. And perhaps that's how
I shall be remembered by posterity. And if it is I shall
be content."

Never before had Audrey heard anybody connect himself
with posterity, and she was very much impressed. Monsieur
Dauphin was resigned and yet brave. By no means convinced that posterity would do the right thing, he nevertheless had no grudge against posterity.

Just then there was a sharp scream at the top of the
spiral staircase. With a smile that condoned the scream
and excused his flight, Monsieur Dauphin ran to the
staircase, and up it, and disappeared on to the roof.
Nobody seemed to be perturbed. Audrey was left alone
and conspicuous on the dais.

"Charming, isn't he?" said Miss Thompkins, arriving with Miss Ingate in front of the flower-screened
platform.

"Oh! he is!" answered Audrey with sincerity, leaning
downwards.

"Has he told you all about the Russian princesses?"

"Oh, yes," said Audrey, pleased.

"I thought he would," said Miss Thompkins, with a
peculiar intonation.

Audrey knew then that Miss Thompkins, having first

maliciously made sure that she was a ninny, was now telling her to her face that she was a ninny.

Tommy continued:

"Then I guess he told you he'd given Musa to the world."

Audrey nodded.

"Ah! I knew he would. Well, when he comes back he'll tell you that you must come to one of his *real* entertainments here, and that this one is nothing. Then he'll tell you about all the nobs he knows in London. And at last he'll say that you have a strangely expressive face, and he'd like to paint it and show the picture in the Salon. But he won't tell you it'll cost you forty thousand francs. So I'll tell you that, because perhaps later on, if you don't know, you might find yourself making a noise like a tenderfoot. You see, Miss Ingate hasn't concealed that you're a lady millionaire."

"No, I haven't," said Miss Ingate, glowing and yet sarcastic. "I couldn't bring myself to, because I was so anxious to see if human nature in Paris is anything like what it is in Essex."

"And why should you hide it, Winnie?" Audrey stoutly demanded.

"Well, au revoir," Tommy murmured delicately, with a very original gesture. "He's coming back."

As Monsieur Dauphin, having apparently established peace on the roof, approached again, Audrey discreetly examined his face and his demeanour, to see if she could perceive in him any of the sinister things that Tommy had implied. She was unable to make up her mind whether she could or not. But in the end she decided that she was as shrewd as anybody in the place.

"Have you been to my roof-garden, Mrs. Moncreiff?" he asked in a persuasive voice, raising his eyebrows.

She said she had, and that she thought the roof was heavenly.

Then from the corner of her eye she saw Miss Ingate

and Tommy sidling mischievously away, like conspirators who have lighted a time fuse. She considered that Tommy, with her red hair and freckles, and strange glances and strange tones full of a naughty and malicious sweetness, was even more peculiar than Miss Ingate. But she was not intimidated by them nor by the illustrious Monsieur Dauphin, so perfectly master of his faculties. Rather she was exultant in the contagion of their malice. Once more she felt as if she had ceased to be a girl a very long time ago. And she was aware of agreeable and exciting temptations.

"Are you taking a house in Paris?" inquired Monsieur Dauphin.

Audrey answered primly:

"I haven't decided. Should you advise me to do so?"

He waved a hand.

"Ah! It depends on the life you wish to lead. Who knows—with a young woman who has all experience behind her and all life before her! But I do hope I may see you again. And I trust I may persuade you to come to my studio again." Audrey felt the thrill of drama as he proceeded. "This is scarcely a night for you. I ought to tell you that I give three entertainments during the autumn. To-night is the first. It is for students and those English and Americans who think they are seeing Paris here. Then I give another for the political and dramatic worlds. Each is secretly proud to meet the other. The third I reserve to my friends. Some of my many friends in London are good enough to come over specially for it. It is on Christmas Eve. I do wish you would come to that one."

"I suppose," she said, catching the diabolic glances of Miss Ingate and Tommy, "I suppose you know almost more people in London than in Paris?"

He answered:

"Well, I count among my friends more than two-thirds of the subscribers to Covent Garden Opera. . . . By the

way, do you happen to be connected with the Moncreiffs
of Suddon Wester? They have a charming house in Hyde
Park Terrace. But probably you know it?"

Audrey burst out laughing. She laughed loud and
violently till the tears stood in her eyes.

"Well," he said, at a loss, deprecatingly. "Perhaps
these Moncreiffs *are* rather weird."

"I was only laughing," she said in gasps, but with a
complete secret composure. "Because we had such an awful
quarrel with them last year. I couldn't tell you the details.
They're too shocking."

He gave a dubious smile.

"D'you know, dear young lady," he recommenced after
a brief pause, "I should adore to paint a portrait of you
laughing. It would be very well hung in the Salon. Your
face is so strangely expressive. It is utterly different, in
expression, from any other face I ever saw—and I have
studied faces."

Heedless of the general interest which she was arousing,
Audrey leaned on the rail of the screen of flowers, and
gave herself up afresh to laughter. Monsieur Dauphin
was decidedly puzzled. The affair might have ended in
hysteria and confusion had not Miss Ingate, with Nick
and Tommy, come hurrying up to the dais.

CHAPTER XI

A POLITICAL REFUGEE

"Rosamund has come to my studio and wants to see me at once. *She has sent for me.* Miss Ingate says she shall go, too."

It was these words in a highly emotionalised voice from Miss Nickall that, like a vague murmured message of vast events, drew the entire quartet away from the bright inebriated scene created by Monsieur Dauphin.

The single word "Rosamund" sufficed to break one mood and induce another in all bosoms save that of Audrey, who was in a state of permanent joyous exultation that she scarcely even attempted to control. The great militant had a surname, but it was rarely used save by police magistrates. Her Christian name alone was more impressive than the myriad cognomens of queens and princesses. Miss Nickall ran away home at once. Miss Thompkins was left to deliver Miss Ingate and Audrey at Nick's studio, which, being in the Rue Delambre, was not far away. And not the shedding of the kimono and the re-assumption of European attire could affect Audrey's spirits. Had she been capable of regret in that hour, she would have regretted the abandonment of the ball, where the refined, spiritual, strange faces of the men, and the enigmatic quality of the women, and the exceeding novelty of the social code had begun to arouse in her sentiments of approval and admiration. But she quitted the staggering frolic without a sigh; for she carried within her a frolic surpassing anything exterior or physical.

The immense flickering boulevard with its double

roadway stretched away to the horizon on either hand,
empty.

"What time is it?" asked Miss Ingate.

Tommy looked at her wrist-watch.

"Don't tell me! Don't tell me!" cried Audrey.

"We might get a taxi in the Rue de Babylone," Tommy
suggested. "Or shall we walk?"

"We *must* walk," cried Audrey.

She knew the name of the street. In the distance she
could recognise the dying lights of the café-restaurant where
they had eaten. She felt already like an inhabitant of
the dreamed-of city. It was almost inconceivable to her
that she had been within it for only a few hours, and that
England lay less than a day behind her in the past, and
Moze less than two days. And Aguilar the morose, and
the shuttered rooms of Flank Hall, shot for an instant into
her mind and out again.

The other two women walked rather quickly, mesmerised
possibly by the magic of the illustrious Christian name,
and Audrey gave occasional schoolgirlish leaps by their
side. A little policeman appeared inquisitive from a by-street,
and Audrey tossed her head as if saying: "Pooh! I belong
here. All the mystery of this city is mine, and I am as
at home as in Moze Street."

And as they surged through the echoing solitude of
the boulevard, and as they crossed the equally tremendous
boulevard that cut through it east and west, Tommy told
the story of Nick's previous relations with Rosamund. Nick
had met Rosamund once before through her English chum,
Betty Burke, an art student who had ultimately sacrificed
art to the welfare of her sex, but who with Mrs. Burke
had shared rooms and studio with Nick for many months.
Tommy's narrative was spotted with hardly perceptible
sarcasms concerning art, women, Betty Burke, Mrs. Burke,
and Nick; but she put no barb into Rosamund. And
when Miss Ingate, who had never met Rosamund, asked
what Rosamund amounted to in the esteem of Tommy,

Tommy evaded the question. Miss Ingate remembered, however, what she had said in the café-restaurant.

Then they turned into the Rue Delambre, and Tommy halted them in the deep obscurity in front of another of those huge black doors which throughout Paris seemed to guard the secrets of individual life. An automobile was waiting close by. A little door in the huge one clicked and yielded, and they climbed over a step into black darkness.

"Thompkins!" called Miss Thompkins loudly to the black darkness, to reassure the drowsy concierge in his hidden den, shutting the door with a bang behind them; and, groping for the hands of the others, she dragged them forward stumbling.

"I never have a match," she said.

They blundered up tenebrous stairs.

"We're just passing my door," said Tommy. "Nick's is higher up."

Then a perpendicular slit of light showed itself—and a portal slightly open could be distinguished.

"I shall quit here," said Tommy. "You go right in."

"You aren't leaving us?" exclaimed Miss Ingate in alarm.

"I won't go in," Tommy persisted in a quiet satiric tone. "I'll leave my door open below, and see you when you come down."

She could be heard descending.

"Why, I guess they're here," said a voice, Nick's, within, and the door was pulled wide open.

"My legs are all of a tremble!" muttered Miss Ingate.

Nick's studio seemed larger than reality because of its inadequate illumination. On a small paint-stained table in the centre was an oil-lamp beneath a round shade that had been decorated by some artist's hand with. a series of reclining women in many colours. This lamp made a moon in the midnight of the studio, but it was a moon almost without rays; the shade seemed to imprison the light, s've that which escaped from its superior orifice. Against the table stood a tall thin woman in black. Her face was lit by the rays escaping upward; a pale, firm, bland face, with rather prominent cheeks, loose grey hair above, surmounted by a toque. The dress was dark, and the only noticeable feature of it was that the sleeves were finished in white linen; from these the hands emerged calm and veined under the lampshade; in one of them a pair of gloves were clasped. On the table lay a thin mantle.

At the back of the studio there sat another woman, so engloomed that no detail of her could be distinguished.

"As I was saying," the tall upright woman resumed as soon as Miss Ingate and Audrey had been introduced. "Betty Burke is in prison. She got six weeks this morning. She may never come out again. Almost her last words from the dock were that you, Miss Nickall, should be asked to go to London to look after Mrs. Burke, and perhaps to take Betty's place in other ways. She said that her mother preferred you to anybody else, and that she was sure you would come. Shall you?"

The accents were very clear, the face was delicately smiling, the little gestures had a quite tranquil quality. Rosamund did not seem to care whether Miss Nickall obeyed the summons or not. She did not seem to care about anything whatever except her own manner of existing. She was the centre of Paris, and Paris was naught but a circumference for her. All phenomena beyond the individuality of the woman were reduced to the irrelevant and the negligible. It would have been absurd to mention to her costume balls. The frost of her indifference would have wilted them into nothingness.

"Yes, of course, I shall go," Nick answered.

"When?" was the implacable question.

"Oh! By the first train," said Nick eagerly. As she approached the lamp, the gleam of the devotee could be seen in her gaze. In one moment she had sacrificed Paris and art and Tommy and herself, and had risen to the sacred ardour of a vocation. Rosamund was well accustomed to watching the process, and she gave not the least sign of satisfaction or approval.

"I ought to tell you," she went on, "that I came over from London suddenly by the afternoon service in order to escape arrest. I am now a political refugee. Things have come to this pass. You will do well to leave by the first train. That is why I decided to call here before going to bed."

"Where's Tommy?" asked Nick, appealing wildly to Miss Ingate and Audrey. Upon being answered she said, still more wildly: "I must see her. Can you—No, I'll run down myself." In the doorway she turned round: "Mrs. Moncreiff, would you and Miss Ingate like to have my studio while I'm away? I should just love you to. There's a very nice bed over there behind the screen, and a fair sort of couch over here. Do say you will! *Do!*"

"Oh! We will!" Miss Ingate replied at once, reassuringly, as though in haste to grant the supreme request of some condemned victim. And indeed Miss Nickall appeared ready to burst into tears if she should be thwarted.

As soon as Nick had gone, Miss Ingate's smiling face, nervous, intimidated, audacious, sardonic, and good humoured, moved out of the gloom nearer to Rosamund.

"You knew I played the barrel organ all down Regent Street?" she ventured, blushing.

"Ah!" murmured Rosamund, unmoved. "It was you who played the barrel-organ? So it was."

"Yes," said Miss Ingate. "But I'm like you. I don't care passionately for prison. Eh! Eh! I'm not so vehy, vehy fond of it. I don't know Miss Burke, but what a pity she has got six weeks, isn't it? Still, I was vehy much struck by what someone said to me to-day—that you'd be vehy sorry if women *did* get the vote. I think I should be sorry, too—you know what I mean."

"Perfectly," ejaculated Rosamund, with a pleasant smile.

"I hope I'm not skidding," said Miss Ingate still more timidly, but also with a sardonic giggle, looking round into the gloom. "I do skid sometimes, you know, and we've just come away from a——"

She could not finish.

"And Mrs. Moncreiff, if I've got the name right, is she with us, too? " asked Rosamund, miraculously urbane. And added : "I hear she has wealth and is the mistress of it."

Audrey jumped up, smiling, and lifting her veil. She could not help smiling. The studio, the lamp, Rosamund with her miraculous self-complacency, Nick with her soft, mad eyes and wistful voice, the blundering ruthless Miss Ingate, all seemed intensely absurd to her. Everything seemed absurd except dancing and revelry and coloured lights and strange disguises and sensuous contacts. She had the most careless contempt, stiffened by a slight loathing, for political movements and every melancholy effort to reform the world. The world did not need reforming and did not want to be reformed.

"Perhaps you don't know my story," Audrey began, not realising how she would continue. "I am a widow. I made an unhappy marriage. My husband on the day after our wedding-day began to eat peas with his knife. In a week I was forced to leave him. And a fortnight later I heard that he was dead of blood-poisoning. He had cut his mouth."

And she thought :

"What is the matter with me? I have ruined myself." All her exultation had collapsed.

But Rosamund remarked gravely :

"It is a common story."

Suddenly there was a movement in the obscure corner where sat the unnamed and unintroduced lady. This lady rose and came towards the table. She was very elegant in dress and manner, and she looked maturely young.

"Madame Piriac," announced Rosamund.

Audrey recoiled. . . . Gazing hard at the face, she saw

in it a vague but undeniable resemblance to certain admired photographs which had arrived at Moze from France.

"Pardon me!" said Madame Piriac in English with a strong French accent. "I shall like very much to hear the details of this story of *petits pois*." The tone of Madame Piriac's question was unexceptionable; it took account of Audrey's mourning attire, and of her youthfulness; but Audrey could formulate no answer to it. Instead of speaking she gave a touch to her veil, and it dropped before her piquant, troubled, inscrutable face like a screen.

Miss Ingate said with noticeable calm, but also with the air of a conspirator who sees danger to a most secret machination :

"I'm afraid Mrs. Moncreiff won't care to go into details."

It was neatly done. Madame Piriac brought the episode to a close with a sympathetic smile and an apposite gesture. And Audrey, safe behind her veil, glanced gratefully and admiringly at Miss Ingate, who, taken quite unawares, had been so surprisingly able thus to get her out of a scrape. She felt very young and callow among these three women, and the mere presence of Madame Piriac, of whom years ago she had created for herself a wondrous image, put her into a considerable flutter. On the whole she was ready to believe that the actual Madame Piriac was quite equal to the image of her founded on photographs and letters. She set her teeth, and decided that Madame Piriac should not learn her identity—yet! There was little risk of her discovering it for herself, for no photograph of Audrey had gone to Paris for a dozen years, and Miss Ingate's loyalty was absolute.

As Audrey sat down again, the illustrious Rosamund took a chair near her, and it could not be doubted that the woman had the mien and the carriage of a leader.

"You are very rich, are you not?" asked Rosamund, in a tone at once deferential and intimate, and she smiled very attractively in the gloom. Impossible not to reckon with that smile, as startling as it was seductive !

Evidently Nick had been communicative.

"I suppose I am," murmured Audrey, like a child, and feeling like a child. Yet at the same time she was asking herself with fierce curiosity: "What has Madame Piriac got to do with this woman?"

"I hear you have eight or ten thousand a year and can do what you like with it. And you cannot be more than twenty-three. . . . What a responsibility it must be for you! You are a friend of Miss Ingate's and therefore on our side. Indeed, if a woman such as you were not on our side, I wonder whom we *could* count on. Miss Ingate is, of course, a subscriber to the Union——"

"Only a very little one," cried Miss Ingate.

Audrey had never felt so abashed since an ex-parlourmaid at Flank Hall, who had left everything to join the Salvation Army, had asked her once in the streets of Colchester whether she had found salvation. She knew that she, if any one, ought to subscribe to the Suffragette Union, and to subscribe largely. For she was a convinced suffragette by faith, because Miss Ingate was a convinced suffragette. If Miss Ingate had been a Mormon, Audrey also would have been a Mormon. And, although she hated to subscribe, she knew also that if Rosamund demanded from her any subscription, however large—even a thousand pounds—she would not know how to refuse. She felt before Rosamund as hundreds of women, and not a few men, had felt.

"I may be leaving for Germany to-morrow," Rosamund proceeded. "I may not see you again—at any rate for many weeks. May I write to London that you mean to support us?"

Audrey was giving herself up for lost, and not without reason. She foreshadowed a future of steely self-sacrifice, propaganda, hammers, riots, and prison; with no self-indulgence in it, no fine clothes, no art, and no young men save earnest young men. She saw herself in the iron clutch of her own conscience and sense of duty. And she was frightened. But at that moment Nick rushed into the room, and the spell was broken. Nick considered that she had the right to monopolise Rosamund, and she monopolised her.

Miss Ingate prudently gathered Audrey to her side, and was off with her. Nick ran to kiss them, and told them that Tommy was waiting for them in the other studio. They groped downstairs, guided by a wisp of light from Tommy's studio.

"Why didn't you come up?" asked Miss Ingate of Tommy in Tommy's antechamber. "Have you and *she* quarrelled?"

"Oh no!" said Tommy. "But I'm afraid of her. She'd grab me if she had the least chance, and I don't want to be grabbed."

Tommy was arranging to escort them home, and had already got out on the landing, when Rosamund and Madame Piriac, followed by Nick holding a candle aloft, came down the stairs. A few words of explanation, a little innocent blundering on the part of Nick, a polite suggestion by Madame Piriac, and an imperious affirmative by Rosamund—and the two strangers to Paris found themselves in Madame Piriac's waiting automobile on the way to their rooms!

In the darkness of the car the four women could not distinguish each other's faces. But Rosamund's voice was audible in a monologue, and Miss Ingate trembled for Audrey and for the future.

"This is the most important political movement in the history of the world," Rosamund was saying, not at all in a speechifying manner, but quite intimately and naturally. "Everybody admits that, and that's what makes it so extraordinarily interesting, and that is why we have had such magnificent help from women in the very highest positions who wouldn't dream of touching ordinary politics. It's a marvellous thing to be in the movement, if we can only realise it. Don't you think so, Mrs. Moncreiff?"

Audrey made no response. The other two sat silent. Miss Ingate thought:

G

"What's the girl going to do next? Surely she could mumble something."

The car curved and stopped.

"Here we are," said Miss Ingate, delighted. "And thank you so much. I suppose all we have to do is just to push the bell and the door opens. Now Audrey, dear."

Audrey did not stir.

"*Mon Dieu!*" murmured Madame Piriac. "What has she, little one?"

Rosamund said stiffly and curtly:

"She is asleep. . . . It is very late. Four o'clock."

Excellent as was Audrey's excuse for her lapse, Rosamund was not at all pleased. That slumber was one of Rosamund's rare defeats.

CHAPTER XII

WIDOWHOOD IN THE STUDIO

AUDREY was in a white piqué coat and short skirt, with pale blue blouse and pale blue hat—and at the extremity blue stockings and white tennis shoes. She picked up a tennis racket in its press, and prepared to leave the studio. She had bought the coat, the skirt, the blouse, the hat, the tennis shoes, the racket, the press, and practically all she wore, visible and invisible, at that very convenient and immense shop, the Bon Marché, whose only drawback was that it was always full. Everybody in the Quarter, except a few dolls not in earnest, bought everything at the Bon Marché, because the Bon Marché was so comprehensive and so reliable. If you desired a toothbrush, the Bon Marché not only supplied it, but delivered it in a 30-h.p. motor-van manned by two officials in uniform. And if you desired a bedroom suite, a pair of corsets, a box of pastels, an anthracite stove, or a new wallpaper, the Bon Marché would never shake its head.

And Audrey was now of the Quarter. Many simple sojourners in the Quarter tried to imply the Latin Quarter when they said the Quarter. But the Quarter was only the Montparnasse Quarter. Nevertheless, it sufficed. It had its own boulevards, restaurants, cafés, concerts, theatres, palaces, shops, gardens, museums, and churches. There was no need to leave it, and if you were a proper amateur of the Quarter, you never did leave it save to scoff at other Quarters. Sometimes you fringed the Latin Quarter in the big cafés of the Boulevard St. Michel, and sometimes you strolled northwards as far as the Seine, and occasionally even crossed the Seine in order to enter the Louvre, which lined the other bank, but you did not go any farther. Why should you?

Audrey had become so acclimatised to the Quarter that Miss Nickall's studio seemed her natural home. It was very typically a woman's studio of the Quarter. About thirty feet each way and fourteen feet high, with certain irregularities of shape, it was divided into corners. There were the two bed-corners, which were lounge-corners during the day; the afternoon-tea corner, with a piece or two of antique furniture and some old silk hangings, where on high afternoons tea was given to droves of visitors; and there was the culinary corner, with spirit-lamps, gas-rings, kettles, and a bowl or two over which you might spend a couple of arduous hours in ineffectually whipping up a mayonnaise for an impromptu lunch. Artistic operations were carried out in the middle of the studio, not too far from the stove, which never went out from November to May. A large mirror hung paramount on one wall. The remaining spaces of the studio were filled with old easels, canvases, old frames, old costumes and multifarious other properties for pictures, trunks, lamps, boards, tables, and bric-à-brac bought at the Ham-and-Old-Iron Fair. There were a million objects in the studio, and their situations had to be, and were, learnt off by heart. The scene of the toilette was a small attached chamber.

The housekeeping combined the simplicity of the early Christians with the efficient organising of the twentieth century. It began at about half-past seven, when unseen but heard beings left fresh rolls and the *New York Herald* or the *Daily Mail* at the studio door. You made your own bed, just as you cleaned your own boots or washed your own face. The larder consisted of tins of coffee, tea, sugar, and cakes, with an intermittent supply of butter and lemons. The infusing of tea and coffee was practised in perfection. It mattered not in the least whether toilette or breakfast came first, but it was exceedingly important that the care of the stove should precede both. Between ten and eleven the concierge's wife arrived with tools and utensils; she swept and dusted under a considerable percentage of the million objects —and the responsibilities of housekeeping were finished until the next day, for afternoon tea, if it occurred, was a diversion and not a toil.

A great expanse of twelve to fifteen hours lay in front of you. It was not uncomfortably and unchangeably cut into fixed portions by the incidence of lunch and dinner. You ate when you felt inclined to eat, and nearly always at restaurants where you met your acquaintances. Meals were the least important happenings of the day. You had no reliable watch, and you needed none, for you had no fixed programme. You worked till you had had enough of work. You went forth into the world exactly when the idea took you. If you were bored, you found a friend and went to sit in a café. You were ready for anything. The word "rule" had been omitted from your dictionary. You retired to bed when the still small voice within murmured that there was naught else to do. You woke up in the morning amid cups and saucers, lingerie, masterpieces, and boots. And the next day was the same. All the days were the same. Weeks passed with inexpressible rapidity, and all things beyond the Quarter had the quality of vague murmurings and noises behind the scenes.

May had come. Audrey and Miss Ingate had lived in the studio for six months before they realised that they had settled down there and that habits had been formed. Still, they had accomplished something. Miss Ingate had gone back into oils and was attending life classes, and Audrey, by terrible application and by sitting daily at the feet of an oldish lady in black, and by refusing to speak English between breakfast and dinner, had acquired a good accent and much fluency in the French tongue. Now, when she spoke French, she thought in French, and she was extremely proud of the achievement. Also she was acquainted with the names and styles of all known modern painters from pointillistes to cubistes, and, indeed, with the latest eccentricities in all the arts. She could tell who was immortal, and she was fully aware that there was no real painting in England. In brief, she was perhaps more Parisian even than she had hoped. She had absorbed Paris into her system. It was still not the Paris of her early fancy; in particular, it lacked elegance; but it richly satisfied her.

She had on this afternoon of young May an appointment with a young man. And the appointment seemed quite natural, causing no inward disturbance. Less than ever could she understand her father's ukases against young men and against every form of self-indulgence. Now, when she had the idea of doing a thing, she merely did it. Her instincts were her only guide, and, though her instincts were often highly complex, they seldom puzzled her. The old instinct that the desire to do a thing was a sufficient reason against doing it, had expired. For many weeks she had lived with a secret fear that such unbridled conduct must lead to terrible catastrophes, but as nothing happened this fear also expired. She was constantly with young men, and often with men not young; she liked it, but just as much she liked being with women. She never had any difficulties with men. Miss Thompkins insinuated at intervals that she flirted, but she had the sharpest contempt for flirtation, and as a practice put it on a level with embezzlement or arson. Miss Thompkins, however, kept on insinuating. Audrey regarded herself as decidedly wiser than Miss Thompkins. Her opinions on vital matters changed almost weekly, but she was always absolutely sure that the new opinion was final and incontrovertible. Her scorn of the old English Audrey, though concealed, was terrific.

And it is to be remembered that she was a widow. She was never half a second late, now, in replying when addressed as " Mrs. Moncreiff." Frequently she thought that she in fact was a widow. Widowhood was a very advantageous state. It had a free pass to all affairs of interest. It opened wide the door of the world. It recked nothing of girlish codes. It abolished discussions concerning conventional propriety. Its chief defect, for Audrey, was that if she met another widow, or even a married woman, she had to take heed lest she stumbled. Fortunately, neither widows nor wives were very prevalent in the Quarter. And Audrey had attained skill in the use of the state of widowhood. She told no more infantile perilous tales about husbands who ate peas with a knife. In her thankfulness that the tyrannic Rosamund had gone to Germany, and that Madame Piriac had vanished back into unknown Paris, Audrey was at pains to take to heart the lesson of a semi-hysterical blunder.

She descended the dark, dusty oak stairs utterly content. And at the door of the gloomy den of the concierge the concierge's wife was standing. She was a new wife, the young mate of a middle-aged husband, and she had only been illuminating the den (which was kitchen, parlour, and bedroom in a space of ten feet by eight) for about a month. She was plump and pretty, and also she was fair, which was unusual for a Frenchwoman. She wore a striped frock and a little black apron, and her yellow hair was waved with art. Audrey offered her the key of the studio with a smile, and, as Audrey expected, the concierge's wife began to chatter. The concierge's wife loved to chatter with Anglo-Saxon tenants, and she specially enjoyed chattering with Audrey, because of the superior quality of Audrey's French and of her tips. Audrey listened, proud because she could understand so well and answer so fluently.

The sun, which in May shone on the courtyard for about forty minutes in the afternoon on clear days, caught these two creatures in the same beam. They made a delicious sight—Audrey dark, with her large forehead and negligible nose, and the concierge's wife rather doll-like in the regularity of her features. They were delicious not only because of their varied charm, but because they were so absurdly wise and omniscient, and because they had come to settled conclusions about every kind of worldly problem. Youth and vitality equalised their ranks, and the fact that Audrey possessed many ascertained ancestors, and a part of the earth's surface, and much money, and that the concierge's wife possessed nothing but herself and a few bits of furniture, was not of the slightest importance.

The concierge's wife, after curiosity concerning tennis, grew confidential about herself, and more confidential. And at last she lowered her tones, and with sparkling eyes communicated information to Audrey in a voice that was little more than a whisper.

"Oh! truly? I must go," hastily said Audrey, blushing, and off she ran, reduced in an instant to the schoolgirl. Her departure was a retreat. These occasional discomfitures made a faint blot on the excellence of being a widow.

CHAPTER XIII

THE SWOON

In the north-east corner of the Luxembourg Gardens, where the lawn-tennis courts were permitted by a public authority which was strangely impartial and cosmopolitan in the matter of games, Miss Ingate sat sketching a group of statuary with the Rue de Vaugirard behind it. She was sketching in the orthodox way, on the orthodox stool, with the orthodox combined paint-box and easel, and the orthodox police permit in the cover of the box.

The bright and warm weather was tonic; it accounted for the whole temperament of Parisians. Under such a sky, with such a delicate pricking vitalisation in the air, it was impossible not to be Parisian. The trees, all arranged in beautiful perspectives, were coming into leaf, and through their screens could be seen everywhere children shouting as they played at ball and top, and both kinds of nurses, and scores of perambulators and mothers, and a few couples dallying with their sensations, and old men reading papers, and old women knitting and relating anecdotes or entire histories. And nobody was curious beyond his own group. The people were perfectly at home in this grandiose setting of gardens and fountains and grey palaces, with theatres, boulevards and the odour and roar of motor-buses just beyond the palisades. And Miss Ingate in the exciting sunshine gazed around with her subdued Essex grin, as if saying: "It's the most topsy-turvy planet that I was ever on, and why am I, of all people, trying to make this canvas look like a piece of sculpture and a street?"

"Now, Miss Ingate," said tall red-haired Tommy, who was standing over her. "Before you go any farther, do look at the line of roofs and see how interesting it is; it's really full of interest. And you've simply not got on speaking terms with it yet."

"No more I have! No more I have!" cried Miss Ingate, glancing round at Audrey, who was swinging her racket. "Thank you, Tommy. I ought to have thought of it for my own sake, because roofs are so much easier than statues, and I must get an effect somewhere, mustn't I?"

Tommy winked at Audrey. But Tommy's wink was as naught to the great invisible wink of Miss Ingate, the everlasting wink that derided the universe and the sun himself.

Then Musa appeared, with paraphernalia, at the end of a path. Accompanying him was a specimen of the creature known on tennis lawns as "a fourth." He was almost nameless, tall, very young, with the seedlings of a moustache and a space of nude calf between his knicker-bockers and his socks. He was very ceremonious, shy, ungainly and blushful. He played a fair-to-middling game; and nothing more need be said of him.

Musa by contrast was an accomplished man of the world, and the fact that the fourth obviously regarded him as a hero helped Musa to behave in a manner satis-factory to himself in front of these English and American women, so strange, so exotic, so kind, and so disconcerting. Musa looked upon Britain as a romantic isle where people died for love. And as for America, in his mind it was as sinister, as wondrous, and as fatal as the Indies might seem to a bank clerk in Bradford. He had need of every moral assistance in this or any other social ordeal. For, though he was still the greatest violinist in Paris, and perhaps in the world, he could not yet prove this pro-found truth by the only demonstration which the world accepts.

If he played in studios he was idolised. If he played at small concerts in unknown halls he was received with rapture. But he was never lionised. The great concert halls never saw him on their platforms; his name was never in the newspapers; and hospitable personages never fought together for his presence at their tables, even if occasionally they invited him to perform for charity in return for a glass of claret and a sandwich. Monsieur Dauphin had attempted to force the invisible barriers for him, but without success. All his admirers in the Quarter stuck to it that he was in the rank of Kreisler and Ysaye; at the same time they were annoyed with him inasmuch as he did not force the world to acknowledge the prophetic good taste of the Quarter. And Musa made mistakes. He ought to have arrived at studios in a magnificent automobile, and to have given superb and uproarious repasts, and to have rendered innumerable women exquisitely unhappy. Whereas he arrived by tube or bus, never offered hospitality of any sort, and was like a cat with women. Hence the attitude of the Quarter was patronising, as if the Quarter had said: "Yes, he is the greatest violinist in Paris and perhaps in the world; but that's all, and it isn't enough."

The young man and the boy made ready for the game as for a gladiatorial display. Their frowning seriousness proved that they had comprehended the true British idea of sport. Musa came round the net to Audrey's side, but Audrey said in French:

"Miss Thompkins and I will play together. See, we are going to beat you and Gustave."

Musa retired. A few indifferent spectators had collected. Gustave, the fourth, had to serve.

"Play!" he muttered, in a thick and threatening voice, whose depth was the measure of his nervousness.

He served a double fault to Tommy, and then a fault to Audrey. The fourth ball he got over. Audrey played it. The two males rushed with appalling force together on the centre line in pursuit, and a terrible collision occurred. Musa fell away from Gustave as from a wall. When he arose out of the pebbly dust his right arm hung very limp from the shoulder. No sooner had he risen than he sank again, and the blood began to leave his face, and his eyes closed. The fourth, having recovered from the collision, knelt down by his side, and gazed earnestly at him. Tommy and Audrey hurried towards the statuesque group, and Audrey was thinking: "Why did I refuse to let him play with me? If he had played with me there would have been no accident." She reproached herself because she well knew that only out of the most absurd contrariness had she repulsed Musa. Or was it that she had repulsed him from fear of something that Tommy might say or look?

In a few seconds, strongly drawn by this marvellous piece of luck, promenaders were darting with joyous rapidity from north, south, east and west to witness the tragedy. There were nurses with coloured streamers six feet long, lusty children, errand boys, lads, and sundry nondescript men, some of whom carefully folded up their newspapers as they hurried to the cynosure. They beheld the body as though it were a corpse, and the corpse of an enemy; they formulated and discussed theories of the event; they examined minutely the rackets which had been thrown on the ground. They were exercising the immemorial rights of unmoved curiosity; they held themselves as indifferent as gods, and the murmur of their impartial voices floated soothingly over Musa, and the shadow of their active profiles covered him from the sparkling sunshine. Somebody mentioned policemen, in the plural, but none came. All remarked in turn that the ladies were English, as though that were a sufficient explanation of the whole affair.

No one said:

"It is Musa, the greatest violinist in Paris and perhaps in Europe."

Desperately Audrey stooped and seized Musa beneath the armpits to lift him to a sitting position.

"You'd better leave him alone," said Tommy, with a kind of ironic warning and innuendo.

But Audrey still struggled with the mass, convinced that she was showing initiative and firmness of character. The fourth with fierce vigour began to aid her, and another youth from the crowd was joining the enterprise when Miss Ingate arrived from her stool.

"Drop him, you silly little thing!" adjured Miss Ingate. "Instead of lifting his head you ought to lift his feet."

Audrey stared uncertain for a moment, and then let the mass subside. Whereupon Miss Ingate with all her strength lifted both legs to the height of her waist, giving Musa the appearance of a wheelless barrow.

"You want to let the blood run *into* his head," said Miss Ingate with a self-conscious grin at the increasing crowd. "People only faint because the blood leaves their heads—that's why they go pale."

Musa's cheeks showed a tinge of red. You could almost see the precious blood being decanted by Miss Ingate out of the man's feet into his head. In a minute he opened his eyes. Miss Ingate lowered the legs.

"It was only the pain that made him feel queer," she said.

The episode was over, and the crowd very gradually and reluctantly scattered, disappointed at the lack of a fatal conclusion. Musa stood up, smiling apologetically, and Audrey supported him by the left arm, for the right could not be touched.

"Hadn't you better take him home, Mrs. Moncreiff?" Tommy suggested. "You can get a taxi here in the Rue de Vaugirard." She did not smile, but her green eyes glinted.

"Yes, I will," said Audrey curtly.

And Tommy's eyes glinted still more.

"And I shall get a doctor," said Audrey. "His arm may be broken."

"I should," Tommy concurred with gravity.

"Well, if it is, *I* can't set it," said Miss Ingate quizzically. "I was getting on so well with the high lights on that statue. I'll come along back to the studio in about half an hour."

The fourth, who had been hovering near like a criminal magnetised by his crime, bounded off furiously at the suggestion that he should stop a taxi at the entrance to the gardens.

"I hope he has broken his arm and he can never play any more," thought Audrey, astoundingly, as she and the fourth helped pale Musa into the open taxi. "It will just serve those two right." She meant Miss Ingate and Tommy.

No sooner did the taxi start than Musa began to cry. He did not seem to care that he was in the midst of a busy street, with a piquant widow by his side.

CHAPTER XIV

MISS INGATE POINTS OUT THE DOOR

"WHY did you cry this afternoon, Musa?"

Musa made no reply.

Audrey was lighting the big lamp in the Moncreiff-Ingate studio. It made exactly the same moon as it had made on the night in the previous autumn when Audrey had first seen it. She had brought Musa to the studio because she did not care to take him to his own lodgings. (As a fact, nobody that she knew, except Musa, had ever seen Musa's lodgings.) This was almost the first moment they had had to themselves since the visit of the little American doctor from the Rue Servandoni. The rumour of Musa's misfortune had spread through the Quarter like the smell of a fire, and various persons of both sexes had called to inspect, to sympathise, and to take tea, which Audrey was continually making throughout the late afternoon. Musa had had an egg for his tea, and more than one girl had helped to spread the yolk and the white on pieces of bread-and-butter, for the victim of destiny had his right arm in a sling. Audrey had let them do it, as a mother patronisingly lets her friends amuse her baby.

In the end they had all gone; Tommy had enigmatically looked in and gone, and Miss Ingate had gone to dine at the favourite restaurant of the hour in the Rue Léopold Robert. Audrey had refused to go, asserting that which was not true; namely, that she had had an enormous tea, including far too many *petits fours*. Miss Ingate in departing had given a glance at her sketch (fixed on the easel), and another at Audrey, and another at Musa, all equally ironic and kindly.

Musa also had declined dinner, but he had done nothing to indicate that he meant to leave. He sat mournful and passive in a basket chair, his sling making a patch of white in the gloom. The truth was that he suffered from a disability not uncommon among certain natures: he did not know how to go. He could arrive with ease, but he was no expert at vanishing. Audrey was troubled. As suited her age and condition, she was apt to feel the responsibility of the whole universe. She knew that she was responsible for Musa's accident, and now she was beginning to be aware that she was responsible for his future as well. She was sure that he needed encouragement and guidance. She pictured him with his fiddle under his chin, masterful, confident, miraculous, throwing a spell over everyone within earshot. But actually she saw him listless and vanquished in the basket chair, and she perceived that only a strongly influential and determined woman, such as herself, could save him from disaster. No man could do it. His tears had shaken her. She was willing to make allowances for a foreigner, but she had never seen a man cry before, and the spectacle was very disturbing. It inspired her with a fear that even she could not be the salvation of Musa.

"I demanded something of you," she said, after lowering the wick of the lamp to exactly the right point, and staring at it for a greater length of time than was necessary or even seemly. She spoke French, and as she listened to her French accent she heard that it was good.

"I am done for!" came the mournful voice of Musa out of the obscurity behind the lamp.

"What! You are done for? But you know what the doctor said. He said no bone was broken. Only a little strain, and the pain from your——" Admirable though her French accent was, she could not think of the French word for "funny-bone." Indeed she had never learnt it.

So she said it in English. Musa knew not what she
meant, and thus a slight chasm was opened between them
which neither could bridge. She finished: "In one week
you are going to be able to play again."

Musa shook his head.

Relieved as she was to discover that Musa had cried
because he was done for, and not because he was hurt,
she was still worried by his want of elasticity, of resiliency.
Nevertheless she was agreeably worried. The doctor had
disappointed her by his light optimism, but he could not
smile away Musa's moral indisposition. The large vagueness of the studio, the very faint twilight still showing
through the great window, the silence and intimacy, the
sounds of the French language, the gleam of the white
sling, all combined to permeate her with delicious melancholy.
And not for everlasting bliss would she have had Musa
strong, obstinate, and certain of success.

"A week!" he murmured. "It is for ever. A week
of practice lost is eternally lost. And on Wednesday one
had invited me to play at Foa's. And I cannot."

"Foa? Who is Foa?"

"What! You do not know Foa? In order to succeed
it is necessary, it is essential, to play at Foa's. That
alone gives the *cachet*. Dauphin told me last week. He
arranged it. After having played at Foa's all is possible.
Dauphin was about to abandon me when he met Foa.
Now I am ruined. This afternoon after the tennis I was
going to Durand's to get the new Caprice of Roussel—
he is an intimate friend of Foa. I should have studied
it in five days. They would have been ravished by the
attention. . . . But why talk I thus? No, I could not
have played Caprice to please them. I am cursed. I will
never again touch the violin, I swear it. What am I?
Do I not live on the money *lent* to me regularly by
Mademoiselle Thompkins and Mademoiselle Nickall?"

"You don't, Musa?" Audrey burst out in English.

"Yes, yes!" said Musa violently. "But last month,

H

from Mademoiselle Nickall—nothing! She is in London;
she forgets. It is better like that. Soon I shall be
playing in the Opéra orchestra, fourth desk, one hundred
francs a month. That will be the end. There can be
no other."

Instead of admiring the secret charity of Tommy and
Nick, which she had never suspected, Audrey was very
annoyed by it. She detested it and resented it. And
especially the charity of Miss Thompkins. She considered
that from a woman with eyes and innuendoes like Tommy's
charity amounted to a sneer.

"It is extremely unsatisfactory," she said, dropping on
to Miss Ingate's sofa.

Not another word was spoken. Audrey tapped her foot.
Musa creaked in the basket chair. He avoided her eyes,
but occasionally she glared at him like a schoolmistress.
Then her gaze softened—he looked so ill, so helpless, so
hopeless. She wanted to light a cigarette for him, but she
was somehow bound to the sofa. She wanted him
to go—she hated the prospect of his going. He could not
possibly go, alone, to his solitary room. Who would
tend him, soothe him, put him to bed? He was an
infant. . . .

Then, after a long while, Miss Ingate entered sharply.
Audrey coughed and sprang up.

"Oh!" ejaculated Miss Ingate.

"I—I think I shall just change my boots," said Audrey,
smoothing out the short white skirt. And she disappeared
into the dressing-room that gave on to the studio.

As soon as she was gone, Miss Ingate went close up
to Musa's chair. He had not moved.

She said, smiling, with the corners of her mouth well
down :

"Do you see that door, young man?"

And she indicated the door.

When Audrey came back into the studio,

"Audrey," cried Miss Ingate shrilly. "What you been

doing to Musa? As soon as you went out he up vehy
quickly and ran away."

At this information Audrey was more obviously troubled
and dashed than Miss Ingate had ever seen her, in Paris.
She made no answer at all. Fortunately, lying on the table
in front of the mirror was a letter for Miss Ingate which had
arrived by the evening post. Audrey went for it, pretending
to search, and then handed it over with a casual gesture.

"It looks as if it was from Nick," she murmured.

Miss Ingate, as she was putting on her spectacles,
remarked :

"I hope you weren't hurt—me not coming with you and
Musa in the taxi from the gardens this afternoon, dear."

"Me? Oh no !"

"It wasn't that I was so vehy interested in my sketch.
But to my mind there's nothing more ridiculous than
several women all looking after one man. Miss Thompkins
thought so, too."

"Oh ! Did she? . . . What does Nick say?"

Miss Ingate had put the letter flat on the table in the full
glare of the lamp, and was leaning over it, her grey hair
brilliantly illuminated. Audrey kept in the shadow and in
the distance. Miss Ingate had a habit of reading to herself
under her breath. She read slowly, and turned pages over
with a deliberate movement.

"Well," said Miss Ingate twisting her head sideways so
as to see Audrey standing like a ghost afar off. "Well, she
has been going it ! She's broken a window in Oxford
Street with a hammer; she had one night in the cells for
that. And she'd have had to go to prison altogether only
some unknown body paid the fine for her. She says :
' There are some mean persons in the world, and he was
one. I feel sure it was a man, and an American, too.
The owners of the shops are going to bring a law action
against me for the value of the plate-glass. It is such fun.
And our leaders are splendid and so in earnest. They say
we are doing a great historical work, and we are. The

London correspondent of the *New York Times* interviewed
me because I am American. I did not want to be interviewed, but our instructions are—never to avoid publicity.
There is to be no more window breaking for the present.
Something new is being arranged. The hammer is so
heavy, and sometimes the first blow does not break the
window. The situation is *very* serious, and the Government is at its wits' end. This we *know*. We have our
agents everywhere. All the most thoughtful people are
strongly in favour of votes for women; but of course some
of them are afraid of our methods. This only shows that
they have not learnt the lessons of history. I wonder that
you and dear Mrs. Moncreiff do not come and help. Many
women ask after you, and everybody at Kingsway is very
curious to know Mrs. Moncreiff. Since Mrs. Burke's
death, Betty has taken rooms in this house, but perhaps
Tommy has told you this already. If so, excuse. Betty's
health is very bad since they let her out last. With regard
to the rent, will you pay the next quarter direct to the
concierge yourselves? It will save so much trouble. I
must tell you——' "

Slowly Audrey moved up to the table and leaned over the
letter by Miss Ingate's side.

"So you see!" said Miss Ingate. "Well, we must
show it to Tommy in the morning. ' Not learnt the lessons
of history,' eh? I know who's been talking to Nick. *I*
know as well as if I could hear them speaking."

"Do you think we ought to go to London?" Audrey
demanded bluntly.

"Well," Miss Ingate answered, with impartial irony on
her long upper lip. "I don't know. Of course I played the
organ all the way down Regent Street. I feel very strongly
about votes for women, and once when I was helping in the
night and day vigil at the House of Commons and some
Ministers came out smoking their *cigahs* and asked us how
we liked it, I was vehy, vehy angry. However, the next
morning I had a cigarette myself and felt better. But I'm

not a professional reformer, like a lot of them are at Kingsway. It isn't my meat and drink. And I don't think it matters much whether we get the vote next year or in ten years. I'm Winifred Ingate before I'm anything else. And so long as I'm pretty comfortable no one's going to make me believe that the world's coming to an end. I know one thing—if we did get the vote it would take me all my time to keep most of the women I know from voting for something silly."

"Winnie," said Audrey. "You're very sensible sometimes."

"I'm always very sensible," Winnie retorted, "until I get nervous. Then I'm apt to skid."

Without more words they transformed the studio, by a few magical strokes, from a drawing-room into a bedroom. Audrey, the last to retire, extinguished the lamp, and tripped to her bed behind her screen. Only a few slight movements disturbed the silence.

"Winnie," said Audrey suddenly. "I do believe you're one of those awful people who compromise. You're always right in the middle of the raft."

But Miss Ingate, being fast asleep, offered no answer.

CHAPTER XV

THE RIGHT BANK

THE next day, after a studio lunch which contained too much starch and was deficient in nitrogen, Miss Ingate, putting on her hat and jacket, said with a caustic gesture :

"Well, I must be off to my life class. And much good may it do me ! "

The astonishing creature had apparently begun existence again, and begun it on the plane of art, but this did not prevent the observer within her from taking the same attitude towards her second career as she had taken towards her first. Nothing seemed more meet for Miss Ingate's ironic contemplation than the daily struggle for style and beauty in the academies of the Quarter.

Audrey made no reply. The morning had been unusually silent, giving considerable scope for Miss Ingate's faculty for leaving well alone.

"I suppose you aren't coming out? " added Miss Ingate.

"No. I went out a bit this morning. You know I have my French lesson in twenty minutes."

"Of course."

Miss Ingate seized her apparatus and departed. The instant she was alone Audrey began in haste to change into all her best clothes, which were black, and which the Quarter seldom saw. Fashionably arrayed, she sat down and wrote a note to Madame Schmitt, her French instructress, to say that she had been suddenly called away on urgent business, and asking her nevertheless to count the time as a lesson given. This done, she put her credit notes and her cheque-book into her handbag, and, leaving the note with the concierge's wife, who bristled with interesting suspicions, she vanished into Paris.

The weather was even more superb than on the previous day. Paris glittered around her as she drove, slowly, in a horse-taxi, to the Place de l'Opéra on the right bank, where the *grand boulevard* meets the Avenue de l'Opéra and the Rue de la Paix. Here was the very centre of the fashionable and pleasure-ridden district which the Quarter held in noble scorn. She had seen it before, because she had started a banking account (under advice from Mr. Foulger), and the establishment of her bankers was situate at the corner of the Avenue de l'Opéra and the Rue de la Paix. But she knew little of the district, and such trifling information as she had acquired was tinged by the natural hostility of a young woman who for over six months, with no compulsion to do so, had toiled regularly and fiercely in the pursuit of knowledge. She paid off the cab, and went to test the soundness of her bankers. The place was full of tourists, and in one department of it young men in cages, who knew not the Quarter, were counting, and ladling, and pinning together, and engorging, and dealing forth, the currency and notes of all the great nations of the earth. The spectacle was inspiring.

In half a year the restive but finally obedient Mr. Foulger had sent three thousand pounds to Paris in the unpoetic form of small oblong pieces of paper signed with his own dull signature. Audrey desired to experience the thrill of authentic money. She waited some time in front of a cage, with her cheque-book open on the counter, until a young man glanced at her interrogatively through the bars.

" How much money have I got here, please? " she asked. She ought to have said : " What is my balance, please? " But nobody had taught her the sacred formula.

" What name? " said the clerk.

" Moze—Audrey Moze," she answered, for she had not dared to acquaint Mr. Foulger with her widowhood, and his cheques were made out to herself.

The clerk vanished, and in a moment reappeared, silently wrote something on a little form, and pushed it to her under the grille. She read:

"73,065 frs. 50c."

The fact was that in six months she had spent little more than the amount which she had brought with her from London. Having begun in simplicity, in simplicity she had continued, partly because she had been too industrious and too earnest for luxurious caprices, partly because she had never been accustomed to anything else but simplicity, and partly from wilfulness. It had pleased her to think that she was piling tens of thousands upon tens of thousands—in francs.

But in the night she had decided that the moment had arrived for a change in the great campaign of seeing life and tasting it.

She timorously drew a cheque for eleven thousand francs, and asked for ten thousand in notes and a thousand in gold. The clerk showed no trace of either astonishment or alarm; but he insisted on her endorsing the cheque. When she saw the gold, she changed half of it for ten notes of fifty francs each.

Emerging with false but fairly plausible nonchalance from the crowded establishment, where other clerks were selling tickets to Palestine, Timbuctoo, Bagdad, Berlin, and all the abodes of happiness in the world, she saw at the newspaper kiosk opposite the little blue poster of an English daily. It said: "More Suffragette Riots." She had a qualm, for her conscience was apt to be tyrannic, and its empire over her had been strengthened by the long, steady course of hard work which she had accomplished. Miss Ingate's arguments had not placated that conscience. It had said to her in the night: "If ever there was a girl who ought to assist heartily in the emancipation of women, that girl is you, Audrey Moze."

"Pooh!" she replied to her conscience, for she could always confute it with a sharp word—for a time.

And she crossed to the *grand boulevard*, and turned westward along the splendid, humming, roaring thoroughfare gay with flags and gleaming with such plate-glass as Nick the militant would have loved to shatter. Certainly there was nothing like this street in the Quarter. The Quarter could equal it neither in shops, nor in cafés, nor in vehicles, nor in crowds. It was an exultant thoroughfare, and Audrey caught its buoyancy, which could be distinctly seen in the feather on her hat. At the end of it she passed into the cool shade of a music-shop with the name "Durand" on its façade. She had found the address, and another one, in the telephone book at the Café de Versailles that morning. It was an immense shop containing millions of pieces of music for all instruments and all tastes. Yet when she modestly asked for the Caprice for violin of Roussel, the *morceau* was brought to her without the slightest hesitation, together with the pianoforte accompaniment. The price was twelve francs.

Her gloved hand closed round the slim roll with the delicate firmness which was actuating all her proceedings on that magnificent afternoon. She was determined to save Musa not merely from himself, but from Miss Thompkins and everybody. It was not that she was specially interested in Musa. No! She was interested in a clean, neat job—that was all. She had begun to take charge of Musa, and she intended to carry the affair through. He had the ability to succeed, and he should succeed. It would be ridiculous for him not to succeed. From certain hints, and from a deeply sagacious instinct, she had divined that money and management were the only ingredients lacking to Musa's triumph. She could supply both these elements; and she would. And her reward would be the pride of the workman in his job.

Now her firmness hesitated. She retraced the boulevard to the Place de l'Opéra, and then took the Rue de la Paix. In the first shop on the left-hand side, next to her bankers, she saw amid a dazzling collection of jewelled articles for travellers and letter-writers and diary-keepers, a sublime gold handbag, or, as the French say, hand-sack. Its clasp was set with a sapphire. Impulse sent her gliding right into the shop, with the words already on her lips: "How much is that gold hand-sack in the window?" But when she reached the hushed and shadowed interior, which was furnished like a drawing-room with soft carpets and tapestried chairs, she beheld dozens of gold hand-sacks glinting like secret treasure in a cave; and she was embarrassed by the number and variety of them. A well-dressed and affable lady and gentleman, with a quite remarkable similarity of prominent noses, welcomed her in general terms, and seemed surprised, and even a little pained, when she talked about buying and selling. She came out of the shop with a gold hand-sack which had cost twelve hundred francs, and all her money was in it.

Fortified by the impressive bauble, she walked along the street to the Place Vendôme, where she descried in the distance the glittering signs and arms of the Hôtel du Danube. Then she walked up the opposite pavement of the Rue de la Paix, and down again and up again until she had grasped its significance.

It was a street of jewellery, perfumes, antiques, gloves, hats, frocks, and furs. It was a street wherein the lily was painted and gold was gilded. Every window was a miracle of taste, refinement, and costliness. Every article in every window was so dear that no article was ticketed with its price, save a few wafer-like watches and jewelled rings that bore tiny figures, such as 12,500 francs, 40,000 francs. Despite her wealth, Audrey felt poor. The upper windows of nearly all the great buildings were arrayed with plants in full bloom. The roadway was covered with superb automobiles, some of them nearly as long as trains. About half of them stood in repose at the kerb, and Audrey as she strolled could see through their panes of bevelled glass the complex luxury within of toy dogs, clocks, writing-pads, mirrors, powder boxes, parasols, and the lounging arrogance of uniformed menials. At close intervals women passed rapidly across the pavements to or from these automobiles. If they were leaving a shop, the automobile sprang into life, dogs, menials, and all, the door was opened, the woman slipped in like a mechanical toy, the door banged, the menial jumped, and with trumpet tones the entire machine curved and swept away. The aspect of these women made Audrey feel glad that she was wearing her best clothes, and simultaneously made her feel that her best clothes were worse than useless.

She saw an automobile shop with a card at the door : "Town and touring cars for hire by day, week, or month." A gorgeous Mercédès, too spick, too span, altogether too celestial for earthly use, occupied most of the shop.

"Good afternoon, Madame," said a man in bad English. For Audrey had misguided herself into the emporium. She did not care to be addressed in her own tongue ; she even objected to the instant discovery of her nationality, of which at the moment she was ashamed. And so it was with frigidity that she inquired whether cars were to be hired.

The shopman hesitated. Audrey knew that she had committed an indiscretion. It was impossible that cars should be handed out thus unceremoniously to anybody who had the fancy to enter the shop ! Cars were naturally the subject of negotiations and references. . . . And then the shopman, espying the gold bag, and being by it and by the English frigidity humbled to his proper station, fawned and replied that he had cars for hire, and the best cars. Did the lady want a large car or a small car? She wanted a large car. Did she want a town or a touring car? She wanted a town car, and by the week. When did she want it? She wanted it at once—in half an hour.

"I can hire you a car in half an hour, with liveried chauffeur," said the shopman, after telephoning. "But he cannot speak English."

"*Ça m'est égal,*" answered Audrey with grim satisfaction. "What kind of a car will it be?"

"Mercédès, Madame."

The price was eight hundred francs a week, inclusive. As Audrey was paying for the first week the man murmured :

"What address, Madame?"

"Hôtel du Danube," she answered like lightning—indeed far quicker than thought. "But I shall call here for the car. It must be waiting outside."

The dispenser of cars bowed.

"Can you get a taxi for me?" Audrey suggested. "I will leave this roll here and this bag," producing her old handbag which she had concealed under her coat. And she thought : "All this is really very simple."

At the other address which she had found in the telephone book—a house in the Rue d'Aumale—she said to an aged concierge :

"Monsieur Foa—which floor?"

A very dark, rather short and negligently dressed man of nearly middle-age who was descending the staircase, raised his hat with grave ceremony :

"Pardon, Madame. Foa—it is I."

Audrey was not prepared for this encounter. She had intended to compose her face and her speech while mounting the staircase. She blushed.

"I come from Musa—the violinist," she began hesitatingly. "You invited him to play at your flat on Friday night, Monsieur."

Monsieur Foa gave a sudden enchanting smile :

"Yes, Madame. I hear much good of him from my friend Dauphin, much good. And we long to hear him play. It appears he is a great artist."

"He has had an accident," said Audrey. Monsier Foa's face grew serious. "It is nothing—a few days. The elbow —a trifle. He cannot play next Friday. But he will be desolated if he may not play to you later. He has so few friends . . . I came . . . I . . . ."

"Madame, every Friday we are at home, every Friday.

My wife will be ravished. I shall be ravished. Believe
me. Let him be reassured."

"Monsieur, you are too amiable. I shall tell Musa."

"Musa, he may have few friends—it is possible, Madame
—but he is nevertheless fortunate. Madame is English,
is it not so? My wife and I adore England and the
English. For us there is only England. If Madame would
do us the honour of coming when Musa plays. . . . My
wife will send an invitation, to the end of remaining within
the rules. You, Madame, and any of your friends."

"Monsieur is too amiable, truly."

In the end they were standing together on the pavement by the waiting taxi. She gave him her card, and
breathed the words "Hôtel du Danube." He was enchanted. She offered her hand. He took it, raised it,
and kissed the back of it. Then he stood with his hat
off until she had passed from his sight.

Audrey was burning with excitement. She said to
herself:

"I have discovered Paris."

When the taxi turned again into the Rue de la Paix,
she thought:

"The car will not be waiting. It would be too lovely
if it were."

But there the car was, huge, glistening, unreal, incredible. And a chauffeur gloved and liveried in brown,
to match the car, stood by its side, and the shopman
was at the door, holding the Caprice of Roussel and the
old handbag ready in his hand.

"Here is Madame," said he.

The chauffeur saluted.

The car was closed.

"Will Madame have the carriage open or closed?"

"Closed."

Having paid the taxi-driver, Audrey entered the car,
and as she did so, she threw over her shoulder:

"Hôtel du Danube."

While the chauffeur started the engine, the shopman with brilliant smiles delivered the music and the bag. The door clicked. Audrey noticed the clock, the rug, the powder-box, the speaking-tube, and the mirror. She gazed, and saw a face triumphant and delicious in the mirror. The car began to glide forward. She leaned back against the pale grey upholstery, but in her soul she was standing and crying with a wild wave of the hand, to the whole street:

"It is a miracle!"

In a moment the gigantic car stopped in front of the Hôtel du Danube. Two attendants rushed out in uniforms of delicate blue. They did not touch their hats—they raised them. Audrey descended and penetrated into the portico, where a tall dandy saluted and inquired her will. She wanted rooms; she wanted a flat? Certainly. They had nothing but flats. A large flat on the ground-floor was at her disposal absolutely. Two bedrooms, sitting-room, bathroom. It had its own private entrance in the court-yard. She inspected it. The suite was furnished in the Empire style. Herself and maid? No. A friend! Well, the maids could sleep upstairs. It could arrange itself. She had no maid? Her friend had no maid? Ah! So much the better. Sixty francs a day.

"Where is the dining-room?" demanded Audrey.

"Madame," said the dandy, shocked. "We have no dining-room. All meals are specially cooked to order and served in the private rooms. We have the reputation. . . ." He opened his arms and bowed.

Good! Good! She would return with her friend in one hour or so.

"106 Rue Delambre," she bade the chauffeur, after being followed to the pavement by the dandy and a suite.

"Rue de Londres?" said the chauffeur.

"No. Rue Delambre."

It had to be looked out on the map, but the chauffeur, trained to the hour, did not blench. However, when he found the Rue Delambre, the success with which he repudiated it was complete.

"Winnie!" began Audrey in the studio, with assumed indifference. Miss Ingate was at tea.

"Oh! You are a swell. Where you been?"

"Winnie! What do you say to going and living on the right bank for a bit?"

"Well, well!" said Miss Ingate. "So that's it, is it? I've been ready to go for a long time. Of course you want to go first thing to-morrow morning. I know you."

"No, I don't," said Audrey. "I want to go to-night. Now! Pack the trunks quick. I've got the finest auto you ever saw waiting at the door."

CHAPTER XVI

ROBES

On the second following Friday evening, Audrey's suite of rooms at the Hôtel du Danube glowed in every corner with pink-shaded electricity. According to what Audrey had everywhere observed to be the French custom, there was in this flat the minimum of corridor and the maximum of doors. Each room communicated directly with all the other rooms. The doors were open, and three women continually in a feverish elation passed to and fro. Empire chairs and sofas were covered with rich garments of every colour and form and material, from the transparent blue silk *matinée* to the dark heavy cloak of velvet ornamented with fur. The place was in fact very like the showrooms of a cosmopolitan dressmaker after a vast trying-on. Sundry cosmopolitan dressmakers had contributed to the rich confusion. None had hesitated for an instant to execute Audrey's commands. They had all been waiting, apparently since the beginning of time, to serve her. All that district of Paris had been thus waiting. The flat had been waiting, the automobile had been waiting, the chauffeur had been waiting, and purveyors of every sort. A word from her seemed to have released them from an enchantment. For the most part they were strange people, these magical attendants, never mentioning money, but rather deprecating the sound of it, and content to supply nothing but the finest productions of their unquestionable genius. Still, Audrey reckoned that she owed about twenty-five thousand francs to Paris.

The third woman was the maid, Elise. The hotel had invented and delivered Elise, and thereafter seemed easier in its mind. Elise was thirty years of age and not repellent of aspect. On a black dress she wore the smallest white muslin apron that either Audrey or Miss Ingate had ever seen. She kept pins in her mouth, but in other respects showed few eccentricities beyond an extreme excitability. When at eight o'clock Mademoiselle's new gown, promised for seven, had not arrived, Elise begged permission to use Madame's salts. When the bell rang at eight-thirty, and a lackey brought in an oval-shaped box with a long loop to it of leathern strap, she only just managed not to kiss the lackey. The rapid movement of Mademoiselle and Elise with the contents of the box from the drawing-room into Mademoiselle's bedroom was the last rushing and swishing that preceded a considerable peace.

Madame was absolutely ready, in her bedroom. In the large mirror of the dark wardrobe she surveyed her victoriously young face, the magnificent grey dress, the coiffure, the jewels, the spangled shoes, the fan; and the ensemble satisfied her. She was intensely and calmly happy. No thought of the past nor of the future, nor of what was going on in other parts of the earth's surface could in the slightest degree impair her happiness. She had done nothing herself, she had neither earned money nor created any of the objects which adorned her; nor was she capable of doing the one or the other. Yet she felt proud as well as happy, because she was young and superbly healthy, and not unattractive. These were her high virtues. And her attitude was so right that nobody would have disagreed with her.

Her left ear was listening for the sound, through the unlatched window, of the arrival of the automobile with Musa and his fiddle inside it.

Then the door leading from Mademoiselle's bedroom opened sharply, and Mademoiselle appeared, with her grey hair, her pale shining forehead, her sardonic grin, and the new dress of those Empire colours, magenta and green. Elise stood behind, trembling with satisfaction.

"Well——" Audrey began. But she heard the automobile, and told Elise to run and be ready to open the front door of the flat.

"Rather showy, isn't it? Rather daring?" said Miss Ingate, advancing self-consciously and self-deprecating.

"Winnie," answered Audrey. "It's a nice question between you and the Queen of Sheba."

Suddenly Miss Ingate beheld in the mirror the masterpiece of an illustrious male dressmaker—a masterpiece in which no touch of the last fashion was abated—and little Essex Winnie grinning from within it.

She screamed. And forthwith putting her hands behind her neck she began to unhook the corsage.

"What are you doing, Winnie?"

"I'm taking it off."

"But why?"

"Because I'm not going to wear it."

"But you've nothing else to wear."

"I can't help that."

"But you can't come. What on earth shall you do?"

"I dare say I shall go to bed. Or I might shoot myself. But if you think that I'm going outside this room in this dress, you're a perfect simpleton, Audrey. I don't mind being a fool, but I won't look one."

Audrey heard Musa enter the drawing-room.

She pulled the door to, keeping her hand on the knob.

"Very well, Winnie," she said coldly, and swept into the drawing-room.

As she and Musa left the pink rose-shaded flat, she heard a burst of tears from Elise in the bedroom.

"21 Rue d'Aumale," she curtly ordered the chauffeur, who sat like a god obscurely in front of the illuminated interior of the carriage. Musa's violin case lay amid the cushions therein.

The chauffeur approvingly touched his hat. The Rue d'Aumale was a good street.

"I wonder what his surname is?" Audrey thought curiously. "And whether he's in love or married, and has children." She knew nothing of him save that his Christian name was Michel.

She was taciturn and severe with Musa.

CHAPTER XVII

SOIRÉE

"MONSIEUR FOA—which floor?" Audrey asked once again of the aged concierge in the Rue d'Aumale. This time she got an answer. It was the fifth or top floor. Musa said nothing, permitting himself to be taken about like a parcel, though with a more graceful passivity. There was no lift, but at each floor a cushioned seat for travellers to use and a palm in a coloured pot in a niche for travellers to gaze upon as they rested. The quality of the palms, however, deteriorated floor by floor, and on the fourth and fifth floors the niches were empty. A broad embroidered bell-pull, twitched, gave rise to one clanging sound within the abode of the Foas, and the clanging sound reacted upon a small dog which yapped loudly and continued to yap until the visitors had entered and the door been closed again. Monsieur came out of a room into the small entrance-hall, accompanied by a considerable noise of conversation. He beamed his ravishment; he kissed hands; he helped with the dark blue cloak.

"I brought Monsieur Musa in my car," said Audrey. "The weather——"

Monsieur Foa bowed low to Monsieur Musa, and Monsieur Musa bowed low to Monsieur Foa.

"Monsieur!"

"Monsieur!"

"Monsieur, your accident I hope . . ."

And so on.

Cloak, overcoat, hat, stick—everything except the violin case—were thrown pell-mell on to a piece of furniture in the entrance-hall. Monsieur Foa, instead of being in evening dress, was in exactly the same clothes as he had worn at his first meeting with Audrey.

Madame Foa appeared in the doorway. She was a slim blonde Italian of pure descent, whereas only the paternal grandfather of Monsieur Foa had been Italian. Madame Foa, who had called on Audrey at the Danube, exhibited the same symptoms of pleasure as her husband.

"But your friend? But your friend?" cried she.

Audrey, being led gradually into the drawing-room, explained that Miss Ingate had been prevented at the last moment, etc., etc.

The distinction of Madame Foa's simple dress had reassured Audrey to a certain extent, but the size of the drawing-room disconcerted her again. She had understood that the house of the Foas was the real esoteric centre of musical Paris, and she had prepared herself for vast and luxurious salons, footmen, fountains of wine, rare flowers, dandies, and the divine shoulders of operatic sopranos who combined wit with the most seductive charm. The drawing-room of the Foas was not as large as her own drawing-room at the Danube. Still it was full, and double doors leading to an unseen dining-room at right angles to its length produced an illusion of space. Some of the men and some of the women were elegant, and even very elegant; others were not. Audrey instantly with her expert eye saw that the pictures on the walls were of the last correctness, and a few by illustrious painters. Here and there she could see scrawled on them "à mon ami, André Foa." Such phenomena were balm. Everybody in the room was presented to her, and with the greatest particularity, and the host and hostess gazed on her as on an idol, a jewel, an exquisite and startling discovery. Musa found two men he knew. The conversation was resumed with energy.

"And now," said Madame Foa in English, sitting down intimately beside Audrey, with a loving gesture, "We will have a little talk, you and I. I find our friend Madame Piriac met you last year."

"Ah! Yes," murmured Audrey, fatally struck, but admirably dissembling, for she was determined to achieve the evening successfully. "Madame Piriac, will she come to-night?"

"I fear not," replied Madame Foa. "She would if she could."

"I should so like to have seen her again," said Audrey eagerly. She was so relieved at Madame Piriac's not coming that she felt she could afford to be eager.

And Monsieur Foa, a little distance off, threw a sign into the duologue, and called:

"You permit me? Your dress . . . *Exquise! Exquise!* And these pigs of French persist in saying that the English lack taste!" He clapped his hand to his forehead in despair of the French.

Then the clanging sound supervened, and the little fox-terrier yapped, and Monsieur Foa went out, ejaculating "Ah!" and Madame Foa went into the doorway. Audrey glanced round for Musa, but he was out of sight in the dining-room. Several people turned at once and spoke to her, including two composers who had probably composed more impossibilities for amateur pianists than any other two men who ever lived, and a musical critic with large dark eyes and an Eastern air, who had come from the Opera very sarcastic about the Opera. One of the composers asked the critic whether he had not heard Musa play.

"Yes," said the critic. "I heard him in the Ternes Quarter—somewhere. He plays very agreeably. Madame," he addressed Audrey. "I was discussing with these gentle-men whether it be not possible to define the principle of beauty in music. Once it is defined, my trade will be much simplified, you see. What say you?"

How could she discourse on the principle of beauty in music when she had the whole weight of the evening on her shoulders? Musa was the whole weight of the evening. Would he succeed? She was his mother, his manager, his creator. He was her handiwork. If he failed she would have failed. That was her sole interest in him, but it was an overwhelming interest. When would he be asked to play? Useless for them to flatter her about her dress, to treat her like a rarity, if they offered callous, careless, off-hand remarks, such as "He plays very agreeably."

She stammered :

"I—I only know what I like."

One of the composers jumped up excitedly :

"*Voilà!* Madame has said the final word. You hear me, the final word, the most profound. Argue as you will, perfect the art of criticism to no matter what point, and you will never get beyond the final word of Madame."

The critic shrugged his shoulders, and with a smile bowed to the ravishing utterer of last words on the most baffling of subjects. This fluttered person soon perceived that she had been mistaken in supposing that the room was full. The clanging sound kept recurring, the dog kept barking, and new guests continually poured into the room, thereby proving that it was not full. All comers were introduced to Audrey, whose head was a dizzy riot of strange names. Then at last a girl sang, and was applauded. Madame Foa played for her. "Now," thought Audrey, "they will ask Musa." Then one of the composers played the piano, his themes punctuated by the clanging sound and by the dog. The room was asphyxiating, but no one except Audrey seemed to be inconvenienced. Then several guests rang in quick succession.

"Madame!" the suave and ardent voice of Foa could be heard in the entrance-hall. "And thou, Roussel . . . Ippolita, Ippolita!" he called to his wife. "It is Roussel."

Audrey did not turn her head. She could not. But presently Roussel, in a blue suit with a wonderful flowing bow of a black necktie in *crêpe de Chine,* was led before her. And Musa was led before Roussel. Audrey, from nervousness, was moved to relate the history of Musa's accident to Roussel.

The moment had arrived. Roussel sat down to the piano. Musa tuned his fiddle.

"From what appears," murmured Monsieur Foa to nobody in particular, with an ecstatic expectant smile on his face, "this Musa is all that is most amazing."

Then, in the silence, the clanging sound was renewed, and the fox-terrier reacted.

"André, my friend," cried Madame Foa, skipping into the hall. "Will you do me the pleasure of exterminating this dog?"

Delicate osculatory explosions and pretty exclamations in the hall! The hostess was encountering an old friend. There was also a man's deep English voice. Then a hush. The man's voice produced a very strange effect upon Audrey. Roussel began to play. Musa held his bow aloft. Creeping steps in the doorway made Audrey look round. A lady smiled and bowed to her. It was Madame Piriac, resplendent and serene.

Musa played the Caprice. Audrey did not hear him, partly because the vision of Madame Piriac, and the man's deep voice, had extremely perturbed her, and partly because she was so desperately anxious for Musa's triumph. She had decided that she could make his triumph here the prelude to tremendous things. When he had finished she held her breath. . . .

The applause, after an instant, was sudden and extremely cordial. Monsieur Foa loudly clapped, smiling at Audrey. Roussel patted Musa on the back and chattered to him fondly. On each side of her Audrey could catch murmured exclamations of delight. Musa himself was certainly pleased and happy. . . . He had played at Foa's, where it was absolutely essential to play if one intended to conquer Paris and to prove one's pretensions; and he had found favour with this satiated and fastidious audience.

"*Ouf!*" sighed the musical critic Orientally lounging on a chair. "André, has it occurred to you that we are expiring for want of air?"

A window was opened, and a shiver went through the assembly.

The clanging sounded again, but no dog, for the dog had been exterminated.

"Dauphin, my old pig!" Foa's greeting from the entrance floated into the drawing-room, and then a very impressed: "Mademoiselle" from Madame Foa.

"What?" cried Dauphin. "Musa has played? He played well? So much the better. What did I tell you?"

And he entered the drawing-room with the satisfied air of having fed Musa from infancy and also of having taught him all he knew about the violin.

Madame Foa followed him, and with her was Miss Ingate, gorgeous and blushing. The whole company was now on its feet and moving about. Miss Ingate scuttered to Audrey.

"Well," she whispered. "Here I am. I came partly to satisfy that hysterical Elise, and Monsieur Dauphin met me on the stairs. But really I came because I've had another letter from Miss Nickall. She's been and got her arm broken in a street row. I knew those policemen would do it one day. I always said they would."

But Audrey seemed not to be listening. With a side-long gaze she saw Madame Piriac talking with a middle-aged Englishman, whose back alone was visible to her. Madame Piriac laughed and vanished out of sight into the dining-room. The Englishman turned and met Audrey's glance.

Abruptly leaving Miss Ingate, Audrey walked straight up to the Englishman.

"Good evening," she said in a low voice. "What is your name?"

"Gilman," he answered, with a laugh. "I only this instant recognised you."

"Well, Mr. Gilman," said Audrey, "will you oblige me very much by not recognising me? I want us to be introduced. I am most particularly anxious that no one should know I'm the same girl who helped you to jump off your yacht at Lousey Hard last year."

And she moved quickly away.

CHAPTER XVIII

A DECISION

The entire company was sitting or standing round the table in the dining-room. It was a table at which eight might have sat down to dinner with a fair amount of comfort; and perhaps thirty-eight now were successfully claiming an interest in it. Not at the end, but about a third of the way down one side, Madame Foa brewed tea in a copper receptacle over a spirit lamp. At the other extremity was a battalion of glasses, some syphons and some lofty bottles. Except for a border of teacups and glasses the rest of the white expanse was empty, save that two silver biscuit boxes and a silver cigarette box wandered up and down it according to the needs of the community. Audrey was sitting next to the Oriental musical critic, on her left, and on her right she had a beautiful stout woman who could speak nothing but Polish, but who expressed herself very clearly in the language of smiles, nods, and shrugs; to Audrey she seemed to be extremely romantic; the musical critic could converse somewhat in Polish, and occasionally he talked across Audrey to the Pole. Several other languages were flying about. The subject of discussion was feminism, chiefly as practised in England. It was Miss Ingate who had begun it; her striking and peculiar appearance, and in particular her frock, had given importance to her lightest word. People who comprehended naught of English listened to her entranced. The host, who was among these, stood behind her in a state of ecstasy. Her pale forehead reddened; her sardonic grin became deliciously self-conscious. "I know I'm skidding," she cried. "I know I'm skidding."

"What does she say? Skeed—skeed?" demanded the host.

Audrey interpreted. Shouts of laughter!

"Oh! These English! These Englishwomen!" said the host. "I adore them. I adore them all. They alone exist."

"It's vehy serious!" protested Miss Ingate. "It's vehy serious!"

"We shall go to London to-morrow, shan't we, Winnie?" said Audrey across the table to her.

"Yes," agreed Miss Ingate. "I think we ought. We're as free as birds. When the police have broken our arms we can come back to Paris to recover. I shan't feel comfortable until I've been and had my arm broken—it's vehy serious."

"What does she say? What is it that she says?" from the host.

More interpretation. More laughter, but this time an impressed laughter. And Audrey perceived that just as she was regarding the Polish woman as romantic, so the whole company was regarding herself and Miss Ingate as romantic. She could feel the polite, curious eyes of twenty men upon her; and her mind seemed to stiffen into a formidable resolve. She grew conscious of the lifting of all depression, all anxiety. Her conscience was at rest. She had been thinking for more than a week past: "I ought to go to London." How often had she not said to herself: "If any woman should be in this movement, I should be in this movement. I am a coward as long as I stay here, dallying my time away." Now the decision was made, absolutely.

The Oriental musical critic turned to glance upward behind his chair. Then he vacated it. The next instant Madame Piriac was sitting in his place.

She said:

"Are you really going to London to-morrow, Madame?"

"Yes, Madame, really!" answered Audrey firmly, without the least hesitation.

"How I regret it! For this reason. I wished so much to make your acquaintance. I mean—to know you a little. You go perhaps in the afternoon? Could you not do me the great pleasure of coming to lunch with me? I inhabit the Quai Voltaire. It is all that is most convenient."

Audrey was startled and suspicious, but she could not deny the persuasiveness of the invitation.

"Ah! Madame!" she said. "I know not at what hour we go. But even if it should be in the afternoon there is the packing—you know—in a word. . . ."

"Listen," Madame Piriac proceeded, bending even more intimately towards her. "Be very, very kind. Come to see me to-night. Come in my car. I will see that you reach the Rue Delambre afterwards."

"But Madame, we are at the Hôtel du Danube. I have my own car. You are very amiable."

Madame Piriac was a little taken aback.

"So much the better," she said, in a new tone. "The Hôtel du Danube is nearer still. But come in my car. Mademoiselle Ingate can return in yours. Do not desolate me."

"Does she know who I am?" thought Audrey, and then: "What do I care if she does?"

And she said aloud:

"Madame, it is I who would be desolated to deprive myself of this pleasure."

A considerable period elapsed before they could leave, because of the complex discussion concerning feminism which was delicately raging round the edge of the table. The animation was acute, but it was purely intellectual. The guests discussed the psychology of English suffragettes, sympathetically, admiringly; they were even wonderstruck; yet they might have been discussing the psychology of the ancient Babylonians, so perfect was their detachment, so completely unclouded by any prejudice was their desire to reach the truth. Many of the things which they imperturbably and politely said made Audrey feel glad that she

was a widow. Had she not been a widow, possibly they
would not have been uttered.

And when Madame Piriac and Audrey did rise to go,
both host and hostess began to upbraid. The host, indeed,
barred the doorway with his urbane figure. They were not
kind, they were not true friends, to leave so soon. The
morrow had no sort of importance. The hour was scarcely
one o'clock. Other guests were expected. . . . Madame
Piriac alone knew how to handle the situation; she appealed
privately to Madame Foa. Having appealed to Madame
Foa, she disappeared with Madame Foa, and could not be
found when Audrey and Miss Ingate were ready to leave.
While these two waited in the antechamber, Monsieur Foa
said suddenly in a confidential tone to Audrey:

"He is charming, Musa, quite charming."

"Did you like his playing?" Audrey demanded boldly.

She could not understand why it should be necessary for
a violinist to play and to succeed at this house before he could
capture Paris. She was delighted excessively with the
home, but positively it bore no resemblance to what she had
anticipated; nor did it seem to her to possess any of the
attributes of influence; for one of her basic ideas about the
world was that influential people must be dull and formal,
moving about with deliberation in sombrely magnificent
interiors.

"Yes," said Monsieur Foa. "I like it. He plays
admirably." And he spoke sincerely. Audrey, however,
was a little disappointed because Monsieur Foa did not
assert that Musa was the most marvellous genius he had
ever listened to.

"I am very, very content to have heard him," said
Monsieur Foa.

"Do you think he will succeed in Paris?"

"Ah! Madame! There is the Press. There are the
snobs. . . . In fine. . . ."

"I suppose if he had money?" Audrey murmured.

"Ah! Madame! In Paris, if one has money, one has

everything. Paris—it is not London, where to succeed one must be truly successful. But he is a player very highly accomplished. It is miraculous that he should have played so long in a café—Dauphin told me the history."

Musa appeared, and after him Madame Piriac. More appeals, more reproaches, more asseverations that friends who left so early as one o'clock in the morning were not friends—and the host at length consented to open the door. At that very instant the bell clanged. Another guest had arrived.

When, after the long descent of the stairs (which, however, unlike the stairs of the Rue Delambre, were lighted), Audrey saw seven automobiles in the street, she veered again towards the possibility that the Foas might after all be influential. Musa and Mr. Gilman, the yachtsman, had left with the women. Audrey told Miss Ingate to drive Musa home. She said not a word to him about her departure the next afternoon, and he made no reference to it. As the most imposing automobile moved splendidly away, Mr. Gilman held open the door of Madame Piriac's vehicle.

Mr. Gilman sat down opposite to the women. In the enclosed space the rumour of his heavy breathing was noticeable. Madame Piriac began to speak in English—her own English—with a unique accent that Audrey at once loved.

"You commence soon the yachting, my oncle?" said she, and turning to Audrey: "Mistair Gilman is no oncle to me. But he is a great friend of my husband. I call always him oncle. Do not I, oncle? Mistair Gilman lives only for the yachting. Every year in May we lose him, till September."

"Really!" said Audrey.

Her heart was apprehensively beating. She even suspected for an instant that both of them knew who she was, and that Mr. Gilman, before she had addressed him in the drawing-room, had already related to Madame Piriac the episode of Mozewater. Then she said to herself that the idea was absurd; and lastly, repeating within her breast that she didn't care, she became desperately bold.

"I should love to buy a yacht," she said, after a pause. "We used to live far inland and I know nothing of the sea; in fact I scarcely saw it till I crossed the Channel, but I have always dreamed about it."

"You must come and have a look at my new yacht, Mrs. Moncreiff," said Mr. Gilman in his solemn, thick voice. "I always say that no yacht is herself without ladies on board, a yacht being feminine, you see." He gave a little laugh.

"Ah! My oncle!" Madame Piriac broke in. "I see in that no reason. If a yacht was masculine then I could see the reason in it."

"Perhaps not one of my happiest efforts," said Mr. Gilman with resignation. "I am a dull man."

"No, no!" Madame Piriac protested. "You are a dear. But why have you said nothing to-night at the Foas in the great discussion about feminism? Not one word have you said!"

"I really don't understand it," said Mr. Gilman. "Either everybody is mad, or I am mad. I dare say I am mad."

"Well," said Madame Piriac. "I said not much myself, but I enjoyed it. It was better than the music, music, which they talk always there. People talk too much shops in these days. It is out-to-place and done over."

"Do you mean overdone?" asked Mr. Gilman mildly.

"Well, overdone, if you like better that."

"Do you mean shop, Hortense?" asked Mr. Gilman further.

"Shop, shop! The English is impossible!"

The automobile crossed the Seine and arrived in the deserted Quai Voltaire.

CHAPTER XIX

In the setting of her own boudoir Madame Piriac equalled, and in some ways surpassed, the finest pictures which Audrey had imagined of her. Her evening dress made Audrey doubt whether after all her own was the genuine triumph which she had supposed; in Madame Piriac's boudoir, and close by Madame Piriac, it had disconcertingly the air of being an ingenious but unconvincing imitation of the real thing.

But Madame Piriac's dress had the advantage of being worn with the highest skill and assurance; Madame Piriac knew what the least fold of her dress was doing, in the way of effect, on the floor behind her back. And Madame Piriac was mistress, not only of her dress, but of herself and all her faculties. A handsome woman, rather more than slim, but not plump, she had an expression of confidence, of knowing exactly what she was about, of foreseeing all her effects, which Audrey envied more than she had ever envied anything.

As soon as Audrey came into the room she had said to herself: "I will have a boudoir like this." It was an interior in which every piece of furniture was loaded with objects personal to its owner. So many signed photographs, so much remarkable bric-à-brac, so many intimate contrivances of ornamental comfort, Audrey had never before seen within four walls. The chandelier, comprising ten thousand crystals, sparkled down upon a complex aggregate of richness overwhelming to everybody except Madame Piriac, who subdued it, understood it, and had the key to it. Audrey wondered how many servants took how many hours to dust the room. She was sure, however, that whatever the number of servants required, Madame Piriac managed them all to perfection. She longed violently to be as old as Madame Piriac, whom she assessed at twenty-nine and a half, and to be French, and to know all about everything in life as Madame Piriac did. Yet at the same time she was extremely determined to be Audrey, and not to be intimidated by Madame Piriac or by anyone.

Just as they were beginning to suck iced lemonade up straws—a delightful caprice of Madame Piriac's, well suited to catch Audrey's taste—the door opened softly, and a tall, very dark, bearded man, appreciably older than Madame Piriac, entered with a kind of soft energy, and Mr. Gilman followed him.

"Ah! My friend!" murmured Madame Piriac. "You give me pleasure. This is Madame Moncreiff, of whom I have spoken to you. Madame—my husband. We have just come from the Foas."

Monsieur Piriac bent over Audrey's hand, and smiled with vivacity, and they talked a little of the evening, carelessly, as though time existed not. And then Monsieur Piriac said to his wife:

"Dear friend. I have to work with this old Gilman. We shall therefore ask you to excuse us. Till to-morrow, then. Good night."

"Good night, my friend. Do not do harm to yourself. Good night, my oncle."

Monsieur Piriac saluted with formality but with sincerity.

"Oh!" thought Audrey, as the men went away. "I should want to marry exactly him if I did want to marry. He doesn't interfere; he isn't curious; he doesn't want to know. He leaves her alone. She leaves him alone. How clever they are!"

"My husband is now chief of the Cabinet of the Foreign Minister," said Madame Piriac with modest pride. "They

kill themselves, you know, in that office—especially in these
times. But I watch. And I tell Monsieur Gilman to watch.
. . . How nice you are when you sit in a chair like that!
Only Englishwomen know how to use an easy chair. . . .
To say nothing of the frock."

"Madame Piriac," Audrey brusquely demanded with an
expression of ingenuous curiosity. "Why did you bring me
here?" It was the cry of an animal at once rash and
rather desperate, determined to unmask all the secret
dangers that might be threatening.

"I much desired to see you," Madame Piriac answered
very smoothly, "in order to apologise to you for my
indiscreet question on the night when we first met. Your
fairy tale about your late husband was a very proper reply to
the attitude of Madame Rosamund—as you all call her. It
was very clever—so clever that I myself did not appreciate
it until after I had spoken. Ever since that moment I have
wanted to explain, to know you more. Also your pretence
of going to sleep in the automobile showed what in a woman
I call distinguished talent."

"But, Madame, I assure you that I really was asleep."

"So much the better. The fact proves that your
instinct for the right thing is quite exceptional. It is not
that I would criticise Madame Rosamund, who has genius.
Nevertheless her genius causes her to commit errors of
which others would be incapable. . . . So she has captured
you, too."

"Captured me!" Audrey protested—and she was
made stronger by the flattering reference to her distinguished talent. "I've never seen her from that day to
this!"

"No. But she has captured you. You are going."

"Going where?"

"To London, to take part in these riots."

"I shan't have anything to do with riots."

"Within a month you will have been in a riot, Madame
. . . and I shall regret it."

J

"And even if I am, Madame! You are a friend of Rosamund's. You must be in sympathy."

"In sympathy with what?"

"With—with all this suffragism, feminism. *I* am anyway!" Audrey sat up straight. "It's horrible that women don't have the Vote. And it's horrible the things they have to suffer in order to get it. But they *will* get it!"

"Why do you say ' they '?"

"I mean 'we.'"

"Supposing you meant ' they,' after all? And you did, Madame. Let me tell you. You ask me if I sympathise with suffragism. You might as well ask me if I sympathise with a storm or with an earthquake, or with a river running to the sea. Perhaps I do. But perhaps I do not. That has no importance. Feminism is a natural phenomenon; it was unavoidable. You Englishwomen will get your vote. Even we in France will get it one day. It cannot be denied. . . . Sympathy is not required. But let us suppose that all women joined the struggle. What would happen to women? What would happen to the world? Just as nunneries were a necessity of other ages, so even in this age women must meditate. Far more than men they need to understand themselves. Until they understand themselves how can they understand men? The function of women is to understand. Their function is also to preserve. All the beautiful and luxurious things in the world are in the custody of women. Men would never of themselves keep a tradition. If there is anything on earth worth keeping, women must keep it. And the tradition will be lost if every woman listens to Madame Rosamund. That is what she cannot see. Her genius blinds her. You say I am a friend of Madame Rosamund. I am. Madame Rosamund was educated in Paris, at the same school as my aunt and myself. But I have never helped her in her mission. And I never will. My vocation is elsewhere. When she fled over here from the English police, she came to me. I received her. She asked me to drive her to certain addresses. I did so. She

was my guest. I surrounded her with all that she had
abandoned, all that her genius had forced her to abandon.
But I never spoke to her of her work, nor she to me of it.
Still, I dare to think that I was of some value to the woman
in Madame Rosamund."

Audrey felt very young and awkward and defiant. She
felt defiant because Madame Piriac had impressed her,
and she was determined not to be impressed.

"So you wanted to tell me all this," said she, putting
down her glass, with the straws in it, on a small round
table laden with tiny figures in silver. "Why did you
want to tell me, Madame?"

"I wanted to tell you because I want you to do nothing
that you will regret. You greatly interested me the moment
I saw you. And when I saw you in that studio, in that
Quarter, I feared for you."

"Feared what?"

"I feared that you might mistake your vocation—that
vocation which is so clearly written on your face. I saw
a woman young and free and rich, and I was afraid that
she might waste everything."

"But do you know anything about me?"

Madame Piriac paused before replying.

"Nothing but what I see. But I see that you are in
a high degree what all women are to a greater extent
than men—an individualist. You know the feeling that
comes over a woman in hours of complete intimacy with
a man? You know what I mean?"

"Oh, yes!" Audrey agreed, blushing.

"In those moments we perceive that only the individual
counts with us. And with you, above all, the individual
should count. Unless you use your youth and your freedom
and your money for some individual, you will never be
content; you will eternally regret. All that is in your face."

Audrey blushed more, thinking of certain plans formed
in that head of hers. She said nothing. She was both
very pleased and very exasperated.

"I have a relative in England, a young girl," Madame Piriac proceeded, "in some unpronounceable county. We write to each other. She is excessively English."

Audrey was scarlet. Several times during the sojourn in Paris she had sent letters (to Madame Piriac) to be posted in Essex by Mr. Foulger. These letters were full of quaint inventions about winter life in Essex, and other matters.

Madame Piriac, looking reflectively at the red embers of wood in the grate, went on:

"She says she may come to Paris soon. I have often asked her to come, but she has refused. Perhaps next month I shall go to England to fetch her. I should like her to know you—very much. She is younger than you are, but only a little, I think."

"I shall be delighted, if I am here," Audrey stammered, and she rose. "You are a very kind woman. Very, very amiable. You do not know how much I admire you. I wish I was like you. But I am not. You have seen only one side of me. You should see the inside. It is very strange. I must go to London. I am forced to go to London. I should be a coward if I did not go to London. Tell me, is my dress really good? Or is it a deception?"

Madame Piriac smiled, and kissed her on both cheeks.

"It is good," said Madame Piriac. "But your maid is not all that she ought to be. However, it is good."

"If you had simply praised it, and only that, I should not have been content," said Audrey, and kissed Madame Piriac in the English way, the youthful and direct way.

Not another word about the male sex, the female sex, tradition or individualism, passed between them.

Mr. Gilman was summoned to take Audrey across the river to the right bank. They went in a taxi. He was protective and very silent. But just as the cab was turning out of the Rue de Rivoli into the Rue Castiglione he said:

"I shall obey you absolutely, Mrs. Moncreiff. It is

a great pleasure for an old, lonely man to keep a secret
for a young and charming woman. A greater pleasure
than you can possibly imagine. You may count on me.
I am not a talker, but you have put me under an obligation,
and I am very grateful."

She took care that her thanks should reward him.

"Winnie," she burst out in the rose-coloured secrecy
of the bedroom, "has Elise gone to bed? . . . All right.
Well, I'm lost. Madame Piriac is going to England to
fetch me."

CHAPTER XX

"Has anything happened in this town?" asked Audrey of Miss Ingate.

It was the afternoon of the day following their arrival in London from Paris, and it was a fine afternoon. They were walking from the Charing Cross Hotel, where they had slept, to Paget Gardens.

"Anything happened?" repeated Miss Ingate. "What you mean? I don't see anything vehy particular on the posters."

"Everybody looks so sad and worried, compared with people in Paris."

"So they do! So they do!" cried Miss Ingate. "Oh, yes! So they do! I wondered what it was seemed so queer. That's it. Well, of course you mustn't forget we're in England. I always did say it was a vehy peculiar place."

"Do *we* look like that?" Audrey suggested.

"I expect we do."

"I'm quite sure that I don't, Winnie, anyway. I'm really very cheerful. I'm surprisingly cheerful."

It was true. Also she both looked and felt more girlish than ever in Paris. Impossible to divine, watching her in her light clothes, and with her airy step, that she was the relict of a man who had so tragically died of blood-poisoning caused by bad table manners.

"I've a good mind to ask a policeman," said she.

"You'd better not," Miss Ingate warned her.

Audrey instantly turned into the roadway, treating the creosoted wood as though it had been rose-strewn velvet, and reached a refuge where a policeman was standing. The policeman bent with benevolence and politeness to listen to her tale.

"Excuse me," she said, smiling innocently up at him, " but is anything the matter? "

" *What* street, miss? " he questioned, bending lower.

"Is anything the matter? All the people round here are so gloomy."

The policeman glanced at her.

"There will be something the matter," he remarked calmly. "There will be something the matter pretty soon if I have much more of that suffragette sauce. I thought you was one of them the moment I saw you, but I wasn't sure."

This was the first time Audrey had ever spoken to a policeman, save Inspector Keeble, at Moze, who was a friendly human being. And she had a little pang of fear. The policeman was like a high wall of blue cloth, with a marvellous imitation of a human face at the top, and above the face a cupola.

"Thank you," she murmured reproachfully, and hastened back to Miss Ingate, who heard the tale with a grinning awe that was, nevertheless, sardonic. They pressed onwards to Piccadilly Circus, where the only normal and cheerful living creatures were the van horses and the flower-women; and up Regent Street, through crowds of rapt and mystical women and romantical men who had apparently wandered out of a play by Henrik Ibsen.

They then took a motor-bus, which was full of the same enigmatic, far-gazing heroines and heroes. When they got off, the conductor pointed dreamily in a certain direction and murmured the words: "Paget Square." Their desire was Paget Gardens, and, after finding Paget Square, Paget Mansions, Paget Houses, Paget Street, Paget Mews, and Upper Paget Street, they found Paget Gardens. It was a terrace of huge and fashionable houses fronting on an immense, blank brick wall. The houses were very lofty;

so lofty that the architect, presumably afraid of hitting heaven with his patent chimney cowls, had sunk the lowest storey deep into the earth. Looking over the high palisades which protected the pavement from the precipice thus made, one could plainly see the lowest storey and all that was therein.

"Whoever can she be staying with?" exclaimed Miss Ingate. "It's a marchioness at least. There's no doubt the very best people are now in the movement."

Audrey went first up massive steps, and, choosing with marked presence of mind the right bell, rang it, expecting to see either a butler or a footman.

A young woman, however, answered the ring. She wore a rather shabby serge frock, but no apron, and she did not resemble any kind of servant. Her ruddy, heavy, and slightly resentful face fronted the visitors with a steady, challenging stare.

"Does Miss Nickall live here?" asked Audrey.

"Aye! She does!" came the answer, with a northern accent.

"We've come to see how she is."

"Happen ye'd better step inside, then," said the young woman.

They stepped inside to an enormous and obscure interior; the guardian banged the door, and negligently led them forward.

"It is a large house," Miss Ingate ventured, against the silent intimidation of the place.

"One o' them rich uns," said the guardian. "She lends it to the Cause when she doesn't want it herself, to show her sympathy. Saves her a caretaker—they all know I'm one to look right well after a house."

Having passed two very spacious rooms and a wide staircase, she opened the door of a smaller but still a considerable room.

"Here y'are," she muttered.

This room, like the others, was thoroughly sheeted, and

thus presented a misty and spectral appearance. All the chairs, the chandelier, and all the pictures, were masked in close-fitting pale yellow. The curtains were down, the carpet was up, and a dust sheet was spread under the table in the middle of the floor.

"Here's some friends of yours," said the guardian, throwing her words across the room.

In an easy chair near the fireplace sat Miss Nickall, her arm in splints and in a sling. She was very thin and very pallid, and her eyes brightly glittered. The customary kind expression of her face was modified, though not impaired, by a look of vague apprehension.

"Mind how ye handle her," the guardian gave warning, when Nick yielded herself to be embraced.

"You're just a bit of my Paris come to see me," said Nick, with her American accent. Then through her tears: "How's Tommy, and how's Musa, and how's—how's my studio? Oh! This is Miss Susan Foley, sister of Jane Foley. Jane will be here for tea. Susan—Miss Ingate and Mrs. Moncreiff."

Susan gave a grim bob.

"Is Jane Foley coming? Does she live here?" asked Miss Ingate, properly impressed by the name of her who was the St. George of Suffragism, and perhaps the most efficient of all militants. "Audrey, we are in luck!"

When Nick had gathered items of information about Paris, she burst out:

"I can't believe I've only met you once before. You're just like old friends."

"So we are old friends," said Audrey. "Your letters to Winnie have made us old friends."

"And when did you come over?"

"Last night," Miss Ingate replied. "We should have called this morning to see you, but Mrs. Moncreiff had so much business to do and people to see. I don't know what it all was. She's very mysterious."

As a fact, Audrey had had an interview with Mr.

Foulger, who, with laudable obedience, had come up to town from Chelmsford in response to a telegram. Miss Ingate was aware of this, but she was not aware of other and more recondite interviews which Audrey had accomplished.

"And how did this happen?" eagerly inquired Miss Ingate, at last, pointing to the bandaged arm.

Nick's face showed discomfort.

"Please don't let us talk about that," said Nick. "It was a policeman. I don't think he meant it. I had chained myself to the railings of St. Margaret's Church."

Susan Foley put in laconically:

"She's not to be worried. I hope ye'll stay for tea. We shall have tea at five sharp. Janey'll be in."

"Can't they sleep here, Susan?" Nick whimpered.

"Of course they can, and welcome," said Susan. "There's more empty beds in this barracks than they could sleep in if they slept all day and all night."

"But we're staying at an hotel. We can't possibly put you to all this trouble," Audrey protested.

"No trouble. It's my business. It's what I'm here for," said Susan Foley. "I'd sooner have it than mill work any day o' the week."

"You're just going to be very mean if you don't stay here," Nick faltered. Tears stood in her eyes again. "You don't know how I feel." She murmured something about Betty Burke's doings.

"We will stay! We will stay!" Miss Ingate agreed hastily. And, unperceived by Nick, she gave Audrey a glance in which irony and tenderness were mingled. It was as if she had whispered, "The nerves of this angel have all gone to pieces. We must humour the little sentimental simpleton."

CHAPTER XXI

JANE

"WE'VE begun, ye see," said Susan Foley.

It was two minutes past five, and Miss Ingate and Audrey, followed by Nick with her slung arm, entered the sheeted living-room. Tremendous feats had been performed. All the Moncreiff and Ingate luggage, less than two hours earlier lying at the Charing Cross Hotel, was now in two adjoining rooms on the third floor of the great house in Paget Gardens. Drivers and loiterers had assisted, under the strict and taciturn control of Susan Foley. Also Nick, Miss Ingate, and Audrey had had a most intimate conversation, and the two latter had changed their attire to suit the station of campers in a palace.

"It's lovely to be quite free and independent," Audrey had said, and the statement had been acclaimed.

Jane Foley was seated opposite her sister at the small table plainly set for five. She rose vivaciously, and came forward with outstretched hand. She wore a blue skirt and a white blouse and brown boots. She was twenty-eight, but her rather small proportions and her plentiful golden, fluffy hair made her seem about twenty. Her face was less homely than Susan's, and more mobile. She smiled somewhat shyly, with an extraordinary radiant cheerfulness. It was impossible for her to conceal the fact that she was very good-natured and very happy. Finally, she limped.

"Susan *will* have the meals prompt," she said, as they all sat down. "And as Susan left home on purpose to look after me, of course she's the mistress. As far as that goes, she always was."

Susan was spreading jam on a slice of bread-and-butter for the one-armed Nick.

"I dare say you don't remember me playing the barrel organ all down Regent Street that day, do you?" said Miss Ingate.

"Oh, yes; quite well. You were magnificent!" answered Jane, with blue eyes sparkling.

"Well, though I only just saw you—I was so busy—I should remember you anywhere, Miss Foley," said Miss Ingate.

"Do you notice any difference in her?" questioned Susan Foley harshly.

"N-o," said Miss Ingate. "Except, perhaps, she looks even younger."

"Didn't you notice she's lame?"

"Oh, well—yes, I did. But you didn't expect me to mention that, did you? I thought your sister had just sprained her ankle, or something."

"No," said Susan. "It's for life. Tell them about it, Jenny. They don't know."

Jane Foley laughed lightly.

"It was all in the day's work," she said. "It was at my last visit to Holloway."

Audrey, gazing at her entranced, like a child, murmured with awe:

"Have you been to prison, then?"

"Three times," said Jane pleasantly. "And I shall be going again soon. I'm only out while they're trying to think of some new way of dealing with me, poor things! I'm generally watched. It must cost them a fearful lot of money. But what are they to do?"

"But how were you lamed? I can't eat any tea if you don't tell me—really I can't!"

"Oh, all right!" Jane laughed. "It was after that Liberal mass meeting in Peel Park, at Bradford. I'd begun to ask questions, as usual, you know—questions they can't answer—and then some Liberal stewards, with lovely rosettes

in their buttonholes, came round me and started cutting my
coat with their penknives. They cut it all to pieces. You
see that was the best argument they could think of in the
excitement of the moment. I believe they'd have cut up
every stitch I had, only perhaps it began to dawn on them
that it might be awkward for them. Then two of them
lifted me up, one by the feet and the other by the shoulders,
and carried me off. They wouldn't let me walk. I told
them they'd hurt my leg, but they were too busy to listen.
As soon as they came across a policeman they said they had
done it all to save me from being thrown into the lake by
a brutal and infuriated mob. I just had enough breath left
to thank them. Of course, the police weren't going to stand
that, so I was taken that night to London. Everything was
thought of except my tea. But I expect they forgot that on
purpose so that I should be properly hungry when I got to
Holloway. However, I said to myself, ' If I can't eat and
drink when *I* want, I won't eat and drink when *they* want ! '
And I didn't.

"After I'd paid my respects at Bow Street, and was
back at Holloway, I just stamped on everything they offered
me, and wrote a petition to the Governor asking to be
treated as a political prisoner. Instead of granting the petition he kept sending me more and more beautiful food, and
I kept stamping on it. Then three magistrates arrived and
sat on my case, and sentenced me to the punishment cells.
They ran off as soon as they'd sentenced me. I said I
wouldn't go to their punishment cells. I told everybody
again how lame I was. So five wardresses carried me there,
but they dropped me twice on the way. It was a very
interesting cell, the punishment cell was. If it had been
in the Tower, everybody would go to look at it because of
its quaintness. There were two pools of water near to the
bed. I was three days in the cell, and those pools of water
were always there; I could see them because from where I
lay on the bed the light glinted on them. Just one gleam
from the tiny cobwebby window high up. I hadn't any-

thing to read, of course, but even if I'd had something I couldn't see to read. The bed was two planks, just raised an inch or two above the water, and the pillow was wooden. Never any trouble about making beds like that! The entire furniture of this cosy drawing-room was—you'll never guess—a tree-stump, meant for a chair, I think. And on this tree-stump was an india-rubber cup. I could just see it across the cell.

"At night the wardresses were struck with pity, or perhaps it was the Governor. Anyhow, they brought me a mattress and a rug. They told me to get up off the bed, and I told them I couldn't get up, couldn't even turn over. So they said, 'Very well, then; you can do without these things,' and they took them away. The funny thing was that I really couldn't get up. If I tried to move, my leg made me want to shriek.

"After three days they decided to take me to the prison hospital. I shrieked all the way—couldn't help it. They laughed. So then I laughed. In the hospital, the doctor decided that my left ankle was sprained and my right thigh broken. So I had the best of them, after all. They had to admit they were wrong. It was most awkward for them. Then I thought I might as well begin to eat. But they had to be very careful what they gave me. I hadn't had anything for nearly six days, you see. They were in a fearful stew. Doctor was there day and night. And it wasn't his fault. I told him he had all my sympathies. He said he was very sorry I should be lame for life, but it couldn't be helped, as the thigh had been left too long. I said, 'Please don't mention it.'"

"But did they keep you after that?"

"Keep me! They implored my friends to take me away. No man was ever more relieved that the poor dear Governor of Holloway Prison, and the Home Secretary himself, too, when I left in a motor ambulance. The Governor raised his hat to two of my friends. He would have eaten but of my hand if I'd had a few more days to tame him."

Audrey's childlike and intense gaze had become extremely noticeable. Jane Foley felt it upon herself, and grew a little self-conscious. Susan Foley noticed it with eager and grim pride, and she made a sharp movement instead of saying: "Yes, you do well to stare. You've got something worth staring at."

Nick noticed it, with moisture in her glittering, hysteric eyes. Miss Ingate noticed it ironically. "You, pretending to be a widow, and so knowing and so superior! Why, you're a schoolgirl!" said the expressive curve of Miss Ingate's shut lips.

And, in fact, Audrey was now younger than she had ever been in Paris. She was the girl of six or seven years earlier, who, at night at school, used to insist upon hearing stories of real people, either from a sympathetic teacher or from the other member of the celebrated secret society. But she had never heard any tale to compare with Jane Foley's. It was incredible that this straightforward, simple girl at the table should be the world-renowned Jane Foley. What most impressed Audrey in Jane was Jane's happiness. Jane was happy, as Audrey had not imagined that anyone could be happy. She had within her a supply of happiness that was constantly bubbling up. The ridiculousness and the total futility of such matters as motor-cars, fine raiment, beautiful boudoirs and correctness smote Audrey severely. She saw that there was only one thing worth having, and that was the mysterious thing that Jane Foley had. This mysterious thing rendered innocuous cruelty, stupidity and injustice, and reduced them to rather pathetic trifles.

"But I never saw all this in the papers!" Audrey exclaimed.

"No paper—I mean no respectable paper—would print it. Of course, we printed it in our own weekly paper."

"Why wouldn't any respectable paper print it?"

"Because it's not nice. Don't you see that I ought to have been at home mending stockings instead of gallivanting round with Liberal stewards and policemen and prison governors?"

"And why aren't you mending stockings?" asked Audrey, with a delicious quizzical smile that crept gradually through the wonder and admiration in her face.

"You pal!" cried Jane Foley impulsively. "I must hug you!" And she did. "I'll tell you why I'm not mending stockings, and why Susan has had to leave off mending stockings in order to look after me. Susan and I worked in a mill when she was ten and I was eleven. We were 'tenters.' We used to get up at four or five in the morning and help with the housework, and then put on our clogs and shawls and be at the mill at six. We worked till twelve, and then in the afternoon we went to school. The next day we went to school in the morning and to the mill in the afternoon. When we were thirteen we left school altogether, and worked twelve hours a day in the mill. In the evenings we had to do housework. In fact, all our housework was done before half-past five in the morning and after half-past six in the evening. We had to work just as hard as the men and boys in the mill. We got a great deal less money and a great deal less decent treatment; but to make up we had to slave in the early morning and late at night, while the men either snored or smoked. I was all right. But Susan wasn't. And a lot of women weren't, especially young mothers with babies. So I learnt typewriting on the quiet, and left it all to try and find out whether something couldn't be done. I soon found out—after I'd heard Rosamund speak. That's the reason I'm not mending stockings. I'm not blaming anybody. It's no one's fault, really. It certainly isn't men's fault. Only something has to be altered, and most people detest alterations. Still, they do get done somehow in the end. And so there you are!"

"I should love to help," said Audrey. "I expect I'm not much good, but I should love to."

She dared not refer to her wealth, of which, in fact, she was rather ashamed.

"Well, you can help, all right," said Jane Foley, rising. "Are you a member?"

"No. But I will be to-morrow."

"They'll give you something to do," said Jane Foley.

"Oh yes!" remarked Miss Ingate. "They'll keep you busy enough—*and* charge you for it."

Susan Foley began to clear the table.

"Supper at nine," said she curtly.

K

CHAPTER XXII

THE DETECTIVE

AUDREY and Miss Ingate were writing letters to Paris. Jane Foley had gone forth again to a committee meeting, which was understood to be closely connected with a great Liberal demonstration shortly to be held in a Midland fortress of Liberalism. Miss Nickall, in accordance with medical instructions, had been put to bed. Susan Foley was in the basement, either clearing up tea or preparing supper.

Miss Ingate, putting her pen between her teeth and looking up from a blotting-pad, said to Audrey across the table:

"Are you writing to Musa?"

"Certainly not!" said Audrey, with fire. "Why should I write to Musa?" She added: "But you can write to him, if you like."

"Oh! Can I?" observed Miss Ingate, grinning.

Audrey knew of no reason why she should blush before Miss Ingate, yet she began to blush. She resolved not to blush; she put all her individual force into the enterprise of resisting the tide of blood to her cheeks, but the tide absolutely ignored her, as the tide of ocean might have ignored her.

She rose from the table, and, going into a corner, fidgeted with the electric switches, turning certain additional lights off and on.

"All right," said Miss Ingate; "I'll write to him. I'm sure he'll expect something. Have you finished your letters?"

"Yes."

"Well, what's this one on the table, then?"

"I shan't go on with that one."

"Any message for Musa?"

"You might tell him," said Audrey, carefully examining the drawn curtains of the window, "that I happened to meet a French concert agent this morning who was very interested in him."

"Did you?" cried Miss Ingate. "Where?"

"It was when I was out with Mr. Foulger. The agent asked me whether I'd heard a man named Musa play in Paris. Of course I said I had. He told me he meant to take him up and arrange a tour for him. So you might tell Musa he ought to be prepared for anything."

"Wonders will never cease!" said Miss Ingate. "Have I got enough stamps?"

"I don't see anything wonderful in it," Audrey sharply replied. "Lots of people in Paris know he's a great player, and those Jew concert agents are always awfully keen—at least, so I'm told. Well, perhaps, after all, you'd better not tell him. It might make him conceited. . . . Now, look here, Winnie, do hurry up, and let's go out and post those letters. I can't stand this huge house. I keep on imagining all the empty rooms in it. Hurry up and come along."

Shortly afterwards Miss Ingate shouted downstairs into the earth:

"Miss Foley, we're both just going out to post some letters."

The faint reply came:

"Supper at nine."

At the farther corner of Paget Square they discovered a pillar-box standing solitary in the chill night among the vast and threatening architecture.

"Do let's go to a café," suggested Audrey.

"A café?"

"Yes. I want to be jolly. I must break loose somewhere to-night. I can't wait till to-morrow. I was feeling splendid till Jane Foley went. Then the house began to get on my nerves, not to mention Susan Foley, with her supper at nine. Do all people in London fix their meals hours and hours beforehand? I suppose they do. We used to at Moze. But I'd forgotten. Come *along*, Winnie."

"But there are no cafés in London."

"There must be some cafés somewhere."

"Only public-houses and restaurants. Of course, we could go to a teashop, but they're all shut up now."

"Well, then, what do people do in London when they want to be jolly? I always thought London was a terrific town."

"They never want to be jolly," said Miss Ingate. "If they feel as if they couldn't help being jolly, then they hire a private room somewhere and draw the blinds down."

With no more words, Audrey seized Miss Ingate by the arm and they walked off, out of the square and into empty and silent streets where highly disciplined gas-lamps kept strict watch over the deportment of colossal houses. In their rapid stroll they seemed to cover miles, but they could not escape from the labyrinth of tremendous and correct houses, which in squares and in terraces and in crescents displayed the everlasting characteristics of comfort, propriety and self-satisfaction. Now and then a wayfarer passed them. Now and then a taxicab sped through the avenues of darkness like a criminal pursued by the impalpable. Now and then a red light flickered in a porch instead of a white one. But there was no surcease from the sinister spell until suddenly they emerged into a long, wide, illumined thoroughfare of shut shops that stretched to infinity on either hand. And a vermilion motor-bus meandered by, and this motor-bus was so sad, so inexpressibly wistful, in the solemn wilderness of the empty artery, that the two women fled from the strange scene and penetrated once more into the gigantic and fearful maze from which they had for an instant stood free. Soon they were quite lost. Till that day and night Audrey had had a notion that Miss Ingate, though bizarre, did indeed know every street in London. The delusion was destroyed.

"Never mind," said Miss Ingate. "If we keep on we're bound to come to a cabstand, and then we can take a taxi and go wherever we like—Regent Street, Piccadilly, anywhere. That's the convenience of London. As soon as you come to a cabstand you're all right."

And then, in the distance, Audrey saw a man apparently tampering with a gate that led to an area.

"Why," she said excitedly, "that's the house we're staying in!"

"Of course it isn't!" said Miss Ingate. "This isn't Paget Gardens, because there are houses on both sides of it and there's a big wall on one side of Paget Gardens. I'm sure we're at least two miles off our beds."

"Well, then, how is it Nick's hairbrushes are on the window-sill there, where she put them when she went to bed? I can see them quite plain. This is the side street—what's-its-name? There's the wall over there at the end. Don't you remember—it's a corner house. This is the side of it."

"I believe you're right," admitted Miss Ingate. "What can that man be doing there?"

They plainly saw him open the gate and disappear down the area steps.

"It's a burglar," said Audrey. "This part must be a regular paradise for burglars."

"More likely a detective," Miss Ingate suggested.

Audrey was thrilled.

"I do hope it is!" she murmured. "How heavenly! Miss Foley said she was being watched, didn't she?"

"What had we better do?" Miss Ingate faltered.

"Do, Winnie?" Audrey whispered, tugging at her arm. "We must run in at the front door and tell Supper-at-nine-o'clock."

They kept cautiously on the far side of the street until the end of it, when they crossed over, nipped into the dark porch of the house and rang the bell.

Susan Foley opened for them. There was no light in the hall.

"Oh, is there?" said Susan Foley, very calmly, when she heard the news. "I think I know who it is. I've seen him hanging round my scullery door before. How did he climb over those railings?"

"He didn't. He opened the gate."

"Well, I locked the gate myself this afternoon. So he's got a key. I shall manage him all right. We'll get the fire-extinguishers. There's about a dozen of 'em, I should think, in this house. They're rather heavy, but we can do it."

Turning on the light in the hall, she immediately lifted from its hook a red-coloured metal cone about twenty inches long and eight inches in diameter at the base. "In case of fire drive in knob by hard blow against floor, and let liquid play on flames," she read the instructions on the side. "I know them things," she said. "It spurts out like a fountain, and it's a rather nasty chemistry sort of a fluid. I shall take one downstairs to the scullery, and the others we'll have upstairs in the room over Miss Nickall's. We can put 'em in the housemaid's lift. . . . I shall open the scullery door and leave it a bit open like, and when he comes in I'll be ready for him behind the door with this. If he thinks he can come spying after our Janey like this——"

"But——" Miss Ingate began.

"You aren't feeling very well, are ye, miss?" Susan Foley demanded, as she put two extinguishers into the housemaid's lift. "Better go and sit down in the parlour. You won't be wanted. Mrs. Moncreiff and me can manage."

"Yes, we can!" agreed Audrey enthusiastically. "Run along, Winnie."

After about two minutes of hard labour Susan ran away and brought a key to Audrey.

"You sneak out," she said, "and lock the gate on him. I lay he'll want a new suit of clothes when I done with him!"

Ecstatically, joyfully, Audrey took the key and departed. Miss Ingate was sitting in the hall, staring about her like an undecided bird. Audrey crept round into the side street. Nobody was in sight. She could not see over the railings, but she could see between them into the abyss of the area. The man was there. She could distinguish his dark form against the inner wall. With every conspiratorial precaution, she pulled the gate to, inserted the key, and locked it.

A light went up in the scullery window, of which the blind was drawn. The man peeped at the sides of the blind. Then the scullery door was opened. The man started. A piece of wood was thrown out on to the floor of the area, and the door swung outwards. Then the light in the scullery was extinguished. The man waited a few moments. He had noticed that the door was not quite closed, and the interstice irresistibly fascinated him. He approached and put his hand against the door. It yielded. He entered. The next instant there was a bang and a cry, and a strong spray of white liquid appeared, in the middle of which was the man's head. The door slammed and a bolt was shot. The man, spluttering, coughing, and swearing, rubbed his eyes and wiped water from his face with his hands. His hat was on the ground. At first he could not see at all, but presently he felt his way towards the steps and began to climb them. Audrey ran off towards the corner. She could see and hear him shaking the gate and then trying to get a key into it. But as Audrey had left her key in the other side of the lock, he failed in the attempt.

The next thing was that a window opened in the high wall-face of the house and an immense stream of liquid descended full on the man's head. Susan Foley was at the window, but only the nozzle of the extinguisher could be seen. The man tried to climb over the railings; he did not succeed; they had been especially designed to prevent such feats. He ran down the steps. The shower faithfully followed him. In no corner of his hiding did the bountiful spray neglect him. As soon as one supply of liquid slackened another commenced. Sometimes there were two at once. The man ran up the steps again and made another effort to reach the safety of the street. Audrey could restrain herself no more. She came, palpitating with joyous vitality, towards the area gate with the innocent mien of a passer-by.

"Whatever is the matter?" she exclaimed, stopping as if thunderstruck. But in the gloom her eyes were dancing fires. She was elated as she had never been.

The man only coughed.

"You oughtn't to take shower-baths like this in the street," she said, veiling the laughter in her voice. "It's not allowed. But I suppose you're doing it for a bet or something."

The downpour ceased.

"Here, miss," said he, between coughs, "unlock this gate for me. Here's the key."

"I shall do no such thing," Audrey replied. "I believe you're a burglar. I shall fetch a policeman."

And she turned back.

In the house, Miss Ingate was coming slowly down the stairs, a fire-extinguisher in her arms, like a red baby. She had a sardonic smile, but there was diffidence in it, which showed, perhaps, that it was directed within.

"I've saved one," she said, pointing to an extinguisher, "in case there should be a fire in the night."

A little later Susan Foley appeared at the door of the living-room.

"Nine o'clock," she announced calmly. "Supper's ready. We shan't wait for Jane."

When Jane Foley arrived, a reconnaissance proved that the martyrised detective had contrived to get away.

CHAPTER XXIII

THE BLUE CITY

In the following month, on a Saturday afternoon, Audrey, Miss Ingate, and Jane Foley were seated at an open-air café in the Blue City.

The Blue City, now no more, was, as may be remembered, Birmingham's reply to the White City of London, and the imitative White City of Manchester. Birmingham, in that year, was not imitative, and, with its chemical knowledge, it had discovered that certain shades of blue would resist the effects of smoke far more successfully than any shade of white. And experience even showed that these shades of blue were improved, made more delicate and romantic, by smoke. The total impression of the show—which it need hardly be said was situated in the polite Edgbaston district—was ethereal, especially when its minarets and towers, all in accordance with the taste of the period, were beheld from a distance. Nor was the exhibition entirely devoted to pleasure. It had a moral object, and that object was to demonstrate the progress of civilisation in our islands. Its official title, indeed, was "The National Progress Exhibition," but the citizens of Birmingham and the vicinity never called it anything but the Blue City.

On that Saturday afternoon a Cabinet Minister historically hostile to the idols of Birmingham was about to address a mass meeting in the Imperial Hall of the Exhibition, which held seven thousand people, in order to prove to Birmingham that the Government of which he was a member had done far more for national progress than any other Government had done for national progress in the same length of time. The presence of the Cabinet Minister accounted for the presence of Jane Foley; the presence of Jane Foley accounted for the presence of Audrey; and the presence of Audrey accounted for the presence of Miss Ingate.

Although she was one of the chief organisers of victory, and perhaps—next to Rosamund and the family trio whose Christian names were three sweet symphonies—the principal asset of the Suffragette Union, Jane Foley had not taken an active part in the Union's arrangements for suitably welcoming the Cabinet Minister; partly because of her lameness, partly because she was writing a book, and partly for secret reasons which it would be unfair to divulge. Nearly at the last moment, however, in consequence of news that all was not well in the Midlands, she had been sent to Birmingham, and, after evading the watch of the police, she had arrived on the previous day in Audrey's motor-car, which at that moment was waiting in the automobile park outside the principal gates of the Blue City.

The motor-car had been chosen as a means of transit for the reason that the railway stations were being watched for notorious suffragettes by members of a police force whose reputations were at stake. Audrey owed her possession of a motor-car to the fact that the Union officials had seemed both startled and grieved when, in response to questions, she admitted that she had no car. It was communicated to her that members of the Union as rich as she reputedly was were expected to own cars for the general good. Audrey thereupon took measures to own a car. Having seen in many newspapers an advertisement in which a firm of middlemen implored the public thus : "Let us run your car for you. Let us take all the worry and responsibility," she interviewed the firm, and by writing out a cheque disembarrassed herself at a stroke of every anxiety incident to defective magnetos, bad petrol, bad rubber, punctures, driving licences, bursts, collisions, damages, and human chauffeurs. She had all the satisfactions of owning a car without any of the cares. One of the evidences of progress in the Blue City was an exhibit of this very firm of middlemen.

From the pale blue tripod table at which sat the three women could be plainly seen the vast Imperial Hall, flanked on one side by the great American Dragon Slide, a side-show loudly demonstrating progress, and cn the other by the unique Joy Wheel side-show. At the doorway of the latter a man was bawling proofs of progress through a megaphone.

Immense crowds had been gathering in the Imperial Hall, and the lines of political enthusiasts bound thither were now thinning. The Blue City was full of rumours, as that the Cabinet Minister was too afraid to come, as that he had been smuggled to the hall inside a tea-chest, and as that he had walked openly and unchallenged through the whole Exhibition. It was no rumour, but a sure fact, that two women had been caught hiding on the roof of the Imperial Hall, under natural shelters formed by the beams and boarding supporting the pediment of the eastern façade, and that they were ammunitioned with flags and leaflets and a silk ladder, and had made a hole in the roof exactly over the platform. These two women had been seen in charge of policemen at the Exhibition police-station. It was under-stood by many that they were the last hope of militancy that afternoon; many others, on the contrary, were convinced that they had been simply a feint.

"Well," said Miss Ingate suddenly, glancing up at the Imperial clock, "I think I shall move outside and sit in the car. I think that'll be the best place for me. I said that night in Paris that I'd get my arm broken, but I've changed my mind about that." She rose.

"Winnie," protested Audrey, "aren't you going to see it out?"

"No," said Miss Ingate.

"Are you afraid?"

"I don't know that I'm afraid. I played the barrel

organ all the way down Regent Street, and it was smashed to pieces. But I don't want to go to prison. Really, I don't *want* to. If me going to prison would bring the Vote a single year nearer, I should say : 'Let it wait a year.' If me not going to prison meant no Vote for ever and ever, I should say : 'Well, struggle on without the Vote.' I've no objection to other people going to prison, if it suits them, but it wouldn't suit me. I know it wouldn't. So I shall go outside and sit in the car. If you don't come, I shall know what's happened, and you needn't worry about me."

The dame duly departed, her lips and eyes equally ironic about her own prudence and about the rashness of others.

"Let's have some more lemonade—shall we?" said Jane Foley.

"Oh, let's !" agreed Audrey, with rapture. "And more sponge-cake, too ! You do look lovely like that !"

"Do I ? "

Jane Foley had her profuse hair tightly bound round her head and powdered grey. It was very advisable for her to be disguised, and her bright hair was usually the chief symptom of her in those disturbances which so harassed the police. She now had the appearance of a neat old lady kept miraculously young by a pure and cheerful nature. Audrey, with a plain blue frock and hat which had cost more than Jane Foley would spend on clothes in twelve months, had a face dazzling by its ingenuous excitement and expectation. Her little nose was extraordinarily pert ; her forehead superb ; and all her gestures had the same vivacious charm as was in her eyes. The white-aproned, streamered girl who took the order for lemonade and sponge-cakes to a covered bar ornamented by advertisements of whisky, determined to adopt a composite of the styles of both the customers on her next ceremonious Sunday. And a large proportion of the other sippers and nibblers and of the endless promenading crowds regarded the pair with pleasure and curiosity, never suspecting that one of them was the most dangerous woman in England.

The new refreshments, which had been delayed by reason of an altercation between the waitress and three extreme youths at a neighbouring table, at last arrived, and were plopped smartly down between Audrey and Miss Foley. Having received half a sovereign from Audrey, the girl returned to the bar for change. "None o' your sauce!" she threw out, as she passed the youths, who had apparently discovered new arguments in support of their case. Audrey was fired by the vigorous independence of the girl against three males.

"I don't care if we are caught!" she murmured low, looking for the future through the pellucid tumbler. She added, however: "But if we are, I shall pay my own fine. You know I promised that to Miss Ingate."

"That's all right, so long as you don't pay mine, my dear," said Jane Foley with an affectionate smile.

"Jenny!" Audrey protested, full of heroine-worship. "How could you think I would ever do such a mean thing!"

There came a dull, vague, voluminous sound from the direction of the Imperial Hall. It lasted for quite a number of seconds.

"He's beginning," said Jane Foley. "I do feel sorry for him."

"Are we to start now?" Audrey asked deferentially.

"Oh, no!" Jane laughed. "The great thing is to let them think everything's all right. And then, when they're getting careless, let go at them full bang with a beautiful surprise. There'll be a chance of getting away like that. I believe there are a hundred and fifty stewards in the meeting, and they'll every one be quite useless."

At intervals a muffled roar issued from the Imperial Hall, despite the fact that the windows were closely shut.

In due time Jane Foley quietly rose from the table, and Audrey did likewise. All around them stretched the imposing blue architecture of the Exhibition, forming vistas that ended dimly either in the smoke of Birmingham or the rustic haze of Worcestershire. And, although the Imperial

Hall was crammed, every vista was thickly powdered with pleasure-seekers and probably pleasure-finders. Bands played. Flags waved. Brass glinted. Even the sun feebly shone at intervals through the eternal canopy of soot. It was a great day in the annals of the Blue City and of Liberalism.

And Jane Foley and Audrey turned their backs upon all that, and—Jane concealing her limp as much as possible— sauntered with affected nonchalance towards the precincts of the Joy Wheel enclosure. Audrey was inexpressibly uplifted. She felt as if she had stepped straight into romance. And she was right—she had stepped into the most vivid romance of the modern age, into a world of disguises, flights, pursuits, chicane, inconceivable adventures, ideals, martyrs and conquerors, which only the Renaissance or the twenty-first century could appreciate.

"Lend me that, will you?" said Jane persuasively to the man with the megaphone at the entrance to the enclosure.

He was, quite properly, a very loud man, with a loud thick voice, a loud purple face, and a loud grey suit. To Audrey's astonishment, he smiled and winked, and gave up the megaphone at once.

Audrey paid sixpence at the turnstile, admittance for two persons, and they were within the temple, which had a roof like an umbrella over the central, revolving portion of it, but which was somewhat open to the skies around the rim. There were two concentric enclosing walls, the inner one was unscalable, and the outer one about five feet six inches high. A second loud man was calling out: "Couples please. Ladies *and* gentlemen. Couples if *you* please." Obediently, numbers of the crowd disposed themselves in pairs in the attitudes of close affection on the circling floor which had just come to rest, while the remainder of the numerous gathering gazed upon them with sarcastic ecstasy. Then the wheel began slowly to turn, and girls to shriek in the plenitude of happiness. And progress was proved geometrically.

Jane, bearing the megaphone, slipped by an aperture into the space between the two walls, and Audrey followed. Nobody gave attention to them except the second loud man, who winked the wink of knowledge. The fact was that both the loud men, being unalterable Tories, had been very willing to connive at Jane Foley's scheme for the affliction of a Radical Minister.

The two girls over the wall had an excellent and appetising view of the upper part of the side of the Imperial Hall, and of its high windows, the nearest of which was scarcely thirty feet away.

"Hold this, will you?" said Jane, handing the megaphone to Audrey.

Jane drew from its concealment in her dress a small piece of iron to which was attached a coloured streamer bearing certain words. She threw, with a strong movement of the left arm, because she was left-handed. She had practised throwing; throwing was one of her several specialties. The bit of iron, trailing its motto like a comet its tail, flew across space and plumped into the window with a pleasing crash and disappeared, having triumphed over uncounted police on the outskirts and a hundred and fifty stewards within. A roar from the interior of the hall supervened, and varied cries.

"Give me the meg," said Jane gently.

The next instant she was shouting through the megaphone, an instrument which she had seriously studied:

"Votes for women. Why do you torture women? Votes for women. Why do you torture women?"

The uproar increased and subsided. A masterful voice resounded within the interior. Many people rushed out of the hall. And there was a great scurry of important and puzzled feet within a radius of a score of yards.

"I think I'll try the next window," said Jane, handing over the megaphone. "You shout while I throw."

Audrey's heart was violently beating. She took the megaphone and put it to her lips, but no sound would come.

Then, as though it were breaking through an obstacle, the sound shot forth, and to Audrey it was a gigantic voice that functioned quite independently of her will. Tremendously excited by the noise, she bawled louder and still louder.

"I've missed," said Jane calmly in her ear. "That's enough, I think. Come along."

"But they can't possibly see us," said Audrey, breathless, lowering the instrument.

"Come along, dear," Jane Foley insisted.

People with open mouths were crowding at the aperture of the inner wall, but, Jane going first, both girls pushed safely through the throng. The wheel had stopped. The entire congregation was staring agog, and in two seconds everybody divined, or had been nudged to the effect, that Jane and Audrey were the authoresses of the pother.

Jane still leading, they made for the exit. But the first loud man rushed chivalrously in.

"Perlice!" he cried. "Two bobbies a-coming."

"Here!" said the second loud man. "Here, misses. Get on the wheel. They'll never get ye if ye sit in the middle back to back." He jumped on to the wheel himself, and indicated the mathematical centre. Jane took the suggestion in a flash; Audrey was obedient. They fixed themselves under directions, dropping the megaphone. The wheel started, and the megaphone rattled across its smooth surface till it was shot off. A policeman ran in, and hesitated; another man, in plain clothes, and wearing a rosette, ran in.

"That's them," said the rosette. "I saw her with the grey hair from the gallery."

The policeman sprang on to the wheel, and after terrific efforts fell sprawling and was thrown off. The rosette met the same destiny. A second policeman appeared, and with the fearless courage of his cloth, undeterred by the spectacle of prostrate forms, made a magnificent dash, and was equally floored.

As Audrey sat very upright, pressing her back against
the back of Jane Foley and clutching at Jane Foley's skirts
with her hands behind her—the locked pair were obliged thus
to hold themselves exactly over the axis of the wheel, for
the slightest change of position would have resulted in their
being flung to the circumference and into the blue grip of
the law—she had visions of all her life just as though she
had been drowning. She admitted all her follies and
wondered what madness could have prompted her remarkable escapades both in Paris and out of it. She remembered Madame Piriac's prophecy. She was ready to wish
the past year annihilated and herself back once more in
parental captivity at Moze, the slave of an unalterable
routine imposed by her father, without responsibility, without initiative and without joy. And she lived again through
the scenes in which she had smiled at the customs official,
fibbed to Rosamund, taken the wounded Musa home in the
taxi, spoken privily with the ageing yacht-owner, and
laughed at the drowned detective in the area of the palace
in Paget Gardens.

Everything happened in her mind while the wheel went
round once, showing her in turn to the various portions
of the audience, and bringing her at length to a second view
of the sprawling policemen. Whereupon she thought
queerly: "What do I care about the vote, really?" And
finally she thought with anger and resentment: "What a
shame it is that women haven't got the vote!" And then
she heard a gay, quiet sound. It was Jane Foley laughing
gently behind her.

"Can you see the big one now, darling?" asked Jane
roguishly. "Has he picked himself up again?"

Audrey laughed.

And at last the audience laughed also. It laughed
because the big policeman, unconquerable, had made
another intrepid dash for the centre of the wheel and fallen
upon his stomach as upon a huge india-rubber ball. The
audience did more than laugh—it shrieked, yelled, and

L

guffawed. The performance to be witnessed was worth ten times the price of entry. Indeed no such performance had ever before been seen in the whole history of popular amusement. And in describing the affair the next morning as "unique" the *Birmingham Daily Post* for once used that adjective with absolute correctness. The policemen tried again and yet again. They got within feet, within inches, of their prey, only to be dragged away by the mysterious protector of militant maidens—centrifugal force. Probably never before in the annals of the struggle for political freedom had maidens found such a protection, invisible, sinister and complete. Had the education of policemen in England included a course of mechanics, these particular two policemen would have known that they were seeking the impossible and fighting against that which was stronger than ten thousand policemen. But they would not give up. At each fresh attempt they hoped by guile to overcome their unseen enemy, as the gambler hopes at each fresh throw to outwit chance. The jeers of the audience pricked them to desperation, for in encounters with females like Jane Foley and Audrey they had been accustomed to the active sympathy of the public. But centrifugal force had rendered them ridiculous, and the public never sympathises with those whom ridicule has covered. The strange and side-splitting effects of centrifugal force had transformed about a hundred indifferent young men and women into ardent and convinced supporters of feminism in its most advanced form.

In the course of her slow revolution Audrey saw the rosetted steward arguing with the second loud man, no doubt to persuade him to stop the wheel. Then out of the tail of her eye she saw the steward run violently from the tent. And then while her back was towards the entrance she was deafened by a prodigious roar of delight from the mob. The two policemen had fled also—probably for reinforcements and appliances against centrifugal force. In their pardonable excitement they had, however, committed the imprudence of departing together. An elementary knowledge of strategy should have warned them against such a mistake. The wheel stopped immediately. The second loud man beckoned with laughter to Jane Foley and Audrey, who rose and hopefully skipped towards him. Audrey at any rate was as self-conscious as though she had been on the stage.

"Here's th' back way," said the second loud man, pointing to a coarse curtain in the obscurity of the nether parts of the enclosure.

They ran, Jane Foley first, and vanished from the regions of the Joy Wheel amid terrific acclamations given in a strong Midland accent.

The next moment they found themselves in a part of the Blue City which nobody had taken the trouble to paint blue. The one blue object was a small patch of sky, amid clouds, overhead. On all sides were wooden flying buttresses, supporting the boundaries of the Joy Wheel enclosure to the south-east, of the Parade Restaurant and Bar to the south-west, and of a third establishment of good cheer to the north. Upon the ground were brick-ends, cinders, bits of wood, bits of corrugated iron, and all the litter and refuse cast out of sight of the eyes of visitors to the Exhibition of Progress.

With the fear of the police behind them they stumbled forward a few yards, and then saw a small ramshackle door swinging slightly to and fro on one hinge. Jane Foley pulled it open. They both went into a narrow passage. On the mildewed wall of the passage was pinned up a notice in red ink: "Any waitress taking away any apron or cap from the Parade Restaurant and Bar will be fined one shilling." Farther on was another door, also ajar. Jane Foley pushed against it, and a tiny room of irregular shape was disclosed. In this room a stout woman in grey was counting a pile of newly laundered caps and aprons, and putting them out of one hamper into another. Audrey remembered seeing the woman at the counter of the restaurant and bar.

"The police are after us. They'll be here in a minute," said Jane Foley simply.

"Oh!" exclaimed the woman in grey, with the carelessness of fatigue. "Are you them stone-throwing lot? They've just been in to tell me about it. What d'ye do it for?"

"We do it for you—amongst others," Jane Foley smiled.

"Nay! That ye don't!" said the woman positively. "I've got a vote for the city council, and I want no more."

"Well, you don't want us to get caught, do you?"

"No, I don't know as I do. Ye look a couple o' bonny wenches."

"Let's have two caps and aprons, then," said Jane Foley smoothly. "We'll pay the shilling fine." She laughed lightly. "And a bit more. If the police get in here we shall have to struggle, you know, and they'll break the place up."

Audrey produced another half-sovereign.

"But what shall ye do with yer hats and coats?" the woman demanded.

"Give them to you, of course."

The woman regarded the hats and coats.

"I couldn't get near them coats," she said. "And if I put on one o' them there hats my old man 'ud rise from the grave—that he would. Still, I don't wish ye any harm."

She shut and locked the door.

In about a minute two waitresses in aprons and streamered caps of immaculate purity emerged from the secret places of the Parade Restaurant and Bar, slipped round the end of the counter, and started with easy indifference to saunter away into the grounds after the manner of restaurant girls who have been gifted with half an hour off. The tabled expanse in front of the Parade erection was busy with people, some sitting at the tables and supporting the establishment, but many more merely taking advantage of the pitch to observe all possible exciting developments of the suffragette shindy.

And as the criminals were modestly getting clear, a loud
and imperious voice called:

"Hey!"

Audrey, lacking experience, hesitated.

"Hey there!"

They both turned, for the voice would not be denied.
It belonged to a man sitting with another man at a table
on the outskirts of the group of tables. It was the voice
of the rosetted steward, who beckoned in a not unfriendly
style.

"Bring us two liqueur brandies, miss," he cried. "And
look slippy, if ye please."

The sharp tone, so sure of obedience, gave Audrey a
queer sensation of being in reality a waitress doomed to
tolerate the rough bullying of gentlemen urgently desiring
alcohol. And the fierce thought that women—especially
restaurant waitresses—must and should possess the Vote
surged through her mind more powerfully than ever.

"I'll never have the chance again," she muttered to herself. And marched to the counter.

"Two liqueur brandies, please," she said to the woman
in grey, who had left her apron calculations. "That's all
right," she murmured, as the woman stared a question at
her. Then the woman smiled to herself, and poured out
the liqueur brandies from a labelled bottle with startling
adroitness, and dashed the full glasses on to a brass tray.

As Audrey walked across the gravel carefully balancing
the tray, she speculated whether the public eye would notice
the shape of her small handbag, which was attached by a
safety pin to her dress beneath the apron, and whether her
streamers were streaming out far behind her head.

Before she could put the tray down on the table, the
rosetted steward, who looked pale, snatched one of the
glasses and gulped down its entire contents.

"I wanted it!" said he, smacking his lips. "I wanted
it bad. They'll catch 'em all right. I should know the
young 'un again anywhere. I'll swear to identify her in

any court. And I will. Tasty little piece o' goods, too!
. . . But not so good-looking as you," he added, gazing
suddenly at Audrey.

"None o' your sauce," snapped Audrey, and walked off,
leaving the tray behind.

The two men exploded into coarse but amiable laughter,
and called to her to return, but she would not. "You can
pay the other young lady," she said over her shoulder,
pointing vaguely to the counter where there was now a
bevy of other young ladies.

Five minutes later Miss Ingate, and the chauffeur also,
received a very appreciable shock. Half an hour later the
car, having called at the telegraph office, and also at the
aghast lodgings of the waitresses to enable them to re-
attire and to pack, had quitted Birmingham.

That night they reached Northampton. At the post
office there Jane Foley got a telegram. And when the three
were seated in a corner of the curtained and stuffy dining-
room of the small hotel, Jane said, addressing herself
specially to Audrey :

"It won't be safe for us to return to Paget Gardens
to-morrow. And perhaps not to any of our places in
London."

"That won't matter," said Audrey, who was now
becoming accustomed to the world of conspiracy and
chicane in which Jane Foley carried on her existence with
such a deceiving air of the matter-of-fact. "We'll go anywhere, won't we, Winnie?"

And Miss Ingate assented.

"Well," said Jane Foley. "I've just had a telegram
arranging for us to go to Frinton."

"You don't mean Frinton-on-Sea?" exclaimed Miss
Ingate, suddenly excited.

"It *is* on the sea," said Jane. "We have to go
through Colchester. Do you know it?"

"Do I know it!" repeated Miss Ingate. "I know
everybody in Frinton, except the Germans. When I'm at

home I buy my bacon at Frinton. Are you going to an hotel there?"

"No," said Jane. "To some people named Spatt."

"There's nobody that is anybody named Spatt living at Frinton," said Miss Ingate.

"They haven't been there long."

"Oh!" murmured Miss Ingate. "Of course if that's it . . . ! I can't guarantee what's happened since I began my pilgrimages. But I think I shall wriggle off home quietly as soon as we get to Colchester. This afternoon's business has been too feverish for me. When the policeman held up his hand as we came through Blisworth I thought you were caught. I shall just go home."

"I don't care much about going to Frinton, Jenny," said Audrey.

Indeed, Moze lay within not many miles of Frinton-on-Sea.

Then Audrey and Miss Ingate observed a phenomenon that was both novel and extremely disturbing. Tears came into the eyes of Jane Foley.

"Don't say it, Audrey, don't say it!" she appealed in a wet voice. "I shall have to go myself. And you simply can't imagine how I hate going all alone into these houses that we're invited to. I'd much sooner be in lodgings, as we were last night. But these homes in quiet places here and there are very useful sometimes. They all belong to members of the Union, you know; and we have to use them. But I wish we hadn't. I've met Mrs. Spatt once. I didn't think you'd throw me over just at the worst part. The Spatts will take all of us and be glad."

("They won't take me," said Miss Ingate under her breath.)

"I shall come with you," said Audrey, caressing the recreant who, while equal to trifles such as policemen, magistrates, and prisons, was miserably afraid of a strange home. In fact Audrey now liked Jane much more than ever, liked her completely—and perhaps admired her rather less, though her admiration was still intense. And the thought in Audrey's mind was: "Never will I desert this girl! I'm a militant, too, now, and I shall stick by her." And she was full of a happiness which she could not understand and which she did not want to understand.

The next morning all the newspaper posters in Northampton bore the words: "Policemen and suffragettes on Joy Wheel," or some variation of these words. And they bore nothing else. And in all the towns and many of the villages through which they passed on the way to Colchester, the same legend greeted their flying eyes. Audrey and Miss Ingate, in the motor-car, read with great care all the papers. Audrey blushed at the descriptions of herself, which were flattering. It seemed that the Cabinet Minister's political meeting had been seriously damaged by the episode, for the reason that rumours of the performance on the Joy Wheel had impaired the spell of eloquence and partially emptied the hall. And this was the more disappointing in that the police had been sure that nothing untoward would occur. It seemed also that the police were on the track of the criminals.

"Are they!" exclaimed Jane Foley with a beautiful smile.

Then the car approached a city of towers on a hill, and as it passed by the station, which was in the valley, Miss Ingate demanded a halt. She got out in the station yard and transferred her belongings to a cab.

"I shall drive home from here," she said. "I've often done it before. After all, I did play the barrel organ all the way down Regent Street. Surely I can rest on the barrel organ, can't I, Miss Foley—at my age? . . . What a business I shall have when I *do* get home, and nobody expecting me!"

And when certain minor arrangements had been made, the car mounted the hill into Colchester and took the Frinton road, leaving Miss Ingate's fly far behind.

CHAPTER XXIV

THE SPATTS

THE house of the Spatts was large, imposing and variegated.
It had turrets, balconies, and architectural nooks in such
quantity that the unaided individual eye could not embrace
it all at once. It overlooked, from a height, the grounds
of the Frinton Sports Club, and a new member of this club,
upon first beholding the residence, had made the immortal
remark : "It wants at least fourteen people to look at it."
The house stood in the middle of an unfinished garden,
which promised ultimately to be as heterogeneous as itself,
but which at present was merely an expanse of sorely
wounded earth.

The time was early summer, and therefore the summer
dining-room of the Spatts was in use. This dining-room
consisted of one white, windowed wall, a tiled floor, and a
roof of wood. The windows gave into the winter dining-
room, which was a white apartment, sparsely curtained and
cushioned with chintz, and containing very few pieces of
furniture or pictures. The Spatts considered, rightly, that
furniture and pictures were unhygienic and the secret lairs
of noxious germs. Had the Spatts flourished twenty-five years
earlier their dining-room would have been covered with
brown paper upon which would have hung permanent photographs of European masterpieces of graphic art, and there
would have been a multiplicity of draperies and specimens
of battered antique furniture, with a warming-pan or so
suspended here and there in place of sporting trophies. But
the Spatts had not begun to flourish twenty-five years ago.
They flourished very few years ago and they still flourish.

As the summer dining-room had only one wall, it follows that it was open to the powers of the air. This result had been foreseen by the Spatts—had indeed been expressly arranged, for they believed strongly in the powers of the air, as being beneficent powers. It is true that they generally had sniffling colds, but their argument was that these maladies had no connection whatever with the powers of the air, which, according to their theory, saved them from much worse.

They and their guests were now seated at dinner. Twilight was almost lost in night. The table was illuminated by four candles at the corners, and flames of these candles flickered in the healthful evening breeze, dropping pink wax on the candlesticks. They were surrounded by the mortal remains of tiny moths, but other tiny moths would not heed the warning and continually shot themselves into the flames. On the outskirts of the table moved with silent stealth the forms of two middle-aged and ugly servants.

Mrs. Spatt was very tall and very thin, and the simplicity of her pale green dress—sole reminder of the brown-paper past—was calculated to draw attention to these attributes. She had an important reddish nose, and a mysterious look of secret confidence, which never left her even in the most trying crises. Mr. Spatt also was very tall and very thin. His head was several sizes too small, and part of his insignificant face, which one was apt to miss altogether in contemplating his body, was hidden under a short grey beard. Siegfried Spatt, the sole child of the union, though but seventeen, was as tall and as thin as his father and his mother; he had a pale face and red hands.

The guests were Audrey, Jane Foley, and a young rubicund gentleman, beautifully clothed, and with fair curly locks, named Ziegler. Mr. Ziegler was far more perfectly at ease than anybody else at the table, which indeed as a whole was rendered haggard and nervous by the precarious state of the conversation, expecting its total

THE SPATTS 179

decease at any moment. At intervals someone lifted the limp dying body—it sank back—was lifted again—struggled feebly—relapsed. Young Siegfried was excessively tongue-tied and self-conscious, and his demeanour frankly admitted it. Jane Foley, acknowledged heroine in certain fields, sat like a schoolgirl at her first dinner-party. Audrey maintained her widowhood, but scarcely with credit. Mr. and Mrs. Spatt were as usual too deeply concerned about the awful condition of the universe to display that elasticity of mood which continuous chatter about nothing in particular demands. And they were too worshipful of the best London conventions not to regard silence at table as appalling. In the part of the country from which Jane Foley sprang, hosts will sit mute through a meal and think naught of it. But Mr. and Mrs. Spatt were of different stuff. All these five appeared to be in serious need of conversation pills. Only Mr. Ziegler beheld his companions with a satisfied equanimity that was insensible to spiritual suffering. Happily at the most acute moments the gentle night wind, meandering slowly from the east across leagues of North Sea, would induce in one or another a sneeze which gave some semblance of vitality and vigour to the scene.

After one of these sneezes it was that Jane Foley, conscience-stricken, tried to stimulate the exchanges by an effort of her own.

"And what are the folks like in Frinton?" she demanded, blushing, and looking up. As she looked up young Siegfried looked down, lest he might encounter her glance and be utterly discountenanced.

Jane Foley's question was unfortunate.

"We know nothing of them," said Mrs. Spatt, pained. "Of course I have received and paid a few purely formal calls. But as regards friends and acquaintances, we prefer to import them from London. As for the holiday-makers, one sees them, naturally. They appear to lead an exclusively physical existence."

"My dear," put in Mr. Spatt stiffly. "The residents

are no better. The women play golf all day on that appalling golf course, and then after tea they go into the town to change their library books. But I do not believe that they ever read their library books. The mentality of the town is truly remarkable. However, I am informed that there are many towns like it."

"You bet!" murmured Siegfried Spatt, and then tried, vainly, to suck back the awful remark whence it had come.

Mr. Ziegler, speaking without passion or sorrow, added his views about Frinton. He asserted that it was the worst example of stupid waste of opportunities he had ever encountered, even in England. He pointed out that there was no band, no pier, no casino, no shelters—and not even a tree; and that there were no rules to govern the place. He finished by remarking that no German state would tolerate such a pleasure resort. In this judgment he employed an excellent English accent, with a scarcely perceptible thickening of the t's and thinning of the d's.

Mr. Ziegler left nothing to be said.

Then the conversation sighed and really did expire. It might have survived had not the Spatts had a rule, explained previously to those whom it concerned, against talking shop. Their attachment to this rule was heroic. In the present instance shop was suffragism. The Spatts had developed into supporters of militancy in a very curious way. Mrs. Spatt's sister, a widow, had been mixed up with the Union for years. One day she was fined forty shillings or a week's imprisonment for a political peccadillo involving a hatpin and a policeman. It was useless for her to remind the magistrate that she, like Mrs. Spatt, was the daughter of the celebrated statesman B——, who in the fifties had done so much for Britain. (Lo! The source of that mysterious confidence that always supported Mrs. Spatt!) The magistrate had no historic sense. She went to prison. At least she was on the way thither when Mr. Spatt paid the fine in spite of her. The same night Mr. Spatt wrote to his favourite evening paper to

point out the despicable ingratitude of a country which would
have imprisoned a daughter of the celebrated B——, and
announced that henceforward he would be an active supporter
of suffragism, which hitherto had interested him only
academically. He was a wealthy man, and his money and
his house and his pen were at the service of the Union—
but always with discretion.

Audrey and Jane Foley had learnt all this privately from
Mrs. Spatt on their arrival, after they had told such part
of their tale as Jane Foley had deemed suitable, and they
had further learnt that suffragism would not be a welcome
topic at their table, partly on account of the servants and
partly on account of Mr. Ziegler, whose opinions were quite
clearly opposed to the movement, but whom they admired
for true and rare culture. He was a cousin of German
residents in First Avenue and, visiting them often,
had been discovered by Mr. Spatt in the afternoon-tea
train.

And just as the ices came to compete with the night
wind, the postman arrived like a deliverer. The postman
had to pass the dining-room *en route* by the circuitous drive
to the front door, and when dinner was afoot he would
hand the letters to the parlourmaid, who would divide
them into two portions, and, putting both on a salver,
offer the salver first to Mrs. and then to Mr. Spatt, while
Mr. or Mrs. Spatt begged guests, if there were any, to
excuse the quaint and indeed unusual custom, pardonable
only on the plea that any tidings from London ought to be
savoured instantly in such a place as Frinton.

After leaving his little pile untouched for some time,
Mr. Spatt took advantage of the diversion caused by the
brushing of the cloth and the distribution of finger-bowls to
glance at the topmost letter, which was addressed in a
woman's hand.

"She's coming!" he exclaimed, forgetting to apologise
in the sudden excitement of news, "Good heavens!" He
looked at his watch. "She's here. I heard the train

several minutes ago! She must be here! The letter's
been delayed."

"Who, Alroy?" demanded Mrs. Spatt earnestly. "Not
that Miss Nickall you mentioned?"

"Yes, my dove." And then in a grave tone to the
parlourmaid: "Give this letter to your mistress."

Mr. Spatt, cheered by the new opportunity for conversation, and in his eagerness abrogating all rules, explained
how he had been in London on the previous day for a performance of Strauss's *Elektra*, and according to his custom
had called at the offices of the Suffragette Union to see
whether he could in any manner aid the cause. He had
been told that a house in Paget Gardens lent to the Union
had been basely withdrawn from service by its owner on
account of some embroilment with the supreme police
authorities at Scotland Yard, and that one of the inmates,
a Miss Nickall, the poor young lady who had had her arm
broken and was scarcely convalescent, had need of quietude
and sea air. Mr. Spatt had instantly offered the hospitality
of his home to Miss Nickall, whom he had seen in a cab
and who was very sweet. Miss Nickall had said that she
must consult her companion. It now appeared that the companion was gone to the Midlands. This episode had
occurred immediately before the receipt of the telegram from
head-quarters asking for shelter for Miss Jane Foley and
Mrs. Moncreiff.

Mr. Spatt's excitement had new communicated itself
to everybody except Mr. Ziegler and Siegfried Spatt. Jane
Foley almost recovered her presence of mind, and Mrs.
Spatt was extraordinarily interested to learn that Miss
Nickall was an American painter who had lived long in
Paris, and that Audrey had first made her acquaintance in
Paris, and knew Paris well. Audrey's motor car had produced a considerable impression on Aurora Spatt, and this
impression was deepened by the touch about Paris. After
breathing mysterious orders into the ear of the parlour-
maid Mrs. Spatt began to talk at large about music in

Paris, and Mr. Spatt made comparisons between the principal opera houses in Europe. He proclaimed for the Scala at Milan; but Mr. Ziegler, who had methodically according to a fixed plan lived in all European capitals except Paris— whither he was soon going, said that Mr. Spatt was quite wrong, and that Milan could not hold a candle to Munich. Mrs. Spatt inquired whether Audrey had heard Strauss's *Elektra* at the Paris Opera House. Audrey replied that Strauss's *Elektra* had not been given at the Paris Opera House.

"Oh!" said Mrs. Spatt. "This prejudice against the greatest modern masterpieces because they are German is a very sad sign in Paris. I have noticed it for a long time."

Audrey, who most irrationally had begun to be annoyed by the blandness of Mr. Ziegler's smile, answered with a rival blandness:

"In Paris they do not reproach Strauss because he is German, but because he is vulgar."

Mrs. Spatt had a martyrised expression. In her heart she felt a sick trembling of her religious belief that *Elektra* was the greatest opera ever composed. For Audrey had the prestige of Paris and of the automobile. Mrs. Spatt, however, said not a word. Mr. Ziegler, on the other hand, after shuffling some seconds for utterance, ejaculated with sublime anger:

"Vulgar!"

His rubicundity had increased and his blandness was dissolved. A terrible sequel might have occurred, had not the crunch of wheels on the drive been heard at that very instant. The huge, dim form of a coach drawn by a ghostly horse passed along towards the front door, just below the diners. Almost simultaneously the electric light above the front door was turned on, casting a glare across a section of the inchoate garden, where no flower grew save the dandelion. Everybody sprang up. Host and hostess, urged by hospitality, spun first into the drive, and came level with the vehicle precisely as the vehicle opened its invisible interior. Jane Foley and Audrey saw Miss Nickall emerge from it rather slowly and cautiously, with her white kind face and her arm all swathed in white.

"Well, Mr. Spatt," came the American benevolent voice of Nick. "How glad I am to see you. And this is Mrs. Spatt? Mrs. Spatt! Delighted. Your husband is the kindest, sweetest man, Mrs. Spatt, that I've met in years. It is perfectly sweet of you to have me. I shouldn't have inflicted myself on you—no, I shouldn't—only you know we have to obey orders. I was told to come here, and here I've come, with a glad heart."

Audrey was touched by the sight and voice of grey-haired Nick, with her trick of seeing nothing but the best in everybody, transforming everybody into saints, angels, and geniuses. Her smiles and her tones were irresistible. They were like the wand of some magical princess come to break a sinister thrall. They nearly humanised the gaunt parlourmaid, who stood grimly and primly waiting until these tedious sentimental preliminaries should cease from interfering with her duties in regard to the luggage.

"We have friends of yours here, Miss Nickall," simpered Mrs. Spatt, after she had given a welcome. She had seen Jane Foley and Audrey standing expectant just behind Mr. Spatt, and outside the field of the electric beam.

Nick glanced round, hesitated, and then with a sudden change of all her features rushed at the girls regardless of her arm. Her joy was enchanting.

"I was afraid—I was afraid——" she murmured as she kissed them. Her eyes softly glistened.

"Oh!" she exclaimed, after a moment. "And I *have* got a surprise for you! I have just! You may say it's some surprise." She turned towards the cab. "Musa, now do come out of that wagon."

And from the blackness of the cab's interior gingerly stepped Musa, holding a violin case in his hand.

"Mrs. Spatt," said Nick. "Let me introduce Mr. Musa.

Mr. Musa is perhaps the greatest violinist in Paris—or in Europe. Very old friend of ours. He came over to London unexpectedly just as I was starting for Liverpool Street station this afternoon. So I did the only thing I could do. I couldn't leave him there—I brought him along, and we want Mr. Spatt to recommend us an hotel in Frinton for him." And while Musa was shyly in his imperfect English greeting Mr. and Mrs. Spatt, she whispered to Audrey : "You don't know. You'd never guess. A big concert agent in Paris has taken him up at last. He's going to play at a lot of concerts, and they actually paid him two thousand five hundred francs in advance. Isn't it a perfect dream?"

Audrey, who had seen Musa's trustful glance at Nick as he descended from the cab, was suddenly aware of a fierce pang of hate for the benignant Nick, and a wave of fury against Musa. The thing was very disconcerting.

After self-conscious greetings, Musa almost dragged Audrey away from the others.

"It's you I came to London to see," he muttered in an unusual voice.

M

CHAPTER XXV

THE MUTE

It was upon this evening that Audrey began alarmingly to develop the quality of being incomprehensible—even to herself. Like most young women and men, she had been convinced from an early age that she was mysteriously unlike all other created beings, and—again like most young men and women—she could find, in the secrecy of her own heart, plenty of proof of a unique strangeness. But now her unreason became formidable. There she sat with her striking forehead and her quite unimportant nose, in the large austere drawing-room of the Spatts, which was so pervaded by artistic chintz that the slightest movement in it produced a crackle—and wondered why she was so much queerer than other girls could possibly be.

Neither the crackling of chintz nor the aspect of the faces in the drawing-room was conducive to clear psychological analysis. Mr. Ziegler, with a glass of Pilsener by his side on a small table and a cigar in his richly jewelled hand, reposed with crossed legs in an easy chair. He had utterly recovered from the momentary irritation caused by Audrey's attack on Strauss, and his perfect beaming satisfaction with himself made a spectacle which would have distracted an Indian saint from the contemplation of eternity and nothingness. Mr. and Mrs. Spatt, seated as far as was convenient from one another on a long sofa, their emaciated bodies very upright and alert, gazed with intense expectation at Musa. Musa stood in the middle of the room, tuning his violin with little twangs and listening to the twangs as to a secret message.

Miss Nickall, being an invalid, had excusably gone to bed, and Jane Foley, sharer of her bedroom, had followed. The happy relief on Jane's face as she said good night to her hosts had testified to the severity of the ordeal of hospitality through which she had so heroically passed. She might have been going out of prison instead of going out of the most intellectual drawing-room in Frinton.

Audrey, too, would have liked to retire, for automobiles and sensations had exhausted her; but just at this point her unreason had begun to operate. She would not leave Musa alone, because Miss Nickall was leaving him alone. Yet she did not feel at all benevolent towards Musa. She was angry with him for having quitted Paris. She was angry with him for having said to her, in such a peculiar tone: "It's you I came to London to see." She was angry with him for not having found an opportunity, during the picnic meal provided for the two new-comers after the regular dinner, to explain why he had come to London to see her. She was angry with him for that dark hostility which he had at once displayed towards Mr. Ziegler, though she herself hated the innocent Mr. Ziegler with the ferocity of a woman of the Revolution. And further, she was glad, ridiculously glad, that Musa had come to London to see her. Lastly she was aware of a most irrational objection to the manner in which Miss Nickall and Musa said good night to one another, and the obvious fact that Musa in less than an hour had reached terms of familiarity with Jane Foley.

She thought:

"I haven't the faintest idea why he has given up his practising in Paris to come to see me. But if it is what I feel sure it is, there will be trouble. . . . Why do I stay in this ghastly drawing-room? I am dying to go to sleep, and I simply detest everybody in the room. I detest Musa more than all, because as usual he has been acting like a child. . . . Why can't you smile at him, Audrey Moze? Why frown and pretend you're cross when you know you aren't, Audrey Moze? . . . I am cross, and he shall suffer. Was this a time to leave his practising— and the concerts soon coming on? I positively prefer this Ziegler man to him. Yes, I do." So ran her reflections, and they annoyed her.

"What would you wish me to play?" asked Musa, when he had definitely finished twanging. Audrey noticed that his English accent was getting a little less French. She had to admit that, though his appearance was extra- vagantly un-British, it was distinguished. The immensity of his black silk cravat made the black cravat of Mr. Spatt seem like a bootlace round his thin neck.

"Whatever you like, Mr. Musa," replied Aurora Spatt. "*Please!*"

And as a fact the excellent woman, majestic now in spite of her red nose and her excessive thinness, did not care what Musa played. He had merely to play. She had decided for herself, from the conversation, that he was a very celebrated performer, and she had ascertained, by direct questioning, that he had never performed in England. She was determined to be able to say to all comers till death took her that "Musa—the great Musa, you know—first played in England in my own humble drawing-room." The thing itself was actually about to occur; nothing could stop it from occurring; and the thought of the immediate realisation of her desire and ambition gave Mrs. Spatt greater and more real pleasure than she had had for years; it even fortified her against the possible resentment of her cherished Mr. Ziegler.

"French music—would you wish?" Musa suggested.

"Is there any French music? That is to say, of artistic importance?" asked Mr. Ziegler calmly. "I have never heard of it."

He was not consciously being rude. Nor was he trying to be funny. His question implied an honest belief. His assertion was sincere. He glanced, blinking slightly, round the room, with a self-confidence that was either terrible or pathetic, according to the degree of your own self-confidence.

Audrey said to herself.

"I'm glad this isn't my drawing-room." And she was almost frightened by the thought that that skull opposite to her was absolutely impenetrable, and that it would go down to the grave unpierced with all its collection of ideas intact and braggart.

As for Mr. and Mrs. Spatt they were both in the state of not knowing where to look. Immediately their gaze met another gaze it leapt away as from something dangerous or obscene.

"I will play Debussy's Toccata for violin solo," Musa announced tersely. He had blushed; his great eyes were sparkling. And he began to play.

And as soon as he had played a few bars, Audrey gave a start, fortunately not a physical start, and she blushed also. Musa sternly winked at her. Frenchmen do not make a practice of winking, but he had learnt the accomplishment for fun from Miss Thompkins in Paris. The wink caused Audrey surreptitiously to observe Mr. and Mrs. Spatt. It was no relief to her to perceive that these two were listening to Debussy's Toccata for solo violin with the trained and appreciative attention of people who had heard it often before in the various capitals of Europe, who knew it by heart, and who knew at just what passages to raise the head, to give a nod of recognition or a gesture of ecstasy. The bare room was filled with the sound of Musa's fiddle and with the high musical culture of Mr. and Mrs. Spatt. When the piece was over they clapped discreetly, and looked with soft intensity at Audrey, as if murmuring: "You, too, are a cultured cosmopolitan. You share our emotion." And across the face of Mrs. Spatt spread a glow triumphant, for Musa now positively had played for the first time in England in her drawing-room, and she foresaw hundreds of occasions on which she could refer to the matter with a fitting air of

casualness. The glow triumphant, however, paled somewhat as she felt upon herself the eye of Mr. Ziegler.

"Where is Siegfried, Alroy?" she demanded, after
having thanked Musa. "I wouldn't have had him miss
that Debussy for anything, but I hadn't noticed that he
was gone. He adores Debussy."

"I think it is like bad Bach," Mr. Ziegler put in
suddenly. Then he raised his glass and imbibed a good
portion of the beer specially obtained and provided for
him by his hostess and admirer, Mrs. Spatt.

"Do you *really*?" murmured Mrs. Spatt, with depre-
cation.

"There's something in the comparison," Mr. Spatt
admitted thoughtfully.

"Why not like good Bach?" Musa asked, glaring in
a very strange manner at Mr. Ziegler.

"Bosh!" ejaculated Mr. Ziegler with a most notable
imperturbability. "Only Bach himself could com-pose good
Bach."

Musa's breathing could be heard across the drawing-
room.

"*Eh bien!*" said Musa. "Now I will play for you
Debussy's Toccata. I was not playing it before. I was
playing the Chaconne of Bach, the most famous composition
for the violin in the world."

He did not embroider the statement. He left it in its
nakedness. Nor did he permit anybody else to embroider
it. Before a word of any kind could be uttered he had
begun to play again. Probably in all the annals of artistic
snobbery, no cultured cosmopolitan had ever been made
to suffer a more exquisite moral torture of humiliation
than Musa had contrived to inflict upon Mr. and Mrs.
Spatt in return for their hospitality. Their sneaped
squirmings upon the sofa were terrible to witness. But
Mr. Ziegler's sensibility was apparently quite unaffected.
He continued to smile, to drink, and to smoke. He seemed
to be saying to himself: "What does it matter to me that

this miserable Frenchman has caught me in a mistake? I could eat him, and one day I shall eat him."

After a little while Musa snatched out of his right-hand lower waistcoat pocket the tiny wooden "mute" which all violinists carry without fail upon all occasions in all their waistcoats; and, sticking it with marvellous rapidity upon the bridge of the violin, he entered upon a pianissimo, but still lively, episode of the Toccata. And simultaneously another melody faint and clear could be heard in the room. It was Mr. Ziegler humming "The Watch on the Rhine" against the Toccata of Debussy. Thus did it occur to Mr. Ziegler to take revenge on Musa for having attempted to humiliate him. Not unsurprisingly, Musa detected at once the competitive air. He continued to play, gazing hard at his violin and apparently entranced, but edging little by little towards Mr. Ziegler. Audrey desired either to give a cry or to run out of the room. She did neither, being held to inaction by the spell of Mr. Ziegler's perfect unconcern as, with the beer glass lifted towards his mouth, he proceeded steadily to work through "The Watch on the Rhine," while Musa lilted out the delicate, gay phrases of Debussy. The enchantment upon the whole room was sinister and painful. Musa got closer to Mr. Ziegler, who did not blench nor cease from his humming. Then suddenly Musa, lowering his fiddle and interrupting the scene, snatched the mute from the bridge of the violin.

"I have put it on the wrong instrument," he said thickly, with a very French intonation, and simultaneously he shoved the mute with violence into the mouth of Mr. Ziegler. In doing so, he jerked up Mr. Ziegler's elbow, and the remains of the beer flew up and baptised Mr. Ziegler's face and vesture. Then he jammed the violin into its case, and ran out of the room.

"*Barbare! Imbécile! Sauvage!*" he muttered ferociously on the threshold.

The enchantment was broken. Everybody rose, and not

the least precipitately the streaming Mr. Ziegler, who, ejecting the mute with much spluttering, and pitching away his empty glass, sprang towards the door, with justifiable homicide in every movement.

"Mr. Ziegler!" Audrey appealed to him, snatching at his dress-coat and sticking to it.

He turned, furious, his face still dripping the finest Pilsener beer.

"If your dress-coat is not wiped instantly, it will be ruined," said Audrey.

"*Ach! Meiner Frack!*" exclaimed Mr. Ziegler, forgetting his deep knowledge of English.   His economic instincts had been swiftly aroused, and they dominated all the other instincts.   "*Meiner Frack!*   Vill you vipe it? " His glance was imploring.

"Oh! Mrs. Spatt will attend to it," said Audrey with solemnity, and walked out of the room into the hall.   There was not a sign of Musa; the disappearance of the violinist was disquieting; and yet it made her glad—so much so that she laughed aloud.   A few moments later Mr. Ziegler stalked forth from the house which he was never to enter again, and his silent scorn and the grandeur of his displeasure were terrific.   He entirely ignored Audrey, who had nevertheless been the means of saving his *Frack* for him.

CHAPTER XXVI

NOCTURNE

Soon afterwards Audrey, who had put on a hat, went out with Mr. Spatt to look for Musa. Not until shortly before the musical performance had the Spatts succeeded in persuading Musa to "accept their hospitality for the night." (The phrase was their own. They were incapable of saying "Let us put you up.") Meanwhile his bag had been left in the hall. This bag had now vanished. The parlourmaid, questioned, said frigidly that she had not touched it because she had received no orders to touch it. Musa himself must therefore have removed it. With bag in one hand and fiddle case in the other, he must have fled, relinquishing nothing but the mute in his flight. He knew naught of England, naught of Frinton, and he was the least practical creature alive. Hence Audrey, who was in essence his mother, and who knew Frinton as some people know London, had said that she would go and look for him. Mr. Spatt, ever chivalrous, had impulsively offered to accompany her. He could indeed do no less. Mrs. Spatt, overwhelmed by the tragic sequel to her innocent triumphant, had retired to the first floor.

The wind blew, and it was very dark, as Audrey and her squire passed along Third Avenue to the front. They did not converse—they were both too shy, too impressed by the peculiarity of the predicament. They simply peered. They peered everywhere for the truant form of Musa balanced on one side by a bag and on the other by a fiddle case. From the trim houses, each without exception new, twinkled discreet lights, with glimpses of surpassingly

correct domesticity, and the wind rustled loudly through the
foliage of the prim gardens, ruffling them as it might have
ruffled the unwilling hair of the daughters of an arch-
deacon. Nobody was abroad. Absurd thoughts ran
through Audrey's head. A letter from Mr. Foulger had
followed her to Birmingham, and in the letter Mr. Foulger
had acquainted her with the fact that Great Mexican Oil
shares had just risen to £2 3s. apiece. She knew that she
had 180,000 of them, and now under the thin protection of
Mr. Spatt she tried to reckon 180,000 times £2 3s. She
could not do the sum. At any rate she could not be sure
that she did it correctly. However, she was fairly well convinced beneath the dark, impenetrable sky that the answer
totalled nearly £400,000, that was, ten million francs.
And the ridiculousness of an heiress who owned over ten
million francs wandering about a place like Frinton with a
man like Mr. Spatt, searching for another man like Musa,
struck her as exceeding the bounds of the permissible. She
considered that she ought to have been in a magnificent
drawing-room of her own in Park Lane or the Avenue du
Bois de Boulogne, welcoming counts, princes, duchesses,
diplomats and self-possessed geniuses of finished manners,
with witty phrase that displayed familiarity with all that
was profoundest and most brilliant in European civilisation.
Life seemed to be disappointing her, and assuredly money
was not the thing that she had imagined it to be.

She thought :

"If this walking lamp-post does not say something soon
I shall scream."

Mr. Spatt said :

"It seems to be blowing up for rain."

She screamed in the silent solitude of Frinton.

"I'm so sorry," she apologised quickly. "I thought I
saw something move."

"One does," faltered Mr. Spatt.

They were now in the shopping street, where in the
mornings the elect encounter each other on expeditions to

purchase bridge-markers, chocolate, bathing costumes and tennis balls. It was a black and empty canyon through which the wind raced.

"He may be down—down on the shore," Mr. Spatt timidly suggested. He seemed to be suggesting suicide.

They turned and descended across the Greensward to the shore, which was lined with hundreds of bathing huts, each christened with a name, and each deserted, for the by-laws of the Frinton Urban District Council judiciously forbade that the huts should be used as sleeping-chambers. The tide was very low. They walked over the wide flat sands, and came at length to the sea's roar, the white tumbling of foamy breakers, and the full force of the southeast wind. Across the invisible expanse of water could be discerned the beam of a lightship. And Audrey was aware of mysterious sensations such as she had not had since she inhabited Flank Hall and used to steal out at nights to watch the estuary. And she thought solemnly : "Musa is somewhere near, existing." And then she thought : "What a silly thought ! Of course he is ! "

"I see somebody coming ! " Mr. Spatt burst out in a dramatic whisper. But the precaution of whispering was useless, because the next instant, in spite of himself, he loudly sneezed.

And about two hundred yards off on the sands Audrey made out a moving figure, which at that distance did in fact seem to have vague appendages that might have resembled a bag and a fiddle case. But the atmosphere of the night was deceptive, and the figure as it approached resolved itself into three figures—a black one in the middle of two white ones. A girl's coarse laugh came down the wind. It could not conceivably have been the laugh of any girl who went into the shopping street to buy bridge-markers, chocolate, bathing costumes or tennis balls. But it might have been—it not improbably was—the laugh of some girl whose mission was to sell such things. The trio meandered past, heedless. Mr. Spatt said no word, but he appreciably winced. The black figure in the midst of the two white ones was that of his son Siegfried, reputedly so fond of Debussy. As the group receded and faded, a fragment of a music-hall song floated away from it into the firmament.

"I'm afraid it's not much use looking any longer," said Mr. Spatt weakly. "He—he may have gone back to the house. Let us hope so."

At the chief garden gate of the Spatt residence they came upon Miss Nickall, trying to open it. The sling round her arm made her unmistakable. And Miss Nickall having allowed them to recover from a pardonable astonishment at the sight of her who was supposed to be exhausted and in bed, said cheerfully :

"I've found him, and I've put him up at the Excelsior Hotel."

Mrs. Spatt had related the terrible episode to her guest, who had wilfully risen at once. Miss Nickall had had luck, but Audrey had to admit that these American girls were stupendously equal to an emergency. And she hated the angelic Nick for having found Musa.

"We tried first to find a café," said Nick. "But there aren't any in this city. What do you call them in England—public-houses, isn't it ? "

"No," agreed Mr. Spatt in a shaking voice. "Public-houses are not permitted in Frinton, I am glad to say." And he began to form an intention, subject to Aurora's approval, to withdraw altogether from the suffrage movement, which appeared to him to be getting out of hand.

As they were all separating for the night Audrey and Nick hesitated for a moment in front of each other, and then they kissed with a quite unusual effusiveness.

"I don't think I've ever really liked her," said Audrey to herself.

What Nick said to herself is lost to history.

CHAPTER XXVII

THE next morning, after a night spent chiefly in thought, Audrey issued forth rather early. Indeed she was probably the first person afoot in the house of the Spatts, the parlourmaid entering the hall just as Audrey had managed to open the front door. As the parlourmaid was obviously not yet in that fullness and spruceness of attire which parlourmaids affect when performing their mission in life, Audrey decided to offer no remark, explanatory or otherwise, and passed into the garden with nonchalance as though her invariable habit when staying in strange houses was to get up before anybody else and spy out the whole property while the helpless hosts were yet in bed and asleep.

Now it was a magnificent morning : no wind, no cloud, and the sun rising over the sea; not a trace of the previous evening's weather. Audrey had not been in the leafy street more than a moment when she forgot that she was tired and short of sleep, and also very worried by affairs both private and public. Her body responded to the sun, and her mind also. She felt almost magically healthy, strong and mettlesome, and, further, she began to feel happy; she rather blamed herself for this tendency to feel happy, calling herself heedless and indifferent. She did not understand what it is to be young. She had risen partly because of the futility of bed, but more because of a desire to inspect again her own part of the world after the unprecedented absence from it.

Frinton was within the borders of her own part of the world, and, though she now regarded it with the condescend-

ing eyes of a Parisian and Londoner, she found pleasure in
looking upon it and in recognising old landmarks and recent
innovations.   She saw, on the Greensward separating the
promenade from the beach, that a rustic seat had been
elaborately built by the Council round the great trunk of the
only tree in Frinton; and she decided that there had been
questionable changes since her time.   And in this way she
went on.   However, the splendour and reality of the sun,
making such an overwhelming contrast with the insub-
stantial phenomena of the gloomy night, prevented undue
cerebral activity.   She reflected that Frinton on a dark night
and Frinton on a bright morning were not like the same
place, and she left it at that, and gazed at the façade of the
Excelsior Hotel, wondering for an instant why she should be
interested in it, and then looking swiftly away.

She had to glance at all the shops, though none of
them was open except the dairy-shop; and in the shopping street, which had a sunrise at one end and the
railway station at the other, she lit on the new palatial
garage.

"My car may be in there," she thought.

After the manner of most car-owners on tour, she had
allowed the chauffeur to disappear with the car in the
evening where he listed, confident that the next morning
he and it would reappear cleansed and in good running
order.

The car was in the garage, almost solitary on a floor
of asphalt under a glass roof.   An untidy youth, with the
end of a cigarette clinging to his upper lip in a way to
suggest that it had clung there throughout the night and
was the last vestige of a jollification, seemed to be dragging
a length of hose from a hydrant towards the car, the while
his eyes rested on a large notice: "Smoking absolutely
prohibited.   By order."

Then from the other extremity of the garage came a
jaunty, dapper, quasi-martial figure, in a new grey uniform,
with a peaked grey cap, bright brown leggings, and bright

brown boots to match—the whole highly brushed, polished, smooth and glittering. This being pulled out of his pocket a superb pair of kid gloves, then a silver cigarette-case, and then a silver match-box, and he ignited a cigarette—the unrivalled, wondrous first cigarette of the day—casting down the match with a large, free gesture. At sight of him the untidy youth grew more active.

"Look 'ere," said the being to the youth, "what the 'ell time did I tell you to have that car cleaned by, and you not begun it!"

Pointing to the clock, he lounged magnificently to and fro, spreading smoke around the intimidated and now industrious youth. The next second he caught sight of Audrey, and transformed himself instantaneously into what she had hitherto imagined a chauffeur always was; but in those few moments she had learnt that the essence of a chauffeur is godlike, and that he toils not, neither does he swab.

"Good morning, madam," in a soft, courtly voice.

"Good morning."

"Were you wanting the car, madam?"

She was not, but the suggestion gave her an idea.

"Can we take it as it is?"

"Yes, madam. I'll just look at the petrol gauge . . . But . . . I haven't had my breakfast, madam."

"What time do you have it?"

"Well, madam, when you have yours."

"That's all right, then. You've got hours yet. I want you to take me to Flank Hall."

"Flank Hall, madam?" His tone expressed the fact that his mind was a blank as to Flank Hall.

As soon as Audrey had comprehended that the situation of Flank Hall was not necessarily known to every chauffeur in England, and that a stay of one night in Frinton might not have been enough to familiarise this particular one with the geography of the entire district, she replied that she would direct him.

They were held up by a train at the railway crossing, and a milk-cart and a young pedestrian were also held up. When Audrey identified the pedestrian she wished momentarily that she had not set out on the expedition. Then she said to herself that really it did not matter, and why should she be afraid . . . etc., etc. The pedestrian was Musa. In French they greeted each other stiffly, like distant acquaintances, and the train thundered past.

"I was taking the air, simply, Madame," said Musa, with his ingenuous shy smile.

"Take it in my car," said Audrey with a sudden resolve. "In one hour at the latest we shall have returned."

She had a great deal to say to him and a great deal to listen to, and there could not possibly be any occasion equal to the present, which was ideal.

He got in; the chauffeur manœuvred to oust the milk-cart from its rightful precedence, the gates opened, and the car swung at gathering speed into the well-remembered road to Moze. And the two passengers said nothing to each other of the slightest import. Musa's escape from Paris was between them; the unimaginable episode at the Spatts was between them; the sleepless night was between them. (And had she not saved him by her presence of mind from the murderous hand of Mr. Ziegler?) They had a million things to impart. And yet naught was uttered save a few banalities about the weather and about the healthfulness of being up early. They were bashful, constrained, altogether too young and inexperienced. They wanted to behave in the grand, social, easeful manner of a celebrated public performer and an heiress worth ten million francs. And they could only succeed in being a boy and a girl. The chauffeur alone, at from thirty to forty miles an hour, was worthy of himself and his high vocation. Both the passengers regretted that they had left their beds. Happily the car laughed at the alleged distance between Frinton and Moze. In a few minutes, as it seemed, with but one false turning, due to the impetuosity of the chauffeur, the vehicle drew up before the gates of Flank Hall. Audrey had avoided the village of Moze. The passengers descended.

"This is my house," Audrey murmured.

The gates were shut but not locked. They creaked as Audrey pushed against them. The drive was covered with a soft film of green, as though it were gradually being entombed in the past. The young roses, however, belonged emphatically to the present. Dewdrops hung from them like jewels, and their odour filled the air. Audrey turned off the main drive towards the garden front of the house, which had always been the aspect that she preferred, and at the same moment she saw the house windows and the thrilling perspective of Mozewater. One of the windows was open. She was glad, because this proved that the perfect Aguilar, gardener and caretaker, was after all imperfect. It was his crusty perfection that had ever set Audrey, and others, against Aguilar. But he had gone to bed and forgotten a window—and it was the French window. While, in her suddenly revived character of a harsh Essex inhabitant, she was thinking of some sarcastic word to say to Aguilar about the window, another window slowly opened from within, and Aguilar's head became visible. Once more he had exasperatingly proved his perfection. He had not gone to bed and forgotten a window. But he had risen with exemplary earliness to give air to the house.

"'d mornin', miss," mumbled the unsmiling Aguilar, impassively, as though Audrey had never been away from Moze.

"Well, Aguilar."

"I didn't expect ye so early, miss."

"But how could you be expecting me at all?"

"Miss Ingate come home yesterday. She said you couldn't be far off, miss."

"Not Miss . . . *Mrs.*—Moncreiff," said Audrey.

"I beg your pardon, madam," Aguilar responded with absolute imperturbability. "She never said nothing at home."

N

And he proceeded mechanically to the next window.

The yard-dog began to bark. Audrey, ignoring Musa, went round the shrubbery towards the kennel. The chained dog continued to bark, furiously, until Audrey was within six feet of him, and then he crouched and squirmed and gave low whines and his tail wagged with extreme rapidity. Audrey bent down, trembling. . . . She could scarcely see. . . . There was something about the green film on the drive, about the look of the house, about the sheeted drawing-room glimpsed through the open window, about the view of Mozewater . . . ! She felt acutely and painfully sorry for, and yet envious of, the young girl in a plain blue frock who used to haunt the house and the garden, and who had somehow made the house and the garden holy for evermore by her unhappiness and her longings. . . . Audrey was crying. . . . She heard a step and stood upright. It was Musa's step.

"I have never seen you so exquisite," said Musa in a murmur subdued and yet enthusiastic. All his faculties seemed to be dwelling reflectively upon her with passionate appreciation.

They had at last begun to talk, really—he in French, and she partly in French and partly in English. It was her tears, or perhaps her gesture in trying to master them, that had loosed their tongues. The ancient dog was forgotten, and could not understand why. Audrey was excusably startled by Musa's words and tone, and by the sudden change in his attitude. She thought that his personal distinction at the moment was different from and superior to any other in her experience. She had a comfortable feeling of condescension towards Nick and towards Jane Foley. And at the same time she blamed Musa, perceiving that as usual he was behaving like a child who cannot grasp the great fact that life is very serious.

"Yes," she said. "That's all very fine, that is. You pretend this, that, and the other. But why are you here? Why aren't you at work in Paris? You've got the chance of a lifetime, and instead of staying at home and practising hard and preparing yourself, you come gadding over to England simply because there's a bit of money in your pocket!"

She was very young, and in the splendour of the magnificent morning she looked the emblem of simplicity; but in her heart she was his mother, his sole fount of wisdom and energy and shrewdness.

Pain showed in his sensitive features, and then appeal, and then a hot determination.

"I came because I could not work," he said.

"Because you couldn't work? Why couldn't you work?" There was no yielding in her hard voice.

"I don't know! I don't know! I suppose it is because you are not there, because you have made yourself necessary to me; or," he corrected quickly, "because *I* have made you necessary to myself. Oh! I can practise for so many hours per day. But it is useless. It is not authentic practice. I think not of the music. It is as if some other person was playing, with my arm, on my violin. I am not there. I am with you, where you are. It is the same day after day, every day, every day. I am done for. I am convinced that I am done for. These concerts will infallibly be my ruin, and I shall be shamed before all Paris."

"And did you come to England to tell me this?"

"Yes."

She was relieved, for she had thought of another explanation of his escapade, and had that explanation proved to be the true one, she was very ready to make unpleasantness to the best of her ability. Nevertheless, though relieved in one direction, she was gravely worried in another. She had undertaken the job of setting Musa grandiosely on his artistic career, and the difficulties of it were growing more and more complex and redoubtable.

She said:

"But you seemed so jolly when you arrived last night. Nobody would have guessed you had a care in the world."

"I had not," he replied eagerly, "as soon as I saw you. The surprise of seeing you—it was that. . . . And you left Paris without saying good-bye! Why did you leave Paris without saying good-bye? Never since the moment when I learnt that you had gone have I had the soul to practise. My violin became a wooden box; my fingers, too, were of wood."

He stopped. The dog sniffed round.

Audrey was melting in bliss. She could feel herself dissolving. Her pleasure was terrible. It was true that she had left Paris without saying good-bye to Musa. She had done it on purpose. Why? She did not know. Perhaps out of naughtiness, perhaps. . . . She was aware that she could be hard, like her father. But she was glad, intensely glad, that she had left Paris so, because the result had been this avowal. She, Audrey, little Audrey, scarcely yet convinced that she was grown up, was necessary to the genius whom all the Quarter worshipped! Miss Thompkins was not necessary to him, Miss Nickall was not necessary to him, though both had helped to provide the means to keep him alive. She herself alone was necessary to him. And she had not guessed it. She had not even hoped for it. The effect of her personality upon Musa was mysterious —she did not affect to understand it—but it was obviously real and it was vital. If anything in the world could surpass the pleasure, her pride surpassed it. All tears were forgotten. She was the proudest young woman in the world; and she was the wisest, and the most harassed, too. But the anxieties were delicious to her.

"I am essential to him," she thought ecstatically. "I stand between him and disaster. When he has succeeded his success will be my work and nobody else's. I have a mission. I must live for it. . . . If anyone had told me a year ago that a great French genius would be absolutely dependent upon me, and that I meant for him all the difference between failure and triumph, I should have laughed. . . . And yet! . . ." She looked at him surreptitiously. "He's an angel. But he's also a baby." The feelings of motherhood were as naught compared to hers.

Then she remarked harshly, icily :

"Well, I shall be much obliged if you will go back to Paris at once—to-day. *Somebody* must have a little sense."

Just at this point Aguilar interrupted. He came slouching round the corner of the clipped bushes, untidy, shabby, implacable, with some set purpose in his hard blue eyes. She could have annihilated him with satisfaction, but the fellow was indestructible as well as implacable.

"Could I have a word with ye, madam?" he mumbled, putting on his well-known air of chicane.

With the unexplained Musa close by her she could not answer: "Wait a little. I'm engaged." She had to be careful. She had to make out especially that she and the young man were up to nothing in particular, nothing that had the slightest importance.

"What is it, Aguilar?" she questioned, inimically.

"It's down here," said Aguilar, who recked not of the implications of a tone. And by the mere force of his glance he drew his mistress away, out of sight of Musa and the dog.

"Is that your motor-car at the gates, madam?" he demanded gloomily and confidentially, his gaze now fixed on the ground or on his patched boots.

"Of course it is," said Audrey. "Why, what's the matter?"

"That's all right then," said he. "But I thought it might belong to another person, and I had to make sure. Now if ye'll just step along a bit farther, I've a little thing as I want to point out to ye, madam. It's my duty to point it out, let others say *what* they will."

He walked ahead doggedly, and Audrey crossly came after, until they arrived nearly at the end of the hedge which, separating the upper from the lower garden, hid from those immediately behind it all view of the estuary. Here, still sheltered by the hedge, he stopped and Audrey stopped, and Aguilar absently plucked up a young plantain from the turf and dropped it into his pocket.

"There's been a man a-hanging round this place since yesterday mornin'," said Aguilar intimately. "I call him a suspicious character—at least, I *did*, till last night. He ain't slept in the village, that I do know, but he's about again this morning."

"Well," said Audrey with impatience. "Why don't you tell Inspector Keeble? Or have you quarrelled with Inspector Keeble again?"

"It's not that as would ha' stopped me from acquainting Inspector Keeble with the circumstances if I thought it my duty so to do," replied Aguilar. "But the fact is I saw the chap talking to Inspector Keeble yesterday evening. He don't know as I saw him. It was that as made me think; now is he a suspicious character or ain't he? Of course Keeble's a rare simple-minded 'un, as we all know."

"And what do you want me to do?"

"I thought you might like to have a look at him yeself, madam. And if you'll just peep round the end of this hedge casual-like, ye'll see him walking across the salting from Lousey Hard. He's a-comin' this way. Casual-like now— and he won't see ye."

Audrey had to obey. She peeped casual-like, and she did in fact see a man on the salting, and this man was getting nearer. She could see him very plainly in the brilliant clearness of the summer morning. After the shortest instant of hesitation she recognised him beyond any doubt. It was the detective who had been so plenteously baptised by Susan Foley in the area of the house at Paget Gardens. Aguilar looked at Audrey, and Audrey annoyed herself somewhat by blushing. However, an agreeable elation quickly overcame the blush.

CHAPTER XXVIII

ENCOUNTER

"Good morning," Audrey cried, very gaily, to the still advancing detective, who, after the slightest hesitation in the world, responded gaily :

"Good morning."

The man's accent struck her. She said to herself, with amusement :

"He's Irish ! "

Audrey had left the astonished but dispassionate gardener at the hedge, and was now emerging from the scanty and dishevelled plantation close to the boundary wall of the estate. She supposed that the police must have been on her track and on the track of Jane Foley, and that by some mysterious skill they had hunted her down. But she did not care. She was not in the least afraid. The sudden vision of a jail did not affright her. On the contrary her chief sensation was one of joyous self-confidence, which sensation had been produced in her by the remarks and the attitude of Musa. She had always known that she was both shy and adventurous, and that the two qualities were mutually contradictory ; but now it appeared to her that diffidence had been destroyed, and that that change which she had ever longed for in her constitution had at least really come to pass.

"You don't seem very surprised to see me," said Audrey.

"Well, madam," said the detective, "I'm not paid to be surprised—in my business."

He had raised his hat. He was standing on the dyke, and from that height he looked somewhat down upon

Audrey leaning against the wall. The watercourse and the strip of eternally emerald-green grass separated them. Though neither tall nor particularly handsome, he was a personable man, with a ready smile and alert, agile movements. Audrey was too far off to judge of his eyes, but she was quite sure that they twinkled. The contrast between this smart, cheerful fellow and the half-drowned victim in the area of the house in Paget Gardens was quite acute.

"Now I've a good mind to hold a meeting for your benefit," said Audrey, striving to recall the proper phrases of propaganda which she had heard in the proper quarters in London during her brief connection with the cause. However, she could not recall them, "But there's no need to," she added. "A gentleman of your intelligence must be of our way of thinking."

"About what?"

"About the vote, of course. And so your conduct is all the more shocking."

"Why!" he exclaimed, laughing. "If it comes to that, your own sex is against you."

Audrey had heard this argument before, and it had the same effect on her as on most other stalwarts of the new political creed. It annoyed her, because there was something in it.

"The vast majority of women are with us," said she.

"My wife isn't."

"But your wife isn't the vast majority of women," Audrey protested.

"Oh yes, she is," said the detective, "so far as I'm concerned. Every wife is, so far as her husband is concerned. Sure, you ought to know that!" In his Irish way he doubled the "r" of the word "sure," and somehow this trick made Audrey like him still more. "My wife believes," he concluded, "that woman's sphere is the home."

("His wife is stout," Audrey decided within herself, on

no grounds whatever. "If she wasn't, she couldn't be a vast majority.")

Aloud she said:

"Well, then, why can't you leave them alone in their sphere, instead of worrying them and spying on them down areas?"

"D'ye mean at Paget Gardens?"

"Of course."

"Oh!" he laughed. "That wasn't professional—if you'll excuse me being so frank. That was just due to human admiration. It's not illegal to admire a young woman, I suppose, even if she is a suffragette."

"What young woman are you talking about?"

"Miss Susan Foley, of course. I won't tell you what I think of her, in spite of all she did, because I've learnt that it's a mistake to praise one woman to another. But I don't mind admitting that her going off to the north has made me life a blank. If I'd thought she'd go, I should never have reported the affair at the Yard. But I was annoyed, and I'm rather hasty." He paused, and ended reflectively: "I committed follies to get a word with the young lady, and I didn't get it, but I'd do the same again."

"And you a married man!" Audrey burst out, startled, and diverted, at the explanation, but at the same time outraged by a confession so cynical.

The detective pulled a silky moustache.

"When a wife is very strongly convinced that her sphere is the home," he retorted slowly and seriously, "you're tempted at times to let her have the sphere all to herself. That's the universal experience of married men, and ye may believe me, miss—madam."

Audrey said:

"And now Miss Foley's gone north, you've decided to come and admire *me* in *my* home!"

"So it is your home!" murmured the detective with an uncontrolled quickness which wakened Audrey's old suspicions afresh—and which created a new suspicion, the

suspicion that the fellow was simply playing with her.
"I assure you I came here to recover; I'd heard it was
the finest climate in England."

"Recover?"

"Yes, from fire-extinguishers. D'ye know I coughed
for twenty-four hours after that reception? . . . And you
should have seen my clothes! The doctor says my lungs
may never get over it. . . . That's what comes of
admiration."

"It's what comes of behaving as no married man ought
to behave."

"Did I say I was married?" asked the detective with
an ingenuous air. "Well, I may be. But I dare say I'm
only married just about as much as you are yourself,
madam."

Upon this remark he raised his hat and departed along
the grassy summit of the sea-wall.

Audrey flushed for the second time that morning, and
more strikingly than before. She was extremely discon-
tented with, and ashamed of, herself, for she had meant
to be the equal of the detective, and she had not been.
It was blazingly clear that he had indeed played with her
—or, as she put it in her own mind: "He just stuffed
me up all through."

She tried to think logically. Had he been pursuing
the motor-car all the way from Birmingham? Obviously
he had not, since according to Aguilar he had been in the
vicinity of Moze since the previous morning. Hence he
did not know that Audrey was involved in the Blue City
affair, and he did not know that Jane Foley was at
Frinton. How he had learnt that Audrey belonged to
Moze, and why and what he had come to investigate at
Moze, she could not guess. Nor did these problems appear
to her to have an importance at all equal to the importance
of hiding from the detective that she had been staying
at Frinton. If he followed her to Frinton he would inevitably discover that Jane Foley was at Frinton, and the

sequel would be more imprisonment for Jane. Therefore Audrey must not return to Frinton. Having by a masterly process of ratiocination reached this conclusion, she began to think rather better of herself, and ceased blushing.

"Aguilar," she demanded excitedly, having gone back through the plantation. "Did Miss Ingate happen to say where I was staying last night?"

"No, madam."

"I must run into the house and write a note to her, and you must take it down instantly." In her mind she framed the note, which was to condemn Miss Ingate to the torture of complete and everlasting silence about the episode at the Blue City and the flight eastwards.

CHAPTER XXIX

FLIGHT

"Fast, madam, did you say?" asked the chauffeur, bending his head back from the wheel as the car left the gates of Flank Hall.

"Fast."

"The Colchester road?"

"Yes."

"It's really just as quick to take the Frinton road for Colchester—it's so much straighter."

"No, no, no! On no account. Don't go near Frinton."

Audrey leaned back in the car. And as speed increased the magnificence of the morning again had its effect on her. The adventure pleased her far more than the perils of it, either for herself or for other people, frightened her. She knew that she was doing a very strange thing in thus leaving the Spatts and her luggage without a word of explanation before breakfast; but she did not care. She knew that for some reason which she did not comprehend the police were after her, as they had been after nearly all the great ones of the movement; but she did not care. She was alive in the rushing car amid the magnificence of the morning. Musa sat next to her. She had more or less incompletely explained the situation to him—it was not necessary to tell everything to a boy who depended upon you absolutely for his highest welfare— such boys must accept, thankfully, what they received. And Musa had indeed done so. He appeared to be quite happy and without anxieties. Ah! That was the worst of Musa—his irresponsibility, his short memory for trouble.

He had wanted to be with her, and he was with her, and he cared for nothing else. He had no interest in what might happen next. He yielded himself utterly to the enjoyment of her presence and of the magnificent morning.

And yet Musa, whom Audrey considered that she understood as profoundly as any mother had ever understood any child—even Musa could surprise.

He said, without any preparation:

"I calculate that I shall have 3,040 francs in hand after the concerts, assuming that I receive only the minimum. That is, after paying the expenses of my living."

"But do you know how much it costs you to live?" Audrey demanded, with careless superiority.

"Assuredly. I write all my payments down in a little book. I have done so since some years."

"Every sou?"

"Yes. Every sou."

"But do you save, Musa?"

"Save!" he repeated the word ingenuously. "Till now to save has been impossible for me. But I have always kept in hand one month's subsistence. I could not do more. Now I shall save. You reproached me with having spent money in order to come to see you in England. But I regarded the money so spent as part of the finance of the concerts. Without seeing you I could not practise. Without practice I could not play. Without playing I could not earn money. Therefore I spent money in order to get money. Such, Madame, was the commercial side. What a beautiful lawn for tennis you have in your garden!"

Audrey was more than surprised, she was staggered by the revelation of the attitude of genius towards money. She had not suspected it. Then she remembered the simple natural tone in which Musa had once told her that both Tommy and Nick contributed to his income. She ought to have comprehended from that avowal more than she, in fact, had comprehended. And now the first hopes of worldly success were strongly developing that unsuspected trait in the young man's character. Audrey was aware of a great fear. Could he be a genius, after all? Was it conceivable that an authentic musical genius should enter up daily in a little book every sou he spent?

A rapid, spitting, explosive sound, close behind the car and a little to the right, took her mind away from Musa and back to the adventure. She looked round, half expecting what she should see—and she saw it, namely, the detective on a motor-cycle. It was an "Indian" machine and painted red. And as she looked, the car, after taking a corner, got into a straight bit of the splendid road and the motor-bicycle dropped away from it.

"Can't you shake off that motor-bicycle thing?" Audrey rather superciliously asked the chauffeur.

Having first looked at his mirror, the chauffeur, who, like a horse, could see in two directions at once, gazed cautiously at the road in front and at the motor-bicycle behind, simultaneously.

"I doubt it, madam," he said. And yet his tone and glance expressed deep scorn of the motor-bicycle. "As a general rule you can't."

"I should have thought you could beat a little thing like that," said Audrey.

"Them things can do sixty when they've a mind to," said the chauffeur, with finality, and gave all his attention to the road.

At intervals he looked at his mirror. The motor-bicycle had vanished into the past, and as it failed to reappear he gradually grew confident and disdainful. But just as the car was going down the short hill into the outskirts of Colchester the motor-bicycle came into view once more.

"Where to, madam?" inquired the chauffeur.

"This is Colchester, isn't it?" she demanded nervously, though she knew perfectly well that it was Colchester.

"Yes, madam."

"Straight through! Straight through!"

"The London road?"

"Yes. The London road," she agreed. London was, of course, the only possible destination.

"But breakfast, madam?"

"Oh! The usual thing," said Audrey. "You'll have yours when I have mine."

"But we shall run out of petrol, madam."

"Never mind," said Audrey sublimely.

The chauffeur, with characteristic skill, arranged that the car should run out of petrol precisely in front of the best hotel in Chelmsford, which was about half-way to London. The motor-bicycle had not been seen for several miles. But scarcely had they resumed the journey, by the Epping road, when it came again into view—in front of them. How had the fellow guessed that they would take the longer Epping road instead of the shorter Romford road?

"When shall we be arriving in Frinton?" Musa inquired, beatific.

"We shan't be arriving in Frinton any more," said Audrey. "We must go straight to London."

"It is like a dream," Musa murmured, as it were in ecstasy. Then his features changed and he almost screamed: "But my violin! My violin! We must go back for it."

"Violin!" said Audrey. "That's nothing! I've even come without gloves." And she had.

She reassured Musa as to the violin, and the chauffeur as to the abandoned Gladstone bag containing the chauffeur's personal effects, and herself as to many things. An hour and twenty minutes later the car, with three people in it, thickly dusted even to the eyebrows, drew up in the courtyard of Charing Cross railway station, and the motor-cycle was visible, its glaring red somewhat paled, in the Strand outside. The time was ten-fifteen.

"We shall take the eleven o'clock boat train for Paris," she said to Musa.

"You also?"

She nodded. He was in heaven. He could even do without his violin.

"How nice it is not to be bothered with luggage," she said.

The chauffeur was pacified with money, of which Audrey had a sufficiency.

And all the time Audrey kept saying to herself:

"I'm not going to Paris to please Musa, so don't let him think it! I'm only going so as to put the detective off and keep Jane Foley out of his clutches, because if I stay in London he'll be bound to find everything out."

While Musa kept watch for the detective at the door of the telegraph office Audrey telegraphed, as laconically as possible, to Frinton concerning clothes and the violin, and then they descended to subterranean marble chambers in order to get rid of dust, and they came up to earth again, each out of a separate cellar, renewed. And, lastly, Audrey slipped into the Strand and bought a pair of gloves, and thereafter felt herself to be completely equipped against the world's gaze.

CHAPTER XXX

ARIADNE

A few days later an automobile—not Audrey's but a large limousine—bumped, with slow and soft dignity, across the railway lines which diversify the quays of Boulogne harbour and, having hooted in a peculiar manner, came to a stop opposite nothing in particular.

"Here we are," said Mr. Gilman, reaching to open the door. "You can see her masthead light."

It was getting dark. Behind, over the station, a very faint flush lightened the west, and in front, across the water, and reflected in the water, the thousand lamps of the own rose in tiers to the lofty church which stood out a dark mass against the summer sky. On the quays the forms of men moved vaguely among crates and packages, and on the water, tugs and boats flitted about, puffing, or with the plash of oars, or with no sound whatever. And from the distance arrived the reverberation of electric trams running their courses in the maze of the town.

Madame Piriac and Audrey descended, after Mr. Gilman, from the car and Mr. Gilman turned off the electric light in the interior and shut the door.

"Do not trouble about the luggage, I beg you," said Mr. Gilman, breathing, as usual, rather noticeably. "*Bon soir*, Leroux. Don't forget to meet the nine-thirty-five." This last to the white-clad chauffeur, who saluted sharply.

At the same moment two sailors appeared over the edge of the quay, and a Maltese cross of light burst into radiance at the end of a sloping gangway, whose summit was just perched on the solid masonry of the port. The sailors were clothed in blue, with white caps, and on their breasts they bore the white-embroidered sign: "*Ariadne, R.T.Y.C.*"

"Look lively, lads, with the luggage," said Mr. Gilman.

"Yes, sir."

Then another figure appeared under the Maltese cross. It was clad in white ducks, with a blue reefer ornamented in gold, and a yachting cap crowned in white: a stoutish and middle-aged figure, much like Mr. Gilman himself in bearing and costume, except that Mr. Gilman had no gold on his jacket.

"Well, skipper!" greeted Mr. Gilman, jauntily and spryly. In one moment, in one second, Mr. Gilman had grown at least twenty years younger.

"Captain Wyatt," he presented the skipper to the ladies. "And this is Mr. Price, my secretary, and Doctor Cromarty," as two youths, clothed exactly to match Mr. Gilman, followed the skipper up the steep incline of the gangway.

And now Audrey could see the *Ariadne* lying below, for it was only just past low water and the tide was scarcely making. At the next berth higher up, with lights gleaming at her innumerable portholes and two cranes hard at work producing a mighty racket on her, lay a Channel steamer, which, by comparison with the yacht, loomed enormous, like an Atlantic liner. Indeed, the yacht seemed a very little and a very lowly and a very flimsy flotation on the dark water, and her illuminated deck-house was no better than a toy. On the other hand, her two masts rose out of the deep high overhead and had a certain impressiveness, though not quite enough.

Audrey thought:

"Is this what we're going on? I thought it was a big yacht." And she had a qualm.

And then a bell rang twice, extremely sweet and mellow, somewhere on the yacht. And Audrey was touched by the beauty of its tone.

"Two bells. Nine o'clock," said Mr. Gilman. "Will

you come aboard? I'll show you the way." He tripped down the gangway like a boy. Behind could be heard the sailors giving one another directions about the true method of handling luggage.

Audrey had met Madame Piriac by sheer hazard in a corset shop in the Rue de la Chaussée-d'Antin. The fugitive from justice had been obliged, in the matter of wardrobe, to begin life again on her arrival trunkless in Paris, and the business of doing so was not disagreeable. Madame Piriac had greeted her with most affectionate warmth. One of her first suggestions had been that Audrey should accompany her on a short yachting trip projected by Mr. Gilman. She had said that though the excellent Gilman was her uncle, and her adored uncle, he was not her real uncle, and that therefore, of course, she was incapable of going unaccompanied, though she would hate to disappoint the dear man. As for Monsieur Piriac, the destiny of France was in his hands, and the moment being somewhat critical, he would not quit the Ministry of Foreign Affairs without leaving a fixed telegraphic address.

On the next day Mr. Gilman and Madame Piriac had called on Audrey at the Hôtel du Danube, and the invitation became formal. It was pressing and flattering. Why refuse it? Mr. Gilman was obviously prepared to be her slave. She accepted, with enthusiasm. And she said to herself that in doing so she was putting yet another spoke in the wheel of the British police. Immediately afterwards she learnt that Musa also had been asked. Madame Piriac informed her, in reply to a sort of protest, that Musa's first concert was postponed by the concert agency until the autumn. "I never heard of that!" Audrey had cried. "And why should you have heard of it? Have you not been in England?" Madame Piriac had answered, a little surprised at Audrey's tone. Whereupon Audrey had said naught. The chief point was that Musa could take a holiday without detriment to his career. Moreover, Mr. Gilman, who possessed everything, possessed a marvellous violin, which he would put at the disposal of Musa on the yacht if Musa's own violin had not been found in the meantime. The official story was that Musa's violin had been mislaid or lost on the Métropolitain Railway, and the fact that he had been to England somehow did not transpire at all.

Mr. Gilman had gone forward in advance to make sure that his yacht was in a state worthy to receive two such ladies, and he had insisted on meeting them in his car at Abbeville on the way to Boulogne. He had not insisted on meeting Musa similarly. He was a peculiar and in some respects a stiff-necked man. He had decided, in his own mind, that he would have the two women to himself in the car, and so indeed it fell out. Nevertheless his attitude to Musa, and Madame Piriac's attitude to Musa, and everybody's attitude to Musa, had shown that the mere prospect of star-concerts in a first-class hall had very quickly transformed Musa into a genuine Parisian lion. He was positively courted. His presence on the yacht was deemed an honour, and that was why Mr. Gilman had asked him. Audrey both resented the remarkable change and was proud of it—as a mother perhaps naturally would do and be. The admitted genius was to arrive the next morning.

On boarding the *Ariadne* in the wake of Mr. Gilman and Madame Piriac, the first thing that impressed Audrey was the long gangway itself. It was made of thin resilient steel, and the handrails were of soft white rope, almost like silk, and finished off with fancy knots; and at the beginning of the gangway, on the dirty quay, lay a beautiful mat bearing the name of the goddess, while at the end, on the pale, smooth deck, was another similar mat. The obvious costliness of that gangway and those superlative mats made Audrey feel poor, in spite of her ten million francs. And the next thing that impressed her was that immediately she got down on deck the yacht, in a very mysterious manner, had grown larger, and much larger. At the forward extremity of the deck certain blue figures lounging about seemed to be quite a long way off, indeed in another world.

Here and there on the deck were circles of yellow or white rope, coiled as precisely and perfectly as Audrey could coil her own hair. Mr. Gilman led them to the door of the deck-house and they gazed within. The sight of the interior drew out of the ravished Audrey an ecstatic exclamation : "What a darling ! " And at the words she saw that Mr. Gilman, for all his assumed nonchalant spryness, almost trembled with pleasure. The deck-house was a drawing-room whose walls were of carved and inlaid wood. Orange-shaded electric bulbs hung on short, silk cords from the ceiling, and flowers in sconces showed brilliantly between the windows, which were draped with curtains of silk matching the thick carpet. Several lounge chairs and a table of bird's-eye maple completed the place, and over the table were scattered newspapers and illustrated weeklies. Everything, except the literature, was somewhat diminished in size, but the smallness of the scale only intensified the pleasure derived from the spectacle.

Then they went "downstairs," as Audrey said ; but Mr. Gilman corrected her and said "below," whereupon Audrey retorted that she should call it the "ground floor," and Mr. Gilman laughed as she had never heard a man of his age laugh. The sight of the ground floor still further increased Audrey's notion of the dimensions of the yacht, whose corridors and compartments appeared to stretch away endlessly in two directions. At the foot of the curving staircase Mr. Gilman, pulling aside a curtain, announced : "This is the saloon." When she heard the word Audrey expected a poky cubicle, but found a vast drawing-room with more books than she had ever seen in any other drawing-room, many pictures, an open piano, with music on it; sofas in every quarter, and about a thousand cupboards and drawers, each with a silver knob or handle. Above all was a dome of multi-coloured glass, and exactly beneath the dome a table set for supper, with the finest napery, cutlery and crystal. The apartment was dazzlingly lighted, and yet not a single lamp could be detected in the act of illumination. A real parlourmaid suddenly appeared at the far end of the room, and behind her two stewards in gilt-buttoned white Eton jackets and black trousers. Mr. Gilman, with seriousness, bade the parlourmaid take charge of the ladies and show them the sleeping-cabins.

"Choose any cabins you like," said he, as Madame Piriac and Audrey rustled off.

There might have been hundreds of sleeping-cabins. And there did, in fact, appear to be quite a number of them, to say nothing of two bathrooms. They inspected all of them save one, which was locked. In an awed voice the parlourmaid said, "That is the owner's cabin." At another door she said, in a different, disdainful voice, "That only leads to the galley and the crew's quarters." Audrey wondered what a galley could be, and the mystery of that name, and the mystery of the two closed doors, merely made the whole yacht perfect. The sleeping-cabins surpassed all else—they were so compact, so complex, so utterly complete. No large bedchamber, within Audrey's knowledge, held so much apparatus, and offered so much comfort and so much wardrobe room as even the least of these cabins. It was impossible, to be sure, that in one's amused researches one had not missed a cupboard ingeniously disguised somewhere. And the multiplicity of mirrors, and the message of the laconic monosyllable "Hot" on silver taps, and the discretion of the lighting, all indicated that the architect and creator of these marvellous microcosms had "understood." The cosy virtue of littleness, and the entire absurdity of space for the sake of space, were strikingly proved, and the demonstration amounted, in Audrey's mind, to a new and delicious discovery.

The largest of the cabins had two berths at right angles to one another, each a lovely little bed with a running screen of cashmere. Having admired it once, they returned to it.

"Do you know, my dear," said Madame Piriac in French, "I have an idea. You will tell me if it is not good. . . . If we shared this cabin . . . ! In this so curious

machine one feels a satisfaction, somehow, in being very
near the one to the other. The ceiling is so low. . . . That
gives you sensations—human sensations. . . . I know not
if you experience the same. . . ."

"Oh! Let's!" Audrey exclaimed impulsively in
English. "Do let's!"

When the parlourmaid had gone, and before the luggage
had come down, Madame Piriac caught Audrey to her and
kissed her fervently on both cheeks, amid the glinting confusion of polished woods and draperies and silver mountings
and bevelled glass.

"I am so content that you came, my little one!"
murmured Madame Piriac.

The next minute the cabin and the corridor outside were
full of open trunks and bags, over which bent the forms of
Madame Piriac, Audrey and the parlourmaid. And all the
drawers were gaping, and the doors of all the cupboards
swinging, and the narrow beds were hidden under piles of
variegated garments. And while they were engaged in the
breathless business of installing themselves in the celestial
domain, strange new thoughts flitted about like mice in
Audrey's head. She felt as though she were in a refuge
from the world, and as though her conscience was being
narcotised. In that cabin, firm as solid land and yet floating
on the water, with Mr. Gilman at hand her absolute slave—
in that cabin the propaganda of women's suffrage presented
itself as a very odd and very remote phenomenon, a phenomenon scarcely real. She had positively everything she
wanted without fighting for it. The lion's share of life was
hers. Comfort and luxury were desirable and beautiful
things, not to be cast aside nor scorned. Madame Piriac
was a wise woman and a good woman. She was a happy
woman. . . . There was a great deal of ugliness in sitting
on Joy Wheels and being chased by policemen. True, as she
had heard, a crew of nineteen human beings was necessary
to the existence of Mr. Gilman and his guests on board the
yacht. Well, what then? The nineteen were undoubtedly

well treated and in clover. And the world was the world; you had to take it as you found it. . . . And then in her mind she had a glimpse of the blissful face of Jane Foley— blissful in a different way from any other face she had met in all her life. Disconcerting, this glimpse, for an instant, but only for an instant! She, Audrey, was blissful, too. The intense desire for joy and pleasure surged up in her. . . . The bell which she had previously heard struck three; its delicate note vibrated long through the yacht, unwilling to expire. Half-past nine, and supper and the chivalry of Mr. Gilman waiting for them in the elegance of the saloon!

As the two women approached the *portière* which screened the forward entrance to the saloon, they heard Mr. Gilman say, in a weary and resigned voice:

"Well, I suppose there's nothing better than a whisky and soda."

And the vivacious reply of a steward:

"Very good, sir."

The owner was lounging in a corner, with a gloomy, bored look on his face. But as soon as the *portière* stirred and he saw the smiles of Madame Piriac and Audrey upon him, his whole demeanour changed in an instant. He sprang up, laughed, furtively smoothed his waistcoat, and managed to convey the general idea that he had a keen interest in life, and that the keenest part of that interest was due to a profound instinctive desire to serve these two beautiful benefactors of mankind—the idea apparently being that the charming creatures had conferred a favour on the human race by consenting to exist. He cooed round them, he offered them cushions, he inquired after their physical condition, he expressed his fear lest the cabins had not contained every convenience that caprice might expect. He was excited; surely he was happy! Audrey persuaded herself that this must, after all, be his true normal condition while aboard the yacht, and that the ennui visible on his features a moment earlier could only have been transient and accidental.

"I am sure the piano is as wonderful as all else on board," said Madame Piriac.

"Do play!" he entreated. "I love to hear music here. My secretary plays for me when I am alone."

"I, who do not adore music!" Madame Piriac protested against the invitation. But she sat down on the clamped music stool and began a waltz.

"Ah!" said Mr. Gilman, dropping into a seat by Audrey. "I wish I danced!"

"But you don't mean to say you don't," said Audrey, with fascination. She felt that she could fascinate him, and that it was her duty to fascinate him.

Mr. Gilman responded to the challenge.

"I suppose I do," he said modestly. "We must have a dance on deck one night. I'll tell my secretary to get the gramophone into order. I have a pretty good one."

"How lovely!" Audrey agreed. "I do think the *Ariadne's* the most heavenly thing, Mr. Gilman! I'd no idea what a yacht was! I hope you'll tell me the proper names for all the various parts—you know what I mean. I hate to use the wrong words. It's not polite on a yacht, is it?"

His smile was entranced.

"You and I will go round by ourselves to-morrow morning, Mrs. Moncreiff," he said.

Just then the steward appeared with the whisky and soda, but Mr. Gilman dismissed him with a sharp gesture, and he vanished back into the unexplored parts of the vessel. The implication was that the society of Audrey made whisky and soda a superfluity for Mr. Gilman. Although she was so young, he treated her with exactly the same deference as he lavished on Madame Piriac, indeed with perhaps a little more. If Madame Piriac was for him the incarnation of sweetness and balm and majesty, so also was Audrey, and Audrey had the advantage of novelty. She was growing, morally, every minute. The confession of Musa had filled her with a good notion of herself. The impulsive flattery of Madame Piriac in the joint cabin, and now the sincere, grave homage of Mr. Gilman, caused her to brim over with consciousness that she was at last somebody.

An automobile hooted on the quay, and at the disturbing sound Madame Piriac ceased to play and swung round on the stool.

"That—that must be our other lady guest," said Mr. Gilman, who had developed nervousness ; his cheeks flushed darkly.

"Ah?" cautiously smiled Madame Piriac, who was plainly taken aback.

"Yes," said Mr. Gilman. "Miss Thompkins. Before I knew for certain that Mrs. Moncreiff could come with you, Hortense, I asked Miss Thompkins if she would care to come. I only got her answer this morning—it was delayed. I meant to tell you. . . . You are a friend of Miss Thompkins, aren't you?" He turned to Audrey.

Audrey replied gaily that she knew Tommy very well.

"I'd better go up," said Mr. Gilman, and he departed, and his back, though a nervous back, seemed to be defying Madame Piriac and Audrey to question in the slightest degree his absolute right to choose his own guests on his own yacht.

"Strange man!" muttered Madame Piriac. It was a confidence to Audrey, who eagerly accepted it as such. "Imagine him inviting Mees Thompkins, without a word to us, without a word! But, you know, my dear uncle was always bizarre, mysterious. Yet—is he mysterious, or is he ingenuous?"

"But how did he come to know Miss Thompkins?" Audrey demanded.

"Ah! You have not heard that? Miss Thompkins gave a—a musical tea in her studio, to celebrate these concerts which are to occur. Musa asked the Foas to come. They consented. It was understood they should bring friends. Thus I went also, and Monsieur Gilman being at my orders that afternoon, he went too. Never have I seen so strange a multitude ! But it was amusing. And all Paris has begun to talk of Musa. Miss Thompkins and my uncle became friends on the instant. I assume that it was her eyes. Also those Americans have vivacity, if not always distinction. Do you not think so ? "

"Oh, yes ! And do you mean to say that on the strength of that he asked her to go yachting ? "

"Well, he had called several times."

"Aren't you surprised she accepted ? " asked Audrey.

"No," said Madame Piriac. "It is another code, that is all. It is a surprise, but she will be amusing."

"I'm sure she will," Audrey concurred. "I'm frightfully fond of her myself."

They glanced at each other very intimately, like long-established allies who fear an aggression—and are ready for it.

Then steps were heard. Miss Thompkins entered.

"Well," drawled Miss Thompkins, gazing first at Audrey and then at Madame Piriac. "Of all the loveliest shocks—— Say, Musa——"

Behind her stood Musa. It appeared that he had been able to get away by the same train as Tommy.

CHAPTER XXXI

THE NOSTRUM

THE hemisphere of heaven was drenched in moonlight, and
—rare happening either on British earth or on the waters
surrounding it, in mid-summer—the night was warm. In
the midst of the glittering sea the yacht moved without the
appearance of motion; only by leaning over the rail and
watching the bubbles glide away from her could you detect
her progress. There were no waves, no ripples, nothing
but a scarcely perceptible swell. The gentle breeze, un-
noticeable on deck, was abaft; all the. sails had been
lowered and stowed except the large square sail bent on a
yard to the mainmast and never used except with such a
wind. The *Ariadne* had a strong flood tide under her, and
her 200-h.p. twin motors were stopped. Hence there
was no tremor in the ship and no odour of paraffin in the
nostrils of those who chanced to wander aft of the engine-
room. The deck awning had been rolled up to the centre,
and at the four corners of its frame had been hung four
temporary electric lights within Chinese lanterns. A
radiance ascended from the saloon skylight; the windows
of the deck-house blazed as usual, but the deck-house was
empty; a very subdued glow indicated where the binnacle
was. And, answering these signs of existence, could be
distinguished the red and green lights of steamers, the firm
rays of lighthouses, and the red or white warnings of gas-
buoys run by clockwork.

The figures of men and women—the women in pale
gowns, the men in blue-and-white—lounged or strolled on
the spotless deck which unseen hands swabbed and stoned

every morning at 6 o'clock; and among these figures passed
the figure of a steward with a salver, staying them with
flagons, comforting them with the finest exotic fruit.
Occasionally the huge square sail gave an idle flap. " Get
that lead out, 'Orace," commanded a grim voice from the
wheel. A splash followed, as a man straddled himself over
the starboard bow, swung a weighted line to and fro and
threw it from him. "Four." Another splash. "Four."
Another splash. "Four." Another splash. "Three-half."
Another splash. "Three-half." Another splash. "Three."
Another splash. "Two-half." Another splash. "Three."
Another splash. "Five." "That'll do, 'Orace," came the
voice from the wheel. Then an entranced silence.

The scene had the air of being ideal. And yet it was
not. Something lacked. That something was the owner.
The owner lay indisposed in the sacred owner's cabin. And
this was a pity because a dance had been planned for that
night. It might have taken place without the owner, but
the strains of the gramophone and especially the shuffling
of feet on the deck would have disturbed him. True, he
had sent up word by Doctor Cromarty that he was not to
be considered. But the doctor had delivered the message
without any conviction, and the unanimous decision was
that the owner must, at all costs, be considered.

It was Ostend, on top of the owner's original offer to
Audrey, that had brought about the suggestion of a dance.
They had coasted up round Gris-Nez from Boulogne to
Ostend, and had reached the harbour there barely in time
to escape from the worst of a tempest that had already
begun to produce in the minds of sundry passengers a grave
doubt whether yachting was, after all, the most delightful
of pursuits. Some miles before the white dome of the
Kursaal was sighted the process of moral decadence had set
in, and passengers were lying freely to each other, and
boastfully lying, just as though somebody had been accusing
them of some dreadful crime of cowardice or bad breeding
instead of merely inquiring about the existence of physical

symptoms over which they admittedly had no control whatever. The security of a harbour, with a railway station not
fifty yards from the yacht's bowsprit, had restored them,
by dint of calming secret fears, to their customary condition of righteousness and rectitude. Several days of
gusty rainstorms had elapsed at Ostend, and the passengers
had had the opportunity to study the method of managing
a yacht, and to visit the neighbourhood. The one was as
wondrous as the other. They found letters and British and
French newspapers on their plates at breakfast. And the
first object they had seen on the quay, and the last object
they saw there, was the identical large limousine which they
had left on the quay at Boulogne. It would have taken
them to Ghent but for the owner's powerful objection to
their eating any meal off the yacht. Seemingly he had a
great and sincere horror of local viands and particularly of
local water. He was their slave; they might demand anything from him; he was the very symbol of hospitality and
chivalry, but somehow they could not compass a meal
away from the yacht. Similarly, he would have them leave
the Kursaal not later than ten o'clock, when the evening had
not veritably begun. They did not clearly understand by
what means he imposed his will, but he imposed it.

The departure from Ostend was accomplished after the
glass had begun to rise, but before it had finished rising, and
there were apprehensions in the saloon and out of it, when
the spectacle of the open sea, and the feel of it under the
feet, showed that, as of old, water was still unstable. The
process of moral decadence would have set in once more
but for the prudence and presence of mind of Audrey, who
had laid in a large stock of the specific which had been of
such notable use to herself and Miss Ingate on previous
occasions. Praising openly its virtues, confessing frankly
her own weakness and preaching persuasively her own
faith, she had distributed the nostrum, and in about a
quarter of an hour had established a justifiable confidence.
Mr. Gilman alone would not partake, and indeed she had

THE NOSTRUM

hardly dared to offer the thing to so experienced a sailor.
The day had favoured her. The sea grew steadily more
tranquil, and after skirting the Belgian and French coasts
for some little distance the *Ariadne*, under orders, had
turned her nose boldly northward for the estuary of the
Thames. The *Ariadne* was now in the midst of that very
complicated puzzle of deeps and shallows. The passengers,
in fact, knew that they were in the region of the North
Edinburgh, but what or where the North Edinburgh was
they had only the vaguest idea. The blot on the voyage
had been the indisposition of Mr. Gilman, who had taken
to his berth early, and who saw nobody but his doctor,
through whom he benignantly administered the world of the
yacht. Doctor Cromarty had a face which imparted nothing
and yet implied everything. He said less and meant more
than even the average pure-blooded Scotsman. It was
imparted that Mr. Gilman had a chronic complaint. The
implications were vast and baffling.

"We shall dance after all," said Miss Thompkins, bending with a mysterious gesture over Audrey, who reclined in
a deck-chair near the companion leading to the deserted
engine-room. Miss Thompkins was dressed in lacy white,
with a string of many tinted beads round her slim neck.
Her tawny hair was arranged in a large fluffiness, and the
ensemble showed to a surprised Audrey what Miss
Thompkins could accomplish when she deemed the occasion
to be worthy of an effort.

"Shall we? What makes you think so, dear?" absently
asked Audrey, in whom the scene had induced profound
reflections upon life and the universe.

"He'll come up on deck," said Miss Thompkins, disclosing her teeth in an inscrutable smile that the moonbeams
made more strange than it actually was. "Like to know
how I know? Sure you'd like to know, Mrs. Simplicity?"
Her beads rattled above Audrey's insignificant upturned
nose. "Isn't a yacht the queerest little self-contained state
you ever visited? It's as full of party politics as

Massachusetts; and that's some.   Well, I didn't use all my
medicine you gave me.   Didn't need it.   So I've shared it
with *him*.   I got the empty packet with all the instructions
on it, and I put two of my tablets in it, and if he hasn't
swallowed them by this time my name isn't Anne Tuckett
Thompkins."

"But you don't mean he's been—— "

"Audrey, you're making a noise like a goose.   'Course
I do."

"But how did you manage to——"

"I gave them to Mr. Price, with instructions to leave
them by the—er—bedside.   Mr. Price is a friend.   I hope
I've made that plain these days to everybody, including Mr.
Gilman.   Mr. Price is a good sample of what painters are
liable to come to after they've found out they don't care
for the smell of oil-tubes.   I knew him when he always
said ' Puvis ' instead of ' Puvis de Chavannes.'   He's cured
now.   If I hadn't happened to know he'd be on board I
shouldn't have dared to come.   He's my lifebuoy."

"But I assure you, Tommy, Mr. Gilman refused the
stuff from me.   He did."

"Oh !   Dove !   Wood-pigeon !   Of course he refused it.
He was bound to.   Owner of a two-hundred-and-fifty-ton
yacht taking a remedy for sea-sickness in public on the two-
hundred-and-fifty-ton yacht !   The very idea makes you
shiver.   But he'll take it down there.   And he won't ask
any questions.   And he'll hide it from the doctor.   And
he'll pretend, and he'll expect everybody else to pretend,
that he's never been within a mile of the stuff."

"Tommy, I don't believe you."

"And he's a lovely man, all the same."

"Tommy, I don't believe you."

"Yes, you do.   You'd like not to, but you can't help it.
I sometimes do bruise people badly in their organ of
illusions-about-human-nature, but it is fun, after all,
isn't it ? "

"What ? "

"Getting down to the facts."

Accompanied by the tattoo of her necklace, Miss Thompkins moved away in the direction of Madame Piriac, who was engaged with Musa.

"Admit I'm rather brilliant to-night," she threw over her shoulder.

The dice seem to be always loaded in favour of the Misses Thompkins of society. Less than a quarter of an hour later Doctor Cromarty, showing his head just above the level of the deck, called out:

"Price, ye can wind up that box o' yours. Mr. Gilman is coming on deck. He's wonderful better."

P

CHAPTER XXXII

THE owner was at the wheel. But he had not got there at once. This singular man, who strangely enough was wearing one of his most effulgent and heterogeneous club neckties, had begun by dancing. He danced with all three ladies, one after the other; and he did not merely dance— he danced modernly, he danced the new dances to the new tunes, given off like intoxicating gas from the latest of gramophones. He knew how to hold the arm of a woman above her head, while coiling his own around it in the manner of a snake, and he knew how to make his very body a vast syncopation. The effect of his arrival was as singular as himself. Captain Wyatt, Doctor Cromarty and Mr. Price withdrew to that portion of the deck about the wheel which convention had always roped off for them with invisible ropes. The captain, by custom, messed by himself, whereas the other two had their meals in the saloon, entering and leaving quickly and saying little while at table. But apart from meals the three formed a separate clan on the yacht. The indisposition of the owner had dissolved this clan into the general population of the saloon. The recovery of the owner re-created it. Mr. Price had suddenly begun to live arduously for the gramophone alone. And when summoned by the owner to come and form half of the third couple for dancing, Doctor Cromarty had the air of arousing himself from a meditation upon medicine. Also, the passengers themselves danced with conscientiousness, with elaborate gusto and with an earnest desire to reach a high standard. And between dances everybody

234

went up to Mr. Gilman and said how lovely it all was. And it really was lovely.

Mr. Gilman had taken the wheel after about the sixth dance. Approaching Audrey, who owed him the next dance, he had said that the skipper had hinted something about his taking the wheel and he thought he had better oblige the old fellow, if Audrey was quite, quite sure she didn't mind, and would she come and sit by him instead—for one dance? . . . As soon as two sailors had fixed cushions for Audrey, and the skipper had given the owner the course, all persons seemed to withdraw respectfully from the pair, who were in the shadow of a great spar, with the glimmer of the binnacle just in front of them. The square sail had been lowered, and the engines started, and a steady, faint throb kept the yacht mysteriously alive in every plank of her. The gramophone and the shuffle of feet continued, because Mr. Gilman had expressly desired that his momentary defection with a lady and in obedience to duty should not bring the ball to an end. Laughter and even giggles came from the ballroom. Males were dancing together. The power of the moon had increased. The binnacle-light, however, threw up a radiance of its own on to Mr. Gilman's lowered face, the face of a kind, a good, and a dependably expert individuality who was watching over the safety, the welfare and the highest interests of every soul on board.

"I was very sorry to be laid up to-day," Mr. Gilman began suddenly, in a very quiet voice, frowning benevolently at the black pointer on the compass. "But, of course, you know my great enemy."

"No, I don't," said Audrey gently.

"Hasn't Doc told you?"

"Doctor Cromarty? No, he doesn't tell much."

"Well," said Mr. Gilman, looking round quickly and shyly, rather in the manner of a boy, "it's liver."

Audrey seemed to read in his face, first, that Doctor Cromarty had received secret orders never to tell anybody anything, and, second, that the great enemy was not liver. And she thought: "So this is human nature! Mature men, wise men, dignified men, do descend to these paltry deceits just in order to keep up appearances, though they must know quite well that they don't deceive anyone who is worth deceiving." The remarkable fact was that she did not feel in the least shocked or disdainful. She merely decided—and found a certain queer pleasure in the decision —that human nature was a curious phenomenon, and that there must be a lot of it on earth. And she felt kindly towards Mr. Gilman.

"If you'd said gout——" she remarked. "I always understood that men generally had gout." And she consciously, with intention, employed a simple, innocent tone, knowing that it misled Mr. Gilman, and wanting it to mislead him.

"No!" he went on. "Liver. All sailors suffer from it, more or less. It's the bugbear of the sea. I have a doctor on board because, with a score or so of crew, it's really a duty to have a doctor."

"I quite see that," Audrey agreed, thinking mildly: "You only have a doctor on board because you're always worrying about your own health."

"However," said Mr. Gilman, "he's not much use to me personally. He doesn't understand liver. Scotsmen never do. Fortunately, I have a very good doctor in Paris. I prefer French doctors. And I'm sure they're right on the great liver question. All English doctors tell you to take plenty of violent exercise if you want to shake off a liver attack. Quite wrong. Too much exercise tires the body and so it tires the liver as well—obviously. What's the result? You can see, can't you? The liver works worse than ever. Now, a French doctor will advise complete rest until the attack is over. *Then* exercise, if you like; but not before. Of course, *you* don't know you've got a liver, and I dare say you think it's very odd of me to talk about my liver. I'm sure you do."

"I don't, honestly. I like you to talk like that. It's very interesting." And she thought: "Suppose Tommy was wrong, after all! . . . She's very spiteful."

"That's you all over, Mrs. Moncreiff. You understand men far better than any other woman I ever saw, unless, perhaps, it's Madame Piriac."

"Oh, Mr. Gilman! How can you say such a thing?"

"It's not the first time you've heard it, I wager!" said Mr. Gilman. "And it won't be the last! Any man who knows women can see at once that you are one of the women who understand. Otherwise, do you imagine I should have begun upon my troubles?"

Now, at any rate, he was sincere—she was convinced of that. And he looked very smart as he spied the horizon for lights and peered at the compass, and moved the wheel at intervals with a strong, accustomed gesture. And, assuredly, he looked very experienced. Audrey blushed. She just had to believe that there must be something in what he said concerning her talent. She had noticed it herself several times.

In an interval of the music the sea washed with a long sound against the bow of the yacht; then silence.

"I do love that sudden wash against the yacht," said Audrey.

"Yes," agreed Mr. Gilman, "so do I. All doctors tell me that I should be better if I gave up yachting. But I won't. I couldn't. Whatever it costs in health, yachting's worth it."

"Oh! It must be!" cried Audrey, with enthusiasm. "I've never been on a yacht before, but I quite agree with you. I feel as if I could live on a yacht for ever—always going to new places, you know; that's how I feel."

"You do?" Mr. Gilman exclaimed and gazed at her for a moment with a sort of ecstasy. Audrey instinctively checked herself. "There's a freemasonry among those who like yachting." His eyes returned to the compass. "I've kept your secret. I've kept it like something precious.

I've enjoyed keeping it. It's been a comfort to me. Now I wonder if you'll do the same for me, Mrs. Moncreiff?"

"Do what?" Audrey asked weakly, intimidated.

"Keep a secret. I shouldn't dream of telling it to Madame Piriac. Will you? May I tell you?"

"Yes, if you think you can trust me," said Audrey, concealing, with amazing ease and skill, her excitement and her mighty pleasure in the scene. . . . "He wouldn't dream of telling it to Madame Piriac." . . . It is doubtful whether she had ever enjoyed anything so much, and yet she was as prim as a nun.

"I'm not a happy man, Mrs. Moncreiff. Materially, I've everything a man can want, I suppose. But I'm not happy. You may laugh and say it's my liver. But it isn't. You're a woman of the world; you know what life is; and yet experience hasn't spoilt you. I could say anything to you; anything! And you wouldn't be shocked, would you?"

"No," said Audrey, hoping, nevertheless, that he would not say "anything, anything," but somehow simultaneously hoping that he would. It was a disconcerting sensation.

"I want you always to remember that I'm unhappy and never to tell anybody," Mr. Gilman resumed.

"But why?"

"It will be a kindness to me."

"I mean, why are you unhappy?"

"My opinions have all changed. I used to think I could be independent of women. Not that I didn't like women! I did. But when I'd left them I was quite happy. You know what the facts of life are, Mrs. Moncreiff. Young as you are you are older than me in some respects, though I have a long life before me. It's just because I have a long life before me—dyspeptics are always long-lived—that I'm afraid for the future. It wouldn't matter so much if I was an old man."

"But," asked Audrey adventurously, "why should you be unhappy because your opinions have changed? What opinions?" She endeavoured to be perfectly judicial and indifferent, and yet kind.

"What opinions? Well, about Woman Suffrage, for instance. You remember that night at the Foas', and what I remarked afterwards about what you all said?"

"Yes, I remember," said Audrey. "But can you remember it? Fancy you remembering a thing like that!"

"I remember every word that was said. It changed me. . . . Not at first. Oh, no! Not for several days, perhaps weeks. I fought against it. Then I said to myself, 'How absurd to fight against it!' . . . Well, I've come to believe in women having the vote. You've no more stanch supporter than I am. I *want* women to have the vote. And you're the first person I've ever said that to. I want *you* to have the vote."

He smiled at her, and she saw scores and scores of excellent qualities in his smile; she could not believe that he had any defect whatever. His secret was precious to her. She considered that he had confided it to her in a manner both distinguished and poetical. He had shown a quality which no youth could have shown. Youths were inferior, crude, incomplete. Not that Mr. Gilman was not young! Emphatically he was young, but her conception of the number of years comprised in youthfulness had been enlarged. She saw, as in a magical enlightenment, that forty was young, fifty was young, any age was young provided it had the right gestures. As for herself, she was without age. The obvious fact that Mr. Gilman was her slave touched her; it saddened her, but sweetly; it gave her a new sense of responsibility.

She said:

"I still don't see why this change of view should make you unhappy. I should have thought it would have just the opposite effect."

"It has altered all my desires," he replied. "Do you know, I'm not really interested in this new yacht now! And that's the truth."

"Mr. Gilman!" she checked him. "How can you say such a thing?"

It now appeared that she was not a nice girl. If she had been a nice girl she would not have comprehended what Mr. Gilman was ultimately driving at. The word "marriage" would never have sounded in her brain. And she would have been startled and shocked had Mr. Gilman even hinted that there was such a word in the dictionary. But not being, after all, a nice girl, she actually dwelt on the notion of marriage with somebody exactly like Mr. Gilman. She imagined how fine and comfortable and final it would be. She admitted that despite her riches and her independence she would be and could be simply naught until she possessed a man and could show him to the world as her own. Strange attitude for a wealthy feminist, but she had the attitude! And, moreover, she enjoyed having it; she revelled in it. She desired, impatiently, that Mr. Gilman should proceed further. She thirsted for his next remark. And her extremely deceptive features displayed only a blend of simplicity and soft pity. Those features did not actually lie, for she was ingenuous without being aware of it and her pity for the fellow-creature whose lot she could assuage with a glance was real enough. But they did suppress about nine-tenths of the truth.

"I tell you," said Mr. Gilman, "there is nothing I could not say to you. And—and—of course, you'll say I scarcely know you—yet——"

Clearly he was proceeding further. She waited as in a theatre one waits for a gun to go off on the stage. And then the gun did go off, but not the gun she was expecting.

Skipper Wyatt's head popped up like a cannon shot out of a hole in the forward deck, and it gazed sharply and apprehensively around the calm, moonlit sea. Mr. Gilman was, beyond question, perturbed by the movements of that head, though he could not see the expression of the eyes. This was the first phenomenon. The second phenomenon was a swirling of water round the after part of the ship, and this swirling went on until the water was white with a thin foam.

"Reverse those d——d engines!" shouted Captain Wyatt, quite regardless of the proximity of refined women. He had now sprung clear of the hole and was running aft. The whole world of the yacht could not but see that he was coatless and that his white shirtsleeves, being rather long, were kept in position by red elastic rings round his arms. "Is that blithering engineer asleep?" continued Captain Wyatt, ignoring the whole system of yacht etiquette. "She's getting harder on every second!"

"Ay, ay, skipper!" came a muffled voice from the engine-room.

"And not too soon either!" snapped the captain.

The yacht throbbed more violently; the swirling increased furiously. The captain stared over the rail. Then, after an interval, he stamped on the deck in disgust.

"Shut off!" he yelled. "It's no good."

The yacht ceased to throb. The swirling came to an end, and the thin white foam faded into flat sombre water. Whereupon Captain Wyatt turned back to the wheel, which, in his extreme haste, he had passed by.

"You've run her on to the sand, sir," said he to Mr. Gilman, respectfully but still accusingly.

"Oh, no! Impossible!" Mr. Gilman defended himself, pained by the charge.

"She's hard on, anyhow, sir. And many a good yacht's left her bones on this Buxey."

"But you gave me the course," protested Mr. Gilman, with haughtiness.

Captain Wyatt bent down and looked at the binnacle. He was contentedly aware that the compass of a yacht hard aground cannot lie and cannot be made to lie. The camera can lie; the speedometer of an automobile after an accident can lie—or can conceal the truth and often does, but the compass of a yacht aground is insusceptible to any blandishment; it shows the course at the moment of striking and nothing will persuade it to alter its evidence.

"What course did I give you, sir?" asked Captain Wyatt.

And as Mr. Gilman hesitated in his reply, the skipper pointed silently to the compass.

"Where's the chart? Let me see the chart," said Mr. Gilman with sudden majesty.

The chart in its little brass frame was handy. Mr. Gilman examined it in a hostile manner; one might say that he cross-examined it, and with it the horizon. "Ah!" he muttered at length, peering at the print under the chart, "'Corrected 1906.' Out of date. Pity they don't re-issue these charts oftener."

His observations had no relation whatever to the matter in hand; considered as a contribution to the unravelling of the matter in hand they were merely idiotic. Nevertheless, such were the exact words he uttered, and he appeared to get great benefit and solace from them. They somehow enabled him to meet, quite satisfactorily, the gaze of his guests who had now gathered in the vicinity of the wheel.

Audrey alone showed a desire to move away from the wheel. The fact was that the skipper had glanced at her in a peculiar way and his eyes had seemed to say, with disdain: "Women! Women again!" Nothing but that! The implications, however, were plain. Audrey may have been discountenanced by the look in the captain's eyes, but at the same time she had an inward pride, because it was undeniable that Mr. Gilman, owing to his extreme and agitated interest in herself, had put the yacht off the course and was thereby imperilling numerous lives. Audrey liked that. And she exonerated Mr. Gilman, and she hated the captain for daring to accuse him, and she mysteriously nursed the wounded dignity of Mr. Gilman far better than he could nurse it himself.

Her feelings were assuredly complex, and they grew more complex when the sense of danger began to dominate them. The sense of danger came to her out of the demeanour of her companions and out of the swift appearance on deck of every member of the crew, including the parlourmaid, and including three men who were incompletely clothed. The yacht was no longer a floating hotel, automobile and dancing-saloon; it was a stranded wreck. Not a passenger on board knew whether the tide was making or ebbing, but, secretly, all were convinced that it was ebbing and that they would be left on the treacherous sand and ultimately swallowed up therein, even if a storm did not supervene and smash the craft to bits in the classical manner. The skipper's words about the bones of many a good yacht had escaped no ear.

Further, not a passenger knew where the yacht was or whither, exactly, she was bound or whether the glass was rising or falling, for guests on yachts seldom concern themselves about details. Of course, signals might be made to passing ships, but signals were often, according to maritime history, unheeded, and the ocean was very large and empty, though it was only the German Ocean. . . . Musa was nervous and angry. Audrey knew from her intimate knowledge of him that he was angry and she wondered why he should be angry. Madame Piriac, on the other hand, was entirely calm. Her calmness seemed to say to those responsible, and even to the not-responsible passenger: "You got me into this and it is inconceivable that you should not get me out of it. I have always been looked after and protected, and I must be looked after and protected now. I absolutely decline to be worried." But Miss Thompkins was worried, she was very seriously alarmed; fear was in her face.

"I do think it's a shame!" she broke out almost loudly, in a trembling voice, to Audrey. "I do think it's a shame you should go flirting with poor Mr. Gilman when he's steering." And she meant all she said.

"Me flirting!" Audrey exclaimed, passionately resentful. Withal, the sense of danger continued to increase. Still there were the boats. There were the motor-launch, the cutter and the dinghy. The sea was—for the present—calm and the moon encouraging.

"Lower the dinghy there and look lively now!" cried the captain.

This command more than ever frightened all the passengers who, in their nervousness and alarm, had tried to pretend to themselves that nervousness and alarm were absurd, and that first-class yachts never did, and could not, get wrecked. The command was a thunderstroke. It proved that the danger was immediate and intense. And the thought of all the beautiful food and drink on board, and all the soft cushions and the electric hair-curlers and the hot-water supply and the ice gave no consolation whatever. The idea of the futility and wickedness of luxury desolated the guests and made them austere, and yet even in that moment they speculated upon what goods they might take with them.

And why the dinghy, though it was a dinghy of large size? Why not the launch?

After the dinghy had been dropped into the sea an old sail was carefully spread amidships over her bottom and she was lugged, by her painter, towards the bow of the yacht where, with much grating of windlasses and of temperaments and voices, an anchor was very gently lowered into her and rested on the old sail. The anchor was so immense that it sank the dinghy up to her gunwale, and then she was rowed away to a considerable distance, a chain grinding after her, and in due time the anchor was pitched with a great splash into the water. The sound of orders and of replies vibrated romantically over the surface of the water. Then a windlass was connected with the engine, and the passengers comprehended that the intention was to drag the yacht off the sand by main force. The chain clacked and strained horribly. The shouting multiplied, as though the vessel had been a great beast that could be bullied into obedience. The muscles of all passengers were drawn taut in sympathy with the chain, and at length there was a lurch and the chain gradually slackened.

"She's off!" breathed the captain. "We've saved a good half-hour."

"She'd have floated off by herself," said Mr. Gilman grandly.

"Yes, sir," said the captain. "But if it had happened to be the ebb, sir——" He left it at that and began on a new series of orders, embracing the dinghy, the engines, the anchor and another anchor.

And all the passengers resumed their courage and their ancient notions about the excellence of luxury, and came to the conclusion that navigation was a very simple affair, and in less than five minutes were sincerely convinced that they had never known fear.

Later, the impressive sight was witnessed of Madame Piriac, on her shoulders such a cloak as certainly had never been seen on a yacht before, bearing Mr. Gilman's valuable violin like a jewel casket. She had found it below and brought it up on deck.

The *Ariadne* was now passing to port those twinkling cities of delight, Clacton and Frinton, and the long pier of Walton stretched out towards it, a string of topazes. The moon was higher and brighter than ever, but clouds had heaped themselves up to windward, and the surface of the water was rippled. Moreover, the yacht was now working over a strong, foul tide. The company, with the exception of Mr. Gilman, who had gone below—apparently in order to avoid being on the same deck with Captain Wyatt—had decided that Musa should be asked to play. Although the sound of his practising had escaped occasionally through the porthole of a locked cabin, he had not once during the cruise performed for the public benefit. Dancing was finished. Why should not the yacht profit by the presence of a great genius on board? The doctor and the secretary were of one mind with the women that there was no good answer to this question, and even the crew obviously felt that the genius ought to show what he was made of.

"Dare we ask you?" said Madame Piriac to the youth, offering him the violin case. Her supplicatory tone and attitude, though they were somewhat assumed, proved to what a height Musa had recently risen as a personage.

He hesitated, leaning against the rail and nervously fingering it.

"I know it is a great deal to ask. But you would give us so much pleasure," said Madame Piriac.

Musa replied in a dry, curt voice:

"I should prefer not to play."

"Oh! But Musa——" There was a general protest.

"I cannot play," Musa exclaimed with impatience, and moved almost savagely away.

The experience was novel for Madame Piriac, left standing there, as it were, respectfully presenting the violin case to the rail. This beautiful and not unpampered lady was accustomed to see her commands received as an honour; and when she condescended to implore, the effect usually was to produce a blissful and deprecatory confusion in the person besought. Her husband and Mr. Gilman had for a number of years been teaching her that whatever she desired was the highest good and the most complete felicity to everybody concerned in the fulfilment of the desire. She bore the blow from Musa admirably, keeping both her smile and her dignity, and with one gesture excusing Musa to all beholders as a capricious and a sensitive artist in whom moodiness was lawful. It was exquisitely done. It could not have been better done. But not even Madame Piriac's extreme skill could save the episode from having the air of a social disaster. The gaiety which had been too feverishly resumed after the salvage of the yacht from the sandbank expired like a pricked balloon. People silently vanished, and only Audrey was left on the after deck.

It was after a long interval that she became aware

of the reappearance of Musa. Seemingly, he had been in the engine-room; since the beginning of the cruise he had shown a fancy for both the engine-room and the engineer. To her surprise, he marched straight towards her deck-chair.

"I must speak to you," he said with emotion.

"Must you?" Audrey replied, full of hot resentment. "I think you've been horrid, Musa. Perfectly horrid! But I suppose you have your own notions of politeness now. Everything has been done for you, and——"

"What is that?" he stopped her. "Everything has been done for me. What is it that has been done for me? I play for years. I am ignored. Then I succeed. I am noticed. Men of affairs offer me immense sums. But am I surprised? Not the least in the world. It is the contrary which would have surprised me. It was inevitable that I should succeed. But note well—it is I myself who succeed. It is not my friends. It is not the concert agent. Do I regard the concert agent as a benefactor? Again, not the least in the world. You say everything has been done for me. Nothing has been done for me, Madame."

"Yes, yes," faltered Audrey, who was in a dilemma, and therefore more resentful than ever. "I—I only mean your friends have always stood by you." She gathered courage, sat up erect in her deck-chair, and finished haughtily: "And now you're conceited. You're insufferably conceited."

"Because I refused to play?" He laughed stridently and grimly. "No. I refused to play because I could not, because I was outside myself with jealousy. Yes, jealousy. You do not know jealousy. Perhaps you are incapable of it. But permit me to tell you, Madame, that jealousy is one of the finest and most terrible emotions. And that is why I must speak to you. I cannot live and see you flirt so seriously with that old idiot. I cannot live."

Audrey jumped up from the chair.

"Musa! I shall never speak to you again. . . . Me
. . . flirt. . . . And you call Mr. Gilman an old idiot!"

"What words would you employ, Madame? He was
so agitated by your intimate conversation that he brought
us all near to death, in any case. Moreover, it jumps
to the eyes that the decrepit satyr is mad about you.
Mad!"

And Musa's voice broke. In the midst of all her fury
Audrey was relieved that it did break, for the reason that
it was getting very loud, and the wheel, with Captain
Wyatt thereat, was not far off.

There was one thing to do, and Audrey did it. She
walked away rapidly. And, as she did so, she was startled
to discover a sob in her throat. The drawn, highly
emotionalised face of Musa remained with her. She was
angry, indignant, infuriated, and yet her feelings were
not utterly unpleasant, though she wanted them to be so.
In the first place, they were exciting. And in the second
place—what was it?—well, she had the strange, sweet
sensation of being, somehow, the mainspring of the universe,
of being immensely important in the scheme of things.

She thought her cup was full. It was not. Staring
blankly over the side of the ship she saw a buoy float
slowly by. She saw it with the utmost clearness, and on
its round black surface was painted in white letters the
word "Flank." There could not be two Flank buoys. It
was the Flank buoy of the Mozewater navigable channel.
. . . She glanced around. The well-remembered shores of
Mozewater were plainly visible under the moon. In the
distance, over the bowsprit, she could discern the mass
of the tower of Mozewater church. She could not distinguish Flank Hall, but she knew it was there. Why
were they threading the Mozewater channel? It had been
distinctly given out that the yacht would make Harwich
harbour. Almost unconsciously she turned in the direction
of the wheel, where Captain Wyatt was. Then, controlling

herself, she moved away. She knew that she could not speak to the captain. She went below, and, before she could escape, found the saloon populated.

"Oh! Mrs. Moncreiff!" cried Madame Piriac. "It is a miraculous coincidence. You will never guess. One tells me we are going to the village of Moze for the night; it is because of the tide. You remember, I told you. It is where lives my little friend, Audrey Moze. To-morrow I visit her, and you must come with me. I insist that you come with me. I have never seen her. It will be all that is most palpitating."

Q

CHAPTER XXXIII

AGUILAR'S DOUBLE LIFE

MADAME PIRIAC came down into the saloon the next afternoon.

"Oh! You are still hiding yourself here!" she murmured gaily to Audrey, who was alone among the cushions.

"I was just resting," said Audrey. "Remember what a night we had!"

It was true that the yacht had not been berthed at Lousey Hard until between two and three o'clock in the morning, and that no guest had slept until after the job was done, though more than one had tried to sleep. It was also true that in consequence the saloon breakfast had been abrogated, that even the saloon lunch lacked vicacity, and that at least one passenger was at that moment dozing in his cabin. But not on account of fatigue and somnolence was Audrey remaining in the saloon instead of taking the splendid summer afternoon on deck under the awning. She felt neither tired nor sleepy. The true secret was that she feared the crowd of village idlers, quidnuncs, tattlers and newsmongers who all day gazed from Lousey Hard at the wonder-yacht.

Examining the line of faces as well as she could through portholes, she recognised nearly every one of them, and was quite sure that every one of them would recognise her face. To go ashore or to stay prominently on deck would, therefore, be to give away her identity and to be forced, sooner or later, to admit that she had practised a long and naughty deception. She could conceive some of those villagers greeting her loudly from the Hard if she should appear; for Essex manners were marked by strange freedoms. Her situation would be terrible. It, in fact, was terrible. Risks surrounded her like angry dogs. Musa, for example, ought surely to have noticed that the estuary in which the yacht lay was the same estuary which he had seen not long before from the garden of the house stated by Audrey to be her own, and he ought to have commented eagerly on the marvellous coincidence. Happily, he had not yet done so—no doubt because he had spent most of the time in bed. If and when he did so there would naturally be an excited outcry and a heavy rain of amazed questions which simply could not be answered.

"I am going almost at once to call on my little friend Audrey Moze, at Flank Hall," said Madame Piriac. "The house looks delicious from the deck. If you will come up I will show it to you. It is precisely like the picture post card which the dear little one sent to me last year. Are you ready to come with me?"

"But, darling, hadn't you better go alone?"

"But certainly not, darling! You are not serious. The meeting will be very agitating. With a third person, however, it will be less so. I count on you absolutely, as I have said already. Nay, I insist. I invoke your friendship."

"She may be out. She may be away altogether."

"In that case we shall return," said Madame Piriac briefly, and, not giving Audrey time to reply further, she vanished, with a firm carriage and an obstinate look in her eyes, towards the sleeping-cabins.

The next instant Mr. Gilman himself entered the saloon.

"Mrs. Moncreiff," he started nervously, in a confidential and deprecating tone, "this is the first chance I have had to tell you. We came into Mozewater without my orders. I won't say against my orders, but certainly not with them. On the plea that I had retired, Captain Wyatt changed our destination last night without going through the formality of consulting me. We ought to have made Harwich, but I am now told that we were running short of paraffin, and that if we had continued to Harwich we should have had the worst of the tide against us, whereas in coming up Mozewater the tide helped us; also that Captain Wyatt did not care about trying to get into Harwich harbour at night with the wind in its present quarter, and rising as it was then. Of course, Wyatt is responsible for the safety of the ship, and it is true that I had her designed with a very light draught on purpose for such waters as Mozewater; but he ought to have consulted me. We might get away again on this tide, but Hortense will not hear of it. She has a call to pay, she says. I can only tell you how sorry I am. And I do hope you will forgive me." The sincerity and alarm of his manly apology were touching.

"But, Mr. Gilman," said Audrey, with the simplicity which more and more she employed in talking to her host, "there is nothing to forgive. What can it matter to me whether we come here or go to Harwich?"

"I thought, I was afraid——" Mr. Gilman hesitated. "In short . . . your secret, Mrs. Moncreiff, which you asked me to keep, and which I have kept. It was here, at this very spot, with my old barge-yacht, that I first had the pleasure of meeting you. And I thought . . . perhaps you had reasons. . . . However, your secret is safe."

"How nice you are, Mr. Gilman!" Audrey said, with a gentle smile. "You're kindness itself. But there is nothing to trouble about, really. Keep my little secret by all means, if you don't mind. As for anything else—that's perfectly all right. . . . Shall we go on deck?"

He thanked her without words.

She was saying to herself, rather desperately:

"After all, what do I care? I haven't committed a crime. It's nobody's business but my own. And I'm worth ten million francs. And if the fat's in the fire, and anything is found out, and people don't like it—well, they must do the other thing."

Thus she went on deck, and her courage was rewarded by the discovery of a chair on the starboard side of the deck-house, from which she could not possibly be seen by any persons on the Hard. She took this chair like a gift from heaven. The deck was busy enough. Mr. Price, the secretary, was making entries in an account book. Dr. Cromarty was pacing to and fro, expectant. Captain Wyatt was arguing with the chauffeur of a vast motor-van from Clacton, and another motor-van from Colchester was also present on the Hard. Rows of paraffin cans were ranged against the engine-room hatchway, and the odour of paraffin was powerfully conflicting with the odour of ozone and possibly ammonia from the marshes. Parcels kept coming down by hand from the village of Moze. Fresh water also came in barrels on a lorry, and lumps of ice in a dog-cart. The arrival of six bottles of aspirin, brought by a heated boy on a bicycle, from Clacton, and seized with gusto by Dr. Cromarty, completed the proof that money will not only buy anything, but will infallibly draw it to any desired spot, however out of the way the spot may be. The probability was that neither paraffin nor ice nor aspirin had ever found itself on Lousey Hard before in the annals of the world. Yet now these things forgathered with ease and naturalness owing to the magic of the word "yacht" in telegrams.

And over the scene floated the wavy, inspiring folds of the yacht's immense blue ensign, with the Union Jack in the top inside corner.

Mr. Price went into the deck-house and began to count money.

"Mr. Price," demanded Mr. Gilman urgently, "did you look up the facts about this village?"

"I was just looking up the place in ' East Coast Tours, sir, when the paraffin arrived," replied Mr. Price. "It says that Moze is mentioned in ' Green's Short History of the English People.'"

"Ah! Very interesting. That work is a classic. It

really treats of the English people, and not solely of their kings and queens. Dr. Cromarty, Mr. Price is busy, will you mind bringing me the catalogue of the library up here?"

Dr. Cromarty obeyed, and Mr. Gilman examined the typewritten, calf-bound volume.

"Yes," said he. "Yes. I thought we had Green on board, and we have. I should like extremely to know what Green says about Moze. It must have been in the Anglo-Saxon or Norman period. Dr. Cromarty, will you mind bringing me up the first three volumes of Green? You will find them on shelf Z8. Also the last volume, for the index."

A few moments later Mr. Gilman, with three volumes of Green on his knees and one in his hand, said reproachfully to Mr. Price :

"Mr. Price, I requested you to see that the leaves of all our books were cut. These volumes are absolutely uncut."

"Well, sir, I'm working through them as fast as I can. But I haven't got to shelf Z8 yet."

"I cannot stop to cut them now," said Mr. Gilman, politely displeased. "What a pity! It would have been highly instructive to know what Green says about Moze. I always like to learn everything I can about the places we stop at. And this place must be full of historic interest. Wyatt, have you had that paraffin counted properly?" He spoke very coldly to the captain.

It thus occurred that what John Richard Green said about Moze was never known on board the yacht *Ariadne*.

Audrey listened to the episode in a reverie. She was thinking about Musa's intractability and inexcusable rudeness, and about what she should do in the matter of Madame Piriac's impending visit to Audrey Moze at Flank Hall, and through the texture of these difficult topics she could see, as it were, shining the sprightly simplicity, the utter ingenuousness, the entirely reliable fidelity of Mr. Gilman.

She felt, rather than consciously realised, that he was a dull man. But she liked his dullness; it reassured her; it was tranquillising; it was even adorable. She liked also his attitude towards Moze. She had never suspected, no one had ever hinted to her, that Moze was full of historic interest. But looking at it now from the yacht which had miraculously wafted her past the Flank buoy at dead of night, she perceived Moze in a quite new aspect—a pleasure which she owed to Mr. Gilman's artless interest in things. (Not that he was artless in all affairs! No; in the great masculine affairs he must be far from artless, for had he not made all his money himself?)

Then Madame Piriac appeared on deck, armed and determined. Audrey found, as hundreds of persons had found, that it was impossible to deny Madame Piriac. Beautiful, gracious, elegant, kind, when she would have a thing she would have it. Audrey had to descend and prepare herself. She had to reascend ready for the visit. But at the critical and dreadful moment of going ashore to affront the crowd she had a saving idea. She pointed to Flank Hall and its sloping garden, and to the sea-wall against which the high spring tide was already washing, and she suggested that they should be rowed thither in the dinghy instead of walking around by the sea-wall or through the village.

"But we cannot climb over that dyke," Madame Piriac protested.

"Oh, yes, we can," said Audrey. "I can see steps in it from here, and I can see a gate at the bottom of the garden."

"What a vision you have, darling!" murmured Madame Piriac. "As you wish, provided we get there."

The dinghy, at Audrey's request, was brought round to the side of the yacht opposite from the Hard, and, screening her face as well as she could with an open parasol, she tripped down by the steps into it. If only Aguilar was away from the premises she might be saved, for the place would be shut up, and there would be nothing to do but return. Should Madame Piriac suggest going into the village to inquire—well, Audrey would positively refuse to go into the village. Yes, she would refuse!

As the boat moved away from the yacht, Musa showed himself on deck. Madame Piriac signalled to him a salutation of the finest good humour. She had forgotten his pettishness. By absolutely ignoring it she had made it as though it had never existed. This was her art. Audrey, observing the gesture, and Musa's smiling reply to it, acquired wisdom. She saw that she must treat Musa as Madame Piriac treated him. She had undertaken the enterprise of launching him on a tremendous artistic career, and she must carry it through. She wanted to make a neat, clean job of the launching, and she would do it dispassionately, like a good workwoman. He had admitted—nay, he had insisted—that she was necessary to him. Her pride in that fact had a somewhat superior air. He might be the most marvellous of violinists, but he was also a child, helpless without her moral support. She would act accordingly. It was absurd to be angry with a child, no matter what his vagaries. . . . At this juncture of her reflections she noticed that Mr. Gilman and Miss Thompkins had quitted the yacht together and were walking seawards. They seemed very intimate, impregnated with mutual understanding. And Audrey was sorry that Mr. Gilman was quite so simple, quite so straightforward and honest.

When the dinghy arrived at the sea-wall Audrey won the startled admiration of the sailor in charge of the boat by pointing at once to the best—if not the only—place fit for a landing. The sailor was by no means accustomed to such *flair* in a yacht's guests. Indeed, it had often astonished him that people who, as a class, had so little notion of how to get into or out of a dinghy could have succeeded, as they all apparently had, in any department of life.

With continuing skill, Audrey guided Madame Piriac over the dyke and past sundry other obstacles, including a watercourse, to a gate in the wall which formed the frontier of the grounds of Flank Hall. The gate seemed at first to be unopenably fastened, but Audrey showed that she possessed a genius with gates, and opened it with a twist of the hand. They wandered through a plantation and then through an orchard, and at length saw the house. There was not a sign of Aguilar, but the unseen yard-dog began to bark, hearing which, Madame Piriac observed in French :

"The property seems a little neglected, but there must be someone at home."

"Aguilar is bound to come now!" thought Audrey. "And I am lost!" Then she added to herself : "And I don't care if I *am* lost. What an unheard-of lark!"

And to Madame Piriac she said lightly :

"Well, we must explore."

The blinds were nearly all up on the garden front. And one window—the French window of the drawing-room—was wide open.

"The crisis will be here in one minute at the latest," thought Audrey.

"Evidently Miss Moze is at home," said Madame Piriac, gazing at the house. "Yes, it is distinguished. It is what I had expected. . . . But ought we not to go to the front door?"

"I think we ought," Audrey agreed.

They went round the side of the house, into the main drive, and without hesitation Madame Piriac rang the front door bell, which they could plainly hear. "I must have my cards ready," said she, opening her bag. "One always hears how exigent you are in England about such details, even in the provinces. And, indeed, why not?"

There was no answer to the bell. Madame Piriac rang again, and there was still no answer. And the dog had ceased to bark.

"*Mon Dieu!*" she muttered. "Have you observed, darling, that all the blinds are down on this façade?"

She rang a third time. Then, without a word, they returned slowly to the garden front.

"How mysterious! *Mon Dieu!* How English it all is!" muttered Madame Piriac. "It gives me fear."

Audrey had almost decided definitely that she was saved when she happened to glance through the open window of the drawing-room. She thought she saw a flicker within. She looked again. She could not be mistaken. Then she noticed that all the dust sheets had been removed from the furniture, that the carpet had been laid, that a table had been set for tea, that there were flowers and china and a teapot and bread-and-butter and a kettle and a spirit-lamp on the table. The flicker was the flicker of the blue flame of the spirit-lamp. The kettle over it was puffing out steam.

Audrey exclaimed, within herself:

"Aguilar!"

She had caught him at last. There were two cups and saucers—the best ancient blue-and-white china, out of the glass-fronted china cupboard in that very room! The celibate Aguilar, never known to consort with anybody at all, was clearly about to entertain someone to tea, and the aspect of things showed that he meant to do it very well. True, there was no cake, but the bread-and-butter was expertly cut and attractively arranged. Audrey felt sure that she was on the track of Aguilar's double life, and that a woman was concerned therein. She was angry, but she was also enormously amused and uplifted. She no longer cared the least bit about the imminent danger threatening her incognito. Her sole desire was to entrap Aguilar, and with deep joy she pictured his face when he should come into the room with his friend and find the mistress of the house already installed.

"I think we had better go in here, darling," she said to Madame Piriac, with her hand on the French window. "There is no other entrance."

Madame Piriac looked at her.

"*Eh bien!* It is your country, not mine. You know the habits. I follow you," said Madame Piriac calmly. "After all, my dear little Audrey ought to be delighted to see me. I have several times told her that I should come. All the same, I expected to announce myself. . . . What a charming room ! So this is the English provinces ! "

The room was certainly agreeable to the eye. And Audrey seemed to see it afresh, to see it for the first time in her life. And she thought : "Can this be the shabby old drawing-room that I hated so? "

The kettle continued to puff vigorously.

"If they don't come soon," said Audrey, "the water will be all boiled away and the kettle burnt. Suppose we make the tea? "

Madame Piriac raised her eyebrows.

"It is your country," she repeated. "That appears to be singular, but I have not the English habits."

And she sat down, smiling.

Audrey opened the tea caddy, put three spoonfuls of tea into the pot, and made the tea.

The clock struck on the mantelpiece. The clock was actually going. Aguilar was ever thorough in his actions.

"Four minutes to brew, and if they don't come we'll have tea," said Audrey, tranquil in the assurance that the advent of Aguilar could not now be long delayed.

"Do you take milk and sugar, darling? " she asked Madame Piriac at the end of the four minutes, which they had spent mainly in a curious silence. "I believe you do."

Madame Piriac nodded.

"A little bread-and-butter? I'm sorry there's no cake or jam."

It was while Madame Piriac was stirring her first cup that the drawing-room door opened, and at once there was a terrific shriek.

"Audrey ! "

The invader was Miss Ingate. Close behind Miss Ingate came Jane Foley.

CHAPTER XXXIV

"Did you get my letter?" breathed Miss Ingate weakly, after she had a little recovered from the shock, which had the appearance of being terrific.

"No," said Audrey. "How could I? We're yachting. Madame Piriac, you know Miss Ingate, don't you? And this is my friend Jane Foley." She spoke quite easily and naturally, though Miss Ingate in her intense agitation had addressed her as Audrey, whereas the Christian name of Mrs. Moncreiff, on the rare occasions when a Christian name became necessary or advisable, had been Olivia—or, infrequently, Olive.

"Yachting!"

"Yes. Haven't you seen the yacht at the Hard?"

"No! I did hear something about it, but I've been too busy to run after yachts. We've been too busy, haven't we, Miss Foley? I even have to keep my dog locked up. I don't know what you'll say. Aud—Mrs. Moncreiff! I really don't! But we acted for the best. Oh! How dreadfully exciting my life does get at times! Never since I played the barrel organ all the way down Regent Street have I——! Oh! dear!"

"Have my tea, and do sit down, Winnie, and remember you're an Essex woman!" Audrey adjured her, going to the china cupboard to get more cups.

"*I'll* just tell you all about it, Mrs. Moncreiff, if you'll let me," Jane Foley began with a serene and happy smile, as she limped to a chair. "I'm quite ready to take all the consequences. It's the police again, that's all. I don't

know how exactly they got on the track of the Spatts at
Frinton. But I dare say you've seen that the police have
seized a lot of documents at our head-quarters. Perhaps
that explains it. Anyway I caught sight of our old friend
at Paget Gardens nosing about, and so as soon as it was
dark I left the Spatts. It's a horrid thing to say, but I
never was so glad about anything as I was at leaving the
Spatts. I didn't tell them where I was going, and they
didn't ask. I'm sure the poor things were very relieved to
have me go. Miss Ingate tells me to-day she's heard they've
both resigned from the Union. Mr. Spatt went up to
London on purpose to do it. And can you be surprised?"

"Yes, you can, and yet you can't!" exclaimed Miss
Ingate. "You can, and yet you can't!"

"I met Miss Ingate on Frinton front," Jane Foley proceeded. "She was just getting into her carriage. I had
my bag and I asked her to drive me to the station. 'To the
station?' she said. 'What for? There's no train to-
night.'"

"No more there wasn't!" Miss Ingate put in, "I'd been
dining at the Proctors' and it was after ten, I know it was
after ten because they never let me leave until after ten, in
spite of the long drive I have. Fancy there being a train
from Frinton after ten! So of course I brought Miss Foley
along. Oh! It was vehy interesting. Vehy interesting.
You see we had to think of the police. I didn't want the
police coming poking round my house. It would never do,
in a little place like Moze. I should never hear the last of
it. So I—I thought of Flank Hall. I——"

Jane Foley went on :

"Miss Ingate was sure you wouldn't mind, Mrs. Moncreiff. And personally I was quite certain you wouldn't
mind. We left the carriage at Miss Ingate's, and carried
the bag in turns. And I stood outside while Miss Ingate
woke up Mr. Aguilar. It was soon all right."

"I must say Aguilar was vehy reasonable," said Miss
Ingate. "Vehy reasonable. And he's got a great spite

against my dear Inspector Keeble. He suggested every.
thing. He never asked any questions, so I told him. You
do, you know. He suggested Miss Foley should have a
bed in the tank-room, so that if there was any trouble all
the bedrooms should look innocent."

"Did he tell you I'd come here to see him not long
since?" Audrey demanded.

"And why didn't you pop in to see *me?* I was hurt
when I got your note."

"Did he tell you?"

"Of course he didn't. He never tells anybody anything.
That sort of thing's very useful at times, especially when
it's combined with a total lack of curiosity. He fixed every.
thing up. And he keeps the gates locked, so that people
can't wander in."

"He didn't lock the gate at the bottom of the garden,
because it won't lock," said Audrey. "And so he didn't
keep me from wandering in." She felt rather disappointed
that Aguilar should once more have escaped her reproof and
that the dream of his double life should have vanished away,
but she was determined to prove that he was not perfect.

"Well, I don't know about that," said Miss Ingate.
"It wouldn't startle me to hear that he knew you were in-
tending to come. All I know is that Miss Foley's been
here for several days. Not a soul knows except me and
Aguilar. And it seems to get safer every day. She does
venture about the house now, though she never goes into
the garden while it's light. It was Aguilar had the idea
of putting this room straight for her."

"And it was he who cut the bread-and-butter," added
Jane Foley.

"And this was to be our first tea-party!" Miss Ingate
half shrieked. "I'd come—I do come, you know, to keep
an eye on things as you asked me—I'd come, and we were
just having a cosy little chat in the tank-room. Aguilar's
gone to Colchester to get a duplicate key of the front gates.
He left me his, so I could get in and lock up after myself,

and he put the water on to boil before leaving. I said to Miss Foley, I said, up in the tank-room : ' Was that a ring at the door? ' But she said it wasn't."

"I've been a little deaf since I was in prison," said Jane Foley.

"And now we come down and find you here ! I—I hope I've done right." This, falteringly, from Miss Ingate.

"Of course you have, you silly old thing," Audrey reassured her. "It's splendid ! "

"Whenever I think of the police I laugh," said Miss Ingate in an unsettled voice. "I can't help it. They can't possibly suspect. And they're looking everywhere, everywhere ! I can't help laughing." And suddenly she burst into tears.

"Oh! Now! Winnie, dear. Don't spoil it all ! " Audrey protested, jumping up.

Madame Piriac, who had hitherto maintained the most complete passivity, restrained her.

"Leave her tranquil ! " murmured Madame Piriac in French. "She is not spoiling it. On the contrary ! One is content to see that she is a woman ! "

And then Miss Ingate laughed, and blushed, and called herself names.

"And so you haven't had my letter," said she. "I wish you had had it. But what is this yachting business? I never heard of such goings-on. Is it your yacht? This world is getting a bit too wonderful for me."

The answer to these questions was cut short by rather heavy masculine footsteps approaching the door of the drawing-room. Miss Ingate grew instantly serious. Audrey and Jane looked at each other, and Jane Foley went quickly but calmly to the door and opened it.

"Oh! It's Mr. Aguilar—returned ! " she said, quietly. "Is anything the matter, Mr. Aguilar? "

Aguilar, hat in hand, entered the room.

"Good afternoon, Aguilar," Audrey greeted him.

"'Noon, madam," he responded, exactly as though he

had been expecting to find the mistress there. "It's like this. I've just seen Inspector Keeble and that there detective as was here afore—*you* know, madam" (nodding to Audrey) "and I fancy they're a-coming this way, so I thought I'd better cut back and warn ye. I don't think they saw me. I was too quick for 'em. Was the bread-and-butter all right, Miss Ingate? Thank ye."

Miss Ingate had risen.

"I ought to go home," she said. "I feel sure it would be wiser for me to go home. I never could talk to detectives."

Jane Foley snatched at one of the four cups and saucers on the table, and put it back, all unwashed, into the china cupboard.

"Three cups will be enough for them to see, if they come," she said, with a bright, happy smile to Audrey. "Yes, Miss Ingate, you go home. I'm ever so much obliged to you. Now, I'll go upstairs and Aguilar shall lock me in the tank-room and push the key under the door. We are causing you a lot of trouble, Mrs. Moncreiff, but you won't mind. It might have been so much worse." She laughed as she went.

"And suppose I meet those police on the way out, what am I to say to them?" asked Miss Ingate when Jane Foley and Aguilar had departed.

"If they're very curious, tell them you've been here to have tea with me and that Aguilar cut the bread-and-butter," Audrey replied. "The detective will be interested to see me. He chased me all the way to London not long since. Au revoir, Winnie."

"Dear friend," said Madame Piriac, with admirable though false calm. "Would it not be more prudent to fly back at once to the yacht—if in truth this is the same police agent of whom you recounted to me with such drollness the exploits? It is not that I am afraid——"

"Nor I," said Audrey. "There is no danger except to Jane Foley."

"Ah! You cannot abandon her. That is true. Nevertheless I regret . . ."

"Well, darling," Audrey exclaimed. "You would insist on my coming!"

The continuing presence of Miss Ingate, who had lost one glove and her purse, rendered this brief conversation somewhat artificial. And no sooner had Miss Ingate got away—by the window, for the sake of dispatch—than a bell made itself heard, and Aguilar came back to the drawing-room in the rôle of butler.

"Inspector Keeble and a gentleman to see you, madam."

"Bring them in," said Audrey.

Aguilar's secret glance at Inspector Keeble as he brought in the visitors showed that his lifelong and harmless enemy had very little to hope from his goodwill.

"Wait a moment, you!" called the detective as Aguilar, like a perfect butler, was vanishing. "Good afternoon, ladies. Excuse me, I wish to question this man." He indicated Aguilar with a gesture of apologising for Aguilar.

Inspector Keeble, an overgrown mass of rectitude and kindliness, greeted Audrey with that constraint which always afflicted him when he was beneath any roof more splendid than that of his own police-station.

"Now, Aguilar," said the detective, "it's you that'll be telling me. Ye've got a woman concealed in the house. Where is she?"

He knew, then, this ferreting and divinatory Irishman! Of course Miss Ingate must have committed some indiscretion, or was it that Aguilar was less astute than he gave the impression of being? Audrey considered that all was lost, and she was aware of a most unpleasant feeling of helplessness and inefficiency. Then she seemed to receive inspiration and optimism from somewhere. She knew not exactly from where, but perhaps it was from the shy stiffness of the demeanour of her old acquaintance, Inspector Keeble. Moreover, the Irishman's twinkling eyes were a challenge to her.

R

"Oh! Aguilar!" she exclaimed. "I'm very sorry to hear this. I knew women were always your danger, but I never dreamt you would start carrying on in my absence."

Aguilar fronted her, and their eyes met. Audrey gazed at him steadily. There was no smile in Audrey's eyes, but there was a smile glimmering mysteriously behind them, and after a couple of seconds this phenomenon aroused a similar phenomenon behind the eyes of Aguilar. Audrey had the terrible and god-like sensation of lifting a hired servant to equality with herself. She imagined that she would never again be able to treat him as Aguilar, and she even feared that she would soon begin to cease to hate him. At the same time she observed slight signs of incertitude in the demeanour of the detective.

Aguilar replied coldly, not to Audrey, but to the police:

"If Inspector Keeble or anybody else has been mixing my name up with any scandal about females, I'll have him up for slander and libel and damages as sure as I stand here."

Inspector Keeble looked away, and then looked at the detective—as if for support in peril.

"Do you mean to say, Aguilar, that you haven't got a woman hidden in the house at this very moment?" the detective demanded.

"I'll thank ye to keep a civil tongue in your head," said Aguilar. "Or I'll take ye outside and knock yer face sideways. Pardon me, madam. Of course I ain't got no woman concealed on the premises. And mark ye, if I lose my place through this ye'll hear of it. And I shall put a letter in the *Gardeners' Chronicle,* too."

"Well, ye can go," the detective responded.

"Yes," sneered Aguilar. "I can go. Yes, and I shall go. But not so far but what I can protect my interests. And I'll make this village too hot for Keeble before I've done, police or no police."

And with a look at Audrey like the look of a knight at his lady after a joust, Aguilar turned to leave the room.

"Aguilar," Audrey rewarded him. "You needn't be afraid about your place."

"Thank ye, m'm."

"May I ask what your name is?" Audrey inquired of the detective as soon as Aguilar had shut the door.

"Hurley," replied the detective.

"I thought it might be," said Audrey, sitting down, but not offering seats. "Well, Mr. Hurley, after all your running after Miss Susan Foley, don't you think it's rather unfair to say horrid things about a respectable man like Aguilar? You were funny about that stout wife of yours last time I saw you, but you must remember that Aguilar can't be funny about his wife, because he hasn't got one."

"I really don't know what you're driving at, miss," said Mr. Hurley simply.

"Well, what were you driving at when you followed me all the way to London the other day?"

"Madam," said Mr. Hurley, "I didn't follow you to London. I only happened to arrive at Charing Cross about twenty seconds after you, that was all. As a matter of fact, nearly half of the way you were following me."

"Well, I hope you were satisfied."

"I only want to know one thing," the detective retorted. "Am I speaking to Mrs. Olivia Moncreiff?"

Audrey hesitated, glancing at Madame Piriac, who, in company with the vast Inspector Keeble, was carefully inspecting the floor. She invoked wisdom and sagacity from heaven, and came to a decision.

"Not that I know of," she answered.

"Then, if you please, who are you?"

"What!" exclaimed Audrey. "You're in the village of Moze itself and you ask who I am. Everybody knows me. My name is Audrey Moze, of Flank Hall, Moze,

Essex. Any child in Moze Street will tell you that. Inspector
Keeble knows as well as anybody."

Madame Piriac proceeded steadily with the inquiry into
the carpet. Audrey felt her heart beating.

"Unmarried?" pursued the detective.

"Most decidedly," said Audrey with conviction.

"Then what's the meaning of that ring on your finger,
if you don't mind my asking?" the detective continued.

Certainly Audrey was flustered, but only for a moment.

"Mr. Hurley," said she; "I wear it as a protection
from men of all ages who are too enterprising."

She spoke archly, with humour; but now there was no
answering humour in the features of Mr. Hurley, who
seemed to be a changed man, to be indeed no longer even
an Irishman. And Audrey grew afraid. Did he, after all,
know of her share in the Blue City enterprise? She had
long since persuaded herself that the police had absolutely
failed to connect her with that affair, but now uncertainty
was born in her mind.

"I must search the house," said the detective.

"What for?"

"I have to arrest a woman named Jane Foley," answered
Mr. Hurley, adding somewhat grimly: "The name will be
known to ye, I'm thinking. . . . And I have reason to
believe that she is now concealed on these premises."

The directness of the blow was terrific. It was almost
worse than the blow itself. And Audrey now believed
everything that she had ever heard or read about the
miraculous ingenuity of detectives. Still, she did not
regard herself as beaten, and the thought of the yacht
lying close by gave her a dim feeling of security. If she
could only procure delay! . . .

"I'm not going to let you search my house," she said
angrily. "I never heard of such a thing! You've got
no right to search my house."

"Oh yes, I have!" Mr. Hurley insisted.

"Well, let me see your paper—I don't know what you

call it. But I know you can't do anything without a paper. Otherwise any bright young man might walk into my house and tell me he meant to search it. Keeble, I'm really surprised at *you*."

Inspector Keeble blushed.

"I'm very sorry, miss," said he contritely. "But the law's the law. Show the lady your search-warrant, Mr. Hurley." His voice resembled himself.

Mr. Hurley coughed. "I haven't got a search-warrant yet," he remarked. "I didn't expect——"

"You'd better go and get one, then," said Audrey, calculating how long it would take three women to transport themselves from the house to the yacht, and perpending upon the probable behaviour of Mr. Gilman under a given set of circumstances.

"I will," said Mr. Hurley. "And I shan't be long. Keeble, where is the nearest justice of the peace? . . . You'd better stay here or hereabouts."

"I got to go to the station to sign on my three constables," Inspector Keeble protested awkwardly, looking at his watch, which also resembled himself.

"You'd better stay here or hereabouts," repeated Mr. Hurley, and he moved towards the door. Inspector Keeble, too, moved towards the door.

Audrey let them get into the passage, and then she was vouchsafed a new access of inspiration.

"Mr. Hurley," she called, in a bright, unoffended tone. "After all, I see no reason why you shouldn't search the house. I don't really want to put you to any unnecessary trouble. It is annoying, but I'm not going to be annoyed." The ingenuous young creature expected Mr. Hurley to be at once disarmed and ashamed by this kind offer. She was wrong. He was evidently surprised, but he gave no evidence of shame or of the sudden death in his brain of all suspicions.

"That's better," he said calmly. "And I'm much obliged."

"I'll come with you," said Audrey. "Madame Piriac," she addressed Hortense with averted eyes. "Will you excuse me for a minute or two while I show these gentlemen the house?" The fact was that she did not care just then to be left alone with Madame Piriac.

"Oh! I beg you, darling!" Madame Piriac granted the permission with overpowering sweetness.

The procedure of Mr. Hurley was astonishing to Audrey; nay, it was unnerving. First he locked the front door and the garden door and pocketed the keys. Then he locked the drawing-room on the passage side and pocketed that key. He instructed Inspector Keeble to remain in the hall at the foot of the stairs. He next went into the kitchen and the sculleries and locked the outer doors in that quarter. Then he descended to the cellars, with Audrey always in his wake. Having searched the cellars and the ground floor, he went upstairs, and examined in turn all the bedrooms with a thoroughness and particularity which caused Audrey to blush. He left nothing whatever to chance, and no dust sheet was undisturbed. Audrey said no word. The detective said no word. But Audrey kept thinking: "He is getting nearer to the tank-room." A small staircase led to the attic floor, upon which were only servants' bedrooms and the tank-room. After he had mounted this staircase and gone a little way along the passage he swiftly and without warning dashed back and down the staircase. But nothing seemed to happen, and he returned. The three doors of the three servants' bedrooms were all ajar. Mr. Hurley passed each of them with a careless glance within. At the end of the corridor, in obscurity, was the door of the tank-room.

"What's this?" he asked abruptly. And he knocked nonchalantly on the door of the tank-room.

Audrey was acutely alarmed lest Jane Foley should respond, thinking the knock was that of a friend. She saw how idiotic she had been not to warn Jane by means of loud conversation with the detective.

"That's the tank-room," she said loudly. "I'm afraid it's locked."

"Oh!" murmured Mr. Hurley negligently, and he turned the searchlight of his gaze upon the three bedrooms, which he examined as carefully as he had examined anything in the house. The failure to discover in any cupboard or corner even the shadow of a human being did not appear to discourage him in the slightest degree. In the third bedroom—that is to say, the one nearest the head of the stairs and farthest from the tank-room—he suddenly beckoned to Audrey, who was standing in the doorway. She went within the room and he pushed the door to, without, however, quite shutting it.

"Now about the tank-room, Miss Moze," he began quietly. "You say it's locked?"

"Yes," said the quaking Audrey.

"As a matter of form I'd better just look in. Will you kindly let me have the key?"

"I can't," said Audrey.

"Why not?"

Audrey acquired tranquillity as she went on : "It's at Frinton. Friends of mine there keep a punt on Moze-water, and I let them store the sail and things in the tank-room. There's plenty of room. I give them the key because that's more satisfactory. The tank-room isn't wanted at all, you see, while I'm away from home."

"Who are these friends?"

"Mr. and Mrs. Spatt," said Audrey at a venture.

"I see," said the detective.

They came downstairs, and the detective made it known that he would re-visit the drawing-room. Inspector Keeble followed them. In that room Audrey remarked :

"And now I hope you're satisfied."

Mr. Hurley merely said :

"Will you please ring for Aguilar?"

Audrey complied. But she had to ring three times before

the gardener's footsteps were heard on the uncarpeted stone floor of the hall.

"Aguilar," Mr. Hurley demanded. "Where is the key of the tank-room?"

Audrey sank into a chair, knowing profoundly that all was lost.

"It's at Mrs. Spatt's at Frinton," replied Aguilar glibly. "Mistress lets her have that room to store some boat-gear in. I expected she'd ha' been over before this to get it out. But the yachting season seems to start later and later every year these times."

Audrey gazed at the man as at a miracle-worker.

"Well, I think that's all," said Mr. Hurley.

"No, it isn't," Audrey corrected him. "You've got all my keys in your pocket—except one."

When the police had gone Audrey said to Aguilar in the hall:

"Aguilar, how on earth did you——"

But she was in such a state of emotion at the realisation of dangers affronted and past that she could not finish.

"I'm sorry I was so long answering the bell, m'm," replied Aguilar strangely. "But I'd put my list slippers on—them as your father made me wear when I come into the house, mornings, to change the plants, and I thought it better to put my boots on again before I come. . . . Shall I put the keys back in the doors, madam?"

So saying he touched his front hair, after his manner, and took the keys and retired. Audrey was as full of fear as of gratitude. Aguilar daunted her.

CHAPTER XXXV

THE THIRD SORT OF WOMAN

"It was quite true what I told the detective. So I suppose you've finished with me for evermore!" Audrey burst out recklessly, as soon as she and Madame Piriac were alone together. The supreme moment had come, and she tried to grasp it like a nettle. Her adventurous rashness was, she admitted, undeniable. She had spoken the truth to the police officer about her identity and her spinsterhood because with unusual wisdom she judged that fibs or even prevarication on such a subject to such an audience might entangle her in far more serious difficulties later on. Moreover, with Inspector Keeble present, she could not successfully have gone very far from the truth. It was a pity that Madame Piriac had witnessed the scene, for really, when Audrey came to face it, the deception which she had practised upon Madame Piriac was of a monstrous and inexcusable kind. And now that Madame Piriac knew the facts, many other people would have to know the facts—including probably Mr. Gilman. The prospect of explanations was terrible. In vain Audrey said to herself that the thing was naught, that she had acted within her rights, and that anyhow she had long ago ceased to be diffident and shy! . . . She was intimidated by her own enormities. And she also thought: "How could I have been silly enough to tell that silly tale about the Spatts? More complications. And poor dear Inspector Keeble will be so shocked."

After a short pause Madame Piriac replied, in a grave but kind tone:

"Why would you that I should have finished with you for ever? You had the right to call yourself by any name you wished, and to wear any ring that pleased your caprice. It is the affair of nobody but yourself."

"Oh! I'm so glad you take it like that," said Audrey with eager relief. "That's just what *I* thought all along!"

"But it *is* your affair!" Madame Piriac finished, with a peculiar inflection of her well-controlled voice. "I mean," she added, "you cannot afford to neglect it."

"No—of course not," Audrey agreed, rather dashed, and with a vague new apprehension. "Naturally I shall tell you everything, darling. I had my reasons. I——"

"The principal question is, darling," Madame Piriac stopped her. "What are you going to do now? Ought we not to return to the yacht?"

"But I must look after Jane Foley!" cried Audrey. "I can't leave her here."

"And why not? She has Miss Ingate."

"Yes, worse luck for her! Winnie would make the most dreadful mess of things if she wasn't stopped. If Winnie was right out of it, and Jane Foley had only herself and Aguilar to count on, there might be a chance. But not else."

"It is by pure hazard that you are here. Nobody expected you. What would this young girl Mees Foley have done if you had not been here?"

"It's no good wasting time about that, darling, because I *am* here, don't you see?" Audrey straightened her shoulders and put her hands behind her back.

"My little one," said Madame Piriac with a certain solemnity. "You remember our conversation in my boudoir. I then told you that you would find yourself in a riot within a month, if you continued your course. Was I right? Happily you have escaped from that horrible complication. Go no farther. Listen to me. You were not created for these adventures. It is impossible that you should be happy in them."

"But look at Jane Foley," said Audrey eagerly. "Is she

not happy? Did you ever see anybody as happy as Jane? I never did."

"That is not happiness," replied Madame Piriac. "That is exaltation. It is morbid. I do not say that it is not right for her. I do not say that she is not justified, and that that which she represents is not justified. But I say that a rôle such as hers is not your rôle. To commence, she does not interest herself in men. For her there are no men in the world—there are only political enemies. Do you think I do not know the type? We have it, *chez nous*. It is full of admirable qualities—but it is not your type. For you, darling, the world is inhabited principally by men, and the time will come—perhaps soon—when for you it will be inhabited principally by one man. If you remain obdurate, there must inevitably arrive a quarrel between that man and these—these riotous adventures."

"No man that I could possibly care for," Audrey retorted, "would ever object to me having an active interest in—er—politics."

"I agree, darling," said Madame Piriac. "He would not object. It is you who would object. The quarrel would occur within your own heart. There are two sorts of women —individualists and fanatics. It was always so. I am a woman, and I know what I'm saying. So do you. Well, you belong to the first sort of woman."

"I don't," Audrey protested. Nevertheless she recollected her thoughts on the previous night, near the binnacle and Mr. Gilman, about the indispensability of a man and about the futility of the state of not owning and possessing a man. The memory of these thoughts only rendered her more obstinate.

"But you will not have the courage to tell me that you are a fanatic?"

"No."

"Then what?"

"There is a third sort of woman."

"Darling, believe me, there is not."

"There's going to be, anyhow!" said Audrey with decision, and in English. "And I won't leave Jane Foley in the lurch, either! . . . Now I'll just run up and have a talk with her, if you don't mind waiting a minute or two."

"But what are you going to do?" Madame Piriac demanded.

"Well," said Audrey. "It is obvious that there is only one safe thing to do. I shall take Jane on board the yacht. We shall sail off, and she'll be safe."

"On the yacht!" repeated Madame Piriac, truly astounded. "But my poor oncle will never agree. You do not know him. You do not know how peculiar he is. Never will he agree! Besides——"

"Darling," said Audrey quietly and confidently. "If he does not agree, I undertake to go into a convent for the rest of my days."

Madame Piriac was silent.

Just as she was opening the door to go upstairs, Audrey suddenly turned back into the room.

"Darling," she said, kissing Madame Piriac. "How calmly you've taken it!"

"Taken what?"

"About me not being Mrs. Moncreiff nor a widow nor anything of that kind."

"But, darling," answered Madame Piriac with exquisite tranquillity. "Of course I knew it before."

"You knew it before!"

"Certainly. I knew it the first time I saw you, in the studio of Mademoiselle Nickall. You were the image of your father! The image, I repeat—except perhaps the nose. Recollect that as a child I saw your father. I was left with my mother's relatives, until matters should be arranged; but he came to Paris. Then before matters could be arranged my mother died, and I never saw him again. But I could never forget him. . . . Then also, in my boudoir that night, you blushed—it was very amusing—when I mentioned Essex and Audrey Moze.   And there were other things."

"For instance? "

"Darling, you were never quite convincing as a widow—at any rate to a Frenchwoman. You may have deceived American and English women. But not myself. You did not say the convincing things when the conversation took certain turns. That is all."

"You knew who I was, and you never told me ! " Audrey pouted.

"Had I the right, darling? You had decided upon your identity. It would have been inexcusable on my part to inform you that you were mistaken in so essential a detail."

Madame Piriac gently returned Audrey's kiss.

"So that was why you insisted on me coming with you to-day ! " murmured Audrey, crestfallen. "You are a marvellous actress, darling."

"I have several times been told so," Madame Piriac admitted simply.

"What on earth did you expect would happen? "

"Not that which has happened," said Madame Piriac.

"Well, if you ask me," said Audrey with gaiety and a renewal of self-confidence. "I think it's all happened splendidly."

CHAPTER XXXVI

IN THE DINGHY

WHEN the pair got back to the sea-wall the tide had considerably ebbed, and where the dinghy had floated there was nothing more liquid than exquisitely coloured mud. Nevertheless water still lapped the yacht, whereas on the shore side of the yacht was now no crowd. The vans and carts had all departed, and the quidnuncs and observers of human nature, having gazed steadily at the yacht for some ten hours, had thought fit to depart also. The two women looked about rather anxiously as though Mr. Gilman had basely marooned them.

"But what must we do?" demanded Madame Piriac.

"Oh! We can walk round on the dyke," said Audrey superiorly. "Unless the stiles frighten you."

"It is about to rain," said Madame Piriac, glancing at the high curved heels of her shoes.

The sky, which was very wide and variegated over Mozewater, did indeed seem to threaten.

At that moment the dinghy appeared round the forefoot of the *Ariadne*. Mr. Gilman and Miss Thompkins were in it, and Mr. Gilman was rowing with gentleness and dignity. They had, even afar off, a tremendous air of intimacy; each leaned towards the other, face to face, and Tommy had her chin in her hands and her elbows on her knees. And in addition to an air of intimacy they had an air of mystery. It was surprising, and perhaps a little annoying, to Audrey that those two should have gone on living to themselves, in their own self-absorbed way, while such singular events had been happening to herself in Flank Hall. She put several fingers in her mouth and produced a piercing long-distance whistle which effectively reached the dinghy.

"My poor little one!" exclaimed Madame Piriac, shocked in spite of her broadmindedness by both the sound and the manner of its production.

"Oh! I learnt that when I was twelve," said Audrey. "It took me four months, but I did it. And nobody except Miss Ingate knows that I can do it."

The occupants of the dinghy were signalling their intention to rescue, and Mr. Gilman used his back nobly.

"But we cannot embark here!" Madame Piriac complained.

"Oh, yes!" said Audrey. "You see those white stones? . . . It's quite easy."

When the dinghy had done about half the journey Madame Piriac murmured :

"By the way, who are you, precisely, for the present? It would be prudent to decide, darling."

Audrey hesitated an instant.

"Who am I? . . . Oh! I see. Well, I'd better keep on being Mrs. Moncreiff for a bit, hadn't I?"

"It is as you please, darling."

The fact was that Audrey recoiled from a general confession, though admitting it to be ultimately inevitable. Moreover, she had a slight fear that each of her friends in turn might make a confession ridiculous by saying: "We knew all along, of course."

The dinghy was close in.

"My!" cried Tommy. "Who did that whistle? It was enough to beat the cars."

"Wouldn't you like to know!" Audrey retorted.

The embarkation, under Audrey's direction, was accomplished in safety, and, save for one tiny French scream, in silence. The silence, which persisted, was peculiar. Each pair should have had something to tell the other, yet nothing was told, or even asked. Mr. Gilman rowed with careful science, and brought the dinghy alongside the yacht in an unexceptionable manner. Musa stood on deck apart, acting indifference. Madame Piriac, having climbed into the *Ariadne,* went below at once. Miss Thompkins, seeing her friend Mr. Price half-way down the saloon companion, moved to speak to him, and they vanished together. Mr. Gilman was respectfully informed by the engineer that the skipper and Dr. Cromarty were ashore.

"How nice it is on the water!" said Audrey to Mr. Gilman in a low, gentle voice. "There is a channel round there with three feet of water in it at low tide." She sketched a curve in the air with her finger.

"Of course you know this part," said Mr. Gilman cautiously and even apprehensively. His glance seemed to be saying: "And it was you who gave that fearful whistle, too! Are you, can you be, all that I dreamed?"

"I do," Audrey answered. "Would you like me to show it you."

"I should be more than delighted," said Mr. Gilman.

With a gesture he summoned a man to untie the dinghy again and hold it, and the man slid down into the dinghy like a monkey.

"I'll pull," said Audrey, in the boat.

The man sprang out of the dinghy.

"One instant!" Mr. Gilman begged her, standing up in the sternsheets, and popping his head through a porthole of the saloon. "Mr. Price!"

"Sir?" From the interior.

"Will you be good enough to play that air with thirty-six variations, of Beethoven's? We shall hear splendidly from the dinghy."

"Certainly, sir."

And Audrey said to herself: "You don't want him to flirt with Tommy while you're away, so you've given him something to keep him busy."

Mr. Gilman remarked under his breath to Audrey:

"I think there is nothing finer than to hear Beethoven on the water."

"Oh! There isn't!" she eagerly concurred.

Ignoring the thirty-six variations of Beethoven, Audrey rowed slowly away, and after about a hundred yards the boat had rounded a little knoll which marked the beginning of a narrow channel known as the Lander Creek. The thirty-six variations, however, would not be denied; they softly impregnated the whole beautiful watery scene.

"Perhaps," said Mr. Gilman suddenly, "perhaps your ladyship was not quite pleased at me rowing about with Miss Thompkins—especially after I had taken her for a walk." He smiled, but his voice was rather wistful. Audrey liked him prodigiously in that moment.

"Foolish man!" she replied, with a smile far surpassing his, and she rested on her oars, taking care to keep the boat in the middle of the channel. "Do you know why I asked you to come out? I wanted to talk to you quite privately. It is easier here."

"I'm so glad!" he said simply and sincerely. And Audrey thought: "Is it possible to give so much pleasure to an important and wealthy man with so little trouble?"

"Yes," she said. "Of course you know who I really am, don't you, Mr. Gilman?"

"I only know you're Mrs. Moncreiff," he answered.

"But I'm not! Surely you've heard *some*thing? Surely it's been hinted in front of you?"

"Never!" said he.

"But haven't you asked—about my marriage, for instance?"

"To ask might have been to endanger your secret," he said.

"I see!" she murmured. "How frightfully loyal you are, Mr. Gilman! I do admire loyalty. Well, I dare say very, very few people do know. So I'll tell you. That's my home over there." And she pointed to Flank Hall, whose chimneys could just be seen over the bank.

"I admit that I had thought so," said Mr. Gilman.

S

"But naturally that was your home as a girl, before your marriage."

"I've never been married, Mr. Gilman," she said. "I'm only what the French call a *jeune fille*."

His face changed; he seemed to be withdrawing alarmed into himself.

"Never—been married?"

"Oh! You *must* understand me!" she went on, with an appealing vivacity. "I was all alone. I was in mourning for my father and mother. I wanted to see the world. I just had to see it! I expect I was very foolish, but it was so easy to put a ring on my finger and call myself Mrs. And it gave me such advantages. And Miss Ingate agreed. She was my mother's oldest friend. . . . You're vexed with me."

"You always seemed so wise," Mr. Gilman faltered.

"Ah! That's only the effect of my forehead!"

"And yet, you know, I always thought there was something very innocent about you, too."

"I don't know what *that* was," said Audrey. "But honestly I acted for the best. You see I'm rather rich. Supposing I'd only gone about as a young marriageable girl—what frightful risks I should have run, shouldn't I? Somebody would be bound to have married me for my money. And look at all I should have missed—without this ring! I should never have met you in Paris, for instance, and we should never have had those talks. . . . And—and there's a lot more reasons—I shall tell you another time—about Madame Piriac and so on. Now do say you aren't vexed!"

"I think you've been splendid," he said, with enthusiasm. "I think the girls of to-day *are* splendid! I've been a regular old fogey, that's what it is."

"Now there's one thing I want you not to do," Audrey proceeded. "I want you not to alter the way you talk to me. Because I'm really just the same girl I was last night. And I couldn't bear you to change."

"I won't! I won't! But of course———"

"No, no! No buts. I won't have it. Do you know why I told you just this afternoon? Well, partly because you were so perfectly sweet last night. And partly because I've got a favour to ask you, and I wouldn't ask it until I'd told you."

"You can't ask me a favour," he replied, "because it wouldn't be a favour. It would be my privilege."

"But if you put it like that I can't ask you."

"You must!" he said firmly.

Then she told him something of the predicament of Jane Foley. He listened with an expression of trouble. Audrey finished bluntly: "She's my friend. And I want you to take her on the yacht to-night after it's dark. Nobody but you can save her. There! I've asked you!"

"Jane Foley!" he murmured.

She could see that he was aghast. The syllables of that name were notorious throughout Britain. They stood for revolt, damage to property, defiance of law, injured policemen, forcible feeding, and all sorts of phenomena that horrified respectable pillars of society.

"She's the dearest thing!" said Audrey. "You've no idea. You'd love her. And she's done as much for Women's Suffrage as anybody in the world. She's a real heroine, if you like. You couldn't help the cause better than by helping her. And I know how keen you are to help." And Audrey said to herself: "He's as timid as a girl about it. How queer men are, after all!"

"But what are we to do with her afterwards?" asked Mr. Gilman. There was perspiration on his brow.

"Sail straight to France, of course. They couldn't touch her there, you see, because it's political. It *is* political, you know," Audrey insisted proudly.

"And give up all our cruise?"

Audrey bent forward, as she had seen Tommy do. She smiled enchantingly. "I quite understand," she said, with a sort of tenderness. "You don't want to do it. And it was a shame of me even to suggest it."

"But I do want to do it," he protested with splendid despairful resolve. "I was only thinking of you—and the cruise. I do want to do it. I'm absolutely at your disposal. When you ask me to do a thing, I'm only too proud. To do it is the greatest happiness I could have."

Audrey replied softly:

"You deserve the Victoria Cross."

"Whatever do you mean?" he demanded nervously.

"I don't know exactly what I mean," she said. "But you're the nicest man I ever knew."

He blushed.

"You mustn't say that to me," he deprecated.

"I shall, and I shall."

The sound of the thirty-six variations still came very faintly over the water. The sun sent cataracts of warm light across all the estuary. The water lapped against the boat, and Audrey was overwhelmed by the inexplicable marvel of being alive in the gorgeous universe.

"I shall have to back water," she said, low. "There's no room to turn round here."

"I suppose we'd better say as little about it as possible," he ventured.

"Oh! Not a word! Not a word till it's done."

"Yes, of course." He was drenched in an agitating satisfaction.

Five bells rang clear from the yacht, overmastering the thirty-six variations.

Audrey thought:

"So he'd never agree, wouldn't he, Madame Piriac!"

CHAPTER XXXVII

AFLOAT

THAT night, which was an unusually dark night for the time of year, Audrey left the yacht, alone, to fetch Jane Foley. She had made a provisional plan with Jane and Aguilar, and the arrangement with Mr. Gilman had been of the simplest, necessitating nothing save a brief order from the owner to the woman whom Audrey could always amuse Mr. Gilman by calling the "parlourmaid," but who was more commonly known as the stewardess. This young married creature had prepared a cabin. For the rest little had been said. The understanding between Mr. Gilman and Audrey was that Mrs. Moncreiff should continue to exist, and that not a word as to the arrival of Jane Foley should escape either of them until the deed was accomplished. It is true that Madame Piriac knew of the probable imminence of the affair, but Madame Piriac was discretion elegantly attired, and from the moment they had left Flank Hall together she had been wise enough not even to mention Jane Foley to Audrey. Madame Piriac appreciated the value of ignorance in a questionable crisis. Mr. Gilman had been less guarded. Indeed he had shown a tendency to discuss the coming adventure with Audrey in remote corners—a tendency which had to be discouraged because it gave to both of them a too obvious air of being tremendous conspirators. Also Audrey had had to dissuade him from accompanying her to the Hall. He had rather conventional ideas about women being abroad alone after dark, and he abandoned them with difficulty even now.

As there were no street lamps alight in summer in the

village of Moze, Audrey had no fear of being recognised; moreover, recognition by her former fellow-citizens could now have no sinister importance; she did not much care who recognised her. The principal gates of Flank Hall were slightly ajar, as arranged with Aguilar, and she passed with a suddenly aroused heart up the drive towards the front entrance of the house. In spite of herself she could not get rid of an absurd fear that either Mr. Hurley or Inspector Keeble or both would jump out of the dark bushes and slip handcuffs upon her wrists. And the baffling invisibility of the sky further affected her nerves. There ought to have been a lamp in the front hall, but no ray showed through the eighteenth century fanlight over the door. She rang the bell cautiously. She heard the distant ting. Aguilar, according to the plan, ought to have opened; but he did not open; nobody opened. She was instantly sure that she knew what had happened. Mr. Hurley had been to Frinton and ascertained that the Spatt story as to the tank-room was an invention, and had returned with a search warrant and some tools. But in another ten seconds she was equally sure that nothing of the sort could have happened, for it was an axiom with her that Aguilar's masterly lying, based on masterly listening at an attic door, had convinced Mr. Hurley of the truth of the story about the tank-room.

Accidentally pushing against the front door with an elbow in the deep obscurity, she discovered that it was not latched. This was quite contrary to the plan. She stepped into the house. The unforeseeing simpleton had actually come on the excursion without a box of matches! She felt her way, aided by the swift returning memories of childhood, to the foot of the stairs, and past the stairs into the kitchen, for in ancient days a candlestick with a box of matches in it had always been kept on the ledge of the small square window that gave light to the passage between the hall and the kitchen. Her father had been most severely particular about that candlestick (with matches) being always ready on that ledge in case of his need. Ridiculous,

AFLOAT 287

of course, to expect a candlestick to be still there! Times
change so. But she felt for it, and there it was, and the
matches too! She lit the candle. The dim scene thus
revealed seemed strange enough to her after the electricity
of the Hôtel du Danube and of the yacht. It made her
want to cry. . . .

She was one of those people who have room in their
minds for all sorts of things at once. And thus she could
simultaneously be worried to an extreme about Jane Foley,
foolish and sad about her immensely distant childhood, and
even regretful that she had admitted the fraudulence of the
wedding-ring on her hand. On the last point she had a
very strong sense of failure and disillusion. When she had
first donned a widow's bonnet she had meant to have wondrous adventures and to hear marvellous conversations as a
widow. And what had she done with her widowhood after
all? Nothing. She could not but think that she ought to
have kept it a little longer, on the chance. . . .

Aguilar made a practice of sleeping in the kitchen; he
considered that a house could only be well guarded at night
from the ground floor. There was his bed, in the corner
against the brush and besom cupboard, all made up. Its
creaselessness, so characteristic of Aguilar, had not been
disturbed. The sight of the narrow bed made Audrey think
what a strange existence was the existence of Aguilar.
. . . Then, with a boldness that was half bluster, she went
upstairs, and the creaking of the woodwork was affrighting.

"Jane! Jane, dear!" she called out, as she arrived
at the second-storey landing. The sound of her voice was
uncanny in the haunted stillness. All Audrey's infancy
floated up the well of the stairs and wrapped itself round
her and tightened her throat. She went along the passage
to the door of the tank-room.

"Jane, Jane!"

No answer! The door was locked. She listened. She
put her ear against the door in order to catch the faintest
sound of life within. But she could only hear the crude,

sharp ticking of the cheap clock which, as she knew,
Aguilar had supplied to Jane Foley. The vision of Jane
lying unconscious or dead obsessed her. Then she thrust
it away and laughed at it. Assuredly Aguilar and Jane
must have received some alarm as to a reappearance of
the police; they must have fled while there had yet been
time. Where could they have gone? Of course, through
the garden and plantation and down to the sea-wall,
whence Jane might steal to the yacht. Audrey turned
back towards the stairs, and the vast intimidating emptiness
of the gloomy house, lit by a single flickering candle,
assaulted her. She had to fight it before she could descend.
The garden door was latched, but not locked. Extinguishing
the candle, she went forth. The gusty breeze from the
estuary was now damp on her cheek with the presage
of rain. She hurried, fumbling as it were, through the
garden. When she achieved the hedge the spectacle of
the yacht, gleaming from stem to stern with electricity,
burst upon her; it shone like something desired and un-
attainable. Carefully she issued from the grounds by the
little gate and crossed the intervening space to the dyke.
A dark figure moved in front of her, and her heart violently
jumped.

"Is that you, madam?"

It was the cold, imperturbable voice of Aguilar. At
once she felt reassured.

"Where is Miss Foley?" she demanded in a whisper.

"I've got her down here, ma'am," said Aguilar. "I
presume as you've been to the house. We had to leave
it."

"But the door of the tank-room was locked!"

"Yes, ma'am. I locked it a-purpose. . . . I thought
as it would keep the police employed a bit when they
come. I seen my cousin Sarah when I went to tell Miss
Ingate as you instructed me. My cousin Sarah seen
Keeble. They been to Frinton to Mrs. Spatt's, and they
found out about *that*. And now the 'tec's back, or nearly.

I reckon it was the warrant as was delaying him. So I out with Miss Foley. I thought I could take her across to the yacht from here. It wouldn't hardly be safe for her to walk round by the dyke. Hurley may have several of his chaps about by this time."

"But there's not water enough, Aguilar."

"Yes, madam. I dragged the old punt down. She don't draw three inches. She's afloat now, and Miss Foley's in her. I was just a-going off. If you don't mind wetting your feet——"

In one minute Audrey had splashed into the punt. Jane Foley took her hand in silence, and she heard Jane's low, happy laugh.

"Isn't it funny?" Jane whispered.

Audrey squeezed her hand.

Aguilar pushed off with an oar, and he continued to use the oar as a punt-pole, so that no sound of their movement should reach the bank. Water was pouring into the old sieve, and they touched ground once. But Aguilar knew precisely what he was about and got her off again. They approached the yacht with the slow, sure inexorability of Aguilar's character. A beam from the portholes of the saloon caught Aguilar's erect figure. He sat down, poling as well as he could from the new position. When they were a little nearer he stopped dead, holding the punt firm by means of the pole fixed in the mud.

"He's there afore us!" he murmured, pointing.

Under the Maltese cross of electric lights at the inner end of the gangway could clearly be seen the form of Mr. Hurley, engaged in conversation with Mr. Gilman. Mr. Hurley was fairly on board.

CHAPTER XXXVIII

When Audrey, having been put ashore in execution of a plan arranged with those naturally endowed strategists, Aguilar and Jane Foley, arrived at the Hard by way of the sea-wall, Mr. Hurley was still in parley with Mr. Gilman under the Maltese cross of electric lights. From the distance Mr. Gilman had an air of being somewhat intimidated by the Irishman, but as soon as he distinguished the figure of Audrey at the shore end of the gangway his muscles became mysteriously taut, and his voice charged with defiance.

"I have already told you, sir," Audrey heard him say, "there is no such person aboard the yacht. And I most certainly will not allow you to search. You have no right whatever to search, and you know it. You have my word. My name is Gilman. You may have heard of me. I'm chairman of the Board of Foodstuffs, Limited. Gilman, sir. And I shall feel obliged if you will leave my decks."

"Are you sailing to-night?" asked Mr. Hurley placidly.

"What the devil has that got to do with you, sir?" replied Mr. Gilman gloriously.

Audrey, standing behind the detective and unseen by him, observed the gloriousness of Mr. Gilman's demeanour and also Mr. Gilman's desire that she should note the same and appreciate it. She nodded violently several times to Mr. Gilman, to urge him to answer the detective in the affirmative.

"Ye-es, sir. Since you are so confoundedly inquisitive, I am sailing to-night. I shall sail as soon as the tide serves," said Mr. Gilman hurriedly and fiercely, and then glanced again at Audrey for further approval.

"Where for?" Mr. Hurley demanded.

"Where I please, sir," Mr. Gilman snorted. By this time he evidently imagined that he was furious, and was taking pleasure in his fury.

Mr. Hurley, having given a little ironic bow, turned to leave and found himself fronting Audrey, who stiffly ignored his salute. The detective gone, Mr. Gilman walked to and fro, breathing more loudly than ever, and unsuccessfully pretending to a scattered audience, which consisted of the skipper, Mr. Price, Dr. Cromarty, and sundry deckhands, that he had done nothing in particular and was not a hero. As Audrey approached him he seemed to lay all his glory with humble pride at her feet.

"Well, he brought that on himself!" said Audrey, smiling.

"He did," Mr. Gilman concurred, gazing at the Hard with inimical scorn.

"She can't come—now," said Audrey. "It wouldn't be safe. He means to stay on the Hard till we're gone. He's a very suspicious man."

Mr. Hurley was indeed lingering just beyond the immediate range of the *Ariadne's* lamps.

"Can't come! What a pity! What a pity!" murmured Mr. Gilman, with an accent that was not a bit sincere. The news was the best he had heard for hours. "But I suppose," he added, "we'd better sail just the same, as I've said we should?" He did not want to run the risk of getting Jane Foley after all.

"Oh! Do!" Audrey exclaimed. "It will be lovely! If it doesn't rain—and even if it does rain! We all like sailing at night. . . . Are the others in the saloon? I'll run down."

"Mr. Wyatt," the owner sternly accosted the captain. "When can we get off?"

"Oh! About midnight," Audrey answered quickly, before Mr. Wyatt could compose his lips.

The men gazed at each other surprised by this show of technical knowledge in a young widow. By the time Mr. Wyatt had replied, Audrey was descending into the saloon. It was Aguilar who, having ascertained the *Ariadne's* draught, had made the calculation as to the earliest possible hour of departure.

And in the saloon Musa was, as it were, being enveloped and kept comfortable in the admiring sympathy of Madame Piriac and Miss Thompkins. Mr. Gilman's violin lay across his knees—perhaps he had been tuning it—and the women inclined towards him, one on either side. It was a sight that somewhat annoyed Audrey, who told herself that she considered it silly. Admitting that Musa had genius, she could not understand this soft flattery of genius. She never flattered genius herself, and she did not approve of others doing so. Certainly Musa was now being treated on the yacht as a celebrity of the first order, and Audrey could find no explanation of the steady growth in the height and splendour of his throne. Her arrival dissolved the spectacle. Within one minute, somehow, the saloon was empty and everybody on deck again.

And then, drawing her away, Musa murmured to Audrey in a disconcerting tone that he must speak to her on a matter of urgency, and that in order that he might do so, they must go ashore and walk seawards, far from interruption. She consented, for she was determined to prove to him at close quarters that she was a different creature from the other two. They moved to the gangway amid discreet manifestations from the doctor and the secretary—manifestations directed chiefly to Musa and indicative of his importance as a notability. Audrey was puzzled. For her, Musa was more than ever just Musa, and less than ever a personage.

"I shall not return to the yacht," he said, with an excited bitterness, after they had walked some distance along one of the paths leading past low bushes into the wilderness of the marsh land that bounded the estuary to the south. The sky was still invisible, but there was now a certain amount of diffused light, and the pale path could easily be distinguished amid the sombreness of green. The yacht was hidden behind one of the knolls. No sound could be heard. The breeze had died. That which was around them—on either hand, above, below— was the universe. They knew that they stood still in the universe, and this idea gave their youth the sensation of being very important.

"What is that which you say?" Audrey demanded sharply in French, as Musa had begun in French. She was aware, not for the first time with Musa, of the sudden possibilities of drama in a human being. She could scarcely make out his face, but she knew that he was in a mood for high follies; she knew that danger was gathering; she knew that the shape of the future was immediately to be moulded by her and him, and chiefly by herself. She liked it. The sensation of her importance was reinforced.

"I say I shall never return to the yacht," he repeated.

She thought compassionately:

"Poor foolish thing!"

She was incalculably older and wiser than this irrational boy. She was the essence of wisdom.

She said, with acid detachment:

"But your luggage, your belongings? What an idea to leave in this manner! It is so polite, so sensible!"

"I shall not return."

"Of course," she said, "I do not at all understand why you are going. But what does that matter? You are going." Her indifference was superb. It was so superb that it might have driven some men to destroy her on the spot.

"Yes, you understand! I told you last night," said Musa, overflowing with emotion.

"Oh! You told me? I forget."

"Naturally Monsieur Gilman is rich. I am not rich, though I shall be. But you can't wait," Musa sneered.

"I do not know what you mean," said Audrey.

"Ah!" said Musa. "Once I told you that Tommy and Nick lent me the money with which to live. For me, since then, you have never been the same being. How stupid I was to tell you! You could not comprehend such a thing. Your soul is too low to comprehend it. Permit me to say that I have already repaid Nick. And at the first moment I shall repay Tommy. My position is secure. I have only to wait. But you will not wait. You are a bourgeoise of the most terrible sort. Opulence fascinates you. Mr. Gilman has opulence. He has nothing else. But he has opulence, and for you that is all."

In an instant her indifference, self-control, wisdom vanished. It was a sad exhibition of frailty; but she enjoyed it, she revelled in it, giving play to everything in herself that was barbaric. The marsh around them was probably as it had been before the vikings had sailed into it, and Audrey rushed back with inconceivable speed into the past and became the primeval woman of twenty centuries earlier. Like almost all women she possessed this wondrous and affrighting faculty.

"You are telling a wicked untruth!" she exploded in English. "And what's more, you know you are. You disgust me. You know as well as I do I don't care anything for money—anything. Only you're a horrid, spoilt beast. You think you can upset me, but you can't. I won't have it, either from you or from anybody else. It's a shame, that's what it is. Now you've got to apologise to me. I absolutely insist on it. You aren't going to bully me, even if you think you are. I'll soon show you the sort of girl I am, and you make no mistake! Are you going to apologise or aren't you?"

The indecorous creature was breathing as loudly as Mr. Gilman himself.

"I admit it," said Musa yielding.

"Ah!"

"I demand your pardon. I knew that what I said was not true. I am outside myself. But what would you? It is stronger than I. This existence is terrible, on the yacht. I cannot support it. I shall become mad. I am ruined. My jealousy is intolerable."

"It is!" said Audrey, using French again, more calmly, having returned to the twentieth century.

"It is intolerable to me." Then Musa's voice changed and grew persuasive, rather like a child's. "I cannot live without you. That is the truth. I am an artist, and you are necessary to me and to my career." He lifted his head. "And I can offer you everything that is most brilliant."

"And what about my career?" Audrey questioned inimically.

"Your career?" He seemed at a loss.

"Yes. My career. It has possibly not occurred to you that I also may have a career."

Musa became appealing.

"You understand me," he said. "I told you you do not comprehend, but you comprehend everything. It is that which enrages me. You have had experience. You know what men are. You could teach me so much. I hate young girls. I have always hated them. They are so tasteless, so insufferably innocent. I could not talk to a young girl as I talk to you. It would be absurd. Now as to my career— what I said——"

"Musa," she interrupted him, with a sinister quietude, "I want to tell you something. But you must promise to keep it secret. Will you?"

He assented, impatient.

"It is not possible!" he exclaimed, when she had told him that she belonged to precisely the category of human beings whom he hated and despised.

"Isn't it?" said she. "Now I hope you see how little you know, really, about women." She laughed.

"It is not possible!" he repeated. And then he said

with deliberate ingenuousness : "I am so content. I am so happy. I could not have hoped for it. It is overwhelming. I am everything you like of the most idiotic, blind, stupid. But now I am happy. Could I ever have borne that you had loved before I knew you? I doubt if I could have borne it. Your innocence is exquisite. It is intoxicating to me."

"Musa," she remarked dryly; "I wish you would remember that you are in England. People do not talk in that way in England. It simply is not done. And I will not listen to it." Her voice grew a little tender. "Why can we not just be friends? "

"It is folly," said he, with sudden disgust. "And it would kill me."

"Well, then," she replied, receding. "You're entitled to die."

He advanced towards her. She kept him away with a gesture.

"You want me to marry you? " she questioned.

"It is essential," he said, very seriously. "I adore you. I can't do anything because of you. I can't think of anything but you. You are more marvellous than anyone can be. You cannot appreciate what you are to me ! "

"And suppose you are nothing to me? "

"But it is necessary that you should love me ! "

"Why? I see no necessity. You want me—because you want me. That's all. I can't help it if you're mad. Your attitude is insulting. You have not given one thought to my feelings. And if I said ' yes ' to you, you'd marry me whatever my feelings were. You think only of yourself. It is the old attitude. And when I offer you my friendship, you instantly decline it. That shows how horribly French you are. Frenchmen can't understand the idea of friendship between a man and a girl. They sneer at it. It shows what brutes you all are. Why should I marry you? I should have nothing to gain by it. You'll be famous. Well, what do I care? Do you think it would be very amusing for me to be the wife of a famous man that was run after by every silly creature in Paris or London or New York? Not quite! And I don't see myself. You don't like young girls. I don't like young men. They're rude and selfish and conceited. They're like babies."

"The fact is," Musa broke in, "you are in love with the old Gilman."

"He is not old!" cried Audrey. "In some ways he is much less worn out than you are. And supposing I am in love with Mr. Gilman? Does it regard you? Do not be rude. Mr. Gilman is at any rate polite. He is not capricious. He is reliable. You aren't reliable. You want someone upon whom you can rely. How nice for your wife! You play the violin. True. You are a genius. But you cannot always be on the platform. And when you are not on the platform . . .! Heavens! If I wish to hear you play I can buy a seat and come and hear you and go away again. But your wife, responsible for your career—she will never be free. Her life will be unbearable. What anxiety! Misery, I should say rather! You would have the lion's share of everything. Now for myself I intend to have the lion's share. And why shouldn't I? Isn't it about time some woman had it? You can't have the lion's share if you are not free. I mean to be free. If I marry I shall want a husband that is not a prison. . . . Thank goodness I've got money. . . . Without that——!"

"Then," said Musa, "you have no feeling for me."

"Love?" she laughed exasperatingly.

"Yes," he said.

"Not that much!" She snapped her fingers. "But " —in a changed tone—"I *should* like to like you. I shall be very disgusted if your concerts are not a tremendous success. And they will not be if you don't keep control over yourself and practise properly. And it will be your fault."

"Then, good-bye!" he said, coldly ignoring all her maternal suggestions. And turned away.

"Where are you going to?"

He stopped.

T

"I do not know. But if I do not deceive myself I have already informed you that in certain circumstances I should not return to the yacht."

"You are worse than a schoolboy."

"It is possible."

"Anyway, *I* shan't explain on the yacht. I shall tell them that I know nothing about it."

"But no one will believe you," he retorted maliciously over his shoulder. And then he was gone.

She at any rate was no longer surrounded by the largeness of the universe. He might still be, but she was not. She was in mind already on the yacht trying to act a surprise equal to the surprise of the others when Musa failed to reappear. She was very angry with him, not because he had been a rude schoolboy and was entirely impossible as a human being, but because she had allowed herself to leave the yacht with him and would therefore be compelled sooner or later to answer questions about him. She seriously feared that Mr. Gilman might refuse to sail unless she confessed to him her positive knowledge that Musa would not be seen again, and that thus she might have to choose between the failure of her plans for Jane Foley and her own personal discomfiture.

Instead of being in the mighty universe she was struggling amid the tiresome littleness of society on a yacht. She hated yachts for their very cosiness and their quality of keeping people close together who wanted to be far apart. And as she watched the figure of Musa growing fainter she was more than ever impressed by the queerness of men. Women seemed to be so logical, so realistic, so understandable, so calculable, whereas men were enigmas of waywardness and unreason. At just that moment her feet reminded her that they had been wetted by the adventure in the punt, and she said to herself sagely that she must take precautions against a chill.

And then she thought she detected some unusual phenomenon behind a clump of bushes to the right which hid a plank-bridge across a waterway. She would have been frightened if she had not been very excited. And in her excitement she marched straight up to the clump, and found Mr. Hurley in a crouching posture. She started, and recovered.

"I might have known!" she said disdainfully.

"We all make mistakes," said Mr. Hurley defensively. "We all make mistakes. I knew I'd made a mistake as soon as I got here, but I couldn't get away quietly enough. And you talked so loud. Ye'll admit I had just cause for suspicion. And being a very agreeable lady ye'll pardon me."

She blushed, and then ceased blushing because it was too dark for him to perceive the blush, and she passed on without a word. When, across the waste, she had come within sight of the yacht again, she heard footsteps behind her, and turned to withstand the detective. But the overtaker was Musa.

"It is necessary that I should return to the yacht," he said savagely. "The thought of you and Monsieur Gilman together, without me. . . . No! I did not know myself. . . . I did not know myself. . . . It is impossible for me to leave."

She made no answer. They boarded the yacht as though they had been for a stroll. Few could have guessed that they had come back from the universe terribly scathed. Accepting deferential greetings as a right, Musa vanished rapidly to his cabin.

Several hours later Audrey and Mr. Gilman, alone among the passengers, were standing together, both tarpaulined, on the starboard bow, gazing seaward as the yacht cautiously felt her way down Mozewater. Captain Wyatt, and not Mr. Gilman, was at the binnacle. A little rain was falling and the night was rather thick but not impenetrable.

"There's the light!" said Audrey excitedly.

"What sharp eyes you have!" said Mr. Gilman. "I can see it, too." He spoke a word to the skipper, and the skipper spoke, and then the engine went still more slowly.

The yacht approached the Flank buoy dead slow, scarcely stemming the tide. The Moze punt was tied up to the buoy, and Aguilar held a lantern on a boathook, while Jane Foley, very wet, was doing a spell of baling. Aguilar dropped the boathook and, casting off, brought the punt alongside the yacht. The steps were lowered and Jane Foley, with laughing, rain-sprinkled face, climbed up. Aguilar handed her bag which contained nearly everything she possessed on earth. She and Audrey kissed calmly, and Audrey presented Mr. Gilman to a suddenly shy Jane. In the punt Miss Foley had been seen to take an affectionate leave of Aguilar. She now leaned over the rail.

"Good-bye!" she said, with warmth. "Thanks ever so much. It's been splendid. I do hope you won't be too wet. Can you row all the way home?" She shivered.

"I shall go back on the tide, Miss Foley," answered Aguilar.

He touched his cap to Audrey, mumbled gloomily a salutation, and loosed his hold on the yacht; and at once the punt felt the tide and began to glide away in the darkness towards Moze. The yacht's engine quickened. Flank buoy faded.

Mr. Gilman and the two girls made a group.

"You're wonderful! You really are!" said Mr. Gilman, addressing apparently the pair of them. He was enthusiastic. . . . He added with grandeur, "And now for France!"

"I do hope Mr. Hurley is still hanging about Moze," said Audrey. "Mr. Gilman, shall I show Miss Foley her cabin? She's rather wet."

"Oh, do! Oh, do, please! But don't forget that we are to have supper together. I insist on supper."

And Audrey thought: "How agreeable he is! How kind-hearted! He hasn't got any 'career' to worry about, and I adore him, and he's as simple as knitting."

CHAPTER XXXIX

THE IMMINENT DRIVE

"Oh!" cried Miss Thompkins. "You can see it from here. It's funny how unreal it seems, isn't it?"

She pointed at one of the large white-curtained windows of the restaurant, through which was visible a round column covered with advertisements of theatres, music-halls, and concert-halls, printed in many colours and announcing superlative delights. Names famous wherever pleasure is understood gave to their variegated posters a pleasant air of distinguished familiarity—names of theatres such as "Variétés," "Vaudeville," "Châtelet," "Théâtre Français," "Folies-Bergère," and names of persons such as "Sarah Bernhardt," "Huegenet," "Le Bargy," "Litvinne," "Lavallière." But the name in the largest type—dark crimson letters on rose paper—the name dominating all the rest, was the name of Musa. The ingenuous stranger to Paris was compelled to think that as an artist Musa was far more important than anybody else. Along the length of all the principal boulevards, and in many of the lesser streets, the ingenuous stranger encountered, at regular distances of a couple of hundred yards or so, one of these columns planted on the kerb; and all the scores of them bore exactly the same legend; they all spoke of nothing but blissful diversions, and they all put Musa ahead of anybody else in the world of the stage and the platform. Sarah Bernhardt herself, dark blue upon pale, was a trifle compared to Musa on the columns. And it had been so for days. Other posters were changed daily—changed by mysterious hands before even bread-girls were afoot with

their yards of bread—but the space given to Musa repeated
always the same tidings, namely that Musa ("the great
violinist") was to give an orchestral concert at the Salle
Xavier, assisted by the Xavier orchestra, on Thursday,
September 24, at 9 P.M.   Particulars of the programme
followed.

Paris was being familiarised with Musa.   His four
letters looked down upon the fever of the thoroughfares;
they were perused by tens of thousands of sitters in cafés
and in front of cafés; they caught the eye of men and
women fleeing from the wrath to come in taxicabs; they
competed successfully with newspaper placards; and on that
Thursday—for the Thursday in question had already run
more than half its course—they had so entered into the
sub-conscious brain of Paris that no habitué of the streets,
whatever his ignorant indifference to the art of music,
could have failed to reply with knowledge, on hearing Musa
mentioned, "Oh, yes!" implying that he was fully acquainted
with the existence of the said Musa.

Tommy was right: there did seem to be a certain un-
reality about the thing, yet it was utterly real.

All the women turned to glance at the name through the
window, and some of them murmured sympathetic and interested exclamations and bright hopes.   There were five
women: Miss Thompkins, Miss Nickall, Madame Piriac,
Miss Ingate and Audrey.   And there was one man—Mr.
Gilman.   And the six were seated at a round table in the
historic Parisian restaurant.   Mr. Gilman had the air
triumphant, and he was entitled to it.   The supreme moment
of his triumph had come.   Having given a luncheon to these
ladies, he had just asked, with due high negligence, for the
bill.   If there was one matter in which Mr. Gilman was a
truly great expert, it was the matter of giving a meal in a
restaurant.   He knew how to dress for such an affair—with
strict conventionality but a touch of devil-may-care youthfulness in the necktie.   He knew how to choose the
restaurant; he had about half a dozen in his répertoire—all

of the first order and for the most part combining the exclusive with the amusing—entirely different in kind from the pandemonium where Audrey had eaten on the night of her first arrival in Paris; he knew how to get the best out of head-waiters and waiters, who in these restaurants were not head-waiters and waiters but worldly priests and acolytes; his profound knowledge of cookery sprang from a genuine interest in his stomach, and he could compose a menu in a fashion to command the respect of head-waiters and to excite the envy of musicians composing a sonata; he had the wit to look in early and see to the flowers; above all he was aware what women liked in the way of wine, and since this was never what he liked in the way of wine, he would always command a half-bottle of the extra dry for himself, but would have it manipulated with such discretion that not a guest could notice it. He paid lavishly and willingly, convinced by hard experience that the best is inestimable, but he felt too that the best was really quite cheap, for he knew that there were imperfectly educated people in the world who thought nothing of paying the price of a good meal for a mere engraving or a bit of china. Withal, he never expected his guests truly to appreciate the marvels he offered them. They could not, or very rarely. Their twittering ecstatic praise, which was without understanding, sufficed for him, though sometimes he would give gentle diffident instruction. This trait in him was very attractive, proving the genuineness of his modesty.

The luncheon was partly to celebrate the return of various persons to Paris, but chiefly in honour of Musa's concert. Musa could not be present, for distinguished public performers do not show themselves on the day of an appearance. Mr. Gilman had learnt this from Madame Piriac, whom he had consulted as to the list of guests. It is to be said that he bore the absence of Musa from his table with stoicism. For the rest, Madame Piriac knew that he wanted no other men, and she had suggested none. She had assumed that he desired Audrey, and had pointed out that Audrey could not well be invited without Miss Ingate, who, sick of her old Moze, had rejoined Audrey in the splendour of the Hôtel du Danube. Mr. Gilman had somehow mentioned Miss Thompkins, whereupon Madame Piriac had declared that Miss Thompkins involved Miss Nickall, who after a complete recovery from the broken arm had returned for a while to her studio. And then Mr. Gilman had closed the list, saying that six was enough, and exactly the right number.

"At what o'clock are you going for the drive?" asked Madame Piriac in her improved, precise English. She looked equally at her self-styled uncle and at Audrey.

"I ordered the car for three o'clock," answered Mr. Gilman. "It is not yet quite three."

The table with its litter of ash-trays, empty cups, empty small glasses, and ravaged sweets, and the half-deserted restaurant, and the polite expectant weariness of the priests and acolytes, all showed that the hour was in fact not quite three—an hour at which such interiors have invariably the aspect of roses overblown and about to tumble to pieces.

And immediately upon the reference to the drive everybody at the table displayed a little constraint, avoiding the gaze of everybody else, thus demonstrating that the imminent drive was a delicate, without being a disagreeable, topic. Which requires explanation.

Mr. Gilman had not been seen by any of his guests during the summer. He had landed them at Boulogne from the *Ariadne*—sound but for one casualty. That casualty was Jane Foley, suffering from pneumonia, which had presumably developed during the evening of exposure spent with Aguilar in the leaking punt and in rain showers. Madame Piriac and Audrey took her to Wimereux and there nursed her through a long and sometimes dangerous illness. Jane possessed no constitution, but she had obstinacy, which saved her. In her convalescence, part of which she spent alone with Audrey (Madame Piriac having to pay visits to Monsieur Piriac), she had proceeded with the writing of a book, and she had also received in conclave the rarely seen

Rosamund, who like herself was still a fugitive from British justice. These two had been elaborating a new plan of campaign, which was to include an incursion by themselves into England, and which had in part been confided by Jane to Audrey, who, having other notions in her head, had been somewhat troubled thereby. Audrey's conscience had occasionally told her to throw herself heartily into the campaign, but her individualistic instincts had in the end kept her safely on a fence between the campaign and something else. The something else was connected with Mr. Gilman.

Mr. Gilman had written to her regularly; he had sent dazzling subscriptions to the Suffragette Union; and Audrey had replied regularly. His letters were very simple, very modest, and quite touching. They were dated from various coastal places. However, he never came near Wimereux, though it was a coastal place. Audrey had excusably deemed this odd; but Madame Piriac having once said with marked casualness, "I hinted to him that he might with advantage stay away," Audrey had concealed her thoughts on the point. And one of her thoughts was that Madame Piriac was keeping them apart so as to try them, so as to test their mutual feelings. The policy, if it was a policy, was very like Madame Piriac; it had the effect of investing Mr. Gilman in Audrey's mind with a peculiar romantic and wistful charm, as of a sighing and obedient victim. Then Jane Foley and Rosamund had gone off somewhere, and Madame Piriac and Audrey had returned to Paris, and had found that practically all Paris had returned to Paris too. And on the first meeting with Mr. Gilman it had been at once established that his feelings and those of Audrey had surmounted the Piriac test. Within forty-eight hours all persons interested had mysteriously assumed that Mr. Gilman and Audrey were coupled together by fate and that a delicious crisis was about to supervene in their earthly progress. And they had become objects of exquisite solicitude. They had also become perfect. A circle of friends and acquaintances waited in excited silence for a palpitating event, as a populace waits for the booming gun-fire which is to inaugurate a national rejoicing. And when the news exuded that he was taking her for a drive to Meudon, which she had never seen, alone, all decided beyond any doubt that *he would do it during the drive.*

Hence the nice constraint at the table when the drive grew publicly and avowedly imminent.

Audrey, as the phrase is, "felt her position keenly," but not unpleasantly, nor with understanding. Not a word had passed of late between herself and Mr. Gilman that any acquaintance might not have listened to. Indeed, Mr. Gilman had become slightly more formal. She liked him for that, as she liked him for a large number of qualities. She did not know whether she loved him. And strange to say, the question did not passionately interest her. The only really interesting questions were: Would he propose to her? And would she accept him? She had no logical ground for assuming that he would propose to her. None of her friends had informed her of the general expectation that he would propose to her. Yet she knew that everybody expected him to propose to her quite soon—indeed within the next couple of hours. And she felt that everybody was right. The universe was full of mysteries for Audrey. As regards her answer to any proposal, she foresaw—another mystery—that it would not depend upon self-examination or upon reason, or upon anything that could be defined. It would depend upon an instinct over which her mind—nay, even her heart—had no control. She was quite certainly aware that this instinct would instruct her brain to instruct her lips to say "Yes." The idea of saying "No" simply could not be conceived. All the forces in the universe would combine to prevent her from saying "No."

The one thing that might have countered that enigmatic and powerful instinct was a consideration based upon the difference between her age and that of Mr. Gilman. It is true that she did not know what the difference was, because she did not know Mr. Gilman's age. And she could not ask him. No! Such is the structure of society that she could not say to Mr. Gilman, "By the way, Mr. Gilman, how old are you?" She could properly ascertain his tastes about all manner of fundamental points, such as the shape of chair-legs, the correct hour for dining, or the comparative merits of diamonds and emeralds; but this trifle of information about his age could not be asked for. And he did not make her a present of it. She might have questioned Madame Piriac, but she could not persuade herself to question Madame Piriac either. However, what did it matter? Even if she learnt his age to a day, he would still be precisely the same Mr. Gilman. And let him be as old or as young as he might, she was still his equal in age. She was far more than six months older than she had been six months ago.

The influence of Madame Piriac through the summer had indirectly matured her. For above all Madame Piriac had imperceptibly taught her the everlasting joy and duty of exciting the sympathy, admiration and gratitude of the other sex. Hence Audrey had aged at a miraculous rate because in order to please Mr. Gilman she wished—possibly without knowing it—to undo the disparity between herself and him. This may be strange, but it is assuredly more true than strange. To the same ends she had concealed her own age. Nobody except Miss Ingate knew how old she was. She only made it clear, when doubts seemed to exist, that she had passed her majority long before. Further, her wealth, magnified by legend, assisted her age. Not that she was so impressed by her wealth as she had been. She had met American women in Paris compared to whom she was at destitution's door. She knew one woman who had kept a 2,000-ton yacht lying all summer in the outer harbour at Boulogne, and had used it during that period for exactly eleven hours.

Few of these people had an establishment. They would rent floors in hotels, or châteaux in Touraine, or yachts, but they had no home, and yet they seemed very content and beyond doubt they were very free. And so Audrey did not

trouble about having a home. She had Moze, which was
more than many of her acquaintances had. She would not
use it, but she had it. And she was content in the knowledge of the power to create a home when she felt inclined
to create one. Not that it would not have been absurd to set
about creating a home with Mr. Gilman hanging over her
like a destiny. It would have been rude to him to do so;
it would have been to transgress against the inter-sexual
code as promulgated by Madame Piriac. . . . She wondered what sort of a place Meudon was, and whether he
would propose to her while they were looking at the view
together. . . . She trembled with the sense of adventure,
which had little to do with happiness or unhappiness. . . .
But *would* he propose to her? Not improbably the whole
conception of the situation was false and she was being
ridiculous !

Still the nice constraint persisted as the women began
to put on their gloves, while Mr. Gilman had a word with
the chief priest. And Audrey had the illusion of being a
dedicated victim. As she self-consciously and yet proudly
handled her gloves she could not help but notice the simple
gold wedding-ring on a certain finger. She had never
removed it. She had never formally renounced her claim
to the status of a widow. That she was not a widow, that
she had been guilty of a fraud on a gullible public, was
somehow generally known; but the facts were not referred
to, save perhaps in rare hints by Tommy, and she had continued to be known as Mrs. Moncreiff. Ignominious close
to a daring enterprise ! And in the circumstances nothing
was more out of place than the ring, bought in cold, wilful,
calculating naughtiness at Colchester.

Just when Miss Ingate was beginning to discuss her own
plans for the afternoon, Mr. Price entered the restaurant,
and as he did so Miss Thompkins, saying something about
the small type on the poster outside, went to the window to
examine it. Mr. Price, disguised as a discreet dandy-about-
town, bore a parcel of music. He removed a most glossy

hat; he bowed to the whole company of ladies, who responded with smiles in which was acknowledge that he was a dandy in addition to being a secretary; and lastly with deference he handed the parcel of music to Mr. Gilman.

"So you did get it! What did I tell you?" said Mr. Gilman with negligent condescension. "A minute later, and we should have been gone. . . . Has Mr. Price got this right?" he asked Audrey, putting the music respectfully in front of her.

It included the reduced score of the Beethoven violin concerto, and other items to be performed that night at the Salle Xavier.

"Oh! Thank you, Mr. Price!" said Audrey. The music was so fresh and glossy and luscious to the eye that it was like a gift of fruit.

"That'll do, then, Price," said Mr. Gilman. "Don't forget about those things for to-night, will you?"

"No, sir. I have a note of all of them."

Mr. Price bowed and turned away, assuming his perfect hat. As he approached the door Tommy intercepted him; and said something to him in a low voice, to which he uncomfortably mumbled a reply. As they had admittedly been friends in Mr. Price's artistic days, exception could not be taken to this colloquy. Nevertheless Audrey, being as suspicious as a real widow, regarded it ill, thinking all manner of things. And when Tommy, humming, came back to her seat on Mr. Gilman's left hand, Audrey thought: "And why, after all, should she be on his left hand? It is of course proper that I should be on his right, but why should Tommy be on his left? Why not Madame Piriac or Miss Ingate?"

"And what am *I* going to do this afternoon?" demanded Miss Ingate, lengthening the space between her nose and her upper lip, and turning down the corners of her lower lip.

"You have to try that new dress on, Winnie," said Audrey rather reprovingly.

"Alone? Me go alone there? I wouldn't do it. It's not respectable the way they look at you and add you up and question you in those trying-on rooms, when they've *got* you."

"Well, take Elise with you."

"Me take Elise? I won't do it, not unless I could keep her mouth full of pins all the time. Whenever we're alone, and her mouth isn't full of pins, she always talks to me as if I was an actress. And I'm not."

"Well, then," said Miss Nickall kindly, "come with me and Tommy. We haven't anything to do, and I'm taking Tommy to see Jane Foley. Jane would love to see you."

"She might," replied Miss Ingate. "Oh! She might. But I think I'll walk across to the hotel and just go to bed and sleep it off."

"Sleep what off?" asked Tommy, with necklace rattling and orchidaceous eyes glittering.

"Oh! Everything! Everything!" shrieked Miss Ingate.

There was one other customer left in the restaurant, a solitary fair, fat man, and as Mr. Gilman's party was leaving, Audrey last, this solitary fair, fat man caught her eye, bowed, and rose. It was Mr. Cowl, secretary of the National Reformation Society. He greeted her with the assurance of an old and valued friend, and he called her neither Miss nor Mrs.; he called her nothing at all. Audrey accepted his lead.

"And is your Society still alive?" she asked with casual polite disdain.

"Going strong!" said Mr. Cowl. "More flourishing than ever—in spite of our bad luck." He lifted his sandy-coloured eyebrows. "Of course I'm here on Society business. In fact, I often have to come to Paris on Society business." His glance deprecated the appearance of the table over which his rounded form was protruding.

"Well, I'm glad to have seen you again," said Audrey, holding out her hand.

"I wonder," said Mr. Cowl, drawing some tickets from his pocket. "I wonder whether you—and your friends—would care to go to a concert to-night at the Salle Xavier. The concierge at my hotel is giving tickets away, and I took some—rather to oblige him than anything else. For one never knows when a concierge may not be useful. I don't suppose it will be anything great, but it will pass the time, and—er—strangers in Paris——"

"Thank you, Mr. Cowl, but I'm not a stranger in Paris. I live here."

"Oh! I beg your pardon," said Mr. Cowl. "Excuse me. Then you won't take them? Pity! I hate to see anything wasted."

Audrey was both desolated and infuriated.

"Remember me respectfully to Miss Ingate, please," finished Mr. Cowl. "She didn't see me as she passed."

He returned the tickets to his pocket.

Outside, Madame Piriac, standing by her automobile, which had rolled up with the silence of an hallucination, took leave of Audrey.

"*Eh bien! Au revoir!*" said she shortly, with a peculiar challenging half-smile, which seemed to be saying, "Are you going to be worthy of my education? Let us hope so."

And Miss Nickall, with her grey hair growing fluffier under a somewhat rakish hat, said with a smile of sheer intense watchful benevolence :

"Well, good-bye!"

While Nick was ecstatically thanking Mr. Gilman for his hospitality, Tommy called Audrey aside. Madame Piriac's car had vanished.

"Have you heard about the rehearsal this morning?" she asked, in a confidential tone, anxious and yet quizzical.

"No! What about it?" Audrey demanded. Various apprehensions were competing for attention in her brain. The episode of Mr. Cowl had agitated her considerably. And now she was standing right against the column bearing Musa's name in those large letters, and other columns up and down the gay, busy street echoed clear the name. And how unreal it was! . . . Tickets being given away in half-dozens! . . . She ought to have been profoundly disturbed by such a revelation, and she was. But here was the drive with Mr. Gilman insisting on a monopoly of all her faculties. And on the top of everything—Tommy with her strange gaze and tone! Tommy carefully hesitated before replying.

"He lost his temper and left it in the middle—orchestra and conductor and Xavier and all! And he swore he wouldn't play to-night."

"Nonsense!"

"Yes, he did."

"Who told you?"

Already the two women were addressing each other as foes.

"A man I know in the orchestra."

"Why didn't you tell us at once—when you came?"

"Well, I didn't want to spoil the luncheon. But of course I ought to have done. You, at any rate, seeing your interest in the concert! I'm sorry."

"My interest in the concert?" Audrey objected.

"Well, my girl," said Tommy, half cajolingly and half threateningly, "you aren't going to stand there and tell me to my face that you haven't put up that concert for him?"

"Put up the concert! Put up the——" Audrey knew she was blushing.

"Paid for it! Paid for it!" said Tommy, with impatience.

CHAPTER XL

AUDREY got away from the group in front of the restaurant with stammering words and crimson confusion. She ran. She stopped a taxi and stumbled into it. There remained with her vividly the vision of the startled, entirely puzzled face of Mr. Gilman, who in an instant had been transformed from a happy, dignified and excusably self-satisfied human male into an outraged rebel whose grievance had overwhelmed his dignity. She had said hurriedly: "Please excuse me not coming with you. But Tommy says something's happened to Musa, and I must go and see. It's very important." And that was all she had said. Had she asked him to drive her to Musa's, Mr. Gilman would have been very pleased to do so; but she did not think of that till it was too late. Her precipitancy had been terrible, and had staggered even Tommy. She had no idea how the group would arrange itself. And she had no very clear idea as to what was wrong with Musa or how matters stood in regard to the concert. Tommy had asserted that she did not know whether the orchestra and its conductor meant to be at their desks in the evening just as though nothing whatever had occurred at the rehearsal. All was vague, and all was disturbing. She had asked Tommy the authority for her assertion that she, Audrey, was financing the concert. To which Tommy had replied that she had "guessed, of course." And seeing that Audrey had only interviewed a concert agent once— and he a London concert agent with relations in Paris —and that she had never uttered a word about the affair

U   313

to anybody except Mr. Foulger, who had been keeping an eye on the expenditure, it was not improbable that Tommy had just guessed. But she had guessed right. She was an uncanny woman. "Have you ever spoken to Musa about—it?" Audrey had passionately demanded; and Tommy had answered also passionately: "Of course not. I'm a white woman all through. Haven't you learnt that yet?"

The taxi, although it was a horse-taxi and incapable of moving at more than five miles an hour, reached the Rue Cassette, which was on the other side of the river and quite a long way off, in no time. That is to say, Audrey was not aware that any time had passed. She had received the address from Tommy, for it was a new address, Musa having admittedly risen in the world. The house was an old one; it had a curious staircase, with china knobs on the principal banisters of the rail, and crimson-tasselled bell cords at all the doors of the flats. Musa lived at the summit of it. Audrey arrived there short of breath, took the crimson-tasselled cord in her hand to pull, and then hesitated in order to think.

Why had she come? The response was clear. She had come solely because she hated to see a job botched, and there was not a moment to lose if it was not to be botched. She had come, not because she had the slightest sympathetic interest in Musa—on the contrary, she was coldly angry with him—but because she had a horror of fiascos. She had found a genius who needed financing, and she, possessing some tons of money, had financed him, and she did not mean to see an ounce of her money wasted if she could help it. Her interest in the affair was artistic and impersonal, and none other. It was the duty of wealthy magnates to foster art, and she was fostering art, and she would have the thing done neatly and completely, or she would know the reason. Fancy a rational creature making a scene at a final rehearsal and swearing that he would not play, and then bolting!

It was monstrous! People really did not do such things. Assuredly no artist had ever done such a thing before. Artists who had a concert all to themselves invariably appeared according to advertised promise. An artist who was only one among several in a programme might fall ill and fail to appear, for such artists are liable to the accidents of earthly existence. But an artist who shared the programme with nobody else was above the accidents of earthly existence and magically protected against colds, coughs, influenza, orange peel, automobiles, and all the other enemies of mankind. But, of course, Musa was peculiar, erratic and unpredictable beyond even the wide range granted by society to genius. And yet of late he had been behaving himself in a marvellous manner. He had never bothered her. On the voyage back to France he had not bothered her. They had separated with punctilious cordiality. Neither of them had written to the other, but she knew that he was working diligently and satisfactorily. He was apparently cured of her. It was perhaps due to the seeming completeness of his cure that her relations with Mr. Gilman had been what they were. . . . And now, suddenly, this!

So with clear conscience she pulled the bell cord.

Musa himself opened the door. He was coatless and in a dressing-gown, under which showed glimpses of a new smartness. As soon as he saw her he went very pale.

"*Bon jour,*" she said.

He repeated the phrase stiffly.

"Can I come in?" she asked.

He silently signified, with a certain annoying resignation, that she might. For one instant she was under a tremendous impulse to walk grandly and haughtily down the stairs. But she conquered the impulse. He was so pale.

"This way, excuse me," he said, and preceded her along a short, narrow passage which ended in an open door leading into a small room. There was no carpet on the floor of the passage, and only a quite inadequate rug on the floor of the room. The furniture was scanty and poor. There was a table, a music stand, a cheap imitation of a Louis Quatorze chair, two other chairs, and some piles of music. No curtains to the window! Not a picture on the walls! On the table a dusty disorder of small objects, including ash-trays, and towards the back of it a little account book, open, with a pencil on it and a low pile of coppers and a silver ten-sou piece on the top of the coppers. Nevertheless this interior represented a novel luxuriousness for Musa; for previously, as Audrey knew, he had lived in one room, and there was no bed here. The flat, indeed, actually comprised three rooms. The account book and the pitiful heap of coins touched her. She had expended much on the enterprise of launching him to glory, and those coins seemed to be all that had filtered through to him. The whole dwelling was pathetic, and she thought of the splendours of her own daily life, of the absolute unimportance to her of such sums as would keep Musa in content for a year or for ten years, and of the grandiose, majestic, dazzling career of herself and Mr. Gilman when their respective fortunes should be joined together. And she mysteriously saw Mr. Gilman's face again, and that too was pathetic. Everything was pathetic. She alone seemed to be hard, dominating, overbearing. Her conscience waked to fresh activity. Was she losing her soul? Where were her ideals? Could she really work in full honesty for the feminist cause as the wife of a man like Mr. Gilman? He was adorable: she felt in that moment that she had a genuine affection for him; but could Mrs. Gilman challenge the police, retort audaciously upon magistrates, and lie in prison? In a word, could she be a martyr? Would Mr. Gilman, with all his amenability, consent? Would she herself consent? Would it not be ridiculous? Thus her flying, shamed thoughts in front of the waiting Musa!

"Then you aren't ill?" she began.

"Ill!" he exclaimed. "Why do you wish that I should be ill?"

As he answered her he removed his open fiddle case, with the violin inside it, from the Louis Quatorze chair, and signed to her to sit down. She sat down.

"I heard that—this morning—at the rehearsal——"

"Ah! You have heard that?"

"And I thought perhaps you were ill. So I came to see."

"What have you heard?"

"Frankly, Musa, it is said that you said you would not play to-night."

"Does it concern you?"

"It concerns everyone. . . . And you have been so good lately."

"Ah! I have been good lately. You have heard that. And did you expect me to continue to be good when you returned to Paris and passed all your days in public with that antique and grotesque Monsieur Gilman? All the world sees you. I myself have seen you. It is horrible."

She controlled herself. And the fact that she was intensely flattered helped her to do so.

"Now Musa," she said, firmly and kindly, as on previous occasions she had spoken to him. "Do be reasonable. I refuse to be angry, and it is impossible for you to insult me, however much you try. But do be reasonable. Do think of the future. We are all wishing for your success. We shall all be there. And now you say you aren't going to play. It is really too much."

"You have perhaps bought tickets," said Musa, and a flush gradually spread over his cheeks. "You have perhaps bought tickets, and you are afraid lest you have been robbed. Tranquillise yourself, Madame. If you have the least fear, I will instruct my agent to reimburse you. And why should I not play? Naturally I shall play. Accept my word, if you can." He spoke with an icy and convincing decision.

"Oh, I'm so glad!" Audrey murmured.

"What right have you to be glad, Madame? If you are glad it is your own affair. Have I troubled you since we last met? I need the sympathy of nobody. I am assured of a large audience. My impresario is excessively optimistic. And if this is so, I owe it to none but myself. You speak of insults. Permit me to say that I regard your patronage as an insult. I have done nothing, I imagine, to deserve it. I crack my head to divine what I have done to deserve it. You hear some silly talk about a rehearsal and you precipitate yourself *chez moi*——"

Without a word Audrey rose and departed. He followed her to the door and held it open.

"*Bon jour*, Madame."

She descended the stairs. Perhaps it was his sudden illogical change of tone; perhaps it was the memory of his phrase, "assured of a large audience," coupled with a picture of the sinister Mr. Cowl unsuccessfully trying to give away tickets—but whatever was the origin of the sob, she did give a sob. As she walked downcast through the courtyard she heard clearly the sounds of Musa's violin, played with savage vigour.

CHAPTER XLI

THE Salle Xavier, or Xavier Hall, had been built, with other people's money, by Xavier in order to force the general public to do something which the general public does not want to do and never would do of its own accord. Namely, to listen to high-class music. It had not been built, and it was not run, strange to say, to advertise a certain brand of piano. Xavier was an old Jew, of surpassing ugliness, from Cracow or some such place. He looked a rascal, and he was one—admittedly; he himself would imply it, if not crudely admit it. He had no personal interest in music, either high-class or low-class. But he possessed a gift for languages and he had mixed a great deal with musicians in an informal manner. Wagner, at Venice, had once threatened Xavier with a stick, and also Xavier had twice run away with great exponents of the rôle of Isolde. His competence as a connoisseur of Wagner's music, and of the proper methods of rendering Wagner's music, could therefore not be questioned, and it was not questioned.

He had a habit of initiating grandiose schemes for opera or concerts and of obtaining money therefor from wealthy amateurs. After a few months he would return the money less ten per cent. for preliminary expenses and plus his regrets that the schemes had unhappily fallen through owing to unforeseen difficulties. And wealthy amateurs were so astonished to get ninety per cent. of their money back from a rascal that they thought him almost an honest man, asked him to dinner, and listened sympathetically to details of his next grandiose scheme. The Xavier Hall was one of the

few schemes—and the only real estate scheme—that had
ever gone through. With the hall for a centre, Xavier laid
daily his plans and conspiracies for persuading the public
against its will. To this end he employed in large numbers
clerks, printers, bill posters, ticket agents, doorkeepers, programme writers, programme sellers, charwomen, and even
artists. He always had some new dodge or hope. The hall
was let several times a week for concerts or other entertainments, and many of them were private speculations of
Xavier. They were nearly all failures. And the hall,
thoroughly accustomed to seeing itself half empty, did not
pay interest on its capital. How could it? Upon occasions
there had actually been more persons in the orchestra than
in the audience. Seated in the foyer, with one eye upon a
shabby programme girl and another upon the street outside,
Xavier would sometimes refer to these facts in conversation
with a titled patron, and would describe the public
realistically and without pretence of illusion. Nevertheless,
Xavier had grown to be a rich man, for percentages were his
hourly food; he received them even from programme sellers.

At nine o'clock the hall was rather less than half full,
and this was rightly regarded as very promising, for the
management, like the management of every place of distrac-
tion in Paris, held it a point of honour to start from twenty
to thirty minutes late—as though all Parisians had many
ages ago decided that in Paris one could not be punctual,
and that, long since tired of waiting for each other, they
had entered into a competition to make each other wait, the
individual who arrived last being universally regarded as
the winner. The members of the orchestra were filing
negligently in from the back of the vast terraced platform,
yawning, and ravaged by the fearful ennui of eternal high-
class music. They entered in dozens and scores, and they
kept on entering, and as they gazed inimically at each other,
fingering their instruments, their pale faces seemed to be
asking: "Why should it be necessary to collect so many
of us in order to prove that just one single human being

can play the violin? We can all play the violin, or something else just as good. And we have all been geniuses in our time."

In strong contrast to their fatigued and disastrous indifference was the demeanour of a considerable group of demonstrators in the gallery. This body had crossed the Seine from the sacred Quarter, and, not owning a wardrobe sufficiently impressive to entitle it to ask for free seats, it had paid for its seats. Hence naturally its seats were the worst in the hall. But the group did not care. It was capable of exciting itself about high-class music. Moreover it had, for that night, an article of religious faith, to wit, that Musa was the greatest violinist that had ever lived or ever could live, and it was determined to prove this article of faith by sheer force of hands and feet. Therefore it was very happy, and just a little noisy.

In the main part of the hall the audience could be divided into two species, one less numerous than the other. First, the devotees of music, who went to nearly every concert, extremely knowing, extremely blasé, extremely disdainful and fastidious, with precise views about every musical composition, every conductor, and every performer; weary of melodious nights at which the same melodies were ever heard, but addicted to them, as some people are addicted to vices equally deleterious. These devotees would have had trouble with their conscience or their instincts had they not, by coming to the concert, put themselves in a position to affirm exactly and positively what manner of a performer Musa was. They had no hope of being pleased by him. Indeed they knew beforehand that he was yet another false star, but they had to ascertain the truth for themselves, because—you see—there was a slight chance that he might be a genuine star, in which case their careers would have been ruined had they not been able to say to succeeding generations: "I was at his first concert. It was a memorable," etc. etc. They were an emaciated tribe, and in fact had the air of mummies temporarily revived and escaped out of museums. They were shabby, but not with the gallery shabbiness; they were shabby because shabbiness was part of their unworldly refinement; and it did not matter—they would have got their free seats even if they had come in sacks and cerements.

The second main division of the audience—and the larger—consisted of the jolly pleasure seekers, who had dined well, who respected Beethoven no more than Oscar Straus, and who demanded only one boon—not to be bored. They had full dimpled cheeks, and they were adequately attired, and they dropped cigarettes with reluctance in the foyer, and they entered adventurously with marked courage, well aware that they had come to something queer and dangerous, something that was neither a revue nor a musical comedy, and, while hoping optimistically for the best, determined to march boldly out again in the event of the worst. They had seven mortal evenings a week to dispose of somehow, and occasionally they were obliged to take risks. Their expressions for the most part had that condescension which is characteristic of those who take a risk without being paid for it.

All around the hall ran a horseshoe of private boxes, between the balcony and the gallery. These boxes gradually filled. At a quarter-past nine over half of them were occupied; which fact, combined with the stylishness of the hats in them, proved that Xavier had immense skill in certain directions, and that on that night, for some reason or other, he had been doing his very best.

At twenty minutes past nine the audience had coalesced and become an entity, and the group from the Quarter was stamping an imitation of the first bars of the C minor Symphony, to indicate that further delay might involve complications.

Audrey sat with Miss Ingate modestly and inconspicuously in the fifth row of the stalls. Miss Ingate, prodigious in crimson, was in a state of beatitude, because she never went to concerts and imagined that she had inadvertently slipped into heaven. The mere size of the orchestra so overwhelmed her that she was convinced that it was an orchestra specially enlarged to meet the unique importance of Musa's genius. "They *must* think highly of him!" she said. She employed the time in looking about her. She had already found, besides many other Anglo-Saxon acquaintances, Rosamund, in black, Tommy with Nick, and Mr. Cowl, who was one seat to Audrey's left in the sixth row of the stalls. Also Mr. Gilman and Madame Piriac and Monsieur Piriac in a double box. Audrey and herself ought to have been in that box, and had the afternoon developed otherwise they probably would have been in that box. Fortunately at the luncheon, Audrey, who had bought various lots of seats, had with the strange cautiousness of a young girl left herself free to utilise or not to utilise the offered hospitality of Mr. Gilman's double box, and Mr. Gilman had not pressed her for a decision. Was it not important that the hall should seem as full as possible? When Miss Ingate, pushing her investigations farther, had discovered not merely Monsieur Dauphin, but Mr. Ziegler, late of Frinton and now resident in Paris, her cup was full.

"It's vehy wonderful, *vehy* wonderful!" said she.

But it was Audrey who most deeply had the sense of the wonderfulness of the thing. For it was Audrey who had created it. Having months ago comprehended that a formal and splendid debut was necessary for Musa if he was to succeed within a reasonable space of time, she had willed the debut within her own brain. She alone had thought of it. And now the realisation seemed to her to be absolutely a miracle. Had she read of such an affair a year earlier in a newspaper—with the words "Paris," "*tout Paris*," "young genius," and so on—she would have pictured it as gloriously, thrillingly romantic, and it indeed was gloriously and thrillingly romantic. She thought: "None of these people sitting around me know that I have brought it about, and that it is all mine." The thought was sweet. She felt like an invisible African genie out of the Thousand and One Nights.

And yet what had she done to bring it about? Nothing, simply nothing, except to command it! She had not even signed cheques. Mr. Foulger had signed the cheques! Mr. Foulger, who set down the whole enterprise as incomprehensible lunacy! Mr. Foulger, who had never been to aught but a smoking-concert in his life, and who could not pronounce the name of Beethoven without hesitations! The great deed had cost money, and it would cost more money; it would probably cost four hundred pounds ere it was finished with. An extravagant sum, but Xavier had motor-cars and toys even more expensive than motor-cars to keep up! Audrey, however, considered it a small sum, compared to the terrific spectacular effect obtained. And she was right. The attributes of money seemed entirely magical to her. And she was right again. She respected money with a new respect. And she respected herself for using money with such large grandeur.

And withal she was most horribly nervous, just as nervous as though it was she who was doomed to face the indifferent and exacting audience with nothing but a violin bow for weapon. She was so nervous that she could not listen, could not even follow Miss Ingate's simple remarks; she heard them as from a long distance, and grasped them after a long interval. Still, she was uplifted, doughty, and proud. The humiliation of the afternoon had vanished like a mist. Nay, she felt glad that Musa had behaved to her just as he did behave. His mien pleased her; his wounding words, each of which she clearly remembered, were a source of delight. She had never admired him so much. She had now no resentment against him. He had proved that her hopes of him were, after all, well justified. He would succeed. Only some silly and improbable accident could stop him from succeeding. She was not nervous about his success. She was nervous for him. She became him. She tuned his fiddle, gathered herself together and walked on to the platform, bowed to the dim multitudinous heads in front of him, looked at the conductor, waited for the opening bars, drew his bow across his strings at precisely the correct second, and heard the resulting sound under her ear. And all that before the conductor had appeared! Such were the manifestations of her purely personal desire for the achievement of a neat, clean job.

"See!" said Miss Ingate. "Mr. Gilman is bowing to us. He does look splendid, and isn't Madame Piriac lovely? I must say I don't care so much for these French husbands."

Audrey had to turn and join Miss Ingate in acknowledging the elaborate bow. At any rate, then, Mr. Gilman had not been utterly estranged by her capricious abandonment of him. And why should he be? He was a man of sense; he would understand perfectly when she explained to-morrow. Further, he was her slave. She was sure of him. She would apologise to him. She would richly recompense him by smiles and honey and charming persuasive simplicity. And he would see that with all her innocent and modest ingenuousness she was capable of acting seriously and effectively in a sudden crisis. She would rise higher in his esteem. As for the foreseen proposal, well——

A sporadic clapping wakened her out of those reflections. The conductor was approaching his desk. The orchestra applauded him. He tapped the desk and raised his stick. And there was a loud noise, the thumping of her heart. The concert had begun. Musa was still invisible—what was he doing at that instant, somewhere behind?—but the concert had begun. Stars do not take part in the first item of an orchestral concert. There is a convention that they shall be preluded; and Musa was preluded by the overture to *Die Meistersinger*. In the soft second section of the overture, a most noticeable babble came from a stage-box. "Oh! It's the Foas," muttered Miss Ingate. "What a lot of people are fussing around them!" "Hsh!" frowned Audrey, outraged by the interruption. Madame

Foa took about fifty bars in which to settle herself, and Monsieur Foa chattered to people behind him as freely as if he had been in a café. Nobody seemed to mind.

The overture was applauded, but Madame Foa, instead of applauding, leaned gracefully back, smiling, and waved somebody to the seat beside her.

Violent demonstrations from the gallery! . . . He was there, tripping down the stepped pathway between the drums. The demonstrations grew general. The orchestra applauded after its own fashion. He reached the conductor, smiled at the conductor and bowed very admirably. He seemed to be absolutely at his ease. Then there was a delay. The conductor's scores had got themselves mixed up. It was dreadful. It was enough to make a woman shriek.

"I say!" said a voice in Audrey's ear. She turned as if shot. Mr. Cowl's round face was close to hers. "I suppose you saw the *New York Herald* this morning."

"No," answered Audrey impatiently.

The orchestra started the Beethoven violin Concerto. But Mr. Cowl kept his course.

"Didn't you?" he said. "About the Zacatecas Oil Corporation? It's under a receivership. It's gone smash. I've had an idea for some time it would. All due to these Mexican revolutions. I thought you might like to know."

Musa's bow hung firmly over the strings.

CHAPTER XLII

INTERVAL

THE most sinister feature of entertainments organised by Xavier was the intervals. Xavier laid stress on intervals; they gave repose, and in many cases they saved money. All Paris managers are inclined to give to the interval the importance of a star turn, and Xavier in this respect surpassed his rivals, though he perhaps regarded his cloak-rooms, which were organised to cause the largest possible amount of inconvenience to the largest possible number of people, as his surest financial buttress. Xavier could or would never see the close resemblance of intervals to wet blankets, extinguishers, palls and hostile critics. The Allegro movement of the Concerto was a real success, and the audience as a whole would have applauded even more if the gallery in particular had not applauded so much. The second or Larghetto movement was also a success, but to a less degree. As for the third and last movement, it put the gallery into an ecstasy while leaving the floor in possession of full critical faculties. Musa retired and had to return, and when he returned the floor good-humouredly joined the vociferous gallery in laudations, and he had to return again. Then the interminable interval. Silence! Murmurings! Silence! Creepings towards exits! And in many, very many hearts the secret trouble question: "Why are we here? What have we come for? What is all this pother about art and genius? Honestly, shall we not be glad and relieved when the solemn old thing is over?" . . . And the desolating, cynical indifference of the conductor and the orchestra! Often there is a clearer vision of the truth during the intervals of a classical concert than on a deathbed.

Audrey was extremely depressed in the interval after the Beethoven Concerto and before the Lalo. But she was not depressed by the news of the accident to the Zacatecas Oil Corporation in which was the major part of her wealth. The tidings had stunned rather than injured that part of her which was capable of being affected by finance. She had not felt the blow. Moreover she was protected by the knowledge that she had thousands of pounds in hand and also the Moze property intact, and further she was already reconsidering her newly-acquired respect for money. No! What depressed her was a doubt as to the genius of Musa. In the long dreadful pause it seemed impossible that he should have genius. The entire concert presented itself as a grotesque farce, of which she as its creator ought to be ashamed. She was ready to kill Xavier or his responsible representative.

Then she saw the tall and calm Rosamund, with her grey hair and black attire and her subduing self-complacency, making a way between the rows of stalls towards her.

"I wanted to see you," said Rosamund, after the formal greetings. "Very much." Her voice was as kind and as unrelenting as the grave.

At this point Miss Ingate ought to have yielded her seat to the terrific Rosamund, but she failed to do so, doubtless by inadvertence.

"Will you come into the foyer for a moment?" Rosamund inflexibly suggested.

"Isn't the interval nearly over?" said Audrey.

"Oh, no!"

And as a fact there was not the slightest sign of the interval being nearly over. Audrey obediently rose. But the invitation had been so conspicuously addressed to herself that Miss Ingate, gathering her wits, remained in her chair.

The foyer—decorated in the Cracovian taste—was dotted with cigarette smokers and with those who had fled from the interval. Rosamund did not sit down; she did not try for seclusion in a corner. She stepped well into the foyer, and then stood still, and absently lighted a cigarette, omitting to offer a cigarette to Audrey. Rosamund's air of a deaconess made the cigarette extremely remarkable.

"I wanted to tell you about Jane Foley," began Rosamund quietly. "Have you heard?"

"No! What?"

"Of course you haven't. I alone knew. She has run away to England."

"Run away! But she'll be caught!"

"She may be. But that is not all. She has run away to get married. She dared not tell me. She wrote me. She put the letter in the manuscript of the last chapter but one of her book, which I am revising for her. She will almost certainly be caught if she tries to get married in her own name. Therefore she will get married in a false name. All this, however, is not what I wanted to tell you about."

"Then you shouldn't have begun to talk about it," said Audrey suddenly. "Did you expect me to let you leave it in the middle! Jane getting married! I do think she might have told me. . . . What next, I wonder! I suppose you've—er—lost her now?"

"Not entirely, I believe," said Rosamund. "Certainly not entirely. But of course I could never trust her again. This is the worst blow I have ever had. She says—but why go into that? Well, she does say she will work as hard as ever, nearly; and that her future husband strongly supports us—and so on." Rosamund smiled with complete detachment.

"And who's he?" Audrey demanded.

"His name is Aguilar," said Rosamund. "So she says."

"Aguilar?"

"Yes. I gather—I say I gather—that he belongs to
v

the industrial class. But of course that is precisely the class that Jane springs from. Odd! Is it not? Heredity, I presume." She raised her shoulders.

Audrey said nothing. She was too shocked to speak— not pained or outraged, but simply shaken. What in the name of Juno could Jane see in Aguilar? Jane, to whom every man was the hereditary enemy! Aguilar, who had no use for either man or woman! Aguilar, a man without a Christian name, one of those men in connection with whom a Christian name is impossibly ridiculous. How should she, Audrey, address Aguilar in future? Would he have to be asked to tea? These vital questions naturally transcended all others in Audrey's mind. . . . Still (she veered round), it was perhaps after all just the union that might have been expected.

"And now," said Rosamund at length, "I have a question to put to you."

"Well?"

"I don't want a definite answer here and now." She looked round disdainfully at the foyer. "But I do want to set your mind on the right track at the earliest possible moment—before any accidents occur." She smiled satirically. "You see how frank I am with you. I'll be more frank still, and tell you that I came to this concert to-night specially to see you."

"Did you?" Audrey murmured. "Well!"

The older woman looked down upon her from a superior height. Her eyes were those of an autocrat. It was quite possible to see in them the born leader who had dominated thousands of women and played a drawn game with the British Government itself. But Audrey, at the very moment when she was feeling the overbearing magic of that gaze, happened to remember the scene in Madame Piriac's automobile on the night of her first arrival in Paris, when she herself was asleep and Rosamund, not knowing that she was asleep, had been solemnly addressing her. Miss Ingate's often repeated account of the scene always made her laugh, and the memory of it now caused her to smile faintly.

"I want to suggest to you," Rosamund proceeded, "that you begin to work for me."

"For the suffrage—or for you?"

"It is the same thing," said Rosamund coldly. "I am the suffrage. Without me the cause would not have existed to-day."

"Well," said Audrey, "of course I will. I have done a bit already, you know."

"Yes, I know," Rosamund admitted. "You did very well at the Blue City. That's why I'm approaching you. That's why I've chosen you."

"Chosen me for what?"

"You know that a new great campaign will soon begin. It is all arranged. It will necessitate my returning to England and challenging the police. You know also that Jane Foley was to have been my lieutenant-in-chief—for the active part of the operation. You will admit that I can no longer count on her completely. Will you take her place?"

"I'll help," said Audrey. "I'll do what I can. I dare say I shan't have much money, because one of those 'accidents' you mentioned has happened to me already."

"That need not trouble you," replied Rosamund imperturbable. "I have always been able to get all the money that was needed."

"Well, I'll help all I can."

"That's not what I ask," said Rosamund inflexibly. "Will you take Jane Foley's place? Will you give yourself utterly?"

Audrey answered with sudden vehemence:

"No, I won't. You didn't want a definite answer, but there it is."

"But surely you believe in the cause?"

"Yes."

"It's the greatest of all causes."

"I'm rather inclined to think it is."

"Why not give yourself, then? You are free. I have given myself, my child."

"Yes," said Audrey, who resented the appellation of "child." "But, you see, it's your hobby."

"My hobby, Mrs. Moncreiff!" exclaimed Rosamund.

"Certainly, your hobby," Audrey persisted.

"I have sacrificed everything to it," said Rosamund.

"Pardon me," said Audrey. "I don't think you've sacrificed anything to it. You just enjoy bossing other people above everything, and it gives you every chance to boss. And you enjoy plots too, and look at the chances you get for that! Mind you, I like you for it. I think you're splendid. Only *I* don't want to be a monomaniac, and I won't be." Her convictions seemed to have become suddenly clear and absolutely decided.

"Do you mean to infer that I am a monomaniac?" asked Rosamund, raising her eyebrows—but only a little.

"Well," said Audrey, "as you mentioned frankness— what else would you call yourself but a monomaniac? You only live for one thing—don't you, now?"

"It is the greatest thing."

"I don't say it isn't," Audrey admitted. "But I've been thinking a good deal about all this, and at last I've come to the conclusion that one thing isn't enough for me, not nearly enough. And I'm not going to be peculiar at any price. Neither a fanatic nor a monomaniac, nor anything like that."

"You are in love," asserted Rosamund.

"And what if I am? If you ask me, I think a girl who isn't in love ought to be somewhat ashamed of herself, or at least sorry for herself. And I am sorry for myself, because I am not in love. I wish I was. Why shouldn't I be? It must be lovely to be in love. If I was in love I shouldn't be *only* in love. You think you understand what girls are nowadays, but you don't. I didn't myself until just lately. But I'm beginning to. Girls were supposed to be only interested in one thing—in your time. Monomaniacs, that's what they had to be. You changed all that, or you're trying to change it, but you only mean women to be monomaniacs about something else. It isn't good enough. I want everything, and I'm going to get it— or have a good try for it. I'll never be a martyr if I can help it. And I believe I can help it. I believe I've got just enough common sense to save me from being a martyr —either to a husband or a house or family—or a cause. I want to have a husband and a house and a family, and a cause too. That'll be just about everything, won't it? And if you imagine I can't look after all of them at once, all I can say is I don't agree with you. Because I've got an idea I can. Supposing I had all these things, I fancy I could have a tiff with my husband and make it up, play with my children, alter a dress, change the furniture, tackle the servants, and go out to a meeting and perhaps have a difficulty with the police—all in one day. Only if I did get into trouble with the police I should pay the fine—you see. The police aren't going to have me altogether. Nobody is. Nobody, man or woman, is going to be able to boast that he's got me altogether. You think you're independent. But you aren't. We girls will show you what independence is."

"You're a rather surprising young creature," observed Rosamund with a casual air, unmoved. "You're quite excited."

"Yes. I surprise myself. But these things do come in bursts. I've noticed that before. They weren't clear when you began to talk. They're clear now."

"Let me tell you this," said Rosamund. "A cause must have martyrs."

"I don't see it," Audrey protested. "I should have thought common sense would be lots more useful than martyrs. And monomaniacs never do have common sense."

"You're very young."

"Is that meant for an insult, or is it just a statement?" Audrey laughed pleasantly.

And Rosamund laughed too.

"It's just a statement," said she.

"Well, here's another statement," said Audrey. "You're very old. That's where I have the advantage of you. Still, tell me what I can do in your new campaign, and I'll do it if I can. But there isn't going to be any utterly —that's all."

"I think the interval is over," said Rosamund with finality. "Perhaps we'd better adjourn."

The foyer had nearly emptied. The distant sound of music could be heard.

As she was re-entering the hall, Audrey met Mr. Cowl, who was coming out.

"I have decided I can't stand any more," Mr. Cowl remarked in a loud whisper. "I hope you didn't mind me telling you about the Zacatecas. As I said, I thought you might be interested. Good-bye. So pleasant to have met you again, dear lady." His face had the same enigmatic smile which had made him so formidable at Moze.

Musa had already begun to play the Spanish Symphony of Lalo, without which no genius is permitted to make his formal debut on the violin in France.

CHAPTER XLIII

AFTER the Spanish Symphony not only the conductor but the entire orchestra followed Musa from the platform, and Audrey understood that the previous interval had not really been an interval and that the first genuine interval was about to begin. The audience seemed to understand this too, for practically the whole of it stood up and moved towards the doors. Audrey would have stayed in her seat, but Miss Ingate expressed a desire to go out and "see the fun" in the foyer, and, moreover, she asserted that the Foas from their box had been signalling to her and Audrey an intention to meet them in the foyer. Miss Ingate was in excellent spirits. She said it beat her how Musa's fingers could get through so many notes in so short a time, and also that it made her feel tired even to watch the fingers. She was convinced that nobody had ever handled the violin so marvellously before. As for success, Musa had been recalled, and the applause from the gallery, fired by its religious belief, was obstinate and extremely vociferous. Audrey, however, was aware of terrible sick qualms, for she knew that Musa was not so far dominating his public. Much of the applause had obviously the worst quality that applause can have—it was good-natured. Yet she could not accept failure for Musa. Failure would be too monstrous an injustice, and therefore it could not happen.

The emptiness of the Foas' box indicated that Miss Ingate might be correct in her interpretation of signals, and Audrey allowed herself to be led away from the now forlorn auditorium. As they filed along the gangways she had to listen to the indifferent remarks of utterly unprejudiced and uninterested persons about the performance of genius, and further she had to learn that a fair proportion of them were departing with no intention to return. In the thronged foyer they saw Mr. Gilman, alone, before he saw them. He was carrying a box of chocolates—doubtless one of the little things that Mr. Price had had instructions to provide for the evening. Mr. Gilman perhaps would not have caught sight of them had it not been for the stridency of Miss Ingate's voice, which caused him to turn round.

Audrey experienced once again the sensation—which latterly was apt to recur in her—of having too many matters on her mind simultaneously; in a phrase, the sensation of the exceeding complexity of existence. And she resented it. The interview with Rosamund was quite enough for one night. It had been a triumph for her; she had surprised herself in that interview; it had left her with a conviction of freedom; it had uplifted her. She ought to have been in a state of exaltation after that interview, and she was. Only, while in a state of exaltation, she was still in the old state of depression—about the tendency of the concert, of her concert, and about the rumoured disappearance of her fortune. Also she was preoccupied by the very strange affair of Jane Foley and Aguilar.

And now—a further intricacy of mood—came a whole new set of emotions due to the mere spectacle of Mr. Gilman's august back! She was intimidated by Mr. Gilman's back. She knew horribly that in the afternoon she had treated Mr. Gilman as Mr. Gilman ought never to have been treated. And, quite apart from intimidation, she had another feeling, a feeling which was ghastly and of which she was ashamed. . . . Assuming the disappearance of her fortune, would Mr. Gilman's attitude towards her be thereby changed? . . . She admitted that young girls ought not to have such suspicions against respectable and mature men of established position in the world. Nevertheless, she could not blow the suspicion away.

But the instant Mr. Gilman's eye met hers the suspicion vanished, and not the suspicion only, but all her intimidation. The miracle was produced by something in the gaze of Mr. Gilman as it rested on her, something wistful—not more definable than that, something which she had noticed in Mr. Gilman's gaze on other occasions. It perfectly restored her. It gave her the positive assurance of a fact which marvellously enheartens young girls of about Audrey's years—to wit, that they have a mysterious power surpassing the power of age, knowledge, wisdom, or wealth, that they influence and decide the course of history, and are the sole true mistresses of the world. Whence the mysterious power sprang she did not exactly know, but she surmised—rightly—that it was connected with her youth, with a dimple, with the incredibly soft down on her cheek, with the arch softness of her glance, with a gesture of the hand, with a turn of the shoulder, with a pleat of the skirt. . . . Anyhow, she possessed it, and to possess it was to wield it. It transformed her into a delicious tyrant, but a tyrant; it inspired her with exquisite cruelty, but cruelty. Her thoughts might have been summed up in eight words:

"Pooh! He has suffered. Well, he must suffer."

Ah! But she meant to be very kind to him. He was so reliable, so adorable, and so dependent. She had genuine affection for him. And he was at once a rock and a cushion.

"Isn't it going splendidly—splendidly, Mr. Gilman?" exclaimed Miss Ingate in her enthusiasm.

"Apparently," said Mr. Gilman, with comfort in his voice.

At that moment the musical critic with large, dark Eastern eyes, whom Audrey had met at the Foas', strolled nonchalantly by, and, perceiving Miss Ingate, described a huge and perfect curve in the air with his glossy silk hat,

which had been tipped at the back of his head. Mr.
Gilman had come close to Audrey.

"The Foas started down with me," said Mr. Gilman
mildly. "But they always meet such crowds of acquaintances at these affairs that they seldom get anywhere.
Hortense would not leave the box. She never will."

"Oh! I'm so glad I've seen you," Audrey began
excitedly, but with simplicity and compelling sweetness.
"You've no idea how sorry I am about this afternoon!
I'm frightfully sorry, really! But I was so upset. I
didn't know what to do. You know how anxious everybody was about Musa for to-night. He's the pet of the
Quarter, and, of course, I belong to the Quarter. At
least—I did. I thought he might be ill, or something.
However, it was all right in the end. I was looking
forward tremendously to that drive. Are you going to
forgive me?"

"Please, please!" he eagerly entreated, with a faint
blush. "Of course, I quite understand. There's nothing
whatever to forgive."

"Oh! but there is," she insisted. "Only you're so
good-natured."

She was being magnanimous. She was pretending that
she had no mysterious power. But her motive was quite
pure. If he was good-natured, so was she. She honestly
wanted to recompense him, and to recompense him richly.
And she did. Her demeanour was enchanting in its ingenuous flattery. She felt happy despite all her anxieties,
for he was living up to her ideal of him. She felt happy,
and her resolve to make him happy to the very limit of
his dreams was intense. She had a vision of her future
existence stretching out in front of her, and there was
not a shadow on it. She thought he was going to offer
her the box of chocolates, but he did not.

"I rather wanted to ask your advice," she said.

"I wish you would," he replied.

Just then the Foas arrived, and with them Dauphin,

the great and fashionable painter and the original dis-
coverer of Musa. And as they all began to speak at once
Audrey heard the Oriental musical critic say slowly to an
inquiring Miss Ingate :

"It is not a concert talent that he has."

"You hear! You hear!" exclaimed Monsieur Foa to
Monsieur Dauphin and Madame Foa, with an impressed
air. "You hear what Miquette says. He has not a
concert talent. He has everything that you like, but not
a concert talent."

Foa seemed to be exhibiting the majestic Oriental, nick-
named Miquette, as the final arbiter, whose word settled
problems like a sword, and Miquette seemed to be trying
to bear the high rôle with negligent modesty.

"But, yes, he has! But, yes, he has!" Dauphin protested, sweeping all Miquettes politely away. And then
there was an urbane riot of greetings, salutes, bowings,
smilings, cooings and compliments.

Dauphin was magnificent, playing the part of the
opulent painter à la mode with the most finished skill,
the most splendid richness of detail. It was notorious that
in the evenings he wore the finest silk shirts in Paris,
and his waistcoat was designed to give scope to these
shirts. He might have come—he probably had come—
straight from the bower of archduchesses; but he produced
in Audrey the illusion that archduchesses were a trifle
compared to herself. He had not seen her for a long
time. Gazing at her, he breathed relief; all his features
indicated the sudden, unexpected assuaging of eternal and
intense desires. He might have been travelling through
the desert for many days and she might have been the
oasis—the pool of living water and the palm.

"Now—like that! Just like that!" he said, holding
her hand and, as it were, hypnotising her in the pose in
which she happened to be. He looked hard at her.
"It is unique. Madame, where did you find that
dress?"

"Callot," answered Audrey submissively.

"I thought so. Well, Madame, I can wait no more. I will wait no more. It is Dauphin who implores you to come to his studio. To come—it is your duty. Madame Foa, you will bring her. I count on you absolutely to bring her. Even if it is only to be a sketch—the merest hint. But I must do it."

"Oh, yes, Madame," said Madame Foa with all the Italian charm. "Dauphin must paint you. The contrary is unthinkable. My husband and I have often said so."

"To-morrow?" Dauphin suggested.

"Ah! To-morrow, my little Dauphin, I cannot," said Madame Foa.

"Nor I," said Audrey.

"The day after to-morrow, then. I will send my auto. What address? Half-past eleven. That goes? In any case, I insist. Be kind! Be kind!"

Audrey blushed. Half the foyer was staring at the group. She was flattered. She saw herself remarkable. She thought she would look more particularly, with perfect detachment, at the mirror that night, in order to decide whether her appearance was as striking, as original, as distinguished, as Dauphin's attitude implied. There must surely be something in it.

"About that advice—may I call to-morrow?" It was Mr. Gilman's voice at her elbow.

"Advice?" She had forgotten her announced intention of asking his advice. (The subject was to be Zacatecas.) "Oh, yes. How nice of you! Please do call. Come for tea." She was delightful to him, but at the same time there was in her tone a little of the condescending casualness proper to the tone of a girl openly admired by the confidant and painter of princesses and archduchesses, the man who treated all plain women and women past the prime with a desolating indifference.

She thought:

"I am a rotten little snob."

Mr. Gilman gave thanksgivings and departed, explaining that he must return to Madame Piriac.

Foa and Dauphin and the Oriental resumed the argument about Musa's talent and the concert. Miquette would say nothing as to the success of the concert. Foa asserted that the concert was not and would not be a success. Dauphin pooh-poohed and insisted vehemently that the success was unmistakable and increasing. Moreover, he criticised the hall, the choice of programme, the orchestra, the conductor. "I discovered Musa," said he. "I have always said that he is a great concert player, and that he is destined for a great world-success, and to-night I am more sure of it than ever." Whereupon Madame Foa said with much sympathy that she hoped it was so, and Foa said: "You create illusions for yourself, on purpose." Dauphin bore him down with wavy gestures and warm cries of "No! No! No!" And he appealed to Audrey as a woman incapable of illusions. And Audrey agreed with Dauphin. And while she was agreeing she kept saying to herself: "Why do I pretend to agree with him? He is not sincere. He knows he is not sincere. We all know—except perhaps Winnie Ingate. The concert is a failure. If it were not a failure, Madame Foa would not be so sympathetic. She is more subtle even than Madame Piriac. I shall never be subtle like that. I wish I could be. I wish I was at Moze. I am too Essex for all this. And Winnie here is too comic for words."

An aged and repellent Jew came into sight. He raised Madame Foa's hand to his odious lips and kissed it, and Audrey wondered how Madame Foa could tolerate the formality.

"Well, Monsieur Xavier?"

Xavier shrugged his round shoulders.

"Do not say," said he, in a hoarse voice to the company, "do not say that I have not done my best on this occasion." He lifted his eyes heavenward, and as he did so his passing glance embraced Audrey, and she violently hated him.

"Winnie," said she, "I think we ought to be getting back to our seats."

"But," cried Madame Foa, "we are going round with Dauphin to the artists' room. You do not come with us, Madame Moncreiff?"

"In your place . . ." muttered Xavier discouragingly, with a look at Dauphin, and another shrug of the shoulders. "I have been . . ."

"Ah!" said Dauphin, in a strange new tone. And then very brightly to Audrey: "Now, as to Saturday, dear lady——"

Xavier engaged in private converse with Foa, and his demeanour to Foa was extremely deferential, whereas he almost ignored the Oriental critic. And Audrey puzzled her head once again to discover why the Foas should exert such influence upon the fate of music in Paris. The enigma was only one among many.

CHAPTER XLIV

THE first item after the true interval was the Chaconne of Bach, which Musa had played upon a memorable occasion in Frinton. He stood upon the platform utterly alone, against a background of empty chairs, double-basses and drums. He seemed to be unfriended and forlorn. It appeared to Audrey that he was playing with despair. She wished, as she looked from Musa to the deserted places in the body of the hall, that the piece was over, and that the entire concert was over. How could anyone enjoy such an arid maze of sounds? The whole theory of classical composition and its vogue was hollow and ridiculous. People did not like the classics; they could not and they never would. Now a waltz . . . after a jolly dinner and wine! . . . But the Chaconne! But Bach! But culture! The audience was visibly and audibly restless. For about two hundred years the attempt to force this Chaconne upon the public had been continuous, and it was still boring them. Of course it was! The thing was unnatural.

And she herself was a fool; she was a ninny. And the alleged power of money was an immense fraud. She had thought to perform miracles by means of a banking account. For a moment she had imagined that the miracles had come to pass. But they had not come to pass. The public was too old, too tired, and too wary. It could not thus be tricked into making a reputation. The forces that made reputations were far less amenable than she had fancied. The world was too clever and too experienced for her ingenuous self. Geniuses were not lying about and waiting to be picked up. Musa was not a genius. She had been a simpleton, and the sacred Quarter had been a simpleton. She was rather angry with Musa for not being a genius. And the confidence which he had displayed a few hours earlier was just grotesque conceit! And men and women who were supposed to be friendly human hearts were not so in truth. They were merely indifferent and callous spectators. The Foas, for example, were chattering in their box, apparently oblivious of the tragedy that was enacting under their eyes. But then, it was perhaps not a tragedy; it was perhaps a farce.

And what would these self-absorbed spectators of existence say and do, if and when it was known that she was no longer a young woman of enormous wealth? Would Dauphin have sought to compel her to enter his studio had he been aware that her fortune had gone up in smoke? She was not in a real world. She was in a world of shams. And she was a sham in the world of shams. She wanted to be back again in the honest realities of Moze, where in the churchyard she could see the tombs of her great-great-grandfathers. Only one extraneous interest drew her thoughts away from Moze. That interest was Mr. Gilman. Mr. Gilman was her conquest and her slave. She adored him because he was so wistful and so reliable and so adoring. Mr. Gilman sat intent and straight upright in Madame Piriac's box and behaved just as though Bach himself was present. He understood nothing of Bach, but he could be trusted to behave with benevolence.

The music suddenly ceased. The Chaconne was finished. The gallery of enthusiasts still applauded with vociferation, with mystic faith, with sublime obstinacy. It was carrying on a sort of religious war against the base apathy of the rest of the audience. It was determined to force its belief down the throats of the unintelligent mob. It had made up its mind that until it had had its way the world should stand still. No encore had yet been obtained, and the gallery was set on an encore. The clapping fainted, ex-

pired, and then broke into new life, only to expire again
and recommence.   A few irritated persons hissed.   The
gallery responded with vigour.   Musa, having retired, reappeared, very white, and bowed.   The applause was
feverish and unconvincing.   Musa vanished.   But the
gallery had thick soles and hard hands and stout sticks,
even serviceable umbrellas.   It could not be appeased by
bows alone.   And after about three minutes of tedious
manœuvring, Musa had at last to yield an encore that in
fact nobody wanted.   He played a foolish pyrotechnical
affair of De Bériot, which resembled nothing so much as a
joke at a funeral.   After that the fate of the concert could
not be disputed even by the gallery.   At the finish of the
evening there was, in the terrible idiom of the theatre,
"not a hand."

Whether Musa had played well or ill, Audrey had not
the least idea.   Nor did that point seem to matter.   Naught
but the attitude of the public seemed to matter.   This was
strange, because for a year Audrey had been learning steadily
in the Quarter that the attitude of the public had no importance whatever.   She suffered from the delusion that
the public was staring at her and saying to her : " You, you
silly little thing, are responsible for this fiasco.   We condescended to come—and this is what you have offered us.
Go home, and let your hair down and shorten your skirts,
for you are no better than a schoolgirl, after all."   She
was really self-conscious.   She despised Musa, or rather
she threw to him a little condescending pity.   And yet at
the same time she was furious against that group in the
foyer for being so easily dissuaded from going to see Musa
in the artists' room. . . . Rats deserting a sinking ship !
. . . People, even the nicest, would drop a failure like a
match that was burning out. . . . Yes, and they would
drop her. . . . No, they would not, because of Mr. Gilman.
Mr. Gilman was calling to see her to-morrow.   He was
the rock and the cushion.   She would send Miss Ingate
out for the afternoon.   As the audience hurried eagerly

w

forth she spoke sharply to Miss Ingate. She was indeed very rude to Miss Ingate. She was exasperated, and Miss Ingate happened to be handy.

In the foyer not a trace of the Foa clan nor of Madame Piriac and her husband, nor of Mr. Gilman! But Tommy and Nick were there, putting on their cloaks, and with them, but not helping them, was Mr. Ziegler. The blond Mr. Ziegler greeted Audrey as though the occasion of their previous meeting had been a triumph for him. His self-satisfaction, if ever it had been damaged, was repaired to perfection. The girls were silent; Miss Ingate was silent; but Mr. Ziegler was not silent.

"He played better than I did anticipate," said Mr. Ziegler, lighting a cigarette, after he had nonchalantly acknowledged the presentation to him of Miss Ingate. "But of what use is this French public? None. Even had he succeeded here it would have meant nothing. Nothing. In music Paris does not exist. There are six towns in Germany where success means vorldt-reputation. Not that he would succeed in Germany. He has not studied in Germany. And outside Germany there are no schools. However, we have the intention to impose our culture upon all European nations, including France. In one year our army will be here—in Paris. I should wait for that, but probably I shall be called up. In any case, I shall be present."

"But whatever do you mean?" cried Miss Ingate, aghast.

"What do I mean? I mean our army will be here. All know it in Germany. They know it in Paris! But what can they do? How can they stop us? . . . Decadent! . . ." He laughed easily.

"Oh, my chocolates!" exclaimed Miss Thompkins. "I've left them in the hall!"

"No, here they are," said Nick, handing the box.

To Audrey it seemed to be the identical box that Mr. Gilman had been carrying. But of course it might not be. Thousands of chocolate boxes resemble each other exactly.

Carefully ignoring Mr. Ziegler, Audrey remarked to Tommy with a light-heartedness which she did not feel :

"Well, what did you think of Jane this afternoon?"

"Jane?"

"Jane Foley. Nick was taking you to see her, wasn't she?"

"Oh, yes!" said Tommy with a bright smile. "But I didn't go. I went for a motor drive with Mr. Gilman."

There was a short pause. At length Tommy said :

"So he's got the goods on you at last!"

"Who?" Audrey sharply questioned.

"Dauphin. I knew he would. Remember my words. That portrait will cost you forty thousand francs, not counting the frame."

This was the end of the concert.

CHAPTER XLV

THE next afternoon Audrey sat nervous and expectant, but highly finished, in her drawing-room at the Hôtel du Danube. Miss Ingate had gone out, pretending to be quite unaware that she had been sent out. The more detailed part of Audrey's toilette had been accomplished subsequent to Miss Ingate's departure, for Audrey had been at pains to inform Miss Ingate that she, Audrey, was even less interested than usual in her appearance that afternoon. They were close and mutually reliable friends; but every friendship has its reservations. Elise also was out; indeed, Miss Ingate had taken her.

Audrey had the weight of all the world on her, and so long as she was alone she permitted herself to look as though she had. She had to be wise, not only for Audrey Moze, but for others. She had to be wise for Musa, whose failure, though the newspapers all spoke (at about twenty francs a line) of his overwhelming success, was admittedly lamentable; and she hated Musa; she confessed that she had been terribly mistaken in Musa, both as an artist and as a man; still, he was on her mind. She had to be wise about her share in the new campaign of Rosamund, which, while not on her mind, was on her conscience. She had to be wise about the presumable loss of her fortune; she had telegraphed to Mr. Foulger early that morning for information, and an answer was now due. Finally she had to be wise for Mr. Gilman, whose happiness depended on a tone of her voice, on a single monosyllable breathed through those rich lips. She looked forward with interest to being wise for Mr. Gilman. She felt capable of that. The other necessary wisdoms troubled her brow. She seemed to be more full of responsibility and sagacity than any human being could have been expected to be. She was, however, very calm. Her calmness was prodigious.

Then the bell rang, and she could hear one of the hotel attendants open the outer door with his key. Instantly her calmness, of which she had been so proud, was dashed to pieces and she had scarcely begun in a hurry to pick the pieces up and put them together again when the attendant entered the drawing-room. She was afraid, but she thought she was happy.

Only it was not Mr. Gilman the attendant announced. The man said:

"Mademoiselle Nickall."

Audrey said to herself that she must get Nick very quickly away. She was in no humour to talk even to Nick, and, moreover, she did not want Nick to know that Mr. Gilman was calling upon her.

Miss Nickall was innocent and sweet. Good nature radiated from her soft, tired features, and was somehow also entangled in her fluffy grey hair. She kissed Audrey with affection.

"I've just come to say good-bye, you dear!" she said, sitting down and putting her check parasol across her knees. "How lovely you look!"

"Good-bye?" Audrey questioned. "Do I?"

"I have to cross for England to-night. I've had my orders. Rosamund came this morning. What about yours?"

"Oh!" said Audrey. "I don't take orders. But I expect I shall join in, one of these days, when I've had everything explained to me properly. You see, you and I haven't got the same tastes, Nick. You aren't happy without a martyrdom. I am."

Nick smiled gravely and uncertainly.

"It's very serious this time," said she. "Hasn't Rosamund spoken to you yet?"

"She's spoken to me. And I've spoken to her. It was deuce, I should say. Or perhaps my 'vantage. Anyhow, I'm not moving just yet."

"Well, then," said Nick, "if you're staying in Paris, I hope you'll keep an eye on Musa. He needs it. Tommy's going away. At least I fancy she is. We both went to see him this morning."

"Both of you!"

"Well, you see, we've always looked after him. He was in a terrible state about last night. That's really one reason why I called. Not that I'd have gone without kissing you——"

She stopped. There was another ring at the bell. The attendant came in with great rapidity.

"I'm lost!" thought Audrey, disgusted and perturbed. "Her being here will spoil everything."

But the attendant handed her a card, and the card bore the name of Musa. Audrey flushed. Almost instinctively, without thinking, she passed the card to Nick.

"My land!" exclaimed Nick. "If he sees me heré he'll think I've come on purpose to talk about him and pity him, and he'll be just perfectly furious. Can I get out any other way?" She glanced interrogatively at the half-open door of the bedroom.

"But I don't want to see him, either!" Audrey protested.

"Oh! You must! He'll listen to sense from you, perhaps. Can I go this way?"

Impelled to act in spite of herself, Audrey took Nick into the bedroom, and as soon as Musa had been introduced into the drawing-room she embraced Nick in silence and escorted her on tiptoe through Miss Ingate's bedroom to the vestibule and waved an adieu. Then she retraced her steps and made a grand entry into the drawing-room from her own bedroom. She meant to dispose of Musa immediately. A meeting between him and Mr. Gilman on her hearthrug might involve the most horrible complications.

The young man and the young woman shook hands.

But it was the handshaking of bruisers when they enter the ring, and before the blood starts to flow.

"Won't you please sit down?" said Audrey. He was obliged now to obey her, as she had been obliged to obey him on the previous afternoon in the Rue Cassette.

If Audrey looked as though the whole world was on her shoulders, Musa's face seemed to contradict hers and to say that the world, far from being on anybody's shoulders, had come to an end. All the expression of the violinist showed that in his honest conviction a great mundane calamity had occurred, the calamity of course being that his violin bow had not caused catgut to vibrate in such a way as to affect the ears of a particular set of people in a particular manner. But in addition to this sense of a calamity he was under the influence of another emotion—angry resentment. However, he sat down, holding firmly his hat, gloves, and stick.

"I saw my agent this morning," said he, in a grating voice, in French. He was pale.

"Yes?" said Audrey. She suddenly guessed what was coming, and she felt a certain alarm, which nevertheless was not entirely disagreeable.

"Why did you pay for that concert, and the future concerts, without telling me, Madame?"

"Paid for the concerts?" she repeated, rather weakly.

"Yes, Madame. To do so was to make me ridiculous— not to the world, but to myself. For I believed all the time that I had succeeded in gaining the genuine interest of an agent who was prepared to risk money upon the proper exploitation of my talent. I worked in that belief. In spite of your attitude to me I did work. Your antipathy was bad for me; but I conquered myself, and I worked. I had confidence in myself. If last night I did not have a triumph, it was not because I did not work, but because I had been upset—and again by you, Madame. Even after the misfortune of last night I still had confidence, for I knew that the reasons of my failure were accidental and temporary. But I now know that I was living in a fool's paradise, which you had kindly created for me. You have money. Apparently you have too much money. And with money you possess the arrogance of wealth. You knew that I had accepted assistance from good friends. And you thought in your arrogance that you might launch me without informing me of your intention. You thought it would amuse you to make a little fairy-tale in real life. It was a negligent gesture on the part of a rich and idle woman. It cost you nothing save a few bank-notes, of which you had so many that it bored you to count them. How amusing to make a reputation! How charitable to help a starving player! But you forgot one thing. You forgot my dignity and my honour. It was nothing to you that you exposed these to the danger of the most grave affront. It was nothing to you that I was received just as though I had been a child, and that for months I was made, without knowing it, to fulfil the rôle of a conceited jackanapes. When one is led to have confidence in oneself one is tempted to adopt a certain tone and to use certain phrases, which may or may not be justified. I yielded to the temptation. I was wrong, but I was also victimised. This morning, with a moment's torture under the impertinent tongue of a rascally impresario, I paid for all the spurious confidence which I have felt and for all the proud words I have uttered. I came to-day in order to lay at your feet my thanks for the unique humiliation which I owe to you."

His mien was undoubtedly splendid. It ought to have cowed and shamed Audrey. But it did not. She absolutely refused to acknowledge, even within her own heart, that she had committed any wrong. On the contrary, she remembered all the secret sympathy which she had lavished on Musa, all her very earnest and single-minded desires for his apotheosis at the hands of the Parisian public; and his ingratitude positively exasperated her. She was aroused. But she tried to hide the fact that she was roused, speaking in a guarded and sardonic voice.

"And did this agent of yours—I do not know his name

—tell you that I was paying for the concert—I mean, the concerts?" she demanded with an air of impassivity.

"He did not give your name."

"That's something," Audrey put in, her body trembling. "I am much obliged to him."

"But he clearly indicated that money had been paid— that he had not paid it himself—that the enterprise was not genuine. He permitted himself to sneer until I corrected him. He then withdrew what he had said and told me that I had misunderstood. But he was not convincing. It was too late. And I had not misunderstood. Far from that, I had understood. At once the truth traversed my mind like a flash of lightning. It was you who had paid."

"And how did you guess that?" She laughed carelessly, though she could not keep her foot from shaking on the carpet.

"I knew because I knew!" cried Musa. "It explained all your conduct, your ways of speaking to me, your attitude of a schoolmistress, everything. How ingenuous I have been not to perceive it before!"

"Well," said Audrey firmly. "You are wrong. It is absolutely untrue that I have ever paid a penny, or ever shall, to any agent on your behalf. Do you hear? Why should I, indeed! And now what have you to reply?"

She was aware of not the slightest remorse for this enormous 'and unqualified lie. Nay, she held it was not a lie, because Musa deserved to hear it. Strange logic, but her logic! And she was much uplifted and enfevered, and grandly careless of all consequences.

"You are a woman," said Musa curtly and obstinately.

"That, at any rate, is true."

"Therefore I cannot treat you as a man."

"Please do," she said, rising.

"No. If you were a man I should call you out." And Musa rose also. "And I should be right. As you are a woman I have told you the truth, and I can do no more. I shall not characterise your denial. I have no taste for recrimination. Besides, in such a game, no man can be the equal of a woman. But I maintain what I have said, and I affirm that I know it to be true, and that there is no excuse for your conduct. And so I respectfully take leave." He moved towards the door and then stopped. "There never had been any excuse for your conduct to me," he added. "It has always been the conduct of a rich and capricious woman who amused herself by patronising a poor artist."

"You may be interested to know," she said fiercely, "that I am no longer rich. Last night I heard that my fortune is gone. If I have amused myself, that may amuse you."

"It does amuse me," he retorted grimly and more loudly. "I wish that you had never possessed a sou. For then I might have been spared many mournful hours. All would have been different. Yes! From three days ago when I saw you walking intimately in the Tuileries Gardens with the unspeakable Gilman—right back to last year when you first, from caprice, did your best to make me love you—did it deliberately, so that all the Quarter could see!"

In a furious temper Audrey rushed past Musa to the door, and stood with her back to it, palpitating. She vaguely recalled a similar movement of hers long ago, and the slightly comic figure of Mr. Foulger flitted through her memory.

"You shall apologise for that! You shall apologise before you leave this room!" she exploded. Her chin was aloft and her mouth remained open. "I say you shall apologise for that monstrous untruth!"

He approached her, uttering not a word. She was quite ready to kill him. She had no fear of anything whatever. Not once since his arrival had she given one thought to the imminent advent of Mr. Gilman.

She said to herself, watching Musa intently :

"Yes, he shall apologise. It is shameful, what he says. It's worse than horrid. I am as strong as he is."

Musa dropped his hat, stick and gloves. The hat, being English and hard, bounced on the carpet. Then he put his trembling arms around her waist, and his trembling lips came nearer and nearer to hers.

She thought, very puzzled:

"What is happening? This is all wrong. I am furious with him! I will never speak to him again! What is he doing? This is all wrong. I must stop it. I'm saying nothing to him about my career, and my independence, and how horrid it is to be the wife of a genius, and all that. . . . I must stop it."

But she had no volition to stop it.

She thought:

"Am I fainting?"

       *   *   *   *   *

It was upon this scene that Mr. Gilman intruded. Mr. Gilman looked from one to the other. Perhaps the thought in his mind was that if they added their ages together they could not equal his age. Perhaps it was not. He continued to look from one to the other, and this needed some ocular effort, for they were as far apart as two persons in such a situation usually get when they are surprised. Then he caught sight of the hat, stick and gloves on the floor.

"I've been expecting you for a long time," said Audrey, with that miraculous bland tranquillity of which young girls alone have the secret when the conventions are imperilled. "I was just going to order tea."

Mr. Gilman hesitated and then replied:

"How kind of you! But please don't order tea for me. The—er—fact is, I have been unexpectedly called away, and I only called to explain that—er—I could not call." After all, he was a man of some experience.

She let him go. His demeanour to Musa, like Musa's to him, was a marvel of high courtesy.

"Musa," said Audrey, with an intimidated, defiant, proud smile, when the door had shut on Mr. Gilman, "I am still frightfully angry with you. If we stay here I shall suffocate. Let us go out for a walk. Besides, other people might call."

Simultaneously there was another ring. It was a cable. She read:

"Sold Zacatecas at an average of six and a quarter dollars three weeks ago. Wrote you at length to Wimereux. Writing again as to new investments.

"FOULGER."

"This comes of having no fixed address," she said, throwing the blue cablegram carelessly down in front of Musa. "I'm not quite ruined, after all. But I might have known—with Mr. Foulger." Then she explained.

"I wish——" he began.

"No, you don't," she stopped him. "So you needn't start on that line. You are brilliant at figures. At least I long since suspected you were. How much is one hundred and eighty thousand times six and a quarter?"

Notwithstanding his brilliance, it took two pencils, two heads, and one piece of paper to solve the problem. They were not quite certain, but the answer seemed to be £225,000 in English money.

"We cannot starve," said Audrey, and then paused. . . . "Musa, are we friends? We shall quarrel horribly. Do you know, I never knew that proposals of marriage were made like that!"

"I have not told you one thing," said Musa. "I am going to play in Germany, instead of further concerts in Paris. It is arranged."

"Not in Germany," she pleaded, thinking of Ziegler.

"Yes, in Germany," said Musa masterfully. "I have a reputation to make. It is the agent who has suggested it."

"But the concerts in London?"

"You are English. I wish not to wound you."

When Audrey stood up again, she had to look at the floor in order to make sure that it was there. Once she had tasted absinthe. She had had to take the same precaution then.

"Stop! I entreat thee!" said Musa suddenly, just as, all arrayed in her finery, she was opening the door for the walk.

"What is it?"

He kissed her, and with his lips almost on hers he murmured:

"Thou shalt not go out without avowing. And if thou art angry—well, I adore thy anger. The concerts were . . . thy enterprise? I guessed well?"

"You see," she replied like a shot, "you weren't sure, although you pretended you were."

In the Rue de Rivoli, and in the resplendent Champs Elysées they passed column after column of entertainment posters. But the name of Musa had been mysteriously removed from all of them.

CHAPTER XLVI

AN EPILOGUE

AUDREY was walking along Piccadilly when she overtook Miss Ingate, who had been arrested by a shop window, the window of one of the shops recently included in the vast edifice of the Hotel Majestic.

Miss Ingate gave a little squeal of surprise. The two kissed very heartily in the street, which was full of spring and of the posters of evening papers bearing melodramatic tidings of the latest nocturnal development of the terrible suffragette campaign.

"You said eleven, Audrey. It isn't eleven yet."

"Well, I'm behind time. I meant to be all spruced up and receive you in state at the hotel. But the boat was three hours late at Harwich. I jumped into a cab at Liverpool Street, but I got out at Piccadilly Circus because the streets looked so fine and I felt I really must walk a bit."

"And where's your husband?"

"He's at Liverpool Street trying to look after the luggage. He lost some of it at Hamburg. He likes looking after luggage, so I just left him at it."

Miss Ingate's lower lip dropped at the corners.

"You've had a tiff."

"Winnie, we haven't."

"Did you go to all his concerts?"

"All. I heard all his practising, and I sat in the stalls at all his concerts. Quite contrary to my principles, of course. But, Winnie, it's very queer, I *wanted* to do it. So naturally I did it. We've never been apart—until now."

"And it's not exaggerated, what you've written me about his success?"

"Not a bit. I've been most careful not to exaggerate. In fact, I've tried to be gloomy. No use, however! It was a triumph. . . . And how's all this business?" Audrey demanded, in a new key, indicating an orange-tinted newspaper bill that was being flaunted in front of her.

"Oh! I believe it's dreadful. Of course, you know Rosamund's in prison. But they'll have to let her out soon. Jane Foley—she still calls herself Foley—hasn't been caught. And that's funny. I doubled my subscription. We had to, you see. But that's all I've done. They don't have processions and things now, and barrel organs are *quite* out of fashion. What with that, and my rheumatism! . . . I used to think I should live to vote myself. I feel I shan't now. So I've gone back into water-colours. They're very soothing, if you let the paper dry after each wash and don't take them seriously. . . . Now, I'm a very common-sense woman, Audrey, as you must have noticed, and I'm not subject to fancies. Will you just look at the girl on the left hand in this window here, and tell me whether I'm dreaming or not?"

Miss Ingate indicated the shop window which had arrested her. The establishment was that of a hair specialist, and the window was mainly occupied by two girls who sat in arm-chairs with their backs to the glass, and all their magnificent hair spread out at length over the backs of the chairs for the inspection of the public; the implication being that the magnificent hair was due to the specific of the hair specialist. Passers-by continually stopped to gaze at the spectacle, but they never stopped long, because the spectacle was monotonous.

"Well, what about her?" said Audrey, staring.

"Isn't it Lady Southminster?"

"Good heavens!" Audrey's mind went back to the

Channel packet and the rain squall and the scenes on the Paris train. "So it is! Whatever can have happened to her? Let's go in."

And in they went, Audrey leading, and demanding at once a bottle of the specific; Audrey had scarcely spoken when the left-hand girl in the window, who, of course, from her vantage had a full view of the shop, screamed lightly and jumped down from the window.

"Don't give me away!" she whispered appealingly in Audrey's ear. The next moment, not heeding the excitement of the shop manager, she had drawn Audrey and Miss Ingate through another door which led into the entrance-hall of the Majestic Hotel. The shop was thus contrived to catch two publics at once.

"If they knew I was Lady Southminster in there," said Lady Southminster in a feverish murmur—she seemed not averse to the sensation caused by her hair in the twilight of the hotel—"I expect I should lose my place, and I don't want to lose it. *He'll* be coming by presently, and he'll see me, and it'll be a lesson to him. We're always together. Race meetings, dances, golf, restaurants, bridge. Twenty-four hours every day. He won't lose sight of me. He's that fond of me, you know. I couldn't stand it. I'd as lief be in prison—only I'm that fond of him, you know. But I was so homesick, and I felt if I didn't have a change I should burst. This is Constantinopoulos's old shop, you know, where I used to make cigarettes in the window. He's dead, Constantinopoulos is. I don't know what *he'd* have said to hair restorers. I asked for the place, and I showed 'em my hair, and I got it. And me sitting there—it's quite like old times. Only before, you know, I used to have my face to the street. I don't know which I like best. But, anyhow, you can see my profile from the side window. And *he* will. He always looks at that sort of thing. He'll be furious. But it will you him no end of good. Well, good-bye. But come back in and buy a bottle, or I shall

be let in for a shindy. In fact, you might buy two
bottles."

"So that's love!" said Audrey when the transaction
was over and they were in the entrance-hall again.

"No," said Miss Ingate. "That's marriage. And don't
you forget it. . . . Hallo, Tommy!"

"You'd better not let Mr. Gilman hear me called
Tommy in this hotel," laughed Miss Thompkins, who was
attired with an unusual richness, as she advanced towards
Miss Ingate and Audrey. "And what are you doing
here?" she questioned Audrey.

"I'm staying here," said Audrey. "But I've only just
arrived. I'm advance agent for my husband. How are
you? And what are *you* doing here? I thought you hated
London."

"I came the day before yesterday," Tommy replied.
"And I'm very fit. You see, Mr. Gilman preferred us
to be married in London. And I'd no objection. So
here I am. The wedding's to-morrow. You aren't very
startled, are you? Had you heard?"

"Well," said Audrey, "not what you'd call 'heard.'
But I'd a sort of a kind of a——"

"You come right over here, young woman."

"But I want to get my number."

"You come right over here right now," Tommy insisted. And in another corner of the entrance-hall she
spoke thus, and there was both seriousness and fun in
her voice: "Don't you run away with the idea that I'm
taking your leavings, young woman. Because I'm not.
We all knew you'd lost your head about Musa, and it
was quite right of you. But you never had a chance
with Ernest, though you thought you had, after I'd met
him. Admit I'm much better suited for him than you'd
have been. I'd only one difficulty, and that was the nice
boy Price, who wanted to drown himself for my beautiful
freckled face. That's all. Now you can go and get your
number."

x

The incident might not have ended there had not Madame Piriac appeared in the entrance-hall out of the interior of the hotel.

"He exacted my coming," said Madame Piriac privately to Audrey. "You know how he is strange. He asks for a quiet wedding, but at the same time it must be all that is most correct. There are things, he says, which demand a woman. . . . I know four times nothing of the English etiquette. I have abandoned my husband. And here I am. *Voilà!* Listen. She has great skill with him, *cette Tommy.* Nevertheless, I have the intention to counsel her about her complexion. Impossible to keep any man with a complexion like hers!"

They saw Mr. Gilman himself enter the hotel. He was very nervous and very important. As soon as he caught sight of Miss Thompkins he said to the door-keeper :

"Tell my chauffeur to wait."

He was punctiliously attentive to Miss Thompkins, and held her hand for two seconds after he had practically finished with it.

"Are you ready, dear?" he said. "You'll be sorry to hear that my liver is all wrong again. I knew it was because I slept so heavily."

These words were distinctly heard by Audrey herself.

"I think I'll slip upstairs now," she murmured to Madame Piriac. And vanished, before Mr. Gilman had observed her presence.

She thought :

"How he has aged!"

Scarcely ten minutes later, when Audrey was upstairs in her sitting-room, waiting idly for the luggage and her husband to arrive, and thinking upon the case of Lady Southminster, the telephone bell rang out startlingly.

"Mr. Shinner to see you."

"Mr. Shinner? Oh! Mr. Shinner. Send him up, please."

This Mr. Shinner was the concert agent with connections in Paris whom Audrey had first consulted in the enterprise of launching Musa upon the French public. He was a large, dark man, black moustached and bearded, with heavy limbs and features, and an opaque, pimpled skin. In spite of these characteristics, he entered the room soft-footed as a fairy, ingratiating as a dog aware of his own iniquity, reassuring as applause.

"Well, Mr. Shinner. But how did you know we were here? As a matter of fact we aren't here. My husband has not arrived yet."

"Madam," said Mr. Shinner, "I happened to hear that you had telegraphed for rooms, and as I was in the neighbourhood I thought I would venture to call."

"But who told you we had telegraphed for rooms?"

"The manager is a good friend of mine, and as you are now famous—— Ah! I have heard all about the German tour. I mean I have read about it. I subscribe to the German musical papers. One must, in my profession. Also I have had direct news from my correspondents in Germany. It was a triumph there, was it not?"

"Yes," said Audrey. "After Dusseldorf. My husband did not make much money——"

"That will not trouble you," Mr. Shinner smiled easily.

"But somebody did—the agents did."

"Perhaps not so much as you think, madam, if I may say so. Perhaps not so much as you think. And we must all live—unfortunately. Has your husband made any arrangements yet for London or for a provincial tour? I have reason to think that the season will be particularly brilliant. And I can now offer advantages——"

"But, Mr. Shinner, when I last saw you, and it isn't so very long ago, you told me that my husband was not a concert-player, which was exactly what I had heard in Paris."

"I didn't go quite so far as that, surely, did I?" Mr. Shinner softly insinuated. He might have been pouring

honey from his mouth. "Surely I didn't say quite that?
And perhaps I had been too much influenced by Paris."

"Yes, you said he wasn't a concert-player and never
would be——"

"Don't rub it in, madam," said Mr. Shinner merrily.
"*Peccavi.*"

"What's that?"

"Nothing, nothing, madam," he disclaimed.

"And you said there were far too many violinists on the
market, and that it was useless for a French player to offer
himself to the London musical public. And I don't know
what you didn't say."

"But I didn't know then that your husband would have
such a success in Germany."

"What difference does that make?"

"Madam," said Mr. Shinner, "it makes every difference."

"But England and Germany hate each other. At least
they despise each other. And what's more, nearly everybody in Germany was talking about going to war this
summer. I was told they are all ready to invade England
after they have taken Paris and Calais. We heard it
everywhere."

"I don't know anything about any war," said Mr.
Shinner with tranquillity. "But I do know that the London musical public depends absolutely on Germany. The
only first-class instrumentalist that England has ever produced had no success here until he went to Germany and
Germanised his name and himself and announced that he
despised England. Then he came back, and he has caused a
furore ever since. So far as regards London, a success in
Karlsruhe, Wiesbaden, Leipzig, Dusseldorf, and so on, is
worth far more than a success in the Queen's Hall. Indeed—can you get a success in the Queen's Hall without a
success in these places first? I doubt it. Your husband
now has London at his feet. Not Paris, though he may
capture Paris after he has captured London. But London
certainly. He cannot find a better agent than myself. All

artists like me, because I *understand*. You see, my mother was harpist to the late Queen."

"But——"

"Your husband is assuredly a genius, madam!" Mr. Shinner stood up in his enthusiasm, and banged his left fist with his right palm.

"Yes, I know that," said Audrey. "But you are such an expensive luxury."

Mr. Shinner pushed away the accusation with both hands. "Madam, madam, I shall take all the risks. I should not dream, now, of asking for a cheque on account. On the contrary, I should guarantee a percentage of the gross receipts. Perhaps I am unwise to take risks—I dare say I am—but I could not bear to see your husband in the hands of another agent. We professional men have our feelings."

"Don't cry, Mr. Shinner," said Audrey impulsively. It was not a proper remark to make, but the sudden impetuous entrance of Musa himself, carrying his violin case, eased the situation.

"There is a man which is asking for you outside in the corridor," said Musa to his wife. "It is the gardener, Aguilar, I think. I have brought all the luggage, not excluding that which was lost at Hamburg." He had a glorious air, and was probably more proud of his still improving English and of his ability as a courier than of his triumphs on the fiddle. "Ah!" Mr. Shinner was bowing before him.

"This is Mr. Shinner, the agent, my love," said Audrey. "I'll leave you to talk to him. He sees money in you."

In the passage the authentic Aguilar stood with Miss Ingate.

"Here's Mr. Aguilar," said Miss Ingate. "I'm just going into No. 37, Madame Piriac's room. Don't you think Mr. Aguilar looks vehy odd in London?"

"Good morning, Aguilar. You in town on business?"

Aguilar touched his forehead. It is possible that he

looked very odd in London, but he was wearing a most respectable new suit of clothes, and might well have passed for a land agent.

"'Mornin', ma'am. I had to come up because I couldn't get delivery of those wallpapers you chose. Otherwise all the repairs and alterations are going on as well as could be expected."

"And how is your wife, Aguilar?"

"She's nicely, thank ye, ma'am. I pointed out to the foreman that it would be a mistake to make the dining-room door open the other way, as the architect suggested. But he would do it. However, I've told you, ma'am. It'll only have to be altered back. Perhaps I ought to tell you that I took the liberty of taking a fortnight's holiday, ma'am. It's the only holiday I ever did take, except the annual day off for the Colchester Rose Show, which is perhaps more a matter of business with a head gardener than a holiday, as ye might say. My wife wanted me in London."

"She's not caught yet?"

"No'm. And I don't think as she will be, not with me about. I never did allow myself to be bossed by police, and I always been too much for 'em. And as I'm on the matter, ma'am, I should like to give you notice as soon as it's convenient. I wouldn't leave on any account till that foreman's off the place; he's no better than a fool. But as soon afterwards as you like."

"Certainly, Aguilar. I was quite expecting it. Where are you going to live?"

"Well, ma'am, I've got hold of a little poultry run business in the north of London. It'll be handy for Hollo-way in case—— And Jane asked me to give you this letter, ma'am. I see her this morning."

Audrey read the note. Very short, it was signed "Jane" and "Nick," and dated from a house in Fitzroy Street. It caused acute excitement in Audrey.

"I shall come at once," said she.

Getting rid of Aguilar, she knocked at the door of No. 37.

"Read that," she ordered Miss Ingate and Madame Piriac, giving them the note jointly.

"And are you going?" said Miss Ingate, nervous and impressed.

"Of course," Audrey answered. "Don't they ask me to go at once? I meant to write to my cousins at Woodbridge and my uncles in the colonies, and tell them all that I was settling down at last. And I meant to look at those new flats in Park Lane with Musa. But I shall have to leave all that for the present. Also my lunch."

"But, darling," put in Madame Piriac, who had been standing before the dressing-table trying on a hat. "But, darling, it is very serious, this matter. What about your husband?"

"He'll keep," said Audrey. "He's had his turn. I must have mine now. I haven't had a day off from being a wife for ever so long. And it's a little enervating, you know. It spoils you for the fresh air."

"I imagined to myself that you two were happy in an ideal fashion," murmured Madame Piriac.

"So we are!" said Audrey. "Though a certain coolness did arise over the luggage this morning. But I don't want to be ideally happy all the time. And I won't be. I want—I want all the sensations there are; and I want to be everything. And I can be. Musa understands."

"If he does," said Miss Ingate, "he'll be the first husband that ever did." Her lips were sardonic.

"Well, of course," said Audrey nonchalantly, "he *is*. Didn't you know that? . . . And didn't you tell me not to forget Lady Southminster?"

"Did I?" said Miss Ingate.

Audrey heard voices in the corridor. Musa was parting from a subservient Shinner. Also the luggage was bumping along the carpet. She called her husband into No. 37 and kissed him rather violently in front of Madame Piriac and Miss Ingate, and showed him the note. Then she whispered to him, smiling.

"What's that you're whispering?" Miss Ingate archly demanded.

"Nothing. I was only asking him to come and help me to open my big trunk. I want something out of it. Au revoir, you two."

"What do you think of it all, Madame Piriac?" Miss Ingate inquired when the pair were alone.

"'All the sensations there are!' 'Everything!'" Madame Piriac repeated Audrey's phrases. "One is forced to conclude that she has an appetite for life."

"Yes," said Miss Ingate, "she wants the lion's share of it, that's what she wants. No mistake. But of course she's young."

"I was never young like that."

"Neither was I! Neither was I!" Miss Ingate assever-ated. "But something vehy, vehy strange has come over the world, if you ask me."

PRINTED BY CASSELL & COMPANY, LIMITED, LA BELLE SAUVAGE, LONDON, E.C.
F.100.816

Printed in Great Britain by
Amazon.co.uk, Ltd.,
Marston Gate.